DEAD AND GONE

A DCI DANNY FLINT BOOK

TREVOR NEGUS

Revised Edition 2021
INKUBATOR BOOKS

www.inkubatorbooks.com

First published as "The Exodus Murders" by Trevor Negus (2017)

PROLOGUE

3.00pm, 10 February 1986
Worksop, Nottinghamshire

'Excuse me, love, you've forgotten your change.'

The woman slowly turned and, without looking up, walked back to the shop counter. She reached out, and the shopkeeper placed the coins into the palm of her hand. He was worried. The woman looked so fragile. He could see that her eyes were bloodshot and red-rimmed, as though she had recently been crying. There was nothing of her. The baggy clothes she wore hung from her slight frame, and she had the appearance of a Victorian workhouse waif. Her jet-black hair was lank and unwashed. It hung down to her shoulders.

The black hair contrasted vividly against her alabaster white complexion.

'Thanks,' she mumbled before closing her hand around the cash and thrusting it into her jeans pocket.

The woman turned to leave.

Gently the elderly shopkeeper took hold of her arm, momentarily halting her progress, 'Are you sure you're okay, love?' he asked, genuine concern in his voice.

'I'm fine, really.'

The shopkeeper released his soft grip on her arm. The young woman walked slowly back out onto the busy High Street. It was three o'clock in the afternoon, and the street was bustling with shoppers taking advantage of the first day of sunshine after a depressing week of rain. It was a beautiful day. The sky was bright blue, and although the sun looked watery and weak, it still felt quite warm.

She walked with her head down, not even looking up when a coach revved loudly right beside her. The large vehicle belched out a dark cloud of diesel fumes just as it passed her by. Wrinkling her nose at the stench of the acrid fumes, she walked on.

The woman now had everything she needed from her little shopping expedition and started to walk briskly out of the town centre. As she strode out, she could feel the handles of the small white carrier bag biting into the palms of her hand. The contents were quite heavy.

After another ten minutes walking, the streets became quieter, and she was approaching the edge of the town. Another five minutes, and she would be at the entrance to Farriers Wood. It was her favourite place in the small market town of Worksop. Farriers Wood was spread over three acres of park and woodland. It was an oasis of calm; she often visited to relax, unwind, and raise her spirits.

As she continued to walk slowly along the quiet streets, she could hear her mother's voice echoing inside her head, *'When you get here, there will be loads of cuddles, my darling. I've missed being with you so much.'* Her mother's voice sounded encouraging. It was seductive and warm.

She missed her mother so much.

Then she could hear the stern voice of her father. He was shouting, talking over her mother, determined to make himself heard. *'You will stay here with me, girl. It's not time for you to leave yet!'*

Her father's voice was strong and dominant now. She hoped that once inside the peaceful surroundings of Farriers Wood, it would become clear to her, what she should do.

Finally, she found herself standing at the entrance to the park. She paused at the large wrought-iron gates that were flung wide open, inviting her in. The park looked beautiful. The snowdrops were starting to open, urged out by the warm sun. The stark, white flowers contrasted against the lush, green grass, and the purple hues of the bluebells.

She walked along the red cinder pathway until she reached the first area of dense woodland. The new leaves of the trees were starting to bud but hadn't yet begun to unfurl. She stepped off the path and made her way into the woods. It was cooler in here, and the woman was grateful for the thin cardigan she wore.

For a young woman, her face bore the lines of a troubled existence, and she looked older than her twenty-eight years. The trauma she had known in her short life had diminished the natural beauty of her face. Even her once-bright blue eyes, which were framed perfectly by her ghostly white complexion, now appeared dull and lifeless.

Walking deeper into the woods, she found a natural clearing next to a large oak tree. The sunlight was streaming through the almost bare branches; it created a welcome pool of light at the bottom of the big tree.

Feeling weary, the woman sat down at the base of the tree and placed the carrier bag by her side. She sat quietly for several minutes. The sun's rays warmed her as she listened to the sound of birdsong and the gentle breeze moving through the branches overhead.

Her mother's voice was stronger here. Her sweet, cajoling tones easily overpowered her father's angry pleadings.

Reaching into the carrier bag, she took out the large bottle of Smirnoff vodka. Unscrewing the cap, she raised the heavy bottle to her lips and took a mouthful of the fiery liquid. Swallowing it greedily, she felt the harsh spirit burn her throat, then the warmth spread through her body as the alcohol seeped into every nerve ending.

She shuddered and took another mouthful. The burn in her throat was slightly less this time. Feeling light-headed, she propped the bottle upright, between her legs, abandoning the screw cap on the ground next to her.

The only voice she could hear now was her mother's.

In that instant, she knew exactly what she should do. Moving carefully so she didn't disturb the vodka bottle, she reached into the carrier bag again. This time, she took out four white boxes.

Each box contained a blister pack of twenty paracetamol tablets.

She began to take two or three tablets at a time, washing them down with a sip of the fiery vodka.

After ten minutes, both the vodka bottle and the packets of pills were empty.

The woman hurled the empty bottle into the bracken, turned over and lay down on the warm grass.

She felt a few spasms in her stomach, but the vodka she had consumed made the pain dull. Easily bearable.

She curled up into the foetal position, drawing her knees up to her chest, and closed her eyes.

The tablets and the vodka were already killing her. She drifted into a sleep she would never wake from.

The woman was finally at peace, and there was a smile on her face.

She knew her mother was waiting.

1

5.00pm 20 March 1986
Underwood, Nottinghamshire

It was the third day.
The Watcher lay motionless in the hide he'd created. Heavily camouflaged and under the cover of darkness, he'd crawled into the patch of gorse bushes three days ago. He had brought enough food and water to last him a week. He hoped his mission wouldn't take that long. The prickly gorse provided fantastic cover; he knew from experience the harsh plants would also deter any passing dogs from investigating his presence too closely.

As the days passed, he'd gradually refined the hide. This was natural habitat for the Watcher. A large part of his adult life had been spent in similar hides, doing exactly this.

The stalking and killing of prey came naturally to

him. Whether that prey was animal or human was immaterial.

He was used to foul and inclement weather. The constant rain that had fallen and the cold nights didn't concern him. The camouflage overalls and the head and shoulders of his ghillie suit did little to keep him warm; but he knew he could draw on the rage burning within him to help keep out the cold and the wet.

The roll of dark green tarpaulin he lay on kept most of the damp from the sodden earth at bay. The tools he would need later were all in a leather grip bag that was protected against the weather by a black plastic bin liner. The bag was never more than an arm's length away.

From his elevated position in the hide, he had an unobstructed view of the large detached bungalow below. His target hadn't returned home for two nights now, but he remained totally focussed. Maybe tonight would be the night.

The previous night, he'd used the time the bungalow was empty to do a complete recce of the premises. Without leaving any trace, he had forced entry into the property and examined every room. He took great care over the alarm system; it was a simple one that utilised the telephone line. With his specialist skills, it had been an easy task to bypass the system. On the night of the operation, he wouldn't bother to bypass it. He would simply sever the telephone line. People would be aware soon enough that the property had been entered.

He'd been surprised at the opulence of the bungalow. Everything about the interior was perfect. The appliances were all top of the range, and it had been decorated throughout by somebody with exquisite taste.

The reason for his surprise was because he knew his target was male and lived alone, but it was as though the bungalow had been adorned with a feminine touch. He'd been particularly impressed by the low-level lighting in the kitchen. He had made a mental note to use the kitchen as the interrogation and killing room on the night of the operation. As he exited the bungalow, he'd ensured that no telltale signs that would give away his presence had been left inside the property.

He was methodical and professional; these precautionary actions were second nature to him.

Patience was the key; he knew he could only strike when the time was right.

He fully understood what his mission demanded. Once he had made entry to the property, he would need to spend considerable time alone with his target. What he needed to do, in order to get what he required, could take a long time. He could not afford for there to be any interruptions or unexpected visitors.

As dusk fell and twilight replaced daylight, the rain finally abated.

After a couple of hours, the Watcher began to drift into a fitful sleep.

Suddenly, he heard a car being driven at speed along the country lanes. Instantly awake, he now concentrated fully on the luxurious detached bungalow below.

A sporty-looking Jaguar car was driven onto the driveway.

The engine was switched off, but the car remained ticking loudly. Evidence that it had been driven at speed along the winding roads that surrounded the property.

Two men jumped out of the front seats of the car and made their way towards the main entrance of the property. This door was located at the side of the bungalow and was in full view of the Watcher.

The porch light came on automatically as one of the men fumbled in his pockets for the door key. The other man was holding a bottle of wine in his left hand. He said something, stepped forward and placed his right hand on the nape of the other man's neck.

The Watcher was shocked when he saw the man holding the wine bottle lean forward and kiss the other man passionately on the lips. The man with the door keys returned the kiss, slipping his arms around the other man's waist.

From his hide, the Watcher studied the two men. He was satisfied that the dark-haired man with the door keys was his target.

The other man was blonde, but in every other physical way like the target.

He could clearly hear both men giggling as they went inside the bungalow.

After a few minutes, the porch light went off.

He remained alert and watching. A few hours later, the last light inside the bungalow was switched off. The Watcher now knew that his target had company who would be staying the night.

Lying motionless in his gorse hide, on the edge of the wooded copse, he settled down for another long night.

Maybe tomorrow night would be the night.

2

2.00pm, 17 March 1986
Mansfield Cemetery, Nottinghamshire

It was a bitterly cold day; the strong winds drove the freezing rain across the large open cemetery. The headstones and the few scattered trees offered scant protection against the inclement conditions.

For the twenty or so mourners at the open grave, the atrocious weather had turned an already desperately sad day into a horrendous ordeal.

The pall-bearers, with ice-cold rain dripping from their faces, slowly lowered the heavy wooden casket down into the open grave.

The vicar spoke loudly, raising his voice to be heard above the howling wind: 'Man that is born of a woman, hath but a short time to live, and is full of misery. He cometh up, and is cut down, like a flower; he fleeth as it were a shadow, and never continueth in one stay. In the midst of life, we are in death.'

Danny Flint stood at the head of the grave, flanked by his girlfriend, Sue Rhodes, and his best friend and work colleague, Rob Buxton. As he listened to the flat monotonous tone of the vicar, he felt his mind begin to meander away.

As the coffin was slowly lowered down into the muddy maw of the open grave, Danny became transfixed by the rain bouncing off the brass plate on the lid of the casket. His eyes bored into the name engraved on the dull, yellow metal plate: "FRANK EDWARD FLINT".

The vicar's voice cut through into his consciousness again: 'Thou knowest, Lord, the secrets of our hearts; shut not thy merciful ears to our prayer, but spare us, Lord most holy, O God most mighty, O holy and merciful Saviour, thou most Judge eternal, suffer us not, at our last hour, for any pains of death to fall from thee.'

The coffin reached the bottom of the grave, and the pall-bearers began to remove the straps.

So that was it, thought Danny. Both his mother and father were now dead. His father would now be interred in the same grave his mother had occupied for the last ten years.

Danny felt numb, both physically and emotionally. He could feel the tears streaming down his face, and he swallowed hard. He felt Sue's reassuring presence beside him as she squeezed his hand tightly. Then another surge of overwhelming grief as he thought of his impending wedding to her. The celebration his father would not now be able to witness.

For a while, the vicar's words were lost against the strident wind; he had given up trying to talk over it. Danny could see his mouth moving, but did not hear the words. Then he saw the elderly vicar turn and walk directly towards him. In his bony hand, he was carrying a small wooden box that contained soil. With his long robes being buffeted by the strong winds, the clergyman held out the box to Danny, urging him to join in the melancholy ritual.

Now the vicar was closer, he could once again hear his voice above the wind: 'For as much as it hath pleased Almighty God of his great mercy to take unto himself the soul of our dear brother who has departed, we therefore commit his body to the ground; earth to earth, ashes to ashes, dust to dust; in sure and certain hope of the resurrection to eternal life through our Lord Jesus Christ.'

Danny shuddered as he thrust his fingers deep into the freezing cold soil. Taking a handful of the black dirt, he stepped forward to the edge of the open grave and allowed the dirt to drop down onto the top of the coffin. Having carried out his part of the solemn ritual, he stepped back and allowed the other mourners to follow suit.

The vicar completed the blessing, saying the Lord's Prayer first, then the collect, as the final acts of committing Danny's father's body into the care of the Lord. The vicar then urged everybody at the graveside to take immediate shelter from the atrocious conditions.

Sue walked across to the vicar and invited him to join the rest of the mourners at the wake in a nearby public house.

Rob and Sue walked either side of Danny as they left the graveside and headed back to the car park. Sue slipped her arm through Danny's and tried to comfort him.

As they made the short car ride from the cemetery to the Rushley public house for the wake, Danny reflected on the previous year. It had been an emotional roller-coaster for them all.

It was almost a year ago, to the day, when he'd received the amazing telephone call from Dave Smedley in Australia. Smedley had informed Danny that Jimmy Wade, the man dubbed the Coal Killer by the nation's press, was to be found working at a coal mine near Sydney.

Danny had immediately arranged for the Australian police to locate and detain Wade. It had been a simple task to then arrange the extradition of Wade back to the United Kingdom. He'd felt an overwhelming sense of relief and euphoria when he travelled with Rob Buxton to Sydney, to meet the murderer he had worked so hard to bring to justice. The two detectives had then escorted the killer back to England for trial.

Wade never uttered a single word throughout the long aeroplane journey. He sat between the two detectives and maintained a stony silence. He even refused to acknowledge the air stewardess when she enquired if he would like any refreshments.

After they had arrived at Heathrow, a full armed police escort was provided to convey Wade and the detectives back to Nottinghamshire. Jimmy Wade was now considered to be one of the country's most dangerous criminals.

The killer maintained his silence during every interview with the detectives. When questioned at length about the atrocious murders he was suspected of committing with Police Sergeant Michael Reynolds, Wade showed no remorse. Throughout the long interviews, his bright blue eyes stared into the middle distance and never once betrayed an inner emotion.

The fingerprint that Wade had inadvertently left on the base of a glass vase, at the home of DC Rachel Moore, proved to be the final evidential nail in his coffin. He was subsequently charged with the murders of Albert Jones, Mandy Stokes, June Hayes, Police Sergeant Michael Reynolds and the attempted murder of Detective Constable Rachel Moore. The trial at Leicester Crown Court began in October 1985 and lasted for four weeks. Once again, throughout the entire duration of the trial, Wade never uttered a word. He declined to offer any evidence in his defence. It had only taken the jury three hours of deliberations to return guilty verdicts on all the charges.

Having been found guilty by a jury of his peers, Wade was sentenced to life imprisonment. Only when sentence had been passed did Wade finally show any emotion. He allowed the faintest hint of a smile to fleetingly pass over his face as he was being led down the steps.

As he was sentenced, the trial judge had made it clear to Wade that the maximum-security hospital at Rampton in Nottinghamshire would be where he would spend the rest of his life. His Honour Judge Winterbourne considered Wade would continue to be a danger to the public. He ordered that the former coal miner should never be considered for release.

For Jimmy Wade, life imprisonment meant life imprisonment. Declared to be criminally insane, he would grow old and die within the walls of Rampton Hospital.

The immediate aftermath of the trial saw Nottinghamshire Constabulary heavily criticised over their handling of the Coal Killer murders. The public had been outraged at the lack of manpower deployed to investigate the killings.

Even at the height of the criticism of the force generally, His Honour Judge Winterbourne had commended Detective Inspector Danny Flint and his small team of detectives for their efforts in trying to track down the serial killer. Having commended the individual detectives involved in the manhunt, the judge then laid the blame for the fact Wade had evaded capture squarely at the door of the chief constable. He was ignoring, in doing so, the constraints on manpower that the yearlong miner's strike had forced on the Nottinghamshire Constabulary.

The chief constable responded to this direct criticism by forming a specialist Major Crime Investigation Unit to undertake prolonged investigation into murder and other specified serious crime. The head of this new department would be Detective Chief Superintendent Wainwright, a well-regarded, straight-talking Scot who hailed from the tough, granite city of Aberdeen.

The MCIU, as it was to be known, would consist of a detective chief inspector responsible for supervising two investigation teams, each led by a detective inspector. The two teams would be made up of two detective sergeants and twelve detectives.

These investigation teams would be supported by dedicated Scenes of Crime personnel who would be drawn from both the force and civilian resources, as required.

The chief constable, on the forthright recommendation of Chief Superintendent Wainwright, had promoted Danny Flint to detective chief inspector and Rob Buxton to detective inspector. Both men had then been transferred immediately to the new investigation unit. DC Rachel Moore had also transferred onto the MCIU, but DC Andy Wills, the last remaining member of the small team who had worked so hard to bring Jimmy Wade to justice, had been promoted to sergeant and was now working at Beeston in a uniform role.

The feeling of euphoria and satisfaction Danny had felt upon gaining promotion and being asked to head up the new unit had quickly disappeared when his father suffered another stroke. As a result of this second catastrophic stroke, his father had been hospitalised in order to receive round-the-clock care. The prognosis was a poor one; there was absolutely no prospect of him returning to the Pleasley nursing home, where he had been so happy.

It was during this period of emotional turmoil that Danny found himself being drawn ever closer to Sue Rhodes. It had seemed a natural progression to elevate their commitment to one another. So, on Christmas Day, Danny had proposed marriage. Sue readily accepted, and the couple had set their wedding day for the seventh of May 1986.

Then, on the sixth of March, just after the doctors at the hospital had noticed some telltale signs of a gradual recovery, Danny had received the devastating news that his beloved father had contracted pneumonia and was close to death. He'd immediately driven to the hospital to be with his father. He could still tangibly recall the feeling of helplessness that had overwhelmed him as he sat by his father's bedside, holding his hand, watching him pass peacefully away.

Thinking about that moment, Danny could now feel the grief closing in around him again.

As the dark mood enveloped him, his mouth became dry, and he found it difficult to swallow. Once again, he could feel the sting of new tears filling his eyes.

Rob pulled the car into the car park of the Rushley public house.

Danny squeezed Sue's hand gently and said, 'Can you go inside with Rob? I just need a few minutes by myself before I come in.'

Sue smiled and said, 'Of course, take as long as you

need, sweetheart. We'll be waiting inside when you're ready.'

Danny walked out of the car park and along Nottingham Road towards Mansfield town centre. Five minutes later, he was standing outside his father's old house on Garth Road. Danny had sold the house in November last year, after he'd moved in to live with Sue at her house, on the other side of town. The money raised from the sale of the property had originally been intended to help pay for the nursing home where his father had lived happily until the second stroke.

As he stood looking at the front of the house, Danny could see how the new owners had altered things. The planting in the garden was different, the curtains had changed, and the windows had all been replaced with brown UPVC frames.

Danny smiled to himself, turned away from the house, and started to walk briskly back to the pub.

Seeing the changes to the house had helped him realise that life never stands still; it keeps moving forward relentlessly. He'd been understandably devastated at the loss of his father, and that wouldn't change, but he now knew that his future with Sue would be wonderful. He felt uplifted and thankful for everything his mother and father had given him.

He was energised. The depression he had felt at his father's passing was diminishing with each step.

He now felt eager to embrace life. He couldn't wait to marry Sue and spend the rest of his life with her. He also realised how much he was looking forward to making a success of the newly formed Major Crime Investigation Unit.

3

9.00pm, 21 March 1986
Underwood, Nottinghamshire

The Watcher stared down as the metallic grey Jaguar sports car was driven slowly onto the driveway of the bungalow. It was much later than the previous night, nearly nine o'clock, and already dark. He watched as his target got out of the driver's door of the sleek car. He waited patiently to see if the passenger door would open.

It didn't.

Finally, his target was alone at the secluded property. The Watcher felt the usual rush of adrenaline course through his body as he realised the time for action had finally arrived.

He continued to observe the man as, once again, he was illuminated by the automatic porch light. No bottle of wine and no lover to complicate things tonight.

Tonight, Cavalie Naylor would pay for his sins.

The porch light went off. Seconds later, the light in the lounge came on.

The Watcher knew every room of the house after his meticulous recce. With a tinge of excitement, he began to prepare the kit he would need for his night's work.

Silently, he dragged the black leather grip bag towards him and made a check of the contents. Inside the grip bag was a black daysack that contained a black woollen ski mask, surgical latex gloves, a roll of brown gaffer tape, two long lengths of thin but very strong nylon cord, a two-inch paintbrush with a red handle, a small crowbar, a teaspoon that had a long pointed bowl, clear plastic ziplock bags, the razor-sharp Suminagashi skinning knife in its leather scabbard … and, finally, a loaded Smith & Wesson .38 revolver with a black rubber grip.

A grim smile of satisfaction played across his lips as he felt the weight of the loaded revolver in his hands.

Deep down, he knew he wouldn't need the firearm.

It would be an easy task for him to overpower his target, using his own massive physical strength. Although only slight in stature, the Watcher was extremely powerful and naturally strong. He carried the firearm as a contingency, should his meticulous plan go awry.

He continued to observe the bungalow until every light had been switched off. The property was now in darkness.

The Watcher made a last check of the hide, which had been his home for four days. He had left nothing behind. The leather grip bag now contained everything he had used in the hide. Small plastic bags, containing his own excrement, had been gathered up and placed in the bag. Apart from a slight indentation in the ground and some crushed vegetation, it was as if he'd never been there. The tools he needed for his mission were already in the black daysack, which he carried over his shoulder. It was now after midnight.

Stealthily, he made his way towards the rear of the bungalow. A black ski mask had replaced the head and shoulders of his ghillie suit. The camouflage headgear now returned to the black leather grip bag.

When he reached the rear of the bungalow, he stashed the grip bag beneath one of the rhododendron bushes dotted along the rear of the property. He made his way to the small junction box that contained the telephone line. He attached the razor-sharp skinning knife to his belt and used it to sever the telephone line.

Being careful how he placed his feet on the loose gravel, to avoid any unnecessary noise, he made his way to the weak French doors that opened out from the kitchen. He'd previously identified these flimsy wooden doors as the best point of access into the bungalow. He used the small crowbar to prise open the doors.

Having opened the doors, he crouched outside and waited.

After two minutes of silence, he stepped through the open doors and into the luxurious kitchen. Moving into the hallway, he located the alarm panel on the wall.

Satisfied there had been no activation, the Watcher made his way through the bungalow and into the master bedroom. Cavalie Naylor was already in a deep sleep. As soon as his eyes had adjusted fully to the low levels of light in the bedroom, the Watcher stepped over to the bed. He landed a single concussive blow with the clenched fist of his right hand onto the forehead of the sleeping man.

Pulling back the duvet, the Watcher removed the now-unconscious Naylor's boxer shorts. He lifted the naked man from the bed and carried him back through the bungalow. Once inside the kitchen, he used the two lengths of thin nylon cord to bind him securely to one of the sturdy wooden chairs.

The Watcher then wrapped sticky brown gaffer tape over Naylor's mouth before standing back and waiting patiently. Confident in his planning, he removed the woollen gloves and placed them back in the daysack. He adjusted the blue latex gloves that he wore below the woollen ones, before closing the venetian blinds on all the windows. He then flicked on the low-level lighting in the kitchen.

After almost ten minutes, Naylor finally started to stir from his unconscious state. As he slowly drifted back to full consciousness, the Watcher stared at him. He could see the fear in the man's eyes as the realisation of what had happened became apparent.

Naylor was shocked and frightened. He panicked and began to struggle against his bindings. He looked around the room and, for the first time, saw the Watcher standing to his left.

Illuminated only by the low-level, subdued lighting, the Watcher was a terrifying sight.

Naylor could see the figure was dressed from head to foot in dirty camouflage clothing. He wore blue latex gloves, and his face was covered by a black woollen ski mask. The only parts of the face that Naylor could see were the staring, crystal clear blue eyes and the cruel mouth.

He was terrified by the vision and started to hyperventilate beneath the gaffer tape, making a wheezing, panting noise.

The Watcher stepped forward and ripped the brown tape from Naylor's mouth. He gripped the bound man's throat and growled softly, 'If you scream or make a sound, I'll kill you right now. Co-operate with me and you'll live. Do you understand?'

Frantically, Naylor nodded.

Very slowly, the Watcher eased the pressure on Naylor's throat.

Finding his voice, Naylor muttered, 'Who are you? What do you want?'

In his soft Scottish accent, the Watcher replied, 'What I want from you is information. Before I leave here tonight, you'll tell me the names and everything else I need to know about your three friends from Nottingham University.'

'I don't know who you mean ... what friends? I've got no friends from my university days.'

Without speaking, the Watcher stepped forward and wrapped more of the sticky brown gaffer tape around Naylor's head. The tape covered his mouth, but left his nose clear.

He stood before Naylor and held up the razor-sharp skinning knife in front of the terrified man's eyes. The keen blade on the bone-handled knife glinted in the subdued lighting.

'You'll soon learn that it's pointless to try to lie to me, laddie. You will give me those names and the information I want, eventually. It's entirely a matter of your own choosing how much pain you want to endure before you do.'

The razor-sharp blade of the skinning knife was then expertly used to remove a six-inch-by-three-inch strip of flesh from Naylor's chest. The upper layers of the skin had been peeled off with a deft hand. A hand that was totally at ease skinning animals. Blood started to seep from the large wound, and Naylor let out an agonised, muffled scream into the gaffer tape.

The Watcher repeated this process three more times.

Very carefully, he laid each strip of flayed flesh over the back of another wooden chair, strategically placed so that Naylor could see the strips of his own flesh.

The excruciating pain of being flayed alive caused the tortured man to lapse in and out of consciousness.

Finally, Naylor returned to full consciousness. Once again, the Watcher removed the tape from his victim's mouth.

Naylor panted, then started to softly whimper. Sweat was beading on his forehead.

The Watcher moved close to his face and whispered gruffly, 'Are you ready to talk to me now? Or have I got to peel off more of your worthless skin?'

Naylor sobbed, 'Please, no more. I'll give you their names, but they're not my friends. I don't know what they've done to you, but whatever it is, it's nothing to do with me.'

'Boy, just give me their names, NOW!'

Naylor blurted out the three names, then mumbled a response to each of the Watcher's questions. When the questioning had been exhausted, more tape was placed over Naylor's mouth. Even though his body was racked with pain, he started to struggle against the nylon cord and grunted into the clinging tape. His eyes were now wide with fear.

The Watcher reached into the breast pocket of his camouflage overalls and took out a small laminated photograph. He held the image directly in front of Naylor's face, forcing him to look at it.

As he looked at the photograph, Naylor began to weep. Tears streamed down his face, and his body convulsed, racked with sobs. Naylor now knew exactly why this was happening to him. Through the gaffer tape, he tried to scream the words, *I'm sorry!*

The noise that emerged from his mouth behind the

tape was unintelligible.

The Watcher wasn't there for apologies.

He took the pointed teaspoon out of the daysack. Holding it in his left hand, he pressed it hard into the side of Naylor's right eye socket. He exerted pressure on the back of Naylor's head with his right hand, until the metal bowl of the spoon slid in and behind the eyeball. With a deft flick of the spoon , the Watcher popped Naylor's right eyeball out of its socket and onto his cheek.

The pain was overwhelming, and momentarily Naylor blacked out.

He quickly regained consciousness, but was now totally disoriented. His right eyeball was lying on his right cheek, facing down towards the floor. Naylor could still see the images through the eye, but they were no longer aligned with the images being seen by his left eye.

The Watcher used the keen blade of the skinning knife to slice through the optic nerve of the right eye. He held the severed eyeball by the stringy nerve and dangled it in front of Naylor. Growling with contempt, he said, 'Now you're sorry, laddie.'

Frantically, Naylor nodded in agreement, whimpering behind the tape.

The pointed spoon was then used in the same way to remove the left eyeball from its socket. Naylor experienced another brief moment of disorientation as he continued to see the world through the eye that was now lying on his cheek.

The Watcher sliced through the optic nerve of the left eye, and Naylor was instantly plunged into a sightless darkness. Beneath the gag, he started to mutter the word, 'No,' repeatedly.

Having dropped both the severed eyes into a clear

plastic ziplock bag, the Watcher placed the eyes into the daysack.

Moving silently, he manoeuvred around Naylor until he stood directly behind him. Naylor was numb with shock. His body convulsed as he sobbed behind the cloying gag.

With his left hand, the Watcher grabbed a handful of Naylor's dark hair. He pulled his head sharply back and savagely sliced the skinning knife across the exposed throat. The razor-sharp knife easily sliced through windpipe, tendons, muscles, nerves and arteries.

The blood loss from the gaping wound was massive.

Still bound to the wooden chair, Naylor was quickly surrounded by a pool of his own blood. The dark viscous liquid spread rapidly across the polished white marble floor tiles.

For Cavalie Naylor, death came quickly as he bled out.

The Watcher surveyed the scene of carnage and smiled.

He felt satisfied that the first part of his pilgrimage was now complete. He stretched his arms out in front of him, raised his blood-soaked palms to the sky and said a quiet prayer, thanking the Lord God Almighty for guiding his hand.

He moved around the kitchen and methodically gathered all the tools he'd used, placing them back into the daysack. Finally, he took the two-inch paintbrush out of the daysack. There was one last thing he needed to do before he could leave the bungalow.

Bending forward, he dipped the paintbrush into the already congealing pool of Cavalie Naylor's blood.

4
___

9.00am, 25 March 1986
Arnold, Nottingham

Geoff Naylor was in a foul mood.
He had spent the last two days in London. The important business meetings he'd attended had not gone well.

As he parked the car outside his office, he reflected on the arguments he'd become embroiled in with Malcolm Franklin.

Malcolm was the youngest son of Gregg Franklin, the owner of Franklin & Sons. He had only just joined his father's company and was fresh out of some dishwater university down south. The gobby little shit thought he was God's gift to commerce. What an arrogant jumped-up prick he was, trying to tell Geoff how he could make massive savings if he would only run his company in a more modern fashion. Never mind the fact that he had built his company, by himself, from scratch and had probably forgotten more about running a business than Malcolm would ever learn.

After the first clash and the heated exchanges that followed, Geoff had lost all interest in closing the deal. The result being that he'd come away from London late yesterday evening having told Gregg Franklin, and his cockney dickhead son Malcolm, exactly where they could stick their competitively priced electrical cabling.

The consequence of this rash act meant he would have to start urgently ringing round other suppliers for the cabling he needed. Geoff knew in his heart that he'd behaved unprofessionally. That his anger and his spur-of-the-moment decision to pull the plug on the deal would end up costing Naylor Properties Limited a great deal of money. He was now worried that it might even affect the costings for the pending contract with Notts County Council, to build the new Mansfield Woodhouse Police Station.

He slammed his car door and, with an air of defiance, said, 'Who gives a fuck! It will cost that prick, Franklin, far more than it will cost me!'

He chuckled briefly, but the smile evaporated immediately when he noticed that his son's car was not in the car park.

He stormed into the building and walked straight into his office. He ignored the two personal assistants who sat outside the office. Their greetings, made in unison, of 'Good morning, Mr Naylor' fell on deaf ears today.

He sat down heavily in his leather chair and hurled his briefcase onto the settee just the other side of the desk. He felt a familiar heaviness begin to spread across his chest. He knew that feeling only too well.

Reaching into his jacket pocket, he took out a small, solid silver pillbox. He flicked open the lid and took out a single black pill, which he popped into his mouth. He allowed the pill to dissolve beneath his tongue, then closed his eyes and willed himself to calm down.

After a few minutes, the feeling of tightness in his chest passed, and his breathing became deeper.

Feeling calmer, he picked up the telephone and dialled the number for his son's home. He heard the continuous tone that told him the phone was engaged. On the third try, and still getting the same tone, Naylor slammed the phone down and picked up his car keys. He'd made his mind up. He was going to drive over to Underwood, confront Cavalie and get his slack attitude sorted out once and for all.

His son would have a choice. Either he got rid of that useless, grasping piece of shit Christopher Baker, or he could leave the company. He wasn't going to be pissed about, or disrespected, like this anymore.

No sooner had he grabbed the car keys than the phone on his desk began to ring. That would be typical of Cavalie, he thought, to call right at the point of confrontation.

Still feeling angry, he picked up the phone: 'What?'

He instantly recognised the sing-song tones in the voice. It was the detestable Christopher on the phone. 'I'm sorry to bother you at work, Mr Naylor, but has Cavalie had to go away on business again?'

'No, he hasn't, why?'

'I've been away on a sketching course in Cornwall, and we were supposed to be going out for drinks tomorrow evening, but he's not returning my calls. I've phoned him every night since I arrived in Cornwall. He hasn't returned a single call or left any messages. I'll be honest with you, Mr Naylor; I'm beginning to get worried.'

Geoff Naylor detested every fibre of the man who

was on the phone. Just the sound of his voice made his flesh crawl. Then the enormity of what he was hearing began to worm its way into his brain. It bypassed his foul mood and circled around his hatred for the loathsome man.

A question began to scream through his brain. *Where is Cavalie?*

He dropped the telephone on his desk, ignoring Christopher's cries of, 'Mr Naylor, are you there? Mr Naylor?'

He stormed out of his office and growled at his PA, 'I'm driving over to Cav's house.'

In the time it took him to drive from his offices in Arnold out to the small village of Underwood, Geoff Naylor's mood had gone from angry to extremely worried. He'd assumed that his son was off gallivanting somewhere with that grasping friend of his.

The telephone call he'd received from Christopher had put paid to that idea. If he wasn't on holiday abroad with his friend, where was he? What was he playing at? Why hadn't he been in to work?

Geoff drove at crazy speeds along the country lanes that led to his son's bungalow.

Finally, the modern property came into view, and he slowed his vehicle. He let out an audible gasp when he saw his son's Jaguar was still parked on the driveway. There was an icy dread beginning to creep slowly over him. He had an intuition, only shared between a father and child, that something was dreadfully wrong. Horrific thoughts began to gnaw into his mind.

He parked immediately behind his son's car.

His eyes were locked onto the car in front of him. He sat there staring, almost in disbelief that the car was there.

Frantically, he began searching the glove compartment of his own car for the spare set of keys to Cavalie's bungalow. He found the house keys and got out of the car; a hundred different scenarios were now playing through his mind.

Whenever an innocent explanation came to mind, it was quickly replaced with the idea that some dreadful harm had befallen his only child. His legs felt weak, and his heart was pounding in his chest. It was with a feeling of real trepidation that he slowly made his way to the front door.

He peered through the stained-glass panel at each side of the front door. Listening intently, he couldn't hear a thing, but he noticed several large black house flies on the inside of the glass panes.

He banged on the heavy door with his fist and shouted, 'Cav! Are you in there, son?'

The silence was deafening.

He lifted the heavy brass letterbox in the middle of the door, then leaned forward, intending to shout his son's name again.

The shout never came.

As he lifted the letterbox to shout, he breathed in. He instantly gagged on the smell emanating from within the bungalow.

It was a smell he knew. He remembered it from his days as a soldier, fighting in Korea. It was the sickly-sweet, cloying smell of death, and it was coming from inside his son's bungalow.

He felt his chest tighten; his hands shook as he fumbled with the front door key.

At last, the Yale key slipped into the lock. He gave it the half turn needed to open the door. The bungalow still appeared neat and tidy, but it was full of large flies. The stench inside was overpowering, and he fought hard against an overwhelming urge to vomit.

As he walked through the bungalow, he knew exactly what he was going to find.

Even though he was expecting it, the shock of what he saw as he walked into the kitchen made him almost keel over. He grabbed hold of the granite worktop to prevent himself from collapsing completely.

He began to sob as he saw his beloved Cavalie, bound and gagged, sitting in a chair in the centre of the kitchen.

His son's throat had been cut from ear to ear.

Dried crusty blood covered his naked torso, and a large pool of blood had congealed beneath the chair. Maggots crawled in and around the deep slash wound across the throat. The creamy white larvae stood out against the black of the dried blood.

He couldn't bear to see the horrendous image any longer and looked away. He was immediately confronted with another hideous sight. Long strips of human skin had been laid over the back of one of the other chairs. The edges were beginning to curl inwards now that the flesh had dried.

He looked back at his son's mutilated body and saw that the lengths of skin had been flayed from his chest. There were four strips of skin in all. Whoever had killed his son had tortured him first.

Regaining some of the composure of a veteran soldier who'd seen horrendous wounds and countless mutilated bodies during the heat of battle in Korea, he steeled himself and looked closer at the body of his dead son.

He could now see that both his son's eyes were missing.

The sockets were now gaping black holes. The maggots danced in and out of the voids created, desperately searching for a way into the dead man's skull.

Geoff Naylor looked down on the floor below the chair, expecting to see the eyes. There was nothing lying in the congealed pool of blood.

The eyes were nowhere to be seen.

From the moment he had first walked into what resembled a slaughterhouse, Naylor had remained motionless. Finally, he found the strength in his legs to move; he turned away and now faced the far kitchen wall.

As soon as he turned away from his dead son, he was confronted with another image, one that chilled his blood.

Painted on the cream wall of the kitchen, in letters ten inches high, were a series of numbers and letters. They had been brushed onto the wall using his son's blood. There were streak marks down the wall where the blood had run. The dried rivulets made the whole scene even more macabre.

Geoff Naylor could take no more. He stumbled backwards out of the bungalow onto the York stone driveway. He bent forward, placed his hands on his knees, and ejected his recently consumed breakfast all over the yellow-coloured flagstones.

The action of vomiting strained his stomach. He could now feel a familiar dull pain start to throb in his left armpit. The pain grew steadily, then suddenly shot like a lightning bolt down the length of his left arm.

He staggered back to his car and frantically grabbed for his suit jacket that he'd left on the front seat. From the pocket, he retrieved a small pill case. He instantly slipped a black pill beneath his tongue, picked up the small bottle of water that was on the front seat, then slumped down beside the car.

He sipped the water and slowly waited for the pounding in his temples to stop.

Gradually, the heavy ache in his chest subsided, and the shooting pains in his left arm stopped altogether.

After ten minutes, he got onto his hands and knees and crawled back towards the front door of the bungalow. He knew it was too soon to risk standing, but he needed to raise the alarm. He knew if he pushed it, he would be as dead as his son long before any help arrived.

Progress across the driveway was painfully slow. Eventually, he crawled back into the bungalow. The telephone was on an antique wall unit in the hallway.

Not far to go now.

He lifted the handset of the cream-coloured telephone and dialled three nines.

Nothing.

He held the phone close to his ear; he couldn't hear a dialling tone.

The line was dead.

He slumped from his hands and knees and lay face down on the floor.

Using the last reserves of his energy, he rolled onto his back. His eyes felt heavy now. He knew that if he went to sleep now, he would never wake up. Just as he was losing the battle to keep his eyelids open, he heard a knock on the front door and then a man's voice say, 'Hello, anybody in?'

Naylor saw a man's head look around the heavy door. He saw the man's eyes widen as he saw him lying on the floor in the hallway.

The man rushed into the hallway, bent down at Naylor's side, and said, 'Bloody hell, mate, are you alright? You look like shit.'

Naylor recognised the uniform of the post office; it was the postman.

In a voice that was little more than a croaky whisper,

he gasped, 'Call the police. It's my son; he's been murdered. The phone line here's dead. Go and get help, for God's sake.'

The shocked postman blurted out, 'I'll call the police, mate. Are you gonna be okay? You look terrible.'

'I've got my heart pills with me. I'll be fine. Go and call the police, now!'

The postman stood up and raced back out of the bungalow.

Feeling hopeful now, Naylor propped himself against the wall and took another sip of water. He felt the shooting pain down his left arm again. It was getting worse. He fumbled for his pillbox and took another of the tiny black pills, letting it dissolve below his tongue. He hadn't felt this bad for ages.

The agonising pain in his arm gradually subsided, replaced by a feeling of heaviness across his chest. It felt as though a man were standing on his chest.

His breathing was shallow. He panted, trying to get more oxygen in. He closed his eyes, attempted to shut out the pain, and concentrated on remaining calm.

Finally, in the distance, he could hear sirens approaching.

5

11.00am, 25 March 1986
Underwood, Nottinghamshire

As Danny and Rob parked their cars outside the bungalow at Underwood, it was already a hive of police activity.

Danny parked behind the two large white vans being used by the Scenes of Crime team and the Special Operations Unit. A little further down the quiet lane, there were several dark-coloured cars being used by the team of detectives from the MCIU.

A uniformed constable stood outside the front door of the bungalow, clipboard in hand, guardian of the all-important scene log.

Detective Constable Rachel Moore came out of the bungalow, wearing a pale blue forensic suit and over-shoes, carrying a clipboard. Pulling off her latex gloves, she waved at Danny and Rob as they approached her.

'Hello, boss. DS Mayhew phoned in sick this morning, so I've been into the scene to take notes from the pathologist.'

'That's fine. What have we got?'

Rachel glanced down at the clipboard and said, 'Our victim is Cavalie Naylor, twenty-nine years of age, company director of Naylor Properties Ltd. He lives here alone and was found by his father, Geoff Naylor.'

Danny asked, 'Is his father still here?'

Rachel said, 'The first officer who got here thought he was having a heart attack, so he called for an ambulance. Turns out the old man's on medication for acute angina, so it was a good shout by the cop. He was rushed to hospital with a suspected heart attack.'

'We'll obviously need to talk with Mr Naylor. Which hospital has he been taken to?'

Rachel glanced at the clipboard. 'They've taken him to King's Mill at Mansfield. The young cop said he looked like death when the ambulance took him away.'

'Who's the attending pathologist?'

'It's Seamus Carter.'

'Is the cause of death obvious?'

'The victim's had his throat cut, so there's an awful lot of blood everywhere. It looks like he bled out. There's something very bizarre in there as well. The killer's left us a message.'

'A message,' echoed Rob.

'Some sort of coded message has been written on the wall.'

Danny and Rob exchanged a puzzled glance; then Danny said, 'Come on, Rob, let's get booted and suited and have a look inside.'

He turned back to Rachel and said, 'Thanks for holding the fort. I want you to try to find out from the hospital what the prognosis is for Geoff Naylor. I want to know exactly how soon we can talk to him.'

'Will do, boss.'

The two senior detectives quickly donned forensic suits, overshoes and gloves, then walked along the driveway towards the front door. As he walked along the drive, Danny could see the team of Special Operations Unit officers doing a thorough search of the extensive gardens at the rear of the house.

Both detectives gave their names to the officer maintaining the log, then walked inside. Scenes of Crime officers were already busily working inside the hallway. They had placed two strips of yellow adhesive tape on the floor. From behind his face mask, Tim Donnelly, the Scenes of Crime team leader, said, 'Make sure you stay between the lines of tape, gents. We've already checked there for fibres and stains.'

'Thanks,' said Danny before continuing, 'Is there much forensic evidence?'

'It's early days yet, boss. We haven't really started on the murder scene yet. It's through there in the kitchen; we're just waiting for the pathologist to finish up. We've taken all the photographs we need so far, but we'll be getting more when the body is eventually moved.'

'Okay, keep at it.'

Danny and Rob followed the tape trail until they reached the kitchen, where both men stood and stared at the scene of horror before them.

Cavalie Naylor's mutilated body had been tied to a chair, and his throat sliced open. Both his eye sockets were now just hollow holes. Painted on the far wall, behind the body, was a series of letters and numbers that had been daubed in blood.

The letters and numbers were ten inches high. The message read **EC21V2425**.

Standing to one side of the body, with his back facing them, was a huge man whose body was straining to stay within the confines of his forensic suit. Without turning round, his loud voice boomed, 'Gentlemen, I hope you're either the senior investigating officers, or that you've got a bloody good reason for being in my crime scene.'

'Good morning, Seamus.'

The pathologist spun around. 'Ah! Good morning, Danny. Quite a bizarre scene, I think you'd agree?'

Danny nodded. 'It's certainly that, alright.' He then pointed at the message on the wall and said, 'Any idea what that means?'

'Sorry, I've no idea what that message is all about. Coded messages aren't in my remit, I'm afraid. What I can tell you is that your victim died as a result of massive blood loss after having his throat cut. The wound is huge and severed both major blood vessels in the neck. He would have bled out very quickly.'

Rob said, 'Any idea what type of weapon has been used?'

'Difficult to say with any certainty, but it must have been a large, broad-bladed instrument that's extremely sharp. That's all I can really tell you at the moment. I might have a better idea at the post-mortem examination.'

Danny stepped forward to look closer at the gaping wound and the deep holes of the eye sockets. 'What's happened to his eyes?'

'That's what I was examining when I heard you come in. It appears that his eyes have been put out.'

'What do you mean "put out"?' asked Rob.

'The eye can be popped out of the socket, using a surgical instrument, so it rests on the cheek. It's how ophthalmic surgeons operate on the back of the eye. The optic nerve is quite robust and will stretch a little without causing damage. In a mature adult, it's roughly the thickness of a shoelace. It would appear that the killer has used some sort of instrument to crudely put out the eyes before severing the optic nerves and removing them altogether.'

'Bloody hell,' whispered Danny, 'You mean the poor sod was alive when his eyes were cut out?'

'It certainly appears that way, Detective. I'll know for certain when I can examine the eye sockets and what's left of the optic nerve at the post-mortem. I think I'll find the same with these injuries to his torso. As an educated guess, I reckon he would still have been alive when those strips of skin were flayed from his chest.'

Carter indicated the drying flesh on the chair and continued, 'The strips of skin were laid over the back of that chair and would have been visible to the victim after they had been removed.'

Rob shook his head. 'Would he have been able to stand that level of pain without blacking out?'

'Almost certainly. He would have been in agony, but I doubt it was enough to cause him to pass out.'

'The strips of skin have been left behind; is there any sign of the eyes anywhere?'

'No, they've been removed from the scene.'

Danny said, 'Do you think the killer's taken them as some sort of macabre trophy?'

'It's hard to say. It's a possibility, I suppose.'

'Looking at the level of decomposition and infestation, I would think the victim's been dead for at least a couple of days.'

Seamus Carter nodded. 'My best estimate would be that he was killed three days ago.'

'What time do you think you'll be ready to start the post-mortem examination?'

The big pathologist glanced at his watch. 'There's still a lot of work to do here with your Scenes of Crime people before we can even think about moving the body. I think, realistically, it's not going to be until later tonight. I'll arrange a time at the City Hospital mortuary and let you know.'

'Okay. Rob's staying here to manage the crime scene. If you need anything, just give him a shout.'

Danny retraced his steps out of the kitchen and made his way outside. Rob carefully followed in his footsteps.

As they stepped outside, they signed out of the scene and removed their forensic suits and overshoes. They took off the gloves and placed all the protective clothing in the bin bag at the front door. A note was made in the scene log that the protective garments had been discarded correctly.

Danny turned to Rob and said, 'Get a landline established here as a priority. I want to be able to liaise with you while you're here.'

'Will do, boss.'

There was a shout from the rear garden of the bungalow.

A detective came rushing down from the raised garden and waved to Danny. 'Over here, boss!'

Danny and Rob walked over to the breathless detective, who said, 'The Special Ops lads have found what appears to be the remnants of a hide that looks down over the property.'

'Okay. Rob, get it all photographed. Then get the Special Ops lads to fingertip search it. If it's been used by the killer, and he's left something behind, I don't want to miss it.'

'I'm on it.'

Rob walked off, following the detective with the Special Ops team.

Danny located Rachel Moore on the driveway and said, 'Any news from King's Mill?'

Rachel frowned. 'It doesn't sound good. Geoff Naylor almost died in the ambulance. He's been stabilised now but is heavily sedated. We won't be talking to him for a day or so, at the earliest.'

'Thanks.'

Danny walked back to his car; he was deep in thought. He had seen a lot of murder scenes, but there was something particularly savage and brutal about this one. What was the message left on the wall all about?

None of it made any sense.

6
―――

11.00am, 25 March 1986
Clumber Park, Nottinghamshire

The caravan site, situated in Clumber Park, had served as his base of operation since the start of his pilgrimage. It suited his purpose perfectly. The small caravan he had rented was cheap and easily big enough for his needs. The site itself was very secluded, and only a couple of the other caravans on-site were occupied. The shower block was still in good working order and provided hot and cold running water.

He'd arrived at the site on the seventeenth of March. He'd told the owner he would only need a short-term rental for a month. The cover story he had given was that he was on holiday for the next four weeks and wanted to use the caravan as a base for walking trips in the nearby Derbyshire Dales. He'd explained that he wanted to experience a different walk each day and would often be away from the site.

On his arrival at the Clumber Park site, he'd quickly stowed all his gear in the caravan. He'd then set off that evening to establish the hide at Underwood. Once he'd found a suitable location that overlooked the house, he'd prepared the hide. He'd stashed everything he would need, for both the observations and the operation, within it. Only when everything had been taken care of did he return to the caravan park to rest.

The next day, he'd driven the battered olive-green Land Rover Defender he was using to Jacksdale. Geographically, it was the closest village to Underwood. He'd visited a local newsagent in the village. In the window, he had seen a handwritten notice advertising a single garage to rent.

He removed the advertisement card from the window and drove to the address. The garage was at the side of a private house. The Watcher studied the house carefully. The external paintwork was shabby, and the garden was overgrown. He could see a handrail at the side of the front door. All the indications were that it was an elderly person who lived there.

As daylight was turning to dusk, he knocked on the front door of the decaying house. After a brief wait, the door was opened by an incredibly frail-looking old lady. The Watcher explained to her that he was interested in renting the garage for a week. The old lady explained that her husband had passed away six months ago, and she no longer had any use for the garage. The woman agreed to rent the garage to him for one week, at a cost of ten pounds.

Taking the black leather grip bag, which contained everything he would need that wasn't already stashed at the hide, he locked the Land Rover in the garage at Jacksdale.

Ensuring there were no prying eyes watching him, he then set off on foot, under the cover of darkness, across the fields to the neighbouring village of Underwood.

With the Land Rover safely tucked away out of sight and under lock and key, he could now concentrate solely on the observations at the secluded bungalow.

The day prior to him taking up residence at the caravan, the Watcher had established where Cavalie Naylor lived. He had followed him from his workplace to his home address. The only information he had at the beginning of his pilgrimage was the name Cavalie Naylor and the name of the company he owned and worked for.

It had been an easy task for him, first to locate the company in the Arnold district of Nottingham, then to establish that the Jaguar parked in the bay marked Managing Director belonged to Cavalie Naylor.

The first time he saw Naylor, he'd resisted the massive urge he felt to slaughter him there and then. Before he dispatched him to hell, he needed answers. He knew that he needed information from him to help identify the other three demons who needed to pay before God for their sins.

With the Lord's help, he had managed to stay his hand that day. He had demonstrated the patience required. That patience had been rewarded, and the Almighty had delivered unto him the first of the demons.

He had carried out the Lord's bidding perfectly; he felt at peace.

The first part of his mission had taken four long days, with hardly any sleep and little sustenance. It was nothing to him. He'd spent far longer periods in hides when it had been required.

The Watcher had been trained by the best; he was a total professional. Stalking and killing were his stock-in-trade. He was a cold-blooded assassin who revelled in his work.

On the night he killed Naylor, he had walked – in the pitch black – back across the farmland to Jacksdale. It had been almost three o'clock in the morning when he stealthily stalked through the deserted streets of the small village. The roads of the village had few street-lights and were dimly lit. He hadn't seen or heard a soul. He had felt an overwhelming sense, once again, that the Lord was protecting him. He retrieved the Land Rover from the garage and left the padlock and key, with another ten-pound note stuffed beneath it, outside the old lady's front door.

Having arrived back at the Clumber Park site in the early hours of the morning, he had utilised the rudimentary washing facilities in the deserted shower block to wash his kit before the few other caravaners on the site were awake.

He had then returned to his caravan and placed the ziplock bag that contained Naylor's eyes into the small fridge.

Now as he sat in the caravan, he smiled as he thought about the successful outcome of the first part of his mission. He sipped black coffee and ate warm toast. He scribbled down the information he had extracted from Naylor. He now had sufficient information about the three other demons to carry out the order God had given him. They would all soon be despatched back to hell. Naylor had readily given over their names, occupations, and brief descriptions as he writhed in agony after being cruelly flayed alive.

The Watcher placed the mug and plate into the small sink and pondered his next move. Stepping back to the table, he studied the Ordnance Survey map he'd picked up from a local garage. The map gave detailed information of the area surrounding Clumber Park.

Carefully scanning the detailed map, he soon found the nearest public telephone box.

All it required next was a simple phone call to the operator. He would then be able to establish the exact location of his next target. As soon as he discovered that location, he would be able to proceed with his grim pilgrimage.

Suddenly, tiredness overwhelmed him. He didn't bother to undress; he just climbed straight into the sleeping bag on the small bench that constituted his bed.

Within minutes, the Watcher was fast asleep.

7

9.00pm, 25 March 1986
Nottingham City Hospital Mortuary

The examination room was stark and bathed in white light.

There were several stainless-steel examination tables stretched out along one side of the large room.

Standing to one side of the room were Danny Flint and Rob Buxton. Immediately behind them, with a large notepad at the ready, was Police Sergeant Tina Prowse.

Tina Prowse was a recent addition to the Major Crime Investigation Unit. She was an extremely ambitious young woman, very slight in stature, with blonde hair that she wore in a ponytail. As a graduate entry, she had already taken and passed her sergeant's promotion exam with just over three years' service. After completing her two-year probationary period and passing the qualifying exam, she had been promoted to sergeant immediately. She had since undertaken and passed her inspector's exam and was awaiting the next available accelerated promotion course at Bramshill Police College. On completion of that course, she would be promoted to inspector.

The graduate entry scheme also allowed participating officers the opportunity to serve with specialist departments, and although Tina had never been on a CID course, Danny considered her to be a great asset to the unit. Her intellect was beyond doubt, and she combined that with an exceptionally good work ethic. No one doubted that Tina Prowse was destined for the very top.

In front of the detectives, on the stainless-steel examination table, was the naked, mutilated body of Cavalie Naylor. The level of decomposition and putrefaction of the body was even more apparent now that it was in the sterile environment of the mortuary. The associated smells and odours of death were readily apparent to everyone in the room.

Detective Constable Jeff Williams stood to one side of the room, surrounded by exhibit bags and labels, ready to record and bag anything deemed as evidence by either the pathologist or his senior officers.

Seamus Carter stood on the far side of the examination table and instructed his own assistant to commence taking photographs of the body. Once the photographs had been taken, he then made his own visual study of the cadaver laid out in front of him.

He spoke aloud his observations, recording them on a Dictaphone. Tina Prowse scribbled furiously in her notepad, diligently recording his findings. The pathologist would use the verbal information on the Dictaphone to prepare his written report for the investigation team.

Having completed his visual examination, he turned to Danny and said, 'This is interesting. If you look closely, there's a small area of bruising on the victim's forehead. They look like knuckle marks to me. It looks as though he was initially incapacitated by a single punch to the forehead.'

Danny stepped forward to look for himself.

The bindings that had been used to tie the victim to the chair were then carefully removed from the wrists of the dead man. The cord was exhibited and bagged up for later forensic examination.

Seamus Carter then began to examine the wounds around the eye sockets. The pathologist endeavoured to establish exactly what types of instruments had been used to sever and remove the eyes. Tests confirmed that Cavalie Naylor had been very much alive when his eyes had been removed.

The large gaping wound on Naylor's neck was then minutely examined.

By scrutinising the angle of the large cut, the pathologist established that the sharp bladed instrument had been held in the assailant's right hand, and that the murderer had stood behind his victim.

Seamus Carter offered the opinion that the weapon used to make the wound was a heavy, large-bladed, razor-sharp hunting knife. The pathologist stated he thought it could be a knife like the ones used by hunters to gut and skin their prey.

He then examined the wounds on the chest caused by the removal of the skin.

He turned to Danny and said, 'Whoever did this knows exactly what they are doing. The skin has been flayed very carefully. It's been done by someone skilled in the removal of skin or hide.'

Danny bent forward to look at the areas of flayed skin and said, 'How can you tell?'

'Because the outer skin has been removed without causing massive damage to the underlying flesh. I think the blade used to flay the skin from the body was also extremely sharp.'

Carter then performed a further test that established Naylor had been alive when the strips of skin had been removed.

After working intently for another forty minutes, Carter had completed the post-mortem examination. All the exhibits taken had been labelled, signed and bagged.

Danny said, 'How soon can you let me have your full report?'

'I can have it ready for you by tomorrow afternoon.'

'Thanks. I appreciate that.'

Danny then turned to DC Williams and said, 'Jeff, make sure everything is recorded and the exhibits are stored appropriately before you go off duty, please.'

The detective nodded and began tidying everything away.

Seamus Carter said, 'Any more thoughts on the message left on the kitchen wall?'

'Nothing so far. You?'

The big pathologist shook his head. 'Makes no sense to me. I'll call you tomorrow.'

As the pathologist left the room, a mortuary attendant entered to take the remains of Cavalie Naylor back to the refrigerated drawers in the main part of the mortuary. As he was a victim of foul play, his body would be placed in deep-freeze drawers, in case there was a need for a further examination in the future.

Danny turned to Tina and said, 'Was that your first post-mortem?'

The young sergeant nodded and said, 'It was. I found it interesting, sir.'

Danny smiled and said, 'Thank you for taking such comprehensive notes; they will help with the debrief for the team.'

'No problem, sir.'

As the three detectives walked through the car park of the hospital, Danny turned to Rob and said, 'It's way too late to have a debrief tonight. How about tomorrow morning?'

Rob said, 'I thought it would be a late finish, so I spoke with Brian before coming here. We've already allocated the outstanding, urgent enquiries that need doing tomorrow. Everyone on the team knows exactly what enquiries they need to be looking at. There shouldn't be a need to debrief again until tomorrow evening, if that's okay with you, Danny.'

'I'll have a look at the enquiries you've allocated in the morning, just to make sure we haven't missed anything. Let's schedule the next debrief for six o'clock tomorrow evening.'

As the car was driven slowly out of the car park, Danny was deep in thought. What kind of maniac mutilates a body like that and then writes a message using the blood from their victim on the walls?

8

9.00am, 26 March 1986
Ollerton, Nottinghamshire

The Watcher parked the Land Rover in the car park of the Snooty Fox public house in Old Ollerton. After looking around to check the area, he got out of the vehicle, crossed the road and stepped inside the red telephone box.

It was still early, and the quiet street was deserted. He was relieved to see the telephone box hadn't been vandalised, and the telephone itself was still in good working order.

He phoned directory enquiries and asked the operator for the number of the Royal Grosvenor Hotel in Nottingham. When the automated voice recited the number, he quickly scribbled it down.

Wasting no time, he dialled the number, and when the beeps started, he stuffed loose change into the coin slot. He heard a voice say, 'Royal Grosvenor Hotel, Amanda speaking, how can I help you?'

Calmly, he replied, 'Good morning, Amanda. I was contacted by a friend in Nottingham yesterday, and she asked me to meet her in the foyer of your hotel later today. Like an idiot, I didn't ask her precisely whereabouts in Nottingham your hotel is located?'

Amanda chuckled pleasantly before saying, 'That's no problem, sir. We're by far the biggest hotel in Nottingham; I'm sure you would've found us anyway. We're located on Maid Marian Way in the city centre. Is there anything else I can help you with this morning, sir?'

'No. Thank you. Thanks for all your help.'

He walked back across the road to the Land Rover, then made the short ten-minute drive back to the deserted caravan site.

Once inside his caravan, he went to a large suitcase on the floor and removed a dark blue business suit, white shirt and dark tie. From a holdall, he took out a pair of smart black brogues.

He knew that in order to get close to the second target, he would need a totally different method.

He quickly shaved and washed, then dressed in the smart clothes. He checked his watch and flicked open his copy of the Old Testament. He read a few passages, said a quiet prayer and stepped outside to his Land Rover.

It was time to make the half-hour drive to Nottingham.

Having parked the Land Rover in the hotel car park, the Watcher made his way around to the main entrance of the Grosvenor Hotel. He pushed on the glass revolving doors and stepped inside the plush foyer. He paused for a second, quickly assessing his surroundings, then walked briskly up to the reception desk. Dressed as he was, the Watcher gave the appearance of being a successful businessman.

Smiling broadly, he engaged the pretty female receptionist, saying, 'I'm so sorry to be a bother. I've arranged to meet a potential business contact here this morning. He will be travelling into Nottingham on the ten o'clock train from Birmingham. Would you mind if I wait here in the foyer until he arrives?'

Immediately taken by the stranger's soft voice and the distinctive Scottish accent, the receptionist smiled and replied politely, 'Of course not, sir. Please feel free to wait in any one of the seats in the foyer.'

With a wave of her perfectly manicured hand, she indicated the four cream leather settees that were situated across the foyer, at the furthest point away from the reception desk.

'Thank you so much. I'll make sure I keep out of your way.'

The young receptionist smiled. 'Don't worry, sir, it's no trouble. We often have people arrange business meetings in our foyer. Especially if the clients are from out of town and are staying with us. Can I get you a cup of tea or coffee while you wait?'

With a smile, the Watcher shook his head and declined the offer of a hot drink. He was being very particular about which surfaces he touched. He had also ensured that his back was always facing the foyer's security camera.

He stepped across the slick, cream-coloured marble floor of the foyer and occupied a seat that gave him a clear view of the revolving door into the hotel. It was also the only seat in the foyer that allowed him to remain out of sight from the security camera.

No other guests or businesspeople were waiting in

the foyer, so he settled down on the soft leather of the cream settee. Inwardly, he hoped his target would make himself known soon. He didn't want to wait there too long.

At exactly five minutes past ten, the revolving glass doors flew round, and a harassed-looking individual strode inside. He was a very smart-looking man, dressed in a single-breasted black jacket and grey pinstripe trousers. His hair was jet black and parted down the centre in quite a fashionable style, which was probably just a little too young for a man in his early thirties. He had a copy of the *Daily Telegraph* tucked under his left arm, and he carried a small black leather briefcase in his right hand. After the man had breezed into the reception area, the Watcher detected a strong smell of expensive aftershave.

As the man in the black jacket approached the reception desk, the young woman who had been so accommodating to the Watcher smiled and said, 'Good morning, Mr Hall. Is everything okay?'

The response was terse and belied a certain arrogance. 'No. It bloody well isn't, Amanda! The bloody train was late again! They gave some bullshit excuse about leaves on the line – it's March, for Christ's sake! There aren't any bloody leaves on the trees, let alone on the line!'

The receptionist looked suitably horrified and said, 'Oh no, that's terrible, sir!'

Almost instantly, an easy, affable charm replaced the now-suppressed anger, and the man smiled a greasy, lecherous smile towards the young woman. 'Oh well, I'm here now. This place won't run itself, will it? I've got a stack of work to do today, and I've got to catch the two o'clock train back to Beeston.'

Oblivious to the Watcher's presence in the foyer, the

man leaned forward, resting his briefcase on the counter. He reached out with his left hand and began to caress the young receptionist's long blonde hair, twirling it between his fingers. The young woman remained stony-faced, obviously not enjoying the close attention. He leered at her full breasts, and in a breathy whisper said, 'Unfortunately, it's Vanessa's bridge night at the Ladies Rotary Club. So it's down to me to pick the brats up from school and put them to bed. Once they're tucked up in bed though, I'll be all on my lonesome for the rest of the night.'

Amanda took a strategic pace backwards. Now standing just far enough away to be out of the man's reach, she said in a very businesslike tone, 'That's too bad, Mr Hall.'

Hall immediately straightened up, sniffed loudly and began to stride away. As he walked away from the reception desk, he shouted over his shoulder, 'I'll be in my office if anybody needs me. A cup of coffee, no sugar, would be perfect. Thanks, Amanda!'

The Watcher had seen enough and walked slowly over to the reception desk. It was now almost ten fifteen.

Smiling at the now slightly flushed Amanda, he said, 'Well, it looks like my potential client must have encountered a problem. He should've been here by now, so I'm going to head off back to the office, where I can make a few calls and find out what's happened. Thank you so much for letting me wait.'

She smiled a genuinely warm smile back and said, 'No problem, sir, any time.'

'I thought that was him coming in just now, but I'm guessing that was your boss, right?'

'Yes, that's Mr Hall. He's been my boss for the last three years. He's a lovely guy.'

The Watcher admired the young girl's loyalty. It was

obvious from her body language that she despised her boss, but she was far too professional to say as much to a stranger. He smiled at the young woman and nodded before walking out. Once again, he was very careful not to show his face to the security camera.

Hours later, the Watcher glanced at his wristwatch, then shifted uncomfortably on the hard bench. It was a relic from Victorian times and had been made from wrought iron and wood. He'd been waiting patiently for the arrival of the train to Beeston that was scheduled to depart from Nottingham at two o'clock. He'd filled the time spent on the platform by sipping two large, extremely hot and frothy cappuccinos and reading a copy of the *Daily Mirror* he'd purchased from the shop at the station entrance.

As he waited patiently, he had read almost every word printed in the newspaper. He folded the newspaper and looked around, admiring the architecture of the splendid Victorian platform. There were now only ten other passengers waiting for trains. Several trains had already pulled into and then out of the busy station.

One of his favourite pastimes was people watching. He was fascinated by the passengers, of all ages, alighting from the various trains. He wondered what stories lay behind some of the overjoyed and anguished expressions he could see on different faces.

He glanced anxiously along the station platform. There was still no sign of the reason he was waiting so patiently. He'd clearly overheard the hotel manager, Edward Hall, say to the receptionist that he was catching the two-o'clock train home.

Just as he began to wonder if there had been a problem that necessitated Hall's presence at the hotel, right on cue, he saw a red-faced and flustered Edward Hall racing down the stairs onto the platform. He reached platform 2 at exactly the same time as the train destined for Beeston came to a stop. The service to and from Beeston only consisted of two carriages. Half a dozen passengers got off the train and made their way along the platform towards the station exit.

The Watcher stood up, threw the two empty coffee cups into the nearest waste bin and tucked the newspaper under his arm. He waited until Edward Hall got onto the train before boarding himself. He got into the same carriage and occupied a seat three rows behind the breathless hotel manager.

He reached into his jacket pocket, found the return ticket he'd purchased, then began to scan the newspaper. He wasn't reading it, just using it as a prop to conceal his face in case Hall turned around.

The train pulled out of the station and began to sway gently as it picked up speed, heading for the open countryside between Nottingham and Beeston.

'Tickets, please!' shouted the portly conductor as he lurched along the carriage towards Hall's seat.

The Watcher saw Hall disdainfully hold out his ticket towards the conductor without even looking up at the man. The uniformed man took his ticket and scribbled on it before returning it and moving along the carriage.

'Any more tickets?' he said again. A note of boredom could now clearly be heard in his voice.

The Watcher held out his return ticket and made eye contact with the conductor.

The conductor took the ticket and nodded in a gesture of thanks. Once again, the ticket was taken, scribbled on and returned.

As he moved further along the carriage, he shouted, 'Your next stop is Beeston. Beeston is your next stop!'

The entire journey had only taken fifteen minutes.

The train slowed, then crawled slowly to a stop alongside the platform at the small station. Edward Hall jumped up, clutching his briefcase to his chest, and made his way to the automatic doors. The train finally came to a complete stop, and the doors opened. Hall jumped from the train carriage and onto the platform.

As soon as Hall was on the platform, the Watcher stood and made his way off the train. He loitered on the platform behind Hall and was able to avoid any eye contact with the hotel manager. Three other passengers had also got off the train at Beeston. The Watcher used these people to screen himself from Hall as he followed him out of the station.

Hall walked out of the station building and into the car park.

Immediately, a slim, attractive brunette, wearing a red winter coat and black slacks, got out of a gunmetal grey BMW estate car. The car had been parked in the space nearest to the station entrance. The Watcher loitered in the entrance, standing close enough to hear the conversation between Hall and the young woman.

Hall leaned forward and pecked a kiss on the cheek of the woman. 'Hello, darling. What a day I've had. It's been a bloody nightmare; the train was late this morning. I was waiting on this bloody platform for forty-five minutes after you dropped me off!'

The woman turned away brusquely, not returning the kiss. 'Well, you're back now. Come on, darling, do hurry up. You know it's my bridge night, and I've got stacks to do before I can even think about getting ready.'

'Okay, sweetheart. Give me the keys. I'll drive.'

The woman handed the car keys to Hall, who immediately opened the driver's door. They both got into the BMW, and as soon as both doors were slammed shut, it was driven at speed out of the car park.

The Watcher smiled. He made a mental note of the car and its registration number before turning around and striding back into the small station, ready to catch the next train back to Nottingham.

Both the platform and the station were now empty.

He had no idea when the next train was due to arrive, so once again he sat down on a cold, hard bench and waited. Sitting quietly, he closed his eyes, opened his palms to heaven and muttered a quiet prayer of thanks to God.

9

**6.00pm, 26 March 1986
Major Crime Investigation Unit, Mansfield**

A thick pall of blue smoke hung in the air of the briefing room at the Major Crime Investigation Unit. Everyone was now back from the separate enquiries they had been tasked with throughout the day. Only two uniform constables would remain at the secluded property, to safeguard the scene.

It was time for a full debrief, to establish exactly what progress had been made. To see what evidence had been found by the forensic teams and to determine any new lines of enquiry that would take the investigation forward.

There was the soft murmur of voices as the team of detectives talked among themselves about the savagery of the murder they were now tasked with investigating.

The door to the briefing room opened, and Danny walked in, clutching his blue hardback notebook. Any developments and all the enquiries to be carried out would be noted in this book. That way, Danny would have an up-to-date record on the progress being made in the case.

The large briefing room fell silent, and Danny addressed the gathered detectives. 'Right. I know it's been a long day for everyone, but let's not skimp on any of the detail during this debrief. It's vitally important that everyone in this room is fully aware of every development in this case. That's the only way we'll be able to function as a coherent team. It's also the best way to get this thing cracked as quickly as possible.'

He turned to Rob Buxton and said, 'You managed the scene yesterday, and you've got a good overview of the enquiry so far. What can you tell us?'

Rob Buxton spoke slowly, allowing the gathered detectives time to take down any notes they wanted.

'The deceased is Cavalie Naylor, twenty-nine years, a single man who lived alone. He was one of the two company directors of Naylor Properties Ltd. He was found dead at his home address, which is a large, detached bungalow set on the edge of the rural community of Underwood. The offender gained entry by forcing wooden French doors situated at the rear of the property. The phone lines were cut prior to entry taking place. It would appear that the victim was overpowered in his bedroom, then taken to the kitchen. Once in the kitchen, he was bound to a chair, then killed by having his throat cut. The blood loss was enormous, and he would have quickly bled out. Nothing's been stolen from the property. Anomalies found at the scene. There was the remains of a hide in the rear garden. It looks like the offender spent a period of time there prior to the offence. Police dogs managed to briefly follow a track towards the neighbouring village of Jacksdale. Unfortunately, the track was lost quickly, so that doesn't really take us any further on. The victim had both of his eyes removed, and these were missing from the scene. If that isn't strange enough, probably the single most bizarre thing about this entire case is that the offender took the time to paint the message **EC21V2425** on the kitchen wall, using the victim's blood. You were all aware of this message yesterday. Has anyone got any ideas what it may mean?'

Rob paused, but when the room remained silent, he carried on, 'The deceased was discovered by his father, Geoff Naylor, yesterday morning, after not being seen for a few days. From the state of decomposition, it's likely he was killed approximately three days before he was found. It's now known that he was tortured before he was killed. Found draped over the back of a chair in the kitchen were four strips of skin flayed from his torso while he was still alive. The post-mortem has confirmed that his eyes were also removed while he was still alive.'

Rob paused to allow that macabre point to get through to the gathered detectives, then continued, 'That's everything from the scene. There are albums of photographs of the scene now available for you to look at. Before you leave, make sure you acquaint yourself with the details I have outlined, please. If there are no questions, I'll move on to a more detailed description of the findings from the post-mortem.'

He allowed a pause, but once again the room remained silent, so he continued, 'The cause of death was the severed throat and massive blood loss. Other injuries found are the four strips of skin flayed from the torso, the severing of the optic nerves of both eyes and bruising to the forehead. The pathologist believes this bruising was probably caused by a single punch. The weapon used to cause the wound to the throat is believed to be a razor-sharp, broad-bladed weapon. It's likely this weapon was also used to remove the strips of skin from the victim. The pathologist is of the opinion that it's possibly a large hunting knife.'

Rob closed his notebook, and Danny allowed a pause before saying, 'Thanks.'

He then turned to DC Moore and said, 'Rachel, can you give us any update on the victim's father, please?'

The detective glanced at her notebook before speaking. 'Unfortunately, Geoff Naylor is still being treated at King's Mill Hospital and cannot be spoken to at this time. I spoke with the nurse on the ward just before this briefing, and she tells me that the doctors are satisfied that Mr Naylor is now stable. They are hopeful he will be well enough to be released from hospital in the near future. I've spent most of the day with Mr Naylor's secretary at his business premises. She states that Mr Naylor made the decision to drive over to his son's address at Underwood after Cavalie hadn't been into work for a few days. She knows that Geoff Naylor has a duplicate key for his son's property. She was in quite a state of shock herself and couldn't really tell me much more. I've also located the postman who found Geoff Naylor at the scene. He told me that Mr Naylor told him the phone at the house wasn't working and that he'd run to the neighbouring house to call an ambulance and the police.'

'Thanks, Rachel. I want you to stay in touch with the hospital, please. I want to know the moment Geoff Naylor is either well enough to talk to, or he's released from the hospital.'

'Will do.'

Danny then turned to the Scenes of Crime team leader, Tim Donnelly. 'Right, Tim, what have Scenes of Crime got from Underwood?'

'We've taken casts of two footmarks found at the rear of the property. The marks aren't great, so we may not be able to do much of a comparison with any footwear we later recover. They will give us an indication of size and type, at least. Nothing of any value was found in and around the hide. Whoever was in there left it extremely sterile. Which suggests to me some kind of military training. There were glove marks at the point of entry, as well as inside the property. We've also recovered quite a few fibres at various points within the property. This could be an indicator that our offender isn't all that forensically aware. As DS Buxton mentioned, albums of photographs taken at the scene and the post-mortem are circulating for detectives to view at their leisure.'

'Thanks.'

Individual detectives then outlined what enquiries they had been tasked with and how those enquiries had progressed throughout the day.

At the end of the debrief, Danny took a minute or so to digest all the information he'd been given.

'Right, everyone, listen up. Thanks for all the hard work you've put in today. As a matter of urgency, I need to establish the meaning of the message left on the wall at the scene. I think the torture displayed here could be highly relevant. What was he trying to learn from Naylor? Was it other names or something else? It could mean that other people may be in danger from this man. Moving the enquiry forward, the following are to be considered as urgent enquiries: Rob, I want you and your team to concentrate on the area around Underwood. I'm aware there's not a lot of house-to-house enquiries to be done, but I would like enquiries made in the area to see if we can establish any relevant information on the comings and goings at the Underwood bungalow.'

Rob nodded.

Turning to Detective Inspector Hopkirk, Danny continued, 'Brian, I would like you to organise a team to look deeper into the business dealings of Naylor Properties Ltd. We need to try to establish a motive as soon as possible. Has there been any business rivalry? Has anybody been sacked? That kind of thing. I want to know exactly what Cavalie's role in the company was. Has he made enemies through the business? Finally, I want full background checks carried out on our victim. I want to know everything there is to know about Cavalie Naylor.'

'Okay, boss, no problem,' said Brian.

Danny continued, 'Okay. Be back here tomorrow morning at eight o'clock sharp. Get your thinking caps on, all of you. I want to know the meaning of that bloody message!'

10

7.30am, 27 March 1986
Beeston Railway Station, Beeston

The Watcher drove the battered green Land Rover slowly into the car park at Beeston Railway Station. He parked the vehicle as near to the station entrance as he could and then glanced at his wristwatch. It was now almost seven thirty in the morning.

He'd arrived at the small railway station early. He didn't want to risk missing Edward Hall if his target decided to catch an earlier train.

The previous day, when he'd arrived back at Nottingham Midland Station, he had purchased a train timetable that included the times of the service that ran from Beeston to Nottingham. After examining the timetable, he knew that there were trains scheduled to leave Beeston at seven forty-five, eight fifteen and eight forty-five that morning.

He'd waited patiently for almost three-quarters of an hour yesterday before the train had arrived that took him from Beeston back into Nottingham City. He'd used that time and the rest of the day in researching and planning how he was going to deal with Edward Hall.

He was satisfied with his plan.

It felt good inside, knowing that at some time within the next twenty-four hours, Edward Hall would have answered to God for his sins.

The Watcher would see to it personally.

Once again, he was dressed appropriately for his chosen course of action. He was now wearing a pair of old olive-green combat trousers, a black woollen crew neck sweater and a pair of black trainers that had been meticulously washed clean of Cavalie Naylor's blood.

Passengers began to arrive for the seven forty-five train, and very soon the car park began to fill. There was no sign of Edward Hall's grey BMW.

The Watcher heard the seven-forty-five train arrive amidst a screech of air brakes. He then saw the carriages lurch forward, pick up speed slowly, and leave the station. The car park became quiet again. To pass the time before the next train arrived, he reached over and checked the contents of the black grip bag on the passenger seat next to him.

Everything he would need for his mission was in the bag. Methodically, he checked the items: The loaded Smith & Wesson revolver, the freshly honed Suminagashi skinning knife, four-metre-long lengths of nylon cord, two pairs of latex surgical gloves, a two-inch paintbrush, a roll of gaffer tape, a black woollen ski mask, clear plastic ziplock bags, a pair of sturdy pliers, the specialist locksmith's tool and a Mini Maglite torch. It had been instilled into him during his training that, when it came to equipment, he needed to check, recheck and check again.

As cars started pulling into the car park again, the Watcher glanced at his watch. It was now almost ten minutes past eight.

Just when he began to think that Edward Hall must be catching the later train at eight forty-five, he saw the sleek grey BMW estate sweep into the car park.

The Halls' car had barely stopped before the two front doors flew open. Edward Hall and his wife jumped out, leaving two children in the back of the car. He had been driving the car, and his wife had been the front-seat passenger. Having exited the vehicle, they left the doors wide open and theatrically ran around to the front of the car, where they embraced.

The Watcher wound down the window of the Land Rover an inch or two so he could listen in on the couple's conversation.

Edward Hall quickly kissed his wife. She returned his kiss and said, 'Have a good day, sweetheart. I'll be here at five o'clock. I'll bring the children with me so we can nip into town and have pizza for tea.'

The two children in the back of the car squealed loudly at the prospect of pizza for tea.

Hall again kissed his wife on the cheek before saying, 'That'll be perfect, darling. Pizza it is, kids.'

He waved to the two children in the back of the car, then strode off purposefully towards the station to catch the eight-fifteen train.

Vanessa Hall waved before getting into the driver's side of the BMW. She reached across and closed the passenger door before driving out of the car park. The Watcher started the Land Rover and began to discreetly follow the unsuspecting Vanessa Hall.

As he followed the grey estate, the Watcher was

troubled.

He had heard Hall mention the children yesterday at the hotel, but it was only now that he'd physically seen them that he realised he hadn't factored the two small children into his plan. He needed time to think things through.

After a ten-minute drive, the BMW came to a stop outside the entrance to a very exclusive private school. The two back doors were flung open, and two overly excited children, dressed in smart red-and-black school uniforms, jumped out. The children were quickly followed by their mother. All three walked through the school gates and made their way inside the school building.

The Watcher estimated that Edward Hall's daughter was probably seven years old, maybe eight. The boy looked to be even younger, six years old at the most.

Having delivered the children into school, Vanessa Hall came back to the car and quickly drove off. The Watcher followed her, maintaining a cautious distance between the BMW and the Land Rover.

Five minutes later, both vehicles were being driven along a nice, tree-lined street in Beeston Fields, a very upmarket suburb of Beeston. The houses here were all very grand, detached properties with large, well-established gardens. The Watcher smiled as he saw the BMW turn into the driveway of a particularly large house. The front garden of the property was extensive, and the house itself was set back quite a distance from the road.

He parked the Land Rover directly opposite the property, got out, and walked over to the privet hedge that surrounded the garden. Peering through the hedge, he was just in time to see Vanessa Hall using a key to access the front door of the house.

The Watcher walked slowly back to the Land Rover,

got in and shut the door. He closed his eyes and said aloud, 'Oh Lord, please steel my heart and strengthen my hand; enable me to carry out your will tonight. Amen.'

He then started the vehicle and drove away from the detached property. He already knew the time Vanessa Hall would be picking up her husband, and he was confident that he could do what needed to be done, in the window of opportunity created by the Halls' plans to take the children into town for pizza.

There was no point in him waiting around on this affluent street, where a nosy neighbour could easily notice a scruffy old Land Rover parked up outside the Halls' family home.

Instead, he headed into Beeston town centre and parked the Land Rover in a multistorey car park. After ensuring that his grip bag was now out of sight in the back of the locked vehicle, he walked into the pedestrianised area of the town centre, where he found a small café.

As soon as he walked inside, he could smell the delicious aroma of fried bacon and sausage.

Suddenly, he became aware of just how ravenously hungry he was. He hadn't eaten properly for over two days. He ordered a full English breakfast and a mug of tea. The young waitress brought the breakfast and the mug of tea to his table promptly. Hungrily, he wolfed down the tasty fried food. Once he'd finished the breakfast, he ordered a second mug of tea and asked the waitress if there was a public library in the town centre.

The waitress served him a second mug of strong tea and provided directions to the library.

The Watcher heaped two full teaspoons of sugar into the tea and gave it a good stir. He always liked something sweet after eating a fatty fry-up. He paid for the breakfast and left a good, but not over generous, tip. He didn't want to do anything that would cause the young waitress to remember him.

Walking out of the café, he wandered through the pedestrianised town centre, following the directions he had been given. He needed time to think and refine his plan. There were a couple of other things he also needed to establish while he waited for Edward Hall to return home.

It had been the Watcher's intention to spend the day researching the names he had obtained during the gruesome torture of Cavalie Naylor. Now, as he stood outside the library, he felt desperately disappointed. For a town the size of Beeston, the library was pathetic.

He walked inside the red-brick building, which resembled a large residential bungalow, and spoke to the librarian. She was a shrewlike woman in her sixties, with scraped-back grey hair and thin, mean-looking lips. She was dressed from head to toe in black, in what would best be described as widow's weeds.

'Do you have any sort of reference section I could make use of, please?' he asked politely.

The woman looked up at him, grimaced, and forced a weak smile. 'Is there anything in particular that you're trying to research? Our facilities are spread over different areas of the library.'

'It's local news, really, that sort of thing.'

Without acknowledging his request verbally, she stepped from behind the counter and beckoned him with a bony, clawlike hand to follow her.

He dutifully followed the old woman into a secluded corner of the empty library.

She indicated a rack of wooden shelves in the corner and said in a high-pitched, reedy voice, 'There are copies of the three local papers that serve this area, but they only go as far back as twelve months. There are also telephone directories that cover the main towns of Nottinghamshire and Derbyshire. If you need anything else, young man, you'll have to come back and see me at the desk.'

Without waiting for a response, the old woman walked off, leaving the Watcher alone.

With the meagre facilities on offer, he knew that he wouldn't be able to accomplish too much research into the names he'd got from Naylor. At least the library was empty and warm. It was as good a place as any to wait until the time came for him to return to the Halls' residence.

From a pocket in his combat trousers, he took out the small piece of paper that contained the list of names he'd extracted from Naylor.

As he scanned the names, it confirmed what he already knew from the precious newspaper clipping and photograph he had taken from the old copy of the *Worksop Advertiser*. Naylor had confirmed the last name during his torture. That last name on the list would not be a problem. He knew exactly where he would be able to find him. The clipping itself was safe in a plastic poly pocket back at the caravan. Happy that he would be able to get to the last name easily, the Watcher instead turned his attention to the second name provided by Naylor.

Naylor had told the Watcher that Frederick Reece was a business lawyer. The man was responsible for facilitating contracts between Naylor's building business and various public bodies.

As the Watcher had slowly flayed the skin from Naylor's body, the businessman had readily informed him that Reece had been one of the main instigators of the disgusting event that had happened when they were both students at the university. He had also given him the name and location of Reece's law firm.

Richmond Legal Enterprises Limited had its office in the minster town of Southwell in central Nottinghamshire.

The Watcher scanned the long rows of business phone directories on the shelving and quickly found the one that related to Southwell. He removed the directory from the shelf and sat down at one of the two small tables. Thumbing through the pages, he soon found the entry for Richmond Legal Enterprises Limited. Scanning across the page from the telephone number, he saw the address for the business. Richmond Legal Enterprises could be found at 3 Spittle Row, Southwell, Nottinghamshire.

The Watcher glanced over his shoulder before tearing the entire page out of the book.

He was aware that this third name on the list of devils, Frederick Reece, would prove the most challenging to get close to. Obtaining the business address for his law firm was a great start.

He glanced at his watch; it was now almost time to leave the library. He used the toilet facilities before leaving. As he made his way out of the library, he said goodbye to the librarian. The old woman didn't even glance up from the book she was reading.

He walked back along the pedestrianised town centre and called in at the first newsagent's shop he saw. He purchased a small bottle of water and two Galaxy chocolate bars to sustain him overnight, then made his way back to the multistorey car park where he had left the Land Rover.

It would soon be time for Vanessa Hall to deliver her husband, Edward, to him. The next demon on his list would soon have to answer for his sins before God.

11

10.00am, 27 March 1986
South Lodge, Retford

Stewart Ainsworth sat in his car and flicked through the paperwork he'd brought with him from Rampton Hospital. The first thing he saw was the unsmiling face of Jimmy Wade. Those piercing, hypnotic blue eyes stared back at him out of the photograph.

Ainsworth was twenty-four years old and a newly qualified social worker. He'd been employed at Rampton for just over six months. His role was to support the patients incarcerated at the high-security hospital. It was his responsibility to look after their welfare.

He had been given the dossier on Wade by his supervisor the night before. It was now his intention to visit the woman who had become a regular visitor to Wade in the maximum-security hospital. As he read the paperwork, it soon became apparent to him that his supervisor had some concerns over this particular visitor.

Wade had been incarcerated at the hospital for just over four months. In that time, Melissa Braithwaite had visited him on no less than six occasions. Staff supervising the visits in the Main Hall had noticed that the woman was becoming close to Wade. Their conversations were held in secretive, hushed tones, and they had been observed holding hands across the table, staring into each other's eyes.

It was a routine part of his role to make enquiries about the motives of any person visiting someone considered to be as dangerous as Wade.

Ainsworth had already undertaken enquiries like this on several occasions in relation to other long-term patients. He had visited sad, lonely women who had become fixated on murderers, owing to a confused idea that they were somehow glamorous.

The night before, the young social worker had studied the report that detailed the crimes Jimmy Wade had been convicted for. He wasn't easily spooked, but he'd been disturbed by the ruthless and sadistic nature of the offences.

He finished reading the scant information he'd brought with him and closed the folder.

He intended to talk to Braithwaite and try to gauge her motivation for the visits. He would then make an informed decision whether to recommend that the top-security hospital refuse any further Visiting Orders requested by her.

The staff at Rampton Hospital, at the moment, were showing no more than a general concern over the volume of visits. Apart from the fact that Braithwaite was obviously getting close to Wade, there was nothing he could see in the report that would specifically warrant a ban on any further visits. But it would be down to him to make the final judgement.

Ainsworth had driven his small car along the potholed dirt track that led to the secluded property in the middle of dense woodland on the outskirts of Retford. He parked his vehicle directly behind a dark blue Ford Sierra saloon that was outside the property. This Sierra was also shown in the file as belonging to Braithwaite; it was the same vehicle she had parked at Rampton Hospital when visiting Wade.

He stepped out of his Fiat Uno, not bothering to lock the door.

Although the small stone house was surrounded on all sides by thick forest, Ainsworth shivered as he felt the cold wind bite straight away. He instantly regretted that he hadn't brought a coat with him. He pulled the jacket of his cheap, dark blue suit tighter around him and walked up the short garden path to the front door. The wind whipped his long dark hair around his face, and he frantically tried to smooth it down as he approached the house.

He rang the doorbell and made a quick visual inspection of the property.

The house was an old stone-built lodge, which had at one time been a gatehouse for the nearby Retford Hall estate. There was a neat, well-cared for front garden. The postage-stamp lawn was well trimmed, and the surrounding flower beds were all weed-free. There were clean net curtains at the windows, and the window frames and front door were all freshly painted. There were four smaller stone outbuildings within the grounds of the property. They had probably been used in the past as storehouses of some description. They were crumbling now and had obviously been neglected over the years. At the rear of the property, he could see a stream running across the bottom of the lawn that made up most of the larger back garden.

He pressed the ornate doorbell a second time.

This time there was a reply from inside. He heard a woman's voice shout, 'Just a minute!'

He could now hear footsteps coming towards the door, so he reached into his pocket for his identification badge.

The front door was flung open. He instantly caught the aroma of fresh-ground coffee and toast. Standing in front of him was a woman in her mid-thirties, with blonde hair that had been cut in a neat bob. She wore full make-up and had a very pretty, open face with large blue eyes. She was wearing a pink vest top and grey jogging pants, with the word 'pineapple' in pink letters stretching from hip to toe on the right leg.

Ainsworth held up his identification badge and said, 'Sorry to disturb you; my name's Stewart Ainsworth. I'm a social worker employed at Rampton Hospital. Can I speak to Melissa Braithwaite, please?'

Only now did Stewart realise just how petite the woman was. She was barely five feet tall, very slim, but curvaceous at the same time. He couldn't help but notice that she wasn't wearing a bra beneath the tight vest top.

'I'm Melissa Braithwaite. How can I help you?'

'I need to talk to you about your visits to see James Wade at Rampton Hospital.'

Suddenly, Melissa Braithwaite let out a yell: 'Bloody hell!'

She turned and sprinted off down the hallway, shouting behind her, 'Come in, Mr Ainsworth, and close the door behind you. My bloody toast's burning!'

Stewart chuckled, stepped inside the hallway, and quietly closed the door.

A few minutes later, a now-calm Melissa returned to the hallway. 'Sorry about that- I nearly had to call the fire brigade out. The bloody toaster's playing up. It doesn't stop cooking when the toast's done. I literally have to stand there and watch the bloody thing. Please come through into the lounge. Can I get you a coffee or a cup of tea?'

'A cup of coffee would be lovely, thanks.'

'How do you take it?'

'White, no sugar, thank you.'

'Be two ticks; grab a seat. Please make yourself comfortable.'

Stewart eased his tall, skinny frame down into one of the two large armchairs that dominated the living room. He looked around the room and noted that it had been very well decorated and contained some genuinely nice pieces of furniture. Obviously, money wasn't a problem for Melissa Braithwaite.

On the wall, above the fireplace, he could see a framed photograph of her in a black mortar cap and gown, being presented with a scroll. Next to this photograph was a framed certificate. A first-class degree in psychology, presented by the University of Sheffield.

Braithwaite came back into the room, carrying a tray that held two steaming hot mugs of coffee. She handed the milky one to Stewart and took the black one herself. She sat cross-legged in the other armchair, took a sip of her coffee and said, 'Right, Mr Ainsworth, you said you wanted to talk to me about my visits to Jimmy Wade. Can I ask why the Social Services are so interested in me visiting Jimmy? Is there a problem?'

'Please call me Stewart, and thanks for the coffee, by the way. It's delicious. There's no problem, Mrs Braithwaite; it's a routine enquiry we carry out whenever a patient like Wade has a regular visitor. Before we talk about your visits, I need to establish a few things about you, if I may?'

'No problem, Stewart. Ask away.'

He indicated the framed certificate on the wall and said, 'I noticed you have a degree in psychology. Are you currently working as a psychologist?'

'Not at the moment. I went to university quite late in life. After my parents died in a car crash five years ago, they left me a substantial amount of money. I decided to quit my job as a secretary, return to school and try to better myself. I've always been interested in psychology, in particular the psychology of violent criminals.'

'When did you graduate?'

'I graduated just over a year ago. I'm currently working on my master's. Hence my regular visits to see Jimmy Wade.'

'I see. Is there any particular reason you chose Wade to be the subject of your master's?'

'Not really. There wasn't any one single reason; it was just coincidence. When I started to think about what I should base my research on, the Coal Killer case – and Jimmy Wade in particular – was all very topical. His crimes were being reported widely in all the newspapers and all over the media. Then there was the extradition from Australia and the subsequent trial. It was all perfect timing for me. As soon as he'd been found guilty and sentenced, I immediately made enquiries with Rampton Hospital to see if I could get access to interview him for the final part of my work. It was so convenient; as you know, the hospital isn't that far from here.'

'Is Wade aware that the only reason you're visiting him is for research? So you can achieve your master's?'

'I thought it only fair that I told him the reason for my visits. So, the short answer is, yes, he does know.'

'What was his reaction?'

'He was fine with it. Jimmy is a highly intelligent man; I think he finds our conversations quite stimulating.'

'The staff, supervising your visits, have witnessed the two of you holding hands on a couple of occasions. Why did you feel that level of intimacy was necessary, Mrs Braithwaite?'

'It's Ms Braithwaite. I've never been married. Please just call me Melissa; whenever I hear "Mrs Braithwaite", it reminds me of my mother.'

'Okay, Melissa, why was it necessary to have that level of intimacy, that close physical contact?'

'I would hardly describe it as intimacy. It's only happened on the last couple of visits, when I was asking him about his earliest crimes.'

'You mean the drowning of seven-year-old Billy Daines.'

'Yes, the death of that poor unfortunate child.'

'Wade's never admitted his involvement in the child's death. In fact, he's never spoken one word to the police about that incident or any of his other crimes. Do you have open discussions with him about his crimes? Has he made any admissions to you, Melissa?'

'Good Lord, no! We do speak freely, but he's never made any admissions at all. Just for the record, I genuinely believe he wasn't in any way responsible for Billy Daines's death. Apart, that is, from being unfortunate enough to be there at the time the boy fell into the pond and drowned. It must have been a thoroughly traumatic event for a young child to witness. On the two occasions that we spoke about the death of the young boy, Jimmy became really agitated and upset. I held his hand on a purely altruistic level, to both calm him and reassure him, that's all.'

'How many more visits to the hospital do you think you'll need to complete your research, Melissa?'

'I think one more visit should suffice; two at the most.'

'Okay, I think that's all I need to know for now. Thank you for your time this morning, and I'm so sorry for ruining your toast. I'll let my supervisors at the hospital know the reason for your visits, and that you'll only require one or two more visits to complete your research. I'm sure there won't be a problem about you gaining access to see Wade for that number of visits.'

'Thank you so much. While you're here, Stewart, can I ask you something, strictly off the record?'

'Of course you can.'

'Speaking as someone who has contact with him on an almost daily basis, what's your personal opinion of Jimmy Wade?'

'You said "off the record", so please don't quote me on this in your work. You asked for my personal opinion. It's my belief that Wade should never be allowed out from behind those walls. He is without doubt the coldest, most calculating and dangerous individual I've ever met.'

'Thank you, Stewart. It's so good to get your perspective. I've only ever seen the perfectly charming and polite side to his nature.'

Stewart thought back to the detailed files of Wade's crimes that he'd studied the previous night and said, 'Trust me, Melissa. You never, ever want to see the other side of Wade's nature.'

He stood up and stretched his tall frame before walking out of the lounge, followed by Melissa Braithwaite.

She opened the front door and held out her right hand.

He shook her hand gently, made eye contact, and said, 'Good luck with your research. I hope it all goes well and you achieve your master's. Just do me one favour: Always remember exactly what Wade is.'

It was now her turn to meet the gaze of the young, inexperienced social worker.

'And what, exactly, is that?'

'Wade is a pure psychopath, a monster. I don't have a psychology degree, and I'm not researching for a master's, but trust me, that's exactly what he is. Take care.'

'You too, Stewart.'

She watched the young social worker walk back to his little car, then smiled and waved to him as he drove off down the secluded lane. She closed the front door and returned to the lounge, sitting down heavily in the armchair.

Inside, she was raging.

How dare that young upstart talk about her soul mate in such disparaging terms! Not once had he referred to Jimmy by his Christian name.

They were all wrong.

Only she knew his true nature, his kindness, the way he'd reached out to her when she was in the depths of despair. He was the only person who cared, the only one who'd been there for her.

Her parents hadn't died five years ago. They had been killed just over nine months ago, soon after she graduated from Sheffield. She had felt totally lost after the only two people she'd ever loved were wiped out in a split second of madness. The car they were travelling in had been hit head-on by a car being driven dangerously by a young joyrider. A police patrol car had been in pursuit of the car thief, driving at high speeds, and this had obviously contributed to the subsequent collision.

Why were the police so stupid?

In the depths of her grief, she had seen the reports about the trial of Jimmy Wade, the man the nation's press had dubbed 'the Coal Killer'. Impulsively, she had decided to travel to the Crown Court at Leicester to watch the proceedings.

To this day, she didn't understand why she had gone to the court building, but as soon as she saw Jimmy Wade in person, she knew instantly he was the man destined to be her soul mate. They had spent the entire trial staring intently across the packed courtroom at each other.

While ever she was in his presence, she no longer felt the sharp pain of her loss. She'd been completely devastated when he was found guilty and sentenced to be detained indefinitely at Rampton Hospital. As far as she was concerned, there was no proof that Jimmy had committed those horrendous crimes, or that he was in some way mentally deranged.

Melissa Braithwaite had convinced herself that the police and the justice system wanted a scapegoat to deflect from the fact that the real murderer, Police Sergeant Michael Reynolds, was one of their own. It was convenient for the establishment to blame Jimmy, as Sergeant Reynolds had avoided trial by killing himself in Newstead Abbey woods.

She had been a regular visitor to Wade while he was on remand at Wakefield prison, and had visited him on several occasions, giving an acquaintance's name and details on the Visiting Order. It was only after the trial, when she started visiting Wade at Rampton, that she had given her own details.

During her most recent visit to Rampton, Wade had

warned her that it was only a matter of time before the social services would contact her and ask questions about the regular visits she was making. Between them, they had discussed at length how she should react and what she should say when such a visit happened.

Now that the idiotic, wet-behind-the-ears social worker had left, she felt pleased that she had remembered everything Jimmy had told her to say. She knew that her inquisitive but inexperienced visitor had swallowed every word of it.

The only thing she hadn't lied to Ainsworth about was the fact that she only intended making one more visit to the hospital.

It would only take one more visit to set in motion the chain of events that would eventually lead to the new life she dreamed of.

That new life would be spent with her soul mate, Jimmy Wade.

12

3.15pm, 27 March 1986
Beeston Fields, Beeston

The Watcher loitered by the hedge of a neighbouring house, and from a distance of almost fifty yards, he saw the grey BMW being driven slowly out of the long driveway. He could see Vanessa Hall behind the wheel of the car and that she was alone. She drove off at speed, in the direction of the railway station.

He felt the weight of the daysack, which he'd retrieved from the Land Rover earlier, and smiled. He looked around in all directions to make sure he wasn't being observed. Then he walked slowly towards the open gates of the large house.

He knew there were possible shortcomings in his plan, and that it was by no means perfect, but with God's will, everything would be fine.

That was, with God's will and every ounce of skill

and professionalism he'd acquired and mastered over the last twenty or so years.

For his plan to succeed, he would need to become a ghost, an undetected phantom. His powers of self-discipline would be tested to the maximum. He knew he would need to remain undiscovered and invisible for many hours.

The sky was a slate grey colour, and there wasn't a breath of wind, but he could still detect the pleasant smell of woodsmoke as a neighbour burned garden waste on a bonfire some distance away.

He was now dressed head to toe in drab camouflage clothing. He wore black training shoes and a black woollen hat that doubled as a ski mask, with holes for the eyes and mouth.

He moved stealthily down the long driveway towards the Halls' beautiful home. He stayed close to the neatly trimmed privet hedge. The ground underfoot was dry, which would help later. He couldn't afford to leave muddy footprints, which would betray his presence, inside the house.

He made his way to the rear of the property. The large house was not overlooked by any other properties at the back.

The Watcher knew he was free to do as he wanted, without the risk of any interference.

He put on a pair of blue latex gloves, then took out a small aerosol can of builder's foam from the daysack. With the aerosol can tucked inside his jacket, he climbed up a drainpipe towards the bright yellow alarm box. He sprayed the foam inside the alarm box. The foam quickly set like stone, rendering the alarm box useless.

Using the specialist breakers tools, he worked on the lock of the back door until it opened. He checked the exterior of the door lock, and there were no marks betraying his actions.

Once inside the house, he quickly made his way to the hallway, where he found the alarm box. Dropping the panel to examine the system, he smiled when he saw that the intruder alarm hadn't even been set.

Although he had already disabled the bell box of the alarm, the reason he smiled was that he knew a complicated alarm system, like this one, could activate directly at the local police station. He squatted down on his haunches and remained silent and still for two minutes. He slackened his jaw and allowed his mouth to remain slightly open, as an aid to his already acute hearing. He wanted to be sure there were no unexpected visitors inside the property.

From the hallway, he made his way up the stairs. At the top of the staircase, he saw what he had been hoping for. There was a loft hatch positioned in the ceiling, directly above the stairs. Quickly, he climbed onto the bannister rail and checked the hatch. It was loose, so he applied pressure, and the hatch raised easily. It hadn't been painted over and wasn't sealed.

Climbing back down from the bannister rail, he walked around each of the rooms upstairs. He quickly identified the master bedroom and the two bedrooms used by the children. Leaving no sign of his presence, he moved around the rooms until he was completely familiar with the layout.

The Watcher moved the loft hatch to one side, then stood on the bannister rail and pushed the daysack into the loft before pulling himself up. Once inside the loft, he looked down at the bannister rail. He was satisfied that he'd left no scuff marks that would betray his hiding place.

He allowed a second for his eyes to adjust to the

gloom of the roomy loft space, then flicked on the Mini Maglite torch. He began to move items that might easily be disturbed or that could possibly make a noise. The last thing he wanted was for an accidental noise to give him away.

As soon as he was satisfied that nothing could be unwittingly disturbed, he took out a pair of heavy pliers and two clout nails. He used the steel head of the pliers to gently tap the two nails into the reverse side of the loft hatch. He then carefully placed it back into position. He would use the nails later to lift the hatch.

As always, he had been meticulous in his preparations; it was now time for him to become invisible.

He settled down in the loft to await the arrival of the Hall family. Using the Mini Maglite to illuminate his watch, he saw it was now almost five o'clock. There would be at least another two hours or so to wait before the family returned home. He would use that time to get totally into stealth mode.

From now on, his movements would be kept down to the absolute minimum. Everything he might need had been placed at arm's length and was within easy reach.

He scanned the light from the torch around the loft and made one last inspection of his makeshift lair. The loft space had a slightly musty smell; it was obviously used to store what the family no longer needed.

It smelled quite badly of damp and mould.

The thin beam from the torch picked out myriads of dust particles that had been disturbed by his presence.

As he settled down to wait, he could only hear two sounds. One was the rhythmic tick-tock of a faraway clock, and the other was the slow, steady thump of his own heartbeat.

13

7.15pm, 27 March 1986
Teversal Manor, Cotgrave, Nottingham

Danny parked the car on the gravel driveway outside the impressive Georgian mansion house that was Teversal Manor.

He turned to Rachel Moore in the passenger seat of the car and said, 'Are you sure Mr Naylor is well enough to see us?'

'Yes, sir, he was released from hospital this afternoon. It wasn't a heart attack as such, just a bad bout of his angina. He told me earlier that the doctors are more than happy with him, and that his condition can be controlled with his usual medication. Mr Naylor called us. He said he has urgent information that you need to hear.'

Danny nodded. 'Okay, let's go and hear what he's got to say.'

The two detectives got out of the car and walked

towards the imposing oak doors.

As they approached the building, they were suddenly illuminated by bright white security lighting that had been activated by a motion sensor.

Rachel pulled down hard on the ornate doorbell.

The door was immediately opened by a middle-aged woman wearing a nurse's uniform.

Rachel took out her warrant card, showed it to the woman and said, 'DC Moore and Chief Inspector Flint to see Mr Naylor. He's expecting us.'

Danny was still a little concerned and asked, 'Is he well enough to speak to us?'

The woman smiled and said, 'Yes, of course. I've been employed by Mr Naylor ever since he was diagnosed with his heart condition. He lives here alone, so I call in twice a day to make sure everything's okay. He's perfectly well and asked me to show you in.'

Danny said, 'Thanks, after you.'

The nurse took them inside the house and down a spectacular hallway to another set of oak doors. She tapped politely before opening the right-hand door. She stepped inside and said, 'The police are here, Mr Naylor.'

A voice inside the room said, 'Thanks, Julie, that will be everything tonight.'

She turned and beckoned Danny and Rachel to enter the room.

They stepped inside what was obviously the study of the house. Large bookshelves covered two walls, and Geoff Naylor was seated behind an impressive walnut desk.

He gestured for the two detectives to take a seat on the leather bucket chairs in front of the desk.

Before he sat down, Danny said, 'Mr Naylor, I'm deeply sorry for your loss.'

Geoff Naylor fixed Danny with a steely stare and replied evenly, 'Are you going to catch the evil bastard who did that to my beautiful boy, Chief Inspector?'

'I'll do everything in my power to find whoever's responsible. Have you any idea who might have a reason to harm your son?'

'There can be no reason. Cav wouldn't hurt a fly. He was the kindest, most considerate man you could ever meet.'

Danny paused. 'You obviously saw the message left on the kitchen wall. Does that mean anything to you at all?'

'I'm afraid not. I have no idea what that's all about.'

'It couldn't be a reference to a business deal at all?'

'No, nothing like that.'

'I know your son was a director of your company. Have there been any problems with the business that you're aware of?'

'Nothing at all. Obviously, I'm also a director of the company. I know for a fact there are no problems with the business. I can talk to you about every business deal we've ever had, and every one that's currently ongoing. There are no issues with our business.'

Rachel said, 'Have you had any problems with recently laid-off staff?'

'No. We've got a very settled workforce; we haven't had any redundancies or dismissals for years.'

Danny said softly, 'Was Cavalie having any problems privately that you're aware of?'

'There is something I want to disclose to you about Cav's private life. That's why I wanted to see you tonight.'

'What's that?'

'I think you need to have a look at his friend Christopher Baker.'

The old man virtually spat the name out, contempt heavy in his voice.

'What's the problem with Mr Baker?'

'There's something very strange about Christopher bloody Baker! He's really got his claws into Cav. He's a grasping bastard, and I wouldn't trust him as far as I could throw him. He'll have some involvement in this, you mark my words. He's been hanging around my son like a bad smell for months. I just don't trust him; he's weird.'

'Can you be a little more specific? In what way do you find him weird?'

'He behaves like a child around Cav. Constantly whispering and giggling. Then, whenever I come in the room, he becomes sullen and moody. On top of that, he constantly distracts Cav from his work.'

'Anything else?'

Geoff Naylor raised his voice, saying, 'Yes! There's something bloody else! The man's a total freeloader. Cav pays for everything; he buys him everything. Baker's trying to get Cav's money, I'm sure of it.'

'Have you spoken to Cav about your thoughts?'

'I've tried, Chief Inspector, but Cav didn't have many friends. He always got very defensive, very quickly. Baker has always constantly bad-mouthed me to my own son, trying to turn him against me.'

'Where can we find Mr Baker?'

'He lives over in Nottingham, Hucknall way, I think. His address will be in Cav's office somewhere.'

'Is there anything else you wanted to tell us tonight?'

'That's all, Chief Inspector. Get hold of that bastard Christopher Baker. I guarantee the answer to this horror show won't be far from him.'

Rachel asked, 'When do you intend going back to work, Mr Naylor?'

'If I'm feeling up to it, in a few days' time. Why?'

'I just wanted to let you know that we have officers working through all your paperwork and files at the office. They are trying to find something that could lead us to whoever did this.'

Again, Naylor became agitated, and his face reddened as he spoke. 'Weren't you listening? I've just sat and told you who's behind this. Are you going to speak to Baker or what?'

Danny interjected, 'We'll be having a very close look at Mr Baker and will be speaking to him at some stage. I think we've taken up enough of your time this evening. You still need to rest.'

Naylor snarled, 'I don't need to rest. I *won't* rest until you've got that bastard locked up!'

Danny stood and said, 'We'll see ourselves out, Mr Naylor. I'll keep you informed of developments every day. Once again, I'm sorry for your loss.'

As they walked back to the car, Danny said, 'He really doesn't like Christopher Baker, does he?'

Rachel shook her head. 'I'll start researching Baker as soon as we get back to the office.'

'Good, I think we need to speak to him as soon as we can. I want everything you can find on him. Any criminal history, who he associates with, financial, personal, medical, the works.'

As he drove back to Mansfield, Danny was deep in thought. The allegation against Christopher Baker was tenuous, but right now they had nothing else. At some stage in the enquiry, Baker would need to be located and arrested. He hoped that the enquiries Rachel were about to carry out would give him firmer grounds. The arrest would be lawful, as there was genuine suspicion, but he knew without any evidence it would quickly become a pointless exercise.

14

3.30am, 28 March 1986
Beeston Fields, Beeston

The Watcher flicked on the Mini Maglite and glanced at his watch. It was now almost three thirty in the morning.

Immediately below his position, he could hear loud rhythmic snoring emanating up from the master bedroom. He knew it was the master bedroom from the recce he'd carried out earlier that day.

The Watcher had listened as Vanessa made a quick check on the two young children. He heard her return to the master bedroom and get into bed alongside Edward. He could hear them chatting and giggling. Eventually, the conversation had turned to something more passionate as the couple became aroused.

Above them, in the loft space, the Watcher listened intently as the couple began to make love.

He had heard their cries as they both climaxed, then waited patiently for them to drift off to sleep.

At half past one in the morning, he'd heard somebody half wake from their slumbers and slowly get out of bed. He listened carefully, and from the sound of the footsteps as they crossed the landing directly beneath the loft hatch, he knew it was Edward Hall who was awake. He heard the footsteps head into the family bathroom. There was the sound of the light switch being flicked on, then Hall urinating. The stream eventually abated, and the light was flicked off again. The footsteps padded back to the bedroom; then he heard the bedsprings sag as Hall got back into bed.

There had been no noise at all from either of the bedrooms occupied by the two small children.

It was now three thirty in the morning, time for him to move.

The early hours of the morning are widely regarded as the time when the human body is in its deepest unconscious state. It is the time of deep sleep, which eventually transforms into the dream sleep state.

The Watcher made no sound as he used the pliers to grip the nails that he had knocked into the loft hatch earlier. He lifted out the piece of wood and carefully placed it to one side before slipping the nylon daysack around his neck. Before he moved, he ensured that none of its contents knocked against each other.

Using his powerful, muscular arms, he slowly lowered himself from the loft until he felt his feet gently come to rest on the bannister rail.

With great agility, he got down silently from the rail.

His movements were fluid; he made no sound. The years of specialist training hadn't been in vain. He moved across the landing like a phantom, a fleeting shadow in the moonlight.

He slowly opened the door to the master bedroom and saw the couple fast asleep. Vanessa was lying on her side, facing away from her husband, who was lying flat on his back. It was he who was snoring loudly.

The Halls hadn't closed the bedroom curtains. The room was illuminated by bright moonlight flooding in from outside. He breathed in deeply through his nose. He could still detect the smells from their earlier lovemaking.

Stealthily, he crept to the side of the bed where Edward Hall lay. He rolled down the black hat he was wearing, turning it into a black ski mask. The mask left only his eyes and mouth still visible.

Drawing back his left hand, he bunched it into a massive fist, then smashed it down onto the forehead of the sleeping Hall, instantly knocking him out.

The Watcher stepped onto the bed and knelt across the sleeping woman, effectively pinning her beneath the duvet. As she began to stir, he flipped her over roughly, so she lay on her back. As she awoke and her senses returned, he clamped his gloved hand across her mouth. The first thing she saw when she opened her eyes was the Watcher's masked face illuminated by the white moonlight. Her eyes widened in sheer terror, and she began to writhe beneath the duvet, but was pinned and couldn't move. She tried to scream, but the noise was muffled under the gloved hand.

Finally, her energy spent, she stopped struggling.

The Watcher leaned forward and whispered menacingly, 'If you scream or make any noise at all, I will kill your daughter first, then I will kill your son, and you will watch them die.'

He saw her terrified eyes dart to the left as she looked to her husband for help.

'Your husband's not going to help you. He's unconscious. I don't want to hurt you or your children, but if you leave me with no other choice, I'll kill you all in a heartbeat. Do you understand me?'

Vanessa Hall nodded frantically.

'Are you going to behave, Mrs Hall?'

She was shocked that he'd used her surname. The fact that this monster knew who she was panicked her even more.

Again she nodded, but this time she made eye contact with her attacker. All she wanted was for her children to be spared this horror.

Very slowly, he removed his hand. She made no sound. He reached into the daysack on his shoulders and grabbed the roll of gaffer tape. He deftly wrapped the sticky brown tape twice around her head, covering her mouth but leaving her nostrils clear, allowing her to breathe.

He moved off the bed and pulled the duvet onto the floor. Instinctively, Vanessa drew her knees to her chest to cover her naked body. The Watcher wasn't interested in her sexually. He grabbed her arms and roughly turned her over until she was face down on the bed. He used nylon cord from the daysack to bind the naked woman's hands behind her back, then left her face down on the bed.

Turning his attention to the still-unconscious Edward Hall, he repeated the process, binding him with cord, then using gaffer tape to gag him.

He reached down to his waist, and with his right hand he removed the Suminagashi skinning knife from the scabbard on his belt. Using his left hand, he roughly turned Vanessa over on the bed until she was lying on her back facing him. Any thoughts she had of protecting her modesty were now forgotten.

Holding the knife in front of her eyes, he allowed the

stark, white light of the moon to glint off the honed blade.

He leaned forward and whispered, 'We're going to your children's bedrooms now. If you do exactly as I say and cooperate with me, then your children will see the sun come up tomorrow. If you try to resist me, or cause any other sort of problem, I'll slaughter your son and daughter before your eyes. Then I'll gut you like the devil-worshipping whore you are and leave you to die slowly. Do you understand me, Mrs Hall?'

The horrified woman nodded vigorously; she would do exactly what this maniac wanted. She would do whatever it took to protect her two small children.

The Watcher grabbed Vanessa and pulled her up off the bed until she was standing. Her legs felt weak, and she almost collapsed. The Watcher held her upright until she nodded that she was okay. He then pushed her out onto the landing and into her daughter's bedroom. Swiftly and without fuss, he dragged the terrified young girl from her bed, then bound and gagged her without speaking. He then pushed Vanessa into the boy's bedroom, where he quickly repeated the process, binding and gagging the boy. The small boy was then dragged with his mother back into the daughter's bedroom. The Watcher then used more cord to tie all three to the bedpost of the young girl's bed.

Closing the bedroom door behind him, he stalked back across the landing to the master bedroom. Using his great strength, he lifted the unconscious, naked Edward Hall from the double bed and carried him down the stairs into the large kitchen. He pulled out one of the heavy pine chairs from beneath the large breakfast table and secured Hall to it, using more of the cord.

Moonlight flooded into the kitchen. The room was

covered in lines of shadow caused by the half-closed venetian blinds.

Edward Hall was still unconscious and was slumped forward. The only reason he remained upright was because of the cord binding him to the wooden chair.

The Watcher needed Hall to be awake.

He grabbed a Perspex measuring jug from the draining board and filled it from the cold tap. He then threw the cold water into Hall's face. The shock of the cold water immediately caused Hall to stir, and after a few more minutes, he fully regained his senses.

As the fog in his brain cleared, Hall could finally focus on the terrifying figure of the Watcher. His eyes widened with fear as he took in the sight before him. A squat, powerful man standing in lined shadow, dressed in dark stained clothing and a black ski mask.

Hall instantly focussed on the object being held in the man's right hand. His eyes were fixated on the glinting metal blade of the large skinning knife.

In a state of panic, Hall began to struggle against his bindings and shouted muffled threats.

Holding the lethal knife out in front of him, the Watcher slowly walked towards Hall. He leaned in close to Hall's face and said in a menacing whisper, 'I haven't touched your wife and kids yet, you piece of shit. If you atone for what you've done, right now, then the good Lord will allow them to live beyond today.'

The Watcher reached into his pocket and retrieved a small laminated photograph, which he held in front of Hall's horrified face. He angled the photograph so Hall could clearly see it, as it was illuminated by the moonlight.

'Edward Hall, do you repent your sins?'

After seeing the photograph, Hall knew instantly which sin he was being asked to repent. Tears streamed down his face, and he nodded wildly, screaming, 'Yes,' from beneath the sticky tape.

'The Lord will show mercy and accept your repentance; the innocents will live on after tonight. For you, Edward Hall, it's too late. You're beyond the point of forgiveness; the scriptures in the Old Testament have instructed me clearly what needs to be done.'

Bowing his head, the Watcher whispered aloud, 'Forgive me, Lord, as I do your bidding. Thank you for allowing me to spare the innocents. I know you watch over me. Amen.'

He then walked slowly past Hall, whose eyes strained wildly to see where he was going.

The last thing Edward Hall saw was the flash of the gleaming blade as it slipped in front of his eyes, down towards his throat. He then felt his hair being grabbed roughly from behind. His head was yanked backwards until he was looking directly up at the ceiling of his kitchen. His neck muscles felt taut; then they suddenly slackened as the razor-sharp blade sliced deep into his throat. Hall felt the warmth of his own blood as it gushed from the gaping wound in his throat onto his chest.

Within a minute, he had bled out and was dead on the chair. He sat in an ever-widening pool of his own blood.

The Watcher retrieved the heavy pliers from the daysack, ripped the brown tape from around Hall's head and began to systematically remove every single tooth from his mouth.

Each tooth was dropped into a clear plastic ziplock bag. After removing all of Hall's teeth, he sealed the ziplock bag and placed it back into the daysack. There was still one last thing to do before he left the house. He took the two-inch paintbrush from the daysack and dipped it into the dark pool of Hall's blood.

Having finished his macabre ritual, he made one last check of the kitchen to make sure he'd left nothing behind, then returned to the lounge. From the large teak wall unit, he removed a single framed photograph. He had seen the photographs earlier when he had first broken into the house. There were dozens of framed pictures on the unit, but this particular photograph of four men interested the Watcher. Having placed the framed photograph into his daysack, he stepped out through the front door of the house and into the bright moonlight.

The street was quiet and still. The only noise he could hear was the mournful unanswered hoot of an owl, away in the distance. Stealthily, he crouched low and moved across the lawn at the front of the house. The heavy dew on the grass washed Hall's blood from the soles and welts of his training shoes.

Moving carefully and sticking to the shadows, the Watcher slipped unseen through the deserted streets, back to the multistorey car park. He started the engine of the Land Rover and drove out of the car park. He didn't see another vehicle until he'd been driving fifteen minutes.

The vehicle he saw was one of the bread delivery wagons that race around the streets during the early hours of the morning, the drivers with nothing on their mind except the next scheduled delivery of their fresh-baked bread.

After an uneventful drive from Beeston, he eventually steered the Land Rover onto the near-deserted caravan site at Clumber Park.

Everywhere was still and in complete darkness.

He utilised the quiet time to wash and clean his gear

in the deserted shower block before retiring to his small caravan. He opened the fridge and placed the ziplock bag containing Hall's teeth next to the bag that contained Naylor's eyes. He then took out a carton of long-life milk and a tub of Lurpak butter.

He put the kettle on, put two slices of toast under the grill of the tiny cooker, and dropped a tea bag into a mug.

When the kettle had boiled, he poured the hot water into the mug and buttered the toast.

Sitting on the step of the caravan, he sipped his tea and ate his toast. Then he watched as the sun slipped over the horizon, heralding the start of a new day.

15

8.45am, 28 March 1986
Beeston Fields, Beeston

The house had been quiet for hours now.
Vanessa Hall was stark naked and freezing cold. Although the heating was on in the house, her entire body was starting to ache with the cold. Her two young children were snuggled together, trying to keep warm. They had stopped sobbing beneath their sticky, smelly gags now, but they continually glanced at their mother with scared, confused eyes.

Truth be told, she was as confused and scared as her children. She had racked her brain, but still had no answers to the questions that kept forcing their way into her mind.

Who was that madman?

How did he know her name?

What had she done to be visited by such an evil creature?

Where was her husband, Eddie?

Vanessa continued to try to loosen the thin cord that bound her daughter's hands. She had been trying for well over an hour, but with freezing cold fingers, the thin, slippery cord was almost impossible to grip.

Suddenly, there was the slightest give in the cord. Encouraged, she began to work harder, trying to untie the knot she'd loosened. Her hands and fingers ached with the effort. She leaned forward towards her daughter and mumbled in her ear. She had used her lips and tongue to try to push the tape away from her mouth. It had moved slightly, and she desperately hoped the young girl would understand the garbled message she now spluttered from beneath the cloying brown tape. 'When Mummy unties you, take the brown tape from Mummy's mouth. Do not go out of this room. Do you understand?'

The young girl stared, the fear even more evident in her eyes now.

After several attempts to make her understand, finally she nodded.

'Becky, are you sure you know what Mummy wants you to do?'

The young girl nodded again, a little more vigorously this time.

Vanessa unravelled the final knot in her daughter's bindings. The girl's hands were now free. Instantly, the youngster began to pull at the brown tape around her mother's face. The pain was intense as the girl slowly peeled away the sticky tape, inch by inch. Eventually, the tape was pulled completely off, and Vanessa gulped in air.

'Well done, sweetie. Now I'm going to turn around, and I want you to try to untie Mummy. Can you do that?'

The girl nodded enthusiastically, pleased that her mum was happy with what she had achieved so far.

It took a further twenty minutes for the young girl to loosen Vanessa's bonds enough for her to shake them free. The girl's smaller fingers had fared much better with the thin nylon cord than her mother's.

Once free of the cord that had bound her wrists, Vanessa quickly untied her feet and then undid the remaining ties on the children. Lastly, remembering the pain she had experienced, she carefully removed the brown tape from around their small mouths.

When they were all finally free from their bonds, Vanessa huddled the children close to her, cuddling them both tightly.

Vanessa now had a big decision to make. She needed to summon help, and the only way to do that was to venture out of the room and hope that the maniac had gone.

She looked at her frightened children. 'Okay, children. I want you both to stay here; you must be very, very quiet. Mummy's going outside to find Daddy. I won't be two ticks. Whatever you hear, you must stay here and wait for Mummy to come back for you. Becky, will you look after Hugo for me?'

The young girl nodded enthusiastically and pulled her young brother closer to her.

Vanessa stood up and put her index finger to her lips as she looked into the eyes of her terrified children. The kids knew that signal, and both did the same back, placing tiny index fingers over their own lips.

She wrapped the children beneath a thick duvet, then tiptoed out of the room and closed the bedroom door behind her.

Silently, she crept across the landing, noticing immediately that the loft hatch was no longer in place. A wave of fear crashed over her, and she felt her legs weaken. Remembering her children, she steeled herself and picked up a heavy glass vase that stood on the windowsill at the top of the stairs.

Moving slowly, she checked all the other upstairs rooms.

There was no sign of Eddie.

Calling on the last reserves of her courage, she made her way carefully down the stairs, still clutching the heavy vase. As she made her way down the carpeted stairs, she saw that the front door was wide open.

Suddenly, she felt elated, and a sense of relief washed over her; the monster had gone. All she had to do now was find her husband, untie him, and get the kids out of there.

She stepped by the open front door, walked along the hallway and into the L-shaped kitchen. As she stepped onto the kitchen tiles, she suddenly felt something sticky on her bare feet. This part of the kitchen was little more than a corridor, and the light was poor. She looked down at her feet and could make out something dark on the floor tiles.

There was also a strange metallic odour in the room.

She turned the corner into the main part of the kitchen, and the sight that confronted her was like a scene from the worst kind of horror movie.

Her husband sat naked on one of the wooden chairs. He had been secured to the chair by thin nylon cord. His head was back, and his throat had been cut virtually from ear to ear.

The huge wound caused his neck to gape open in some macabre smile.

The floor tiles around the chair were an inch deep in dark brown jelly.

Suddenly, Vanessa realised that the jelly she stood in

was her husband's congealing blood. She let out a gasp and felt her legs buckle beneath her.

Falling to the floor, she dropped the vase she was holding and desperately began trying to shuffle backwards out of the kitchen, away from her slaughtered husband. As she slipped around in the blood, she could feel the panic rising in her.

Finally, she gained some purchase from the floor, scrambled to her feet and bolted out of the kitchen.

Her adrenalin-fuelled panic caused her to run straight out through the open front door. She sprinted down the driveway, not feeling the sharp gravel as it cut into her bare feet.

Vanessa had totally forgotten she was naked. She had also forgotten that her two young children were still in the house. She was in flight mode and just wanted to get as far away from the horror in that kitchen as she could.

It was daylight now, and her neighbours from the house directly opposite were sitting in their car on the driveway. They were about to drive onto the road when they saw the naked Vanessa Hall, covered in blood, sprinting down the driveway away from her house.

The neighbour, Mr Hughes, immediately stopped his car, jumped out, and intercepted Vanessa just as she reached the road.

He tried to grab her by the arms.

She began to lash out at the old man, catching him with a glancing blow just beneath his left eye. He gamely held on and shouted, 'Vanessa, calm down! It's me, Bill Hughes. Calm down!'

All the fight suddenly evaporated from Vanessa, and once again she felt her legs buckle. Mrs Hughes joined her shaken husband and quickly placed her own coat around a now-shivering Vanessa.

A shaken Bill Hughes turned to his wife and said, 'I've got her, Muriel. I'll bring her up to the house. You go ahead and call the police; something terrible has happened. She's covered in blood.'

The old lady shuffled ahead to call the police while Bill slowly helped Vanessa back to her feet. As he reached the front door of the house, Bill whispered, 'What on earth's happened, Vanessa? Where are the children?'

Suddenly, the shock became too much for Vanessa Hall, and she completely passed out.

Bill Hughes carried her the final couple of steps into his house and laid her down on a sofa.

He turned to his wife and said, 'I'm going over there.'

'No, you're bloody not, you old fool! The police are on their way; they can deal with it. You said yourself she's covered in blood.'

'But the children might still be in danger.'

'And what can you do, old man? Except maybe get yourself killed.'

In the distance, they could hear the sound of sirens approaching.

'They'll be here in a moment,' said Muriel. 'You just wait here.'

'Alright, alright. I'll stay here, woman, but God forbid something awful's happened to those two beautiful children.'

16

9.00am, 28 March 1986
Beeston Fields, Beeston

The two police patrol cars arrived virtually together and screeched to a stop outside the home of Bill Hughes.

A young constable jumped out of the first car and ran down the driveway to the front door of the Hughes residence. Bill Hughes was waiting on the doorstep. He immediately began to explain to the officer what had happened. He described how he'd seen his heavily bloodstained neighbour running from her driveway, totally naked, and in a state of panic.

'Where's your neighbour now, sir?'

'She's in the house, resting. I'm afraid she's passed out, Officer.'

'What's her name?'

'Hall. Her name's Vanessa Hall.'

The sergeant, who'd been driving the second patrol

car, joined them on the doorstep just as the old man said, 'We don't know what's happened to her children, though.'

The sergeant, echoing the old man, asked, 'Children?'

'Mr and Mrs Hall have two young children, a girl and a boy. We can't find out from Vanessa if they're okay.'

The sergeant turned to the young officer and said, 'Jim, stay here with Mrs Hall. Get an ambulance travelling; by the sound of it, she's going to need medical attention. I'll go across the road and see what's happened.'

Bill Hughes was listening to the conversation and said, 'I'll come over with you, Sergeant. You may need some help.'

'Thank you, sir, but that won't be necessary. I'd appreciate it if you stayed here with PC Thorne. It will be good for your neighbour to see a friendly face when she comes round again.'

A crestfallen Bill Hughes nodded his head and showed the young constable inside his home.

Sergeant Andy Wills then sprinted back down the driveway, crossed the road and approached the Hall residence.

He could see that the front door to the house was open. He quickly put on his black leather gloves and drew his truncheon, gripping it in his right hand. Using the back of his left hand, he opened the heavy front door as wide as it would go. He saw the smears of blood all along the walls of the hallway. There were no bloody marks on the walls next to the stairs. All the blood marks appeared to be on the ground floor. There were bloody footprints leading from the kitchen, along the hallway, towards the front door. The sergeant could clearly see the bare footprints of Vanessa Hall. He could also see a larger training shoe print. Both sets of footprints were leading out of the front door.

Quietly, he made his way through the house, holding his truncheon out in front of him, ready to engage any threat he might face. After checking the lounge and the dining room, he made his way towards the kitchen. He could see the blood that had pooled on the floor tiles. He avoided the blood and stepped into the kitchen.

As soon as he entered the kitchen, he fully understood why Vanessa Hall had fled in such a state of sheer panic.

Sergeant Wills could see the dead body of a naked male. He was tied to a heavy wooden chair and had a massive wound across his neck, which had severed both arteries. The blood loss had been quick and catastrophic. He looked down at the pool of blood on the floor. He could see the small footprints that had been made by Mrs Hall and smear marks in the congealed blood where she had fallen.

There was nothing more to be done for the victim. Sergeant Wills knew everything about scene preservation. Very carefully, he retraced his steps out of the kitchen, not touching or disturbing anything. Ordinarily, he would have sealed the property off immediately, but he still had a problem. Somewhere in this charnel house were two small children.

They could only be upstairs.

With a feeling of utter dread at what he might be about to find, he began to climb the stairs one at a time. He ensured his weight remained on the sides of the treads so they didn't creak and betray his approach. He was still acutely aware that whoever had slaughtered the man downstairs could still be in the house.

He got to the top of the stairs and saw that the loft hatch was open.

The doors on the landing were all closed. He had to check the loft space before he went any further. The offender could still be hiding up there.

He looked for any obvious footmarks on the bannister rail and saw none.

Quickly, he put his truncheon back in his trouser pocket, reached up and hauled himself up into the loft. He scanned each corner of the loft and saw nobody. He jumped down, took out his truncheon again and began to check the bedrooms.

The first room he entered was obviously the master bedroom. He checked under the bed and the wardrobes; those places were empty. The second room he checked appeared to be a young boy's room. Pictures of Thomas the Tank Engine and Postman Pat adorned the walls. Again he checked beneath the bed and the single wardrobe; it was empty.

The next door he opened led into the family bathroom. He checked inside: nothing.

There was one room left to check, and the door remained closed.

It had a small nameplate on the door, which declared in baby pink letters, 'Becky's Room'.

Andy Wills gripped his truncheon a little tighter. This was the last room. The children had to be in here. His heart felt like it was beating out of his chest, and he could feel the sweat beading on his forehead. He pushed down on the door handle with his left hand and opened the door.

As soon as he entered the small bedroom, he heard what sounded like a soft whimper, and saw movement beneath the flowery duvet cover. He quickly checked below the bed and looked inside the single wardrobe. Nothing.

There was no obvious threat now, so Andy slipped the truncheon back into his pocket.

In a very soft voice, he said, 'Kids, are you in here? I'm a policeman. You can come out now; it's safe. There's nothing to scare you anymore. Your mum's next door with your neighbours.'

He knelt down at the side of the small single bed and said quietly, 'Come on, Becky, are you under here? I need to get you and your brother back to your mum.'

Slowly, the duvet cover shifted a few inches. Andy could now see two pairs of very frightened eyes staring back at him.

'Is that you, Becky? My name's Andy. Becky, can you see the silver buttons on my jacket? They are silver because I'm a policeman. I've come to get you out of here and take you to your mum. Is your brother with you under there?'

He saw the girl nod.

'Come on then, sweetheart. Let's get you and your brother back to your mum.'

Nothing moved. Then he heard a tiny voice say, 'Has the horrid man gone?'

'Yes, he's gone, Becky. It's just me here now, and I'm your friend. Shall we go and see your mum?'

Slowly, the traumatised children moved the quilt cover, and for the first time, Andy could see exactly how shocked they were. He picked up the small boy, held the young girl's hand, then walked them down the stairs and out of the house of horrors that had once been their home.

As soon as they were outside, he also picked up the young girl, as neither child had anything on their feet. With a child in each arm, he walked across the road, where the first ambulance was just pulling up outside the Hughes house. He immediately passed the traumatised children to the ambulance crew.

Another police car arrived with two female officers on board. Andy began to organise his staff; his heart had stopped racing now. After the tension and stress of the house search, he'd started to calm down again.

He sent PC Thorne across to the Halls' house to begin and maintain the crime scene log. Then he tasked one of the women police officers to stay with Mr and Mrs Hughes and begin taking their first account. The other policewoman was instructed to follow the ambulance containing Vanessa Hall and her two young children to the hospital. They all needed to be checked over after their horrific ordeal.

Having organised his small team, Andy drove back to Beeston Police Station and rang the contact number for the newly formed Major Crime Investigation Unit.

17

9.20am, 28 March 1986
Major Crime Investigation Unit, Mansfield

Danny Flint was just about to start allocating the different enquiry teams with their tasks when the telephone began to ring.

He turned to Rob Buxton and said, 'Rob, can you grab that, please?'

Rob walked into Danny's office and snatched up the telephone. 'MCIU, Detective Inspector Buxton; how can I help you?'

'Hello, Rob, it's me, Andy Wills.'

'Andy, good to hear from you. How's life as a uniformed sergeant treating you?'

'It's all good, thanks. I'm calling you with a referral, though. We've had a murder in Beeston overnight.'

'Right, I see. Exactly what have we got?'

Andy then painstakingly relayed every detail of what he'd encountered at the house.

Having listened to the detailed briefing and made a note of the address, Rob said, 'Get back up to the scene, Andy. Keep it tight; you know the drill. I'll arrange for a Scenes of Crime team and a Home Office pathologist to be travelling to your location. I'll inform Danny and let him know what's happening. From what you've just described to me, it sounds almost identical to a murder we're currently investigating. You did say a message in blood, didn't you?'

'I did. It's horrendous.'

'Okay, Andy. We should be with you in less than an hour. It'll be like the old days when we were all chasing the Coal Killer.'

'Wait until you've seen inside the house. It certainly looks like you've got another maniac to catch.'

18

**10.30am, 28 March 1986
Beeston Fields, Beeston**

Danny Flint and Brian Hopkirk walked towards the front door of the Halls' house in Beeston. Rob Buxton was already standing by the front door; he had his arms folded across his chest and was deep in thought.

Rob had been the first MCIU officer to arrive at the scene. Upon his arrival, he had immediately made the decision to call out the second enquiry team, led by Brian Hopkirk. It had been obvious to him that there would be a lot of house-to-house enquiries to undertake.

Danny asked, 'Right, Rob, who's the victim?'

'Dead man's name is Edward Hall.'

'And what do we know about Edward Hall?'

'Hall is – sorry, was – the manager of the prestigious Grosvenor Hotel in Nottingham city centre. He lived here with his wife, Vanessa, and their two young children.'

Rob glanced down at his notebook, then continued, 'The daughter, Rebecca, is seven, and the son, Hugo, is five.'

'Any physical injuries to the wife and children?'

'They were all bound and gagged for a lengthy period of time. They're all still at the hospital, being checked over. Physically, they're pretty much unscathed; God only knows what the damage will be mentally. Luckily, as far as we know, the children haven't seen the state of their father. This is a bad one, Danny. It's identical to the scene at Underwood. It's like a slaughterhouse in the kitchen. There's blood everywhere.'

'I'll go and have a look for myself in a second. What's been organised so far?'

'Seamus Carter's the on-call Home Office pathologist. He's been here about five minutes and is already inside, examining the body.'

Danny said, 'That's good. If it is the same, it's lucky for us that we've got Seamus again.'

Rob continued, 'I called Brian and his team out straight away to help with the house-to-house enquiries. This is a large residential area, and those enquiries alone will be a massive undertaking. I've also arranged for a Scenes of Crime team to attend. They're currently on their way.'

Danny scowled. 'What's the bloody hold-up with them? I've managed to get here from Mansfield; where are they?'

'Vehicle trouble, boss. Apparently, the van they were originally in has broken down, and they've had to wait for the workshops to attend. They couldn't get it going, so they've had to return to headquarters and get another vehicle. They should be here in ten minutes.'

Danny turned to Brian Hopkirk and said, 'Brian, you might as well wait outside. There's no point in us all going in and disturbing the scene. Come on, Rob, show me what we've got.'

The two men signed into the scene log, then walked into the house, protected by forensic suits, gloves and overshoes.

As they walked along the hallway towards the kitchen, Danny could hear the distinctive Irish brogue of Seamus Carter's voice as he rumbled into his Dictaphone.

Danny let out a low whistle as he surveyed the scene of carnage in the kitchen.

'Good morning, Detective. Doesn't this all look familiar?' asked Seamus.

'Yes, it does. What have we got?'

'I've only been here a few minutes myself, but the obvious cause of death is the massive wound to the throat. Blood loss would have been catastrophic. He would have bled out very quickly, dead within a minute or two.'

'Weapon?' asked Danny.

'Not sure exactly what was used, but whatever it was, it's incredibly sharp. Looks like a broad-bladed weapon similar to the one used at Underwood. I'll maybe know more when it comes to the post-mortem.'

'Can you give an estimated time of death?'

'I'd say sometime after three this morning. A ball-park figure would be between three and four thirty.'

'Any other injuries, apart from the wound to the neck?'

'After the victim's throat was cut and he'd bled out, the killer then extracted all the dead man's teeth. Very crudely, too; no care was taken. They've literally been ripped out of his mouth. I can't see any of the teeth here, which means the killer has taken them with him.'

'More trophies?'

'Possibly.'

'Okay, Seamus. Anything else?'

'Only what's scrawled on the wall.'

The pathologist indicated the wall that was to Danny's right, just out of his line of sight.

Danny took a step to his left; he could now clearly see the series of random letters and numbers that were ten inches high. The killer had written EC21V2425.

'Jesus Christ! Again? What's all that about, Seamus?'

The huge shoulders of the pathologist shrugged. 'Not sure what it means, Danny. What I can tell you is that the message, whatever it is, has been painted on the wall using our victim's blood. If you look closely, you can see that there are brush marks. So I'm guessing a small paintbrush was used. There's no paintbrush to be found here, which makes me think this was all done in order to leave that message.'

'So you're thinking that whoever did this came prepared to leave this message.'

'Exactly that.'

'Thanks, Seamus. Rob will remain in charge of the scene. Let him know if you need anything.'

'Will do.'

Danny said, 'What time will you be ready for the post-mortem?'

The big pathologist looked at his watch. 'If your Scenes of Crime aren't too long in getting here, we should be good to go at around four o'clock this afternoon. It will be the City Hospital again.'

'Thanks, Seamus.'

Danny turned and walked out of the house, followed

by Rob, both men signing the log and disposing of their protective clothing.

Waiting outside was a uniform sergeant standing next to Brian Hopkirk.

Danny recognised the sergeant and said, 'Andy, how are you? Rob told me you were first on the scene.'

'I'm good, thanks, boss. I'd only just come on duty when this call came in. I've just been told that this is identical to the recent murder at Underwood.'

'It certainly looks that way, but that's not for everyone to know, understood?'

Danny turned to Brian and said, 'Get onto the control room and arrange for a section of the Special Operations Unit to help out with the house-to-house enquiries. This estate is vast.'

'Okay, boss, I'm on it,' said Brian.

'Is there anything else you need?'

'A Scenes of Crime team would be nice.'

Right on cue, the large white van turned into the street.

'There you go, Brian; your wish is my command. I want you to get a landline set up here so we can remain in contact. Call the office at three o'clock this afternoon and let me have an update.'

'Will do.'

Danny and Rob walked down the driveway of the house back towards their car, followed by Andy Wills.

At the car, Danny turned to Andy Wills and said, 'Good work today, Andy. When are you going to transfer onto the Major Crime team?'

Andy smiled. 'As soon as you like, boss. I've done six months in uniform now. I could do with getting a suit on again; the shift pattern we have to work is killing me. We've done a week of day shifts, and because it's the last shift, we're working a split today. I've got to work from nine this morning until one o'clock this afternoon, then go home for a few hours and come back for an evening shift tonight. I start again at ten o'clock tonight and work through until two in the morning. Then we get three rest days. It's diabolical. Everybody spends the first rest day in bed.'

'Leave it with me, Andy. I've got a vacancy on Rob's team coming up in a couple of months' time. It's yours if you want it.'

Andy grinned and said, 'Can I wait for a vacancy on Brian's team, boss?'

'Cheeky bugger!' said Rob, grinning.

'Seriously, that would be great. I'm ready to get back to doing some detective work.'

'I'll sort it, Andy. I hope your evening shift later isn't too bad.'

Andy turned and walked away. As soon as he was out of earshot, Danny turned to Rob and said, 'I'll see you later at the post-mortem. I don't need that examination to know these two crimes are identical. For whatever reason, we've got a maniac on our hands. Top priority is to find a link between Cavalie Naylor and Edward Hall. There must be one somewhere; we find that, we find the killer. See you at the City Hospital this afternoon.'

19

4.00pm, 28 March 1986
Nottingham City Hospital Mortuary

Danny Flint and Rob Buxton stood to one side of the stainless-steel examination table that held the mutilated body of Edward Hall.

DC Jeff Williams once again had the task of exhibiting all items recovered during the post-mortem. The only other people in the large examining room were Seamus Carter and his assistant.

Seamus began by doing a visual examination of the body.

His attention was immediately drawn to the forehead of the deceased. 'Look here, Danny, the same bruising as before. Distinct knuckle marks on the forehead. A blow sufficient enough to incapacitate, without a doubt.'

Danny nodded as the assistant moved in closer to photograph the bruising.

As usual, the big Irishman spoke his findings into a Dictaphone as he worked.

The bindings that had been used to tie the victim were then carefully removed from the wrists of the dead man and examined. The cord appeared identical in make-up and colour. Forensic examination would later determine whether the cord was scientifically identical to that used at Underwood.

DC Williams quickly bagged and labelled the cord as it was removed from the body.

Seamus Carter then busied himself examining the gaping maw of Edward Hall.

He said, 'I'm sure the victim was already dead by the time his teeth were ripped out. I use the word "ripped" advisedly. No finesse was used at all. I reckon the killer used common or garden pliers to remove the teeth.'

The large gaping wound of the neck was then minutely examined.

Carter said, 'This wound has been inflicted by someone holding the weapon in his right hand, again identical to the Underwood victim.'

After a few more minutes, the pathologist continued, 'Definitely the same type of heavy, large-bladed, razor-sharp hunting knife.'

Three-quarters of an hour later, Seamus Carter stepped away from the examining table. He turned to Danny and said, 'There are so many similarities; these two murders are definitely linked. I'll let you have my full report by tomorrow afternoon.'

'Thanks, Seamus.'

A sombre-looking Seamus Carter walked out of the examining room. All the exhibits taken during the examination were labelled, signed and bagged by DC Williams.

Danny and Rob waited for the mortuary assistant to

return the body of Edward Hall to the refrigerated drawers before walking back through the hospital. They spoke in hushed tones as they walked along the lengthy corridors.

Danny said, 'I'll have to contact Bill Wainwright when we get back and let him know there's every likelihood we've got a serial killer on the loose.'

Rob nodded. 'Do we inform the press?'

'Let's get Christopher Baker in for questioning first. If that doesn't come to anything, then I'll have to consider a full press disclosure. The last thing we need is to waste time on crap information and rubbish leads. You know as well as I do that when we say the words "serial killer", it brings out all the crazies, who want to admit everything.'

Rob nodded. 'I'll make the arrangements to get Baker in. Hopefully, Rachel will have turned something useful up about him.'

20

7.00pm, 28 March 1986
Major Crime Investigation Unit, Mansfield

Danny Flint raised his arms, and the crowded briefing room fell silent.

'Right, I know it's been a long day for all of us, but it's vitally important that everyone in this room is fully aware of every development in both the Underwood murder and this new case in Beeston.'

He turned to Brian Hopkirk and said, 'Let's get started. I think we already know what's happening as far as the Underwood job is concerned, so let's concentrate this evening on Beeston. Brian, what do we know about the victim?'

'The deceased is Edward Hall. He was the manager of the Grosvenor Hotel in Nottingham city centre. Married to Vanessa. There are two children from the marriage, Rebecca, aged seven, and Hugo, aged five. It would appear that our offender gained entry to the property after the alarm box had been filled with builder's foam to prevent activation. The property is a large, detached dwelling, set back from the road, in a very affluent area of Beeston. The search of the property has revealed that the offender spent a considerable amount of time hiding in the loft before he attacked the family during the early hours of the morning. There are no signs of any forced entry into the property, so it's still a bit of a mystery how the offender gained access. Vanessa and the children were all bound and gagged before being placed in the young girl's bedroom. The offender then took Edward Hall from the master bedroom to the kitchen, where he tied him to a wooden chair. While Hall was tied to the chair, his throat was cut, causing him to bleed to death. Hall's teeth were all crudely extracted, then removed from the scene. The message EC21V2425 has been painted on the kitchen wall, using the victim's blood. As you're all aware, this is identical to the message left at Underwood. Hall's wife and children were not physically harmed in any way, although God only knows what this traumatic episode will do to their mental health. This means it's extremely likely the attack was personal. Targeted specifically at Edward Hall.'

'Thanks, Brian. Rob, can you now brief everyone about the findings from the post-mortem examination of Edward Hall?'

Rob took a deep breath. 'The post-mortem was carried out earlier this evening at the City Hospital. We'll get the full written report from the pathologist and photographs tomorrow. The cause of death was a large wound to the neck that severed both arteries. Blood loss would have been enormous and catastrophic. We must assume that our offender would have been heavily bloodstained after the attack. The weapon used to cause the wound to the victim's neck is believed to be a very sharp, broad-bladed instrument. Possibly a hunting knife. The pathologist has intimated that he thinks it's the same weapon that was used to cause the injuries to Cavalie Naylor. Apart from the later extraction of the teeth, the only other injury found on the body was bruising to the forehead. This was believed to have been caused by a single punch. The bruises can be identified as knuckle marks, which are normally associated with injuries caused by punching. This method of incapacitating the victim is, again, identical to the Underwood murder. The pathologist has also confirmed that the teeth were extracted after the victim was dead. We're still waiting on the toxicology reports.'

'Thanks, Brian. Who's been tasked with organising the house-to-house enquiries at Beeston?'

DC Phil Baxter spoke up. 'I have, boss. I've completed the indexing of every house on all the surrounding streets. I briefed a section of the Special Operations Unit earlier so they can continue the enquiries first thing tomorrow morning. I've asked them to complete personal descriptive forms for every person they speak to. Immediately prior to this briefing, I phoned the sergeant in charge of the Special Ops team to see if there was anything noteworthy to report from today's enquiries. They're well into the task, but as yet, there's nothing to report. They've just finished for the day; it's getting dark, and policy dictates we don't carry out house-to-house enquiries after the hours of darkness.'

Danny said, 'Thanks, Phil. I know it's not an easy task, and you've done a great job. I want you to stay on it. I'd like to get all of them completed by tomorrow if possible.'

'Will do.'

'Who interviewed Vanessa Hall?'

Sergeant Tina Prowse spoke up. 'Vanessa Hall is currently on a ward at the City Hospital under sedation. I've been at the hospital most of the day, waiting to speak to her, boss. Unfortunately, she's so traumatised that doctors have kept her sedated. They wouldn't allow me to speak to her at all. Dr Phoebe Gillender, who's in charge of her care, has assured me that I'll be able to talk to her briefly tomorrow morning.'

'Okay, Tina, I want you to stick with Vanessa Hall. Be at the hospital first thing in the morning. Anything she can tell us about the events of last night will be invaluable. It's a priority enquiry. If you explain that to Dr Gillender, she may give you a little more leeway.'

'Okay, boss.'

'What about the two children; who's been tasked with that enquiry?'

DC Lyn Harris answered, 'I've been trying to get access to them. They're both staying with Vanessa's sister and her family. I'm afraid it's a similar scenario to Tina's. Neither of the children are in any fit state to be questioned yet, however gently. They are totally traumatised.'

'Have you managed to get anything?'

'Nothing from the boy; he doesn't want to talk at all. The girl keeps sobbing and asking if the horrible man is going to come back. So apart from the fact that it would appear to be one man acting alone, we've learned nothing. I daren't push it, boss. They're both so young.'

'Don't worry, Lyn, I totally understand. Just stick with it, please. If either of them volunteers any information, to you or their auntie, I want to know about it straight away, okay?'

'Of course, boss.'

'Scenes of Crime, what have you got?'

A short, stocky man with a full beard and crew cut hair spoke up. 'Hello, sir, we haven't met. My name's Stephen Brewer, senior Scenes of Crime officer. I've just transferred down to Nottinghamshire from the Durham force.'

'Welcome to the MCIU, Stephen. Forensically, what have we got?'

'There's quite a lot going on, sir. My team have recovered glove marks from all over the house. It looks like the offender spent quite a long time inside the house. We've also recovered a lot of fibres from the loft, where he pulled himself in through the hatch. I understand that Sergeant Wills also pulled himself up through the hatch to check the loft, so I'll need his tunic for fibre comparison.'

Danny said, 'Brian, can you make a note of that, please? Arrange for Sergeant Wills to submit his tunic ASAP.'

Brian nodded. 'Will do.'

'What else have you got, Stephen?'

'There's a single training shoe print found in the blood on the kitchen floor. We believe that mark was left by the offender; it's the wrong size for Sergeant Wills. There are fainter marks that match this training shoe, also in blood, in the lounge of the property. So it would appear our offender went into the lounge for some reason after he had committed the murder. There are no fingerprints anywhere, I'm afraid. Everything at the scene has been photographed by Dave Whitham – he's a civilian currently seconded to our team. He's assured me he'll have the first album of photographs ready by tomorrow morning. I've already submitted the fibres recovered from the loft to the forensic lab. I'll keep you posted on any updates.'

'Thanks, Stephen. Make sure I get those scene

photographs and the photographs from the post-mortem tomorrow. Mid-morning at the latest.'

'Will do, sir.'

Danny turned to DC Jeff Williams. 'Jeff, you did another cracking job at the mortuary this afternoon. I want you to concentrate on getting the cord recovered from both scenes forensically tested. Fast-track it, please. If we can match that cord, it proves we're looking for the same man for both crimes.'

'I'm on it, boss.'

'Has anybody got anything else from Beeston?'

DC Simon Paine spoke up. 'Yes, sir. I've spent the day with Bill and Muriel Hughes, the neighbours who initially called the incident in. I've taken statements from them both. The interesting thing is this: Mrs Hughes recalls seeing a battered old Land Rover Defender in the area recently. She saw it being driven along the street a couple of days ago, and she's never seen it before. Unfortunately, she can't remember any of the registration number. All she can say, with any certainty, is that it was a dark green colour and very dirty. She said the only reason it stuck in her mind was because whoever was driving it was travelling really slowly, and it just looked out of place.'

'How sure is Mrs Hughes that it was a Land Rover Defender?'

'She's adamant on that. She grew up on a farm, and her family always used Land Rovers.'

'Good work, Simon. Tomorrow morning, I want you to check any CCTV you can find in the area. Let's see if we can find this vehicle.'

'Will do.'

Danny turned to DC Rachel Moore. 'Rachel, any more on your enquiries into Christopher Baker?'

Rachel glanced at her notebook before speaking. 'For

the benefit of everyone in the briefing room who may not be aware, Geoff Naylor is adamant that one of Cavalie's close friends, Christopher Baker, will in some way be involved in his son's death. However, he's got nothing concrete to base this theory on, and there appears to be a real antipathy between him and Baker. I've spent most of the day researching Christopher Baker. He's got two previous convictions. One was for deception. The circumstances involved him presenting a dud cheque at a hotel. He was convicted but given a suspended sentence, as the value was quite low. The second, more interesting, one is a conviction five years ago for an assault occasioning actual bodily harm. He evidently committed an unprovoked assault on an acquaintance of his. This "friend" later refused to give evidence at court, but Baker was still convicted on the evidence of the reporting officer, who had witnessed the facial injuries – a broken nose and black eye. He served three months for the assault. I've done a full financial check, and basically he's on his uppers, with no discernible income.'

'Who are his associates?'

'We have no intelligence reports that link him with any known criminals.'

'Did you find out where Baker lives?'

'He lives in a small flat on the Brindle Estate at Hucknall. His address is 32 Byron Court.'

'Thanks, Rachel. I want you to complete whatever background checks are left to do on Baker. Once you've finished that, I want you to prepare an operational order, ready to arrest him first thing tomorrow morning. Let's get him in custody so we can get an account from him. Contact the Special Operations Unit and arrange for them to be in the area when he's arrested. I want to be able to put a specialist search team in straight away.

Will you need any help to arrange all that by tomorrow morning?'

'No, thanks. I've almost completed the checks on Baker. Do you have a preference for the interview team once he's in custody?'

Danny turned to Rob and said, 'I'd like you and DC Lorimar to carry out the interviews once he's in, okay?'

Rob nodded.

Danny turned back to Rachel and said, 'Just a thought. When you're doing the background checks on Baker, see if you can find anything that links him to Edward Hall. If there's something linking the three of them, that could prove interesting.'

'Will do.'

Danny took a minute or so to digest all the information he'd been given.

'Okay, everyone, listen up. Given the similarities we have highlighted so far, it would be remiss of me not to officially link these two murders. I expect the fibre evidence and the footmarks to confirm this once the comparison tests have been completed. As a matter of urgency, I need to establish two things. Firstly, the meaning of the message left on the wall at both scenes. I want you all to concentrate on that. Secondly, establishing a link between our two victims. I can virtually guarantee there will be one somewhere. I think it's highly unlikely that our killer has targeted two random individuals. The torture of the first victim could also be highly relevant. It could mean that, as well as the second victim, other people could be in danger from this man. Find the meaning of the message and find the link between the two victims, and we'll be getting somewhere. The following are also to be considered as urgent enquiries; Rob, I want you and your team to concentrate on the arrest and interview of Christopher Baker. We need to establish if this man had a motive to kill Cavalie Naylor, as soon as possible.'

Rob nodded. 'Okay.'

Danny continued: 'Brian, I want your team to concentrate on following up the enquiries with Vanessa Hall. We need Tina to obtain a statement from her as soon as possible. Follow up the CCTV enquiries. Let's see if we can spot this scruffy Land Rover anywhere, and continue with the house-to-house enquiries. I also want you to arrange a full search of the office used by Edward Hall at the Grosvenor Hotel, and I want all the staff at the hotel interviewed to see if Hall has upset anybody recently. A disgruntled guest, a previous employee – you know what I'm looking for.'

Brian nodded and said, 'I'll sort it.'

'Okay, everybody. Finish up what you've got to do tonight, then get off home. I want everyone back on duty at six o'clock tomorrow morning. I'll say it again; I need two things as a matter of urgency. One, I need to find a link between our two victims, and two, I need to know what that bloody message means!'

21

**11.30pm, 28 March 1986
Beeston Police Station**

Sergeant Andy Wills sat in his office at Beeston Police Station. It was his last shift of a very eventful week. The week of day shifts always ended with a split shift, which meant that he and his colleagues would not be going off duty until two o'clock tomorrow morning.

Because of the events at the Halls' house in Beeston Fields, none of his shift had been allowed to go off duty until two thirty that afternoon. He had gone home, grabbed a couple of hours' sleep, got ready and returned to work. He'd paraded his shift back on duty at ten o'clock that night.

He made himself a cup of tea and was just about to start clearing his desk of all urgent paperwork, in readiness for his impending rest days, when there was a quiet, almost timid, knock on the door.

Andy shouted, 'Come in!'

The door opened to reveal an extremely nervous-looking PC Gerry Standish.

Gerry was the newest member of the shift. He'd only been at Beeston Police Station for four months, having recently completed his training at Dishforth Police Training Centre.

He was an accomplished footballer who had joined the police force quite late in life, after a brief spell in the professional ranks of the game. He was slightly built, but very fit and strong. He was nearing thirty and had a mature air about everything he did. He had been working on his own for almost three months and was keen to take on anything new. Andy had been impressed by what he had seen of him so far.

'Come in, Gerry. What's the problem?'

'Sorry to disturb you, Sarge. I was out on my beat earlier, and as I walked past the Man of Trent pub, a bloke stopped me and gave me some information about a crime. I know I need to act on it, but I'm not sure what I can do about it at this time of night.'

'Firstly, you're not disturbing me; that's what I'm here for. Grab a seat. So who was the bloke who gave you the information?'

The young officer flipped open his pocketbook and said, 'He gave his name as Freddie Cox. He told me he regularly gives information to Detective Sergeant Carlisle, but he couldn't get hold of him tonight, and this needed to be sorted out urgently.'

'What exactly is it that needs sorting out?'

'Cox told me that he'd heard there was a burglary two nights ago, at the Yeoman's Army Stores on the High Street. A load of camping equipment was stolen. Apparently, all the stolen gear is being stored at 26 Arkwright Road tonight. The problem is, it's being shifted first thing in the morning. If we don't get into the address tonight, we'll miss it.'

'Okay. Have you done any checks on the information provided by Cox?'

'Yes, I have, Sarge. There was a burglary at Yeoman's two nights ago, and a load of camping gear was stolen. All the property stolen during that burglary is still outstanding. I've checked our systems in the Local Intelligence Office, and 26 Arkwright Road is the current home address of a bloke called Davy Finch. Finch has got previous convictions for handling stolen goods.'

'Right, that's good work and tells us that the information has merit. So what do you think we should do now, Gerry?'

'Well, I thought about getting a warrant under the Theft Act to search for stolen goods, but by the time the Magistrates Courts open in the morning, it will probably be too late.'

'Ordinarily, that's exactly what we would do. We'd go to the Magistrates Court and swear out a warrant before the sitting magistrates. As it's this time of night and urgent, we must use a contingency plan. We can call a magistrate who's on the "out of hours" list. If you contact the control room, they'll give you the telephone number for the current on-call magistrate.'

Andy indicated the telephone on his desk.

PC Standish made the call to the control room and scribbled down the name, telephone number and address of the magistrate he was given.

'Right, Sarge. The magistrate's Mrs Beatrice Hayes; she lives on Oakfield Road up near the Leisure Centre.'

'Give her a call and make the arrangements to go and see her. Give yourself at least an hour to type up the warrant and the information form. Tell her we'll be outside her house at half past midnight. Do you know what's needed on the paperwork?'

'I think so, Sarge. I've done the paperwork for a warrant at court before. Is it the same?'

'Yes, it is. I tell you what, just to be on the safe side, when you've completed the paperwork, bring it to me so I can check it, then I'll come with you to obtain the warrant.'

'Righto, Sarge,' said a now-beaming PC Standish.

Half an hour later, there was another knock on the door of Andy Wills's office.

'I've got everything, Sarge,' Standish said. 'Are you still good to come with me?'

Andy quickly checked over the documents, then stood up and grabbed his car keys. 'That's great, Gerry. There's one last thing I forgot to mention: Have you got a Bible to swear out the information on?'

'Mrs Hayes specifically told me not to bring a Bible, as she prefers to use her own.'

'Okay, let's go.'

Just before half past midnight, both officers were standing on the doorstep at the home address of Mrs Hayes.

PC Standish rang the doorbell.

The door was answered almost immediately by a very frail-looking, grey-haired lady who was obviously well into her seventies.

'Come in, come in, Officers. You're letting all the cold air in.'

'Apologies for the late hour, Mrs Hayes, but we need a warrant as a matter of urgency,' said Andy.

'I was awake anyway, Sergeant. Don't worry about the hour. Now, what do you need from me?'

Andy indicated for Gerry to start talking, and the probationer quickly gave a brief outline of the circumstances. He stressed the fact that if they didn't get into the property that night, by the morning the stolen goods would have been moved on.

Mrs Hayes asked, 'Are there any small children living in the house the warrant is intended for?'

'On the checks I've made, no, ma'am, there are no small children at the house.'

'That's good. Do you have a typed information form for me?'

'Yes, ma'am,' said Gerry.

'I'll get my Bible; then you can take the oath before giving me the information.'

Less than a minute later, Mrs Hayes returned with a leather-bound, antique Bible, which she handed to the officer.

Gerry held the heavy Bible in his right hand, spoke the oath, and laid out the Information to Mrs Hayes, who listened carefully before duly signing the Theft Act warrant.

Andy took the leather-bound Bible from Gerry and was about to hand it back to the elderly magistrate when he noticed a couple of yellow Post-it notes sticking out from the pages. Andy saw that written on some of the notes were a series of letters and numbers that looked familiar.

'Mrs Hayes, I hope you don't mind me asking, but what do these sequences of random letters and numbers refer to?'

'They're Bible references, Sergeant. Friends have given them to me. They highlight beautiful verses from the good book.'

Andy retrieved his own pocketbook and flipped through the pages until he found the note he'd made of the message left at the Halls' house.

'Mrs Hayes, what do you make of this message?'

He opened his pocketbook and showed her the note he had made: EC21V2425.

'That's an easy one, Sergeant. It's a reference to one of the most well-known sections of the Old Testament. It refers to the book of Exodus, chapter 21, verses 24 to 25.'

The old lady quickly thumbed through the Old Testament of her Bible, then opened the book on the relevant page.

'There you are, Sergeant; see for yourself.'

The old lady held out the Bible and said from memory, '"An eye for an eye and a tooth for a tooth." Like I said, it's probably one of the most well-known phrases from the Bible. What most people don't know is that the passage goes on to say, "an arm for an arm and a foot for a foot, burning for burning, wound for wound, stripe for stripe".'

Andy quickly made a note of what he'd been told before saying, 'Thank you so much, Mrs Hayes; we won't take up any more of your time. We need to execute this warrant immediately. That's a beautiful old Bible, by the way.'

'You're more than welcome, Sergeant. I hope you're both successful with the warrant. I'm glad you like my Bible. It's very valuable and has been in my family for generations. It's the King James 1st version. I absolutely adore it.'

The old lady clutched the leather-bound Bible to her chest and closed the door.

Andy was deep in thought as he walked back to the police car. He now fully understood the motive for Edward Hall's murder, and he would need to contact Detective Chief Inspector Flint as soon as possible. But first, he had the small matter of a warrant to execute and a load of stolen camping gear to recover.

22

4.30am, 29 March 1986
Beeston Police Station, Beeston

Sergeant Andy Wills was dog tired.
He looked at his watch. It was now half past four in the morning. The warrant had been a massive success; every item of camping equipment stolen from Yeoman's shop had been recovered. PC Gerry Standish was beaming like a Cheshire cat as he filled in the register for the recovered property. Andy had helped him complete the handover for the arrest of Davy Finch. Detective Sergeant Carlisle was on duty later this morning, so he would be able to continue the enquiry and, hopefully, persuade Finch to give up the name of the burglar.

The arrest of Finch for handling stolen goods, together with the recovery of all the outstanding stolen property, would go a long way towards helping the young officer become a valued member of his shift. It would also help him to get through his two-year probationary period.

Andy was in a quandary. It was now extremely late, but he knew he needed to pass on the information he'd learned from the magistrate, Mrs Hayes, as soon as possible.

He yawned, picked up the telephone on his desk and dialled Danny Flint's home number from memory.

After four rings, a very sleepy Sue Rhodes answered the phone. 'Hello, who's this?'

'Sue, it's Andy Wills. I'm so sorry to call at this time of night, but I need to speak to Danny urgently. Is he there?'

'He's fast asleep. He's got to be up at six. Can't it wait 'til then?'

'I'm really sorry, Sue, but this is vitally important. Danny needs to hear this right now.'

'Okay, Andy, just a minute.'

A few seconds passed before Andy heard Danny's voice on the phone. 'Andy, what's the problem? Don't tell me there's been another murder?'

'No, boss, there hasn't. I had to call you; I've cracked the message left on the wall at the Beeston murder scene. I now know what it means.'

A now fully awake and attentive Danny said, 'Go on.'

'It's a Bible reference. It relates to the book of Exodus from the Old Testament. It refers to the passage that states "an eye for an eye and a tooth for a tooth".'

'That all makes sense, Andy. What you don't know is that the victim at the Underwood murder had both of his eyes gouged out. He was killed before Edward Hall, so it makes sense. It also clearly demonstrates that revenge is probably the motive for both murders.'

'Bloody hell! If that's the case, you also need to know

that there are more verses stipulated in the message. The verses it refers to go on to say, "an arm for an arm and a leg for a leg, burning for burning, wound for wound, stripe for stripe".'

'You think our killer could be stalking more victims?'

'It's got to be a distinct possibility. That's why I needed to call you at this ungodly hour.'

'Don't worry about the time; you were right to call me. Listen, Andy, Detective Sergeant Mayhew, on Rob's team, phoned in long-term sick yesterday. He's got a slipped disc and won't be coming back to work anytime soon. I can't afford to be a man down at this time, with everything that's currently going on. If I can arrange it with Detective Chief Superintendent Wainwright this morning, is there anything preventing you transferring on to the Major Crime Investigation Unit sooner rather than later?'

'Nothing at all. I'm clear here workwise. If you can smooth it over with my gaffers at Beeston, I'd love to join the MCIU and get back in a suit.'

'Okay. I'll call you at three this afternoon to let you know one way or the other. If I can arrange it, I'll need you to be back at work this evening, so it will mean you missing your rest days.'

'Just like old times, then. I'll wait for your call.'

'Nice work, Andy. You can tell me later how you sussed it out. I hadn't got you down as a religious man.'

'It was easy, boss. Although I did have a little help from a lovely old lady and a King James 1st Bible.'

23

6.00am, 29 March 1986
Hucknall, Nottinghamshire

Rob Buxton sat in a car outside the entrance to Byron Court.

A run-down, seedy-looking block of flats, Byron Court was situated on the Brindle Estate in Hucknall. The flats had been built in the late fifties and were already close to being considered slums. The walkways and stairs leading to the first-floor flats were covered in graffiti and smelled strongly of urine. Fortunately, number 32 was on the ground floor, so there would be no stairs to climb.

Sitting alongside Rob was Detective Constable Glen Lorimar, a veteran detective with a flair for interviewing. Danny had specifically chosen him for the job of questioning Christopher Baker, as he considered him to be the most accomplished interviewer on the MCIU. If there was anything amiss with Baker's account, Danny trusted Glen Lorimar to find it out.

A little further down the road, a plain white Ford Transit van waited, with the engine ticking over. This vehicle contained a section of the Special Operations Unit, led by Sergeant Graham Turner. Following the arrest of Baker, he and his team would carry out a meticulous search of the flat.

Rob glanced at his watch. It was now almost six thirty. He picked up his personal radio and spoke to the SOU sergeant: 'Are your men in position at the back of the flat?'

'We're good to go, sir.'

'We're not expecting any trouble from the arrest itself, so you and your men remain in position. We'll go and knock on the front door.'

'Received, sir. I'll wait for your update.'

The two detectives got out of the vehicle and started to walk towards the block of flats.

As they approached Baker's flat, Rob could see there was a light on inside. The window was covered by venetian blinds, but telltale chinks of light could be seen between the slats of the blinds.

Glen Lorimar stepped forward and, using his balled-up fist, banged loudly on the flimsy door.

There was immediate movement inside.

Lorimar continued to hammer on the door.

'Alright, alright, I'm coming. Who's banging?'

'Christopher Baker! It's the police! Open the door right now, or I'm going to put it in!'

No sooner had Glen finished speaking than there was the sound of a key being turned in the lock. The door opened a fraction but remained secure, held by a security chain.

Both detectives held out their warrant cards so the

clearly frightened Baker could see they were police officers.

Lorimar said assertively, 'Open the door, Mr Baker!'

Quickly, Baker removed the security chain from the door. Lorimar pushed the door open and stepped inside the hallway of the small flat.

It was immediately obvious to the detective that Baker had been awake all night. His eyes were bloodshot and red-rimmed; his blonde hair dishevelled. He was dressed in a creased white T-shirt that had the red Levi's emblem across the chest and stonewashed blue denim jeans that were baggy and drawn in at the waist with a brown leather belt. He wore no socks, but had dark blue canvas boat shoes on.

An exhausted Baker said, 'What's this all about? You'd better come through to the living room.'

The two detectives followed him along the narrow hallway. Rob noticed a small suitcase and three cardboard tubes dumped near the front door.

'Are you going somewhere, Mr Baker?' he asked.

'No, just the opposite. I only got back from a trip late last night. I just dumped the case there when I walked in.'

The three men walked into the small, smoke-filled living room. The light that Rob had seen from outside the flat was from a dim table lamp. It sat on a coffee table, in front of a threadbare settee. Next to the table lamp were three half-full coffee mugs. There was a greasy film on the surface of the coffee that suggested it was now stone cold. Alongside the mugs was an ashtray full to overflowing with cigarette butts.

It looked like Baker had been drinking coffee and chain-smoking all night.

In a weary voice, Baker asked, 'You said you were from the police; are you here about Cavalie?'

Rob answered the question with one of his own: 'Yes, Mr Baker, we're here about Cavalie Naylor. Why did you assume that was the reason for our visit?'

'Because I've not heard from him for days; then I had a strange conversation over the phone with his dad a few days ago. His dad suddenly hung up the phone on me, then wouldn't answer when I tried to call him back. I just figured something wasn't right. Is Cav okay?'

'Mr Baker, Cavalie Naylor was found murdered in his home at Underwood four days ago.'

It was said matter-of-factly, and both detectives studied Baker's face to see exactly what his reaction would be.

It was one of stunned silence.

A look of bewilderment crossed his features; then he shook his head slowly and allowed his legs to buckle beneath him, slumping heavily onto the settee.

After two minutes of silence, Baker said softly, 'I don't understand any of this. Cav's the gentlest, sweetest man you'll ever meet. Why would anybody want to hurt him?'

'When did you last see Mr Naylor?' asked Rob.

'I saw him a week ago. He dropped me off here. Why?'

Rob nodded towards Lorimar.

Glen stepped forward. 'Christopher Baker, I'm arresting you on suspicion of the murder of Cavalie Naylor.'

He took hold of Baker firmly and placed his wrists in handcuffs.

Baker started to protest. 'What the fuck are you doing? You don't think I had anything to do with it, do you?'

The detective maintained a calm presence and, in an emotionless voice, cautioned Baker.

Baker replied angrily, 'You've got to be kidding me; this is some kind of sick joke. My best friend's been killed, and you lot think I did it. You're all off your fucking heads!'

In a soft voice, Glen said, 'We need to interview you properly at the police station. Arresting you will protect your rights and give you access to legal advice before we question you. Do you understand?'

Baker nodded.

Rob spoke on his personal radio: 'Sergeant Turner, we've detained Baker. Get your men in here to start searching the flat.'

The room was filled with static from the radio before the reply came: 'On our way, sir.'

As soon as the SOU search team came into the flat, DC Lorimar walked Baker outside to the CID car. Baker was now calm and said, 'Detective, can I take my smokes with me, please?'

Without replying, Rob turned and went back inside the flat, where he retrieved a packet of Embassy cigarettes. He walked back outside and tossed the cigarette packet to Glen Lorimar.

He turned to Sergeant Turner, who remained on the doorstep of the flat. 'I want a full search, Sarge; you know what we're looking for. I'm taking Baker to Hucknall nick. I'll see you back there at nine thirty. I'll want an update on the result of the search by then so we can prepare for the interview.'

'No problem, sir.'

Rob joined Glen and a now very subdued Baker in the CID car. The short drive to Hucknall Police Station was made in stony silence.

As they walked into the cell block, Baker turned to Rob and said quietly, 'You've got this completely wrong, Detective. You've no idea what's going on between me and Cav. I bet it's his old man who's set me up to be fucking arrested. Am I right?'

'Save it for the interview, Christopher. You'll get your chance to tell me exactly how everything is then. You look like you need to rest before we have a little chat.'

Baker stepped into the holding cell, and Rob slammed the heavy steel door.

24

9.00am, 29 March 1986
Southwell Town Centre, Nottinghamshire

Even though the Watcher hadn't seen any news reports about the murders, he knew the police would have discovered at least one of the bodies by now. He'd spent most of yesterday planning his next move; he had to act quickly on the information extracted from his first victim. He knew the police would soon be looking for him if they weren't already.

He'd risen early, and after a meagre breakfast, he had showered, shaved and got dressed. He was wearing the same business suit he'd worn at the Grosvenor Hotel when he was stalking Edward Hall.

His plan today demanded he be dressed in a similar fashion. He checked the information one last time, then studied his Ordnance Survey map, to plan his route from Clumber Park to the minster town of Southwell.

As he stepped out of the caravan, he picked up his

black daysack, which contained a single roll of gaffer tape, a small bag of black plastic cable ties, a Smith & Wesson .38 revolver, a box of .38 ammunition and the small silver-framed photograph that he'd taken from the home of Edward Hall.

As before, when he had dispatched Cav Naylor, he knew that if everything went to plan, he wouldn't need the weapon. He only carried it as a contingency. His military background and training always made him plan for the worst-case scenario.

After a twenty-minute drive, he parked his vehicle on a side street in the centre of Southwell, not far from the famous twin-steepled minster. He walked to a nearby newsagent's, where he purchased a street map of the town. He scanned the map and soon found the location he was searching for.

He took a minute to get his bearings, tucked the street map into the black daysack, then set off on foot, walking across town towards Spittle Row. He walked into the shopping area of the town centre, passing the Saracens Head public house. Spittle Row was little more than a yard, situated just off the main road. Walking into the yard, he saw it contained three small shops. On one side was a craft shop and an artisan bakery. The other side contained a single office, which displayed a navy-blue sign above a plate-glass window. In gold lettering on the dark blue background, the sign read Richmond Legal Enterprises Limited.

Having found the premises he was looking for, the Watcher quickly looked around him. Across the road from the entrance to Spittle Row was a small car park that still had empty spaces.

He walked back through town to where he had parked. In less than five minutes, he was reversing the Land Rover into a parking space that afforded him a view of Spittle Row and, more importantly, the front door of Richmond Legal Enterprises.

Only a handful of other vehicles occupied spaces in the car park. One in particular caught his attention. It was a gleaming, one-year-old black Range Rover with the registration plate 440 FDR.

His target was Frederick Reece.

As he wondered if Reece had a middle name, the door to the legal office opened, and a balding, middle-aged man stepped outside onto the doorstep. He turned and bellowed back into the office, 'Mandy! I'm going over to see my mum at the nursing home.'

He closed the door and walked across the street to the car park.

The Watcher glanced down at the silver-framed photograph on the passenger seat. He compared the balding man's features to the four men in the photograph. The man striding purposefully towards the car park was definitely in the photograph. He was unmistakeable. He had the same podgy, fat build now as he did when he was smiling for the camera in his black graduation gown.

The hair that had already started to recede when he was at university had now gone completely. It was Frederick Reece. He was a man ageing before his time due to poor diet, sloth and excessive drinking.

Unsurprisingly, Reece opened the door of the Range Rover and climbed in, heaving his bulky, overweight frame up into the high vehicle.

The Watcher waited for the Range Rover to start moving before turning the ignition of the Land Rover on. Very slowly, and at a discreet distance, he began to follow the Range Rover through the streets of Southwell.

As the two vehicles passed the magnificent Southwell Minster, the Watcher glanced over towards the distinctive, grey-tiled twin steeples. He muttered a quiet prayer of thanks, then said aloud, 'You truly are directing me, heavenly Father. Please don't allow me to fail you.'

25

9.30am, 29 March 1986
Hucknall Police Station, Nottinghamshire

The two detectives waited patiently in the CID office at Hucknall Police Station. They had spent the morning since the arrest of Baker discussing, at length, exactly how they were going to tackle the suspect's interview.

At exactly nine thirty, Sergeant Turner from the Special Operations Unit walked into the CID office. With an almost resigned air, he said, 'Right, sir, the search of the flat hasn't yielded much at all, I'm afraid.'

'Bollocks! Have we got anything?' asked Rob.

'Nothing that would be of any relevance to the murder scene at Underwood. No weapons, blood-stained clothing, eyeballs, etc. What we have recovered that might be of interest are a load of personal letters sent by Cavalie Naylor to Baker. Some of them are quite explicit in content. We've also recovered bank statements from Baker's NatWest current account. There's nothing of any interest in them; no massive sums being transferred in. Basically, Christopher Baker doesn't have a pot to piss in.'

'What was in the suitcase and the cardboard tubes I saw in the hallway?'

'Dirty washing in the suitcase; rolled-up charcoal drawings in the tubes.'

'So when he told me he'd just come back from somewhere rather than just going, it looks like he was telling the truth.'

'It looks that way. There was also a pamphlet in the case, extolling the virtues of a place called the Tranquil Waters Retreat for Artists. The retreat is based at a farmhouse in Cornwall, located just outside the town of Bude. It offers residential courses to budding artists who want to improve on their sketching and painting skills.'

'Have you recovered the pamphlet?' asked Glen Lorimar.

'We have. I thought it could be relevant if that's where he's just come back from.'

'Nice one. Anything else that might be useful?'

'No, that's it. As you saw for yourselves, the flat's very spartan. The living area has a settee, a television and a coffee table. The bedroom's tiny. There's just a wardrobe and a double bed in there. The clothes in the wardrobe are fashionable and smart, but there's not many of them. The kitchen has a cooker, a fridge, a washing machine and a small table and two chairs. It's extremely basic. The spare bedroom's done out like some half-arsed artist's studio. It has an easel, oil paints and a load of shit paintings stuck up on the walls and scattered all over the floor.'

Rob grinned. 'That's a bit harsh, Sergeant. Remember, art is always in the eye of the beholder.'

'I take your point, boss, but this stuff really is crap. Unless you consider paintings of dismembered bodies and body parts in general as art. It's all just a bit too fucking weird!'

'That's interesting, though. Did any of the paintings depict bodies lacking eyes or teeth?' asked Glen.

'No. When I first saw the paintings, that thought did occur to me. These are dismembered bodies, arms and legs missing, that kind of thing.'

Rob asked, 'Has everything you've recovered been bagged up and exhibited properly? Have all the labels been signed?'

'Everything's been done correctly, sir. The guys are downstairs finishing off their statements now. I'll leave the search log with you. The letters, bank statements and other documents have already been booked into the property store.'

'Thanks for a good job this morning.'

'No problem, sir. I'll bring the statements up to you as soon as they're finished.'

Sergeant Turner left the office to rejoin his men, and Glen Lorimar walked down to the property store to retrieve the recovered documents.

Half an hour had passed before Sergeant Turner returned to the CID office with the completed statements from his team. He found Rob and Glen busy reading the pile of letters that had been sent from Cavalie to Chris. Rather than disturb the two detectives, the burly SOU sergeant quietly placed the statements on the desk in front of them and left the office.

26

10.00am, 29 March 1986
Edingley, Nottinghamshire

The Watcher raced through the winding country lanes on the short journey from Southwell to Edingley. As soon as Reece had left the town, he had accelerated and driven at speed. The Watcher had struggled to keep up with the new Range Rover in his older vehicle, and had been relieved when Reece had slowed his vehicle down again as he entered Edingley.

Edingley was a small village. It consisted of two large farms, a row of houses each side of the main road, a whitewashed pub called the Plough Inn, and a small shop. Just through the village, on the road to Farnsfield, stood a magnificent red-brick building. This two-storey building was set back from the road, in its own pretty grounds. The property had previously been the country house of the local squire. It was now the Belle Vue nursing home.

The home was quite isolated, surrounded by open fields. The road that ran past the front of the building was little more than a country lane.

The indicator on the Range Rover came on, and Reece steered the vehicle into the small car park of the nursing home.

The Watcher drove by and parked his Land Rover on the grass verge a little further down the lane, away from the main entrance to the nursing home. From his location, he still had an unobstructed view of the large oak front doors of the nursing home as well as the small car park where Reece had left his vehicle.

He settled down for what he knew might be a lengthy wait.

Almost two hours had passed slowly by before his attention was drawn to movement near the front doors of the nursing home. He saw Reece step outside onto the doorstep and light up a cigarette. As he drew hard on the cigarette, he was joined by a young woman. She looked to be in her late teens, her auburn hair tied back in a ponytail. She wore black trousers and a thin, cream-coloured cardigan over her care assistant's uniform.

The young woman also lit up a cigarette, took a long drag, then spoke to Reece.

Both smokers then moved away from the main entrance, walked to a wooden bench and sat down next to each other. The bench, surrounded by shrubbery, could not be seen by anyone inside the home, but was still within the view of the Watcher.

The two smokers talked quite animatedly, gesturing with their hands. They both pulled hard on their cigarettes, exhaling the last of the smoke, before throwing the butts to the ground and grinding them out with their shoes. Reece reached out and grabbed the young woman by the hair. He pulled her violently towards him. The woman did not resist. Instead she placed her hand around the back of his neck and kissed him hard on the mouth.

Somewhat surprised at what was happening, the Watcher continued to observe.

Reece slid his hand between the legs of the woman. She squirmed and pulled his hand away; she then placed her own hands on Reece's crotch. Glancing around, she quickly unzipped his trousers, exposed his erect penis and began masturbating him. It took a couple of minutes for Reece to climax. Then, just as deftly, the young woman replaced his penis back inside his trousers and did up the zip. They separated and sat each end of the bench before lighting up more cigarettes.

Reece took a long pull on his cigarette before getting out a wallet from his jacket pocket. He smiled and handed the girl several banknotes, which she quickly stuffed into the pocket of her black trousers.

Having finished her cigarette, the young girl stood up, pecked Reece on the cheek and walked away. The Watcher saw her go back inside the nursing home.

With a look of smug satisfaction on his face, Reece leaned back on the wooden bench, looked up to the sky and exhaled the last of the blue smoke from his cigarette.

The Watcher smiled as he saw Reece stand up and walk back inside the nursing home.

Watching Reece go back inside, he said aloud, 'Playing the dutiful son who visits his sick mother, are you? Your visits are all about paying that poor young woman to pleasure you. Reece, you're an ungodly devil; the time for you to be dispatched back to hell is almost here.'

Another hour slowly passed. He checked his watch; it was now almost one o'clock in the afternoon.

His eye was automatically drawn to more movement at the large wooden doors. Frederick Reece stepped out of the doorway, then turned to speak to an elderly woman who had followed him outside. The woman wore the dark navy-blue uniform of a matron. There was a brief conversation; then he shook hands with her briskly and walked off towards the car park.

He walked to the black Range Rover, opened the driver's door, and started the engine.

The Watcher started up his Land Rover and waited.

As Reece drove the Range Rover out of the car park and onto Whipgate Street, the Watcher pulled out and followed the gleaming black vehicle at a discreet distance.

The Range Rover headed towards the village of Farnsfield.

The fact that Reece obviously had no intention of going back to his office in Southwell suited the Watcher. He continued to follow the Range Rover as it moved slowly through the village of Farnsfield. The black vehicle then accelerated as it left the village and headed back out into the countryside.

Less than half a mile out of Farnsfield, the road once again turned into little more than a country lane, with very little traffic.

It was the perfect location for the Watcher.

He mouthed a silent prayer of thanks to the Lord, then began flashing the headlights of the Land Rover, trying to get the attention of Reece in the Range Rover.

The Watcher saw brake lights on the vehicle in front of him. The Range Rover was driven off the road and came to a stop in a small layby. The Watcher followed and parked the Land Rover directly behind the Range Rover. The layby was barely big enough to accommodate both vehicles.

With an anxious expression on his face, the Watcher jumped out of his vehicle and walked towards the Range Rover.

Reece wound down the driver's window, leaned out and scowled. He then shouted towards the approaching Watcher, 'What the hell's the matter, man?'

'Thank goodness you've stopped; the back bumper of your motor's virtually hanging off. I reckon it'll drop off completely if you go much further.'

'Don't be ridiculous. What on earth are you talking about?'

'Seriously, I'm surprised you can't hear it dragging along the road. Have a look for yourself!'

With an air of impatience, Reece left the engine running and got out of the Range Rover. With a face like thunder, he stomped round to the back of the vehicle.

The Watcher quickly checked around for any approaching vehicles. He decided against a physical attack and instead reached for the .38 Smith & Wesson revolver in his jacket pocket.

Reece had by now reached the back of the Range Rover. When he saw there was no damage, he was incandescent with rage and spun round to face the Watcher. 'Are you completely fucking insane, man! There's nothing wrong with the bumper!'

He was so angry, it was only as he finished his rant that he realised the stranger was holding a handgun and pointing the barrel at his stomach.

Undeterred and losing none of his arrogant bluster, he demanded, 'What the hell do you think you're doing?'

The Watcher now pointed the handgun directly at the face of Reece and said quietly, 'Listen to me very carefully. If you say one more word, I'll pull the trigger and spread your brains across this lane. Do you understand me?'

The menace in his voice made it clear to Reece that he needed to do exactly as he was told.

'Walk to the back of my Land Rover, now.'

Reece did as he was instructed.

Still pointing the handgun at Reece, the Watcher undid the back door of the Land Rover.

He gestured with the handgun and said, 'Get in.'

Reece started to protest: 'You won't get away with this, you fucking moron!'

'I won't tell you again; get in.'

Reece climbed clumsily into the rear of the Land Rover. Once he was inside, the Watcher stepped forward and, using the pistol grip of the handgun, dealt him a crushing blow on the back of the head. The force of the blow rendered Reece unconscious.

The Watcher put the handgun back in his jacket pocket. He then bound Reece with cable ties, gagged him using gaffer tape and covered him with old blankets.

He walked to the Range Rover and switched the engine off. He removed the keys from the ignition and locked it before returning to his own vehicle. He started the engine and drove off steadily, back in the direction of Farnsfield. Once he was in the small village, he found the only public car park, which was located at the rear of the Co-op general store.

The car park was busy, and several other vehicles were already parked.

He parked the Land Rover in the far corner of the car park, away from the other vehicles. He got out and checked in the back of the vehicle. Reece was still out cold. He replaced the blankets over Reece and locked the door.

Keeping his head down and avoiding other people using the car park, the Watcher then walked back towards the lane that led out of the village. As soon as he was alone, he broke into a run. His work kept him extremely fit and active. Keeping a steady pace, it took him less than ten minutes to reach the Range Rover parked in the layby.

His intention was to drive the Range Rover back to Farnsfield and park it in the Co-op car park, effectively hiding it in plain sight.

Just as he reached the Range Rover, he heard a car approaching. He looked over his shoulder and saw a marked police car being driven along the lane towards him. He waited at the side of the Range Rover. The police patrol car came to a stop alongside him.

He noted, with a smile, that the police vehicle was single-crewed.

The male officer leaned over, opened the passenger door window of the police car, and said, 'Is everything all right, sir? You don't look too good.'

'I'm fine, Officer. Everything's good, thanks.'

'Is your vehicle alright?'

'It's fine. I was just having a breather.'

'Are you sure everything's okay? You're sweating.'

'Look, I clipped a fox or something as I was driving. When I looked back, I could see it lying in the road. I jumped out to see if it was okay, but every time I get near it, the bloody thing runs off. I've been chasing the bloody creature. That's why I'm sweating.'

The policeman switched off the car engine and got out of the car.

The Watcher noted that the officer was a big man, probably over six feet three inches tall, extremely broad and powerful. He looked to be around twenty-five years old and obviously worked out regularly at the gym. The

Watcher realised if things got physical, he would have a problem overpowering the officer.

The policeman started to examine the Range Rover.

'Is the vehicle registered to you, sir?'

'No, it belongs to a friend of mine. I'm just borrowing it.'

'I hope his insurance covers you. Exactly where did this fox hit the vehicle, sir? I'm struggling to see any damage.'

The policeman then looked squarely at the Watcher, sizing him up. His instincts told him something about the sweating man in the business suit was wrong.

He said bluntly, 'This business about hitting a fox is all bullshit, isn't it? Why don't you stop pissing about and tell me what's really going on here?'

The Watcher realised he was not going to be able to bluff his way out of the situation. For the second time in less than half an hour, he produced the black handgun from his jacket pocket.

In a flat, emotionless voice, he said, 'Do exactly as I tell you and you won't get hurt. Do not make the mistake of thinking I won't use this. The last thing I want to do is kill you, but if you leave me no option, I'll do it in a heartbeat. Do you understand me?'

The policeman nodded, never taking his eyes from the armed stranger.

The Watcher raised the gun a little higher, pointed at the officer's eyes, and said with a growl, 'Stop fucking eyeballing me and throw your radio, car keys and handcuffs on the road behind you.'

The three objects clattered to the ground.

Maintaining eye contact with the Watcher, the officer said, 'You're making a huge mistake, mate. You won't get away with this.'

'Shut up and walk. Go through the layby and into the trees.'

The Watcher followed, two yards behind the policeman, into the trees at the side of the layby.

'Stop. Kneel down and fold your arms across your chest.'

'Don't do this, mate.'

The Watcher stepped forward and smashed the butt of the handgun onto the back of the policeman's head. The officer fell forward, and the Watcher checked to see if he was unconscious.

Satisfied that the officer was indeed unconscious, the Watcher walked back to the road. He located the objects dropped earlier. He picked up the handcuffs and the car keys, then smashed the officer's personal radio on the ground. He returned to the unconscious policeman, sat him up so his back was leaning against the trunk of a tree and restrained him using his own handcuffs.

The last thing the Watcher had wanted to do was injure the officer, but it was a better option than killing him. He was only interested in making the four demons answer for their sins. The young police officer wasn't one of them.

Having handcuffed the still-unconscious policeman, he checked that the wound on the back of his head wasn't bleeding too badly. The Watcher knew that as soon as the officer was missed, his colleagues would start to look for him. By that time, the Watcher would be miles away from the area.

Leaving the officer in the woods, he then walked to the police car. He put on a pair of latex gloves, got in, and drove the vehicle about a hundred yards down the road. He turned off the lane and hid the car behind a tall hawthorn hedge. As he walked back to the Range Rover, he looked back over his shoulder. The police car was well hidden and couldn't be seen from the road.

He got in the Range Rover and, using the keys he had taken from Reece, drove the vehicle back to Farnsfield. He turned into the Co-op car park and parked the vehicle next to his Land Rover. He got out and hurled the Range Rover keys into the small stream that ran alongside the car park.

The Watcher checked in the back of his Land Rover to make sure Reece was still unconscious and secure. Satisfied that the fat solicitor was still out for the count, he covered him with the blankets again. This time, he piled old tools on top of him as well before locking the back door. He got into the driver's seat and slowly drove the vehicle out of the car park.

As he drove out of Farnsfield, a smile played across the Watcher's face. The third of the demons was now in his hands. Before today's events, he had considered the capture of Frederick Reece would prove to be the most challenging. As it turned out, apart from the unfortunate interruption by the police officer, it had been easy.

Just like Naylor and Hall before him, it would soon be time for Reece to pay for his sins.

27

2.00pm, 29 March 1986
Rampton Hospital, Nottinghamshire

Melissa Braithwaite drove her Ford Sierra through Woodbeck, the tiny village where Rampton high-security hospital was located. She flicked on the car's indicator, then took a right turn onto Fleming Drive, passing the two huge pillars that marked the entrance to the hospital.

Directly in front of her, she could see the impressive-looking red-brick buildings that flanked the main entrance and reception. The large buildings housed the doctors, nurses and other staff who worked at the hospital. She parked her vehicle in the main car park, situated just off Fleming Drive.

Before getting out of the car, she checked her Louis Vuitton handbag to ensure her passport was inside. Then she adjusted the bra she wore beneath the thick crew-neck jumper. The small crochet hook she had secreted below the wiring of her bra was extremely uncomfortable, but she knew it wouldn't have to be in there much longer.

On her previous visits to Rampton, she had experienced the pat-down search that was administered to all visitors. She knew if she was patient and waited until almost the end of the queue, the nurses doing the searches would be bored and tired.

The crochet hook Jimmy Wade had asked her to bring was no more than five inches long and made of steel covered in a plastic sheath. She had no reservations about helping Jimmy. The establishment, the lawyers and the police had blatantly used him as a scapegoat to deflect the public's attention away from the horrific murders committed by Police Sergeant Michael Reynolds.

Melissa had always believed this was the case, and now, after speaking with Jimmy on several occasions, she was convinced of it. All she wanted to do was help him get out of this horrendous place so they could spend the rest of their lives together. On her previous visits, they had spoken at length about how this could be achieved. Everything they had planned was now in place. If everything went well today, it would be her final visit to this awful prison.

She got out of the car and put on a thick woollen overcoat. It was a nice spring day, and the sun was shining, but the wind was strong and had a cold edge.

Melissa walked along Fleming Drive, between the two residential blocks, then down the slope towards the main reception. She booked in at the desk, then produced the visiting order and her passport as identification. As usual, she then handed her distinctive brown handbag to the staff on reception for safekeeping. No bags or containers of any description were allowed in the main hall during visits.

There was already a long queue of men and women waiting patiently to visit their loved ones. The afternoon visiting times were always the most popular. Patients from all over the country were detained at the maximum-security hospital, and afternoon visits allowed time for friends and relatives to make the arduous, long journey to the isolated hospital.

The queue of people slowly began filing along the long corridor, being directed towards the main hall by a member of the nursing staff.

Once outside the main hall, there was a further delay as the pat-down searches began. Melissa positioned herself towards the rear of the queue, estimating there were probably a dozen women and a similar number of men in front of her.

By the time she reached the front of the queue, the female nurse responsible for carrying out the searches looked suitably bored.

Although referred to as nurses, the staff all wore uniforms similar to those worn by the prison service. The uniforms made the feeling of overbearing security even more acute. As far as Melissa was concerned, Rampton was a high-security prison and nothing like a hospital.

The young nurse doing the searches looked blankly at Melissa and said, 'Take off your coat.'

Melissa did as she had been instructed.

The nurse continued in a monotone voice: 'Hold your arms out and spread your legs a little, please.'

As soon as Melissa adopted the position, the nurse began the search. Her hands swiftly ran along each of Melissa's arms over the top of the thick jumper, then down each side of her body and across the front and back of her torso. Thanks to the stiff underwire in the sturdy bra she was wearing, there was no sign of the crochet hook beneath it. The nurse then swiftly ran her hands down each of Melissa's legs, over the top of her tight corduroy jeans.

Finally, she ran her hands over the coat Melissa had been wearing before handing the garment back and waving her through.

As she entered the main hall, Melissa could see Jimmy Wade already sitting at a table near the centre of the hall. He smiled when he saw her and waved her over. There were twenty or thirty visitors, being supervised by eight members of staff.

The senior staff nurse stood at the front of the hall. Other staff were positioned at intervals around the hall, looking in towards the area of tables and chairs that had been set out for the visit. A male nurse stood outside the gents' toilet, which was located at the side of the main hall. It was his job to supervise any trips to the lavatory made by visitors or patients. A female nurse had a similar role outside the ladies' toilets.

Melissa sat down opposite Jimmy. She never tired of gazing into those beautiful clear blue eyes. The cobalt blue contrasted wonderfully with his yellow blonde hair. Melissa felt her stomach flip as she looked at him.

Sensing her attraction, Jimmy reached over the small table, held Melissa's hand and whispered, 'Good afternoon, beautiful. How's your auntie's crochet coming along?'

'It's wonderful, sweetheart. Can't you tell I'm wearing it?'

Jimmy smiled. 'I'm getting on really well in here now, and as a reward for being a good little boy, I've been listed for the working party at the concrete plant in two days' time.'

'That's fantastic news, sweetheart. It just so happens that I'm going to have a drive out in my car that day. I'm going to take a picnic with me to a lovely place I've seen not far from here. You might have heard of it? It's called Haggnook Farm.'

'I don't think I've heard of that farm, sweetheart.'

'It's just outside the village, between here and Retford. I'm going to have my picnic there, probably around midday.'

'I wish I could join you there. Who knows, maybe one day?'

Melissa merely smiled.

They both enjoyed talking in riddles. It was a game to them. The message was clear. If everything went to plan, Jimmy would be out on Monday. He would then meet her at Haggnook Farm, where she would be waiting with her car.

When Jimmy Wade had first arrived at Rampton, two of the male nurses had brutalised him at every opportunity, leaving him bruised and battered. At first, he'd resisted the assaults and retaliated, but that just made the beatings worse. Jimmy had adapted. He had taken the decision to become totally subservient. He had become submissive around the nursing staff until they no longer troubled him. Being Jimmy Wade, he had made a mental note of the two sadistic nurses' names and faces. He would bide his time and then exact his revenge.

He'd been working hard towards building up a level of trust so that he would be allowed to go on a working party. In particular, he wanted to get on the working party at the concrete plant.

There was a quite simple reason for this.

The concrete plant was situated adjacent to the lowest perimeter fence at the hospital. The fencing at that location comprised old, flimsy chain link. It was only seven feet high, with two strands of barbed wire on the top. It could easily be scaled in seconds. Beyond that chain-link fence was open countryside as far as the eye could see.

The concrete working parties usually consisted of three male patients, accompanied by six nursing staff, two of whom constantly maintained a position between the patients and the perimeter fence.

If his plan was going to be successful, Jimmy knew he would have to get through the nursing staff. That was where the crochet hook came in.

Melissa stood up and said loudly, 'I'm just nipping to the loo; won't be a minute.'

Jimmy smiled benignly.

She walked over to the toilets and went inside, followed by the supervising nurse.

Inside the toilets, the nurse remained outside the cubicle.

Once inside the cubicle, Melissa took off her coat and quickly removed the crochet hook from beneath her bra and slid it inside the sleeve of her thick jumper. Putting her coat back on, she flushed the toilet and walked out of the cubicle. She walked over to the sinks, watched by the supervising nurse, and thoroughly washed her hands. The door to the toilets opened, and another visitor stepped inside.

The nurse turned to the new arrival and said, 'Wait outside, please! Only one visitor at a time is allowed inside.'

'That's alright. I'm all finished, thanks,' said Melissa, smiling as she stepped out of the toilets.

The nurse was too preoccupied with the second visitor to pay any attention to Melissa, who walked across the hall and back to her seat opposite Jimmy.

Once again, Jimmy reached across the table and held Melissa's hand. Very slowly, his fingers felt for the crochet hook hidden beneath the sleeve of her sweater. Keeping a watchful eye on the supervising nurses, almost imperceptibly, he eased the crochet hook from Melissa's sleeve. In one fluid movement, he slid the hook beneath the sleeve of his own grey V-neck sweater.

Jimmy then stood up and walked over to the gents' toilet, where he spoke to the nurse. 'I'm really sorry, sir, but I desperately need the toilet. I've eaten something that's gone right through me. It's the third time I've had to go today.'

'Alright, Wade, I don't need chapter and bloody verse; be quick. I don't want to stand in a toilet listening to you having a shit!'

'Okay, sir, I'll be as quick as I can. Thank you, sir.'

Once inside the toilet cubicle, Wade removed the crochet hook from beneath his sleeve and placed it into the lining of his left boot. It fitted perfectly, virtually undetectable behind the stiff leather of the boot.

He flushed the chain and came out of the toilet. Smiling at the nurse, he said, 'Bloody hell, that's better. I needed that.'

Just as he reached the door, the staff member said, 'Just a minute, Wade.'

Jimmy froze, wondering if he was about to be caught.

He turned to face the nurse, who said, 'Wash your bloody hands!'

'Sorry, sir, of course.'

Jimmy stepped over to the sinks and washed his hands before walking back out into the main hall.

He walked over to Melissa, sat down, and winked.

It was now time for the second part of their plan.

After a couple of minutes, she suddenly pushed her

chair backwards, causing it to screech across the tiled floor. She stood up and shouted angrily, 'Don't you bloody dare say that to me!'

Wade looked hurt and said, 'I'm sorry, Melissa. I didn't mean it!'

'Yes, you bloody did. I'm not having it!'

Melissa stormed to the front of the hall, stood in front of the staff nurse and demanded, 'I want to leave right now, please.'

The staff nurse in charge signalled for one of the supervising nurses to come over. 'Escort this lady back to reception, then get Wade back to his room.'

The young nurse gently took hold of Melissa's arm and said, 'This way, please, follow me.'

Melissa followed the nurse out of the main hall. She never even glanced in Jimmy Wade's direction as she walked out.

As they walked along the corridor, Melissa turned to the nurse and said, 'I really don't know how you do this job. That's the last time I ever want to see Jimmy Wade. Throw away the key, will you?'

The nurse allowed a grin to play across her mouth and said, 'I wouldn't worry about that, love. Jimmy Wade's key was thrown away a long time ago.'

Melissa retrieved her handbag and passport from reception, then walked outside to her car. She grinned as she drove her car along Fleming Drive, hopefully for the last time. If all went to plan, in just two days' time she would be with her soul mate.

28

3.30pm, 29 March 1986
Hucknall, Nottinghamshire

The two detectives, Buxton and Lorimar, had deliberately taken their time. They'd first read all the letters, then studied the bank statements before finally going through the other documentation recovered from Christopher Baker's flat.

Now, as they sat with Baker in the claustrophobic interview room at Hucknall Police Station, they could see he was nearing exhaustion.

Rob opened his packet of Benson and Hedges cigarettes, offered one to Baker, and said, 'Christopher, are you sure you don't want a solicitor present for this interview?'

Baker accepted the cigarette and a light from Rob. He took a pull on the cigarette and said in his soft, distinctive, sing-song voice, 'I'm sure, thank you.'

Rob put the tapes into the recorder and switched it

on. He announced the time and the date before introducing himself and the other officer present. He then invited Christopher to give his full name and date of birth.

Finally, he cautioned Baker and said, 'Christopher, you've been arrested on suspicion of the murder of Cavalie Naylor. Do you have any knowledge of the events that led to the death of Cavalie Naylor?'

'None at all. Cav is, sorry, was extremely special to me.'

Glen Lorimar leaned forward, placed his elbows on the interview table, and said, 'How long have you known Cavalie?'

'Just under a year.'

'Where did you two first meet?'

'In Nottingham. At the Wimpole Art Gallery on Houndsgate.'

'How did that meeting come about?'

'I was looking at a particular painting, and he stood next to me and passed a comment about it being one of his favourites. We got chatting and ended up going for a glass of wine together. We've been friends ever since.'

'You said earlier that you believed Cav's father was responsible for your arrest today. Why do you think that's the case?'

'Because Geoff Naylor hates my guts, that's why.'

'Why does he hate you?'

'Isn't it obvious, Detective? He thought I was all wrong for his precious Cavalie. He wanted him to meet some gorgeous woman, fall in love, get married and have kids – the whole nine yards.'

'Why was that such a problem?'

Christopher Baker laughed.

'What's so funny, Christopher?'

'I'm amazed you still can't see it; you must have read

the letters at my flat. Cav Naylor didn't need to find someone to fall in love with; he was already in love, with me. We're both gay, for Christ's sake. The only problem was, he couldn't face telling his father. So, consequently, Geoff got it into his head that I was some evil, manipulative bastard who was only interested in fleecing his son for everything he'd got.'

'And were you?'

'Was I what?'

'Trying to fleece Cav for everything he'd got?'

'No, I wasn't. Listen, Detective, I know it's hard for you to understand this, but I genuinely love – loved – Cav. I knew from the beginning of our relationship that we were from completely different backgrounds. But I genuinely believed we would be happy together.'

Tears had never been far away from Christopher's blue eyes. Now, as he spoke, he blinked, and teardrops spilled from his eyes, rolling slowly down each cheek. With a tremor in his soft voice, he said, 'I really loved that man, Detective.'

Glen Lorimar pressed on: 'What happened the last time you saw Cav?'

'He picked me up from my flat last week after work, and we drove out to his bungalow at Underwood. We had a nice meal, drank a bit of wine and chatted about my charcoal-drawing course.'

'Exactly what date was that?'

Christopher was thoughtful for a second, then said, 'It was the night of the twentieth.'

'Did you stay with him all night?'

'Of course I did. We were lovers. It's what lovers do, Detective.'

'How did Cav seem to you that evening?'

'Perfectly normal. We had a lovely night.'

'And the next morning?'

'Everything was fine. We had a bit of breakfast; then he dropped me back at my flat so I could get my things ready to travel down to Cornwall.'

'Let's talk about Cornwall. Tell me about the Tranquil Waters Retreat for Artists.'

'I saw the place advertised in a magazine. I'm currently into drawing with charcoal, and they were advertising a residential course on that very subject at Tranquil Waters. I mentioned it to Cav some time ago and, unbeknown to me, he paid for the course and booked me on it as a surprise gift. Yes, before you ask, Detective, he also paid for my train fare there and back. Cav was an extremely generous man. Which is something else that always pissed his old man off.'

'Exactly when did you travel to Tranquil Waters?'

'The next morning, the twenty-first. I caught the ten o'clock train from Nottingham to St Pancras, where I changed trains. I had a half-hour wait at St Pancras before getting the train down to Bude. I arrived at the retreat around three o'clock in the afternoon.'

'Who can verify your time of arrival?'

'The guy who runs Tranquil Waters is a well-renowned artist called Teddy Blake. He booked me into my room when I arrived. It was Teddy who actually taught the class I attended.'

'And when did you arrive back in Nottingham?'

'I came back late last night. I was still troubled by the strange phone call with Geoff, but I just put it down to his usual rudeness. So, in answer to your question, I arrived back in Nottingham just after eleven o'clock last night.'

'What was it about the telephone conversation with Geoff that made you troubled?'

'It was the last straw, that's all. When I arrived in Bude last week, I was knackered, so I just went to bed and didn't bother calling Cav. The next morning, I called him first thing, but couldn't get through. It sounded as though his phone was constantly engaged. I just thought he had somehow knocked the phone off the hook without realising it. He can be so clumsy at times.'

Christopher brushed a tear from his cheek and continued. 'Anyway, eventually I'd had enough of the engaged tone at his house, so I rang his office. That's when I spoke to his father. I asked him if Cav was there, and the ignorant old bastard hung up on me. It was then I decided that something wasn't right. I intended going over to Underwood to see what was going on this morning. But you arrested me.'

'Are you aware of any enemies Cav might have?'

'Not a single one. Cav was the gentlest, kindest, most loving person you could ever hope to meet.'

'Have you ever discussed Cav's business interests with him?'

'No. I was never bothered about his business. Cav never talked about work after a hard day. All he wanted to do was relax and unwind.'

Glen Lorimar turned to Rob Buxton and said, 'Is there anything you want to ask, sir?'

Rob said, 'Do you know a man by the name of Edward Hall?'

Baker replied, 'No.'

'Has Cav ever mentioned that name to you?'

'No, he hasn't.'

'Have either of you stayed at the Grosvenor Hotel in Nottingham recently?'

'Well, I certainly haven't; it's well out of my price range. I can't say whether Cav has or not, but I don't recall him mentioning anything to me about him staying there.'

Rob then glanced at his watch, said the time out loud, and terminated the interview.

All three men stood up and walked out of the interview room.

Rob turned to Glen and said, 'Make the phone calls to the Tranquil Waters Retreat and verify Christopher's story, especially the timings. Confirm the exact date when the course was booked and who paid for it. If everything checks out, bail him for two weeks. I need to get back over to Mansfield and liaise with the boss.'

'No problem, sir.'

Glen watched Rob walk out of the cell block, then turned to Christopher and said, 'Come on, Chris, let's get you back to your cell while I make these phone calls. Do you want a cup of tea or coffee?'

'Coffee, two sugars, would be great. Thanks, Detective. I really did love Cav; you do know that, don't you?'

'I know you did, Chris; I know you did.'

29

8.00pm, 29 March 1986
Major Crime Investigation Unit, Mansfield

One by one, the weary detectives trailed into the main office of the Major Crime Investigation Unit.

It was time to debrief the day's enquiries. Time for the individual detectives to brief the entire team, how their particular enquiry had gone and whether or not they had learned anything useful.

As soon as everyone was in attendance, Danny addressed them collectively. 'I know you've all been on duty since early this morning, so I won't drag this out. I want you debriefed and away home, ready for another early start tomorrow morning. Before we start the debrief, I want to introduce you to Detective Sergeant Andy Wills, who will be working on DI Buxton's team. Andy's already known to most of you. He'll be replacing DS Mayhew, who has unfortunately slipped a disc and will be off work for the foreseeable future. Andy, I'd like you to start the debrief by enlightening everyone about the exact meaning of the messages found at the murder scenes.'

'Okay,' Andy said. 'The series of numbers and letters written on the walls is a Bible reference. It refers to a passage from the book of Exodus, found in the Old Testament, which is a very well-known quote from the Bible. The passage it refers to famously states, "an eye for an eye and a tooth for a tooth". Everybody in this room has probably heard that expression sometime in their life. What you may not know is the scripture in the reference goes on to state, "hand for hand, foot for foot, burning for burning, wound for wound, stripe for stripe". The two victims so far have lost their eyes and their teeth, respectively. It seems clear that the motive for the killings is vengeance. If the killer is following the scripture to the letter, it could mean there's the potential for several further victims.'

'Thanks, Andy.'

Danny then turned to Rob Buxton. 'How did the arrest and interview of Christopher Baker go?'

'We arrested him at home this morning without a hitch. He's been interviewed at length and has a cast-iron alibi for both murders. At the time of the murders, Baker was attending a residential charcoal-drawing course in Bude, Cornwall. I've released him on bail. DC Lorimar is still with him, obtaining as much background information on Cavalie Naylor as possible. It's true, there was no love lost between Christopher Baker and Geoff Naylor, and it turns out there's a simple reason for this. Christopher Baker is gay. He was in a relationship with Cavalie, who couldn't face admitting his sexual orientation and true feelings for Christopher to his father.'

'Thanks. Is there any suggestion that either Christopher Baker or Cavalie Naylor knew Edward Hall?'

'Definitely not as far as Christopher's concerned. He'd never heard the name Edward Hall.'

There was a pause, which was filled by a woman's voice: 'There is a link between Hall and Naylor, though, sir.'

The voice belonged to Sergeant Tina Prowse.

Danny looked at Tina and said, 'Go on.'

'After I finished getting the statement from Vanessa Hall this morning, I was tasked with doing background checks on Edward Hall. I started by doing comparisons between the two victims. Both men were of a similar age, and both were in professional occupations. So I started thinking about the qualifications they would have needed to achieve their respective positions of employment. Sure enough, I found Edward Hall had attended Nottingham University. I did a quick cross-check and found that Cavalie Naylor had also attended Nottingham University at the same time. I don't know if the two men knew each other at university, but it's definitely common ground and perhaps worthy of a bit more digging.'

Detective Inspector Brian Hopkirk said, 'I think it's a bit more than common ground.'

He turned and addressed his comments to Danny. 'Sir, this afternoon I was tasked with searching the office used by Edward Hall at the Grosvenor Hotel. One of the items recovered was a small framed photograph of four men on their graduation day. One of the men in the photograph was obviously Edward Hall, and I'm fairly sure that one of the other three was Cavalie Naylor. I telephoned Vanessa

Hall and asked her if she knew who the other two men in the photograph were, but she couldn't say. Vanessa asked me if I'd taken the photo from her home, as it was identical to one they kept in the lounge at their house. I've checked the search logs, and no such photo was recovered by the search teams at the Beeston scene. For my own peace of mind, I drove over to the Halls' house and had a look to see if it had been missed by the search teams. There was no sign of any photograph anywhere that was identical, or even similar to, the one recovered from Hall's office. That means either Hall took the photograph from home to the office, or there were two photographs, and one is now missing. Either way, the photograph proves Tina's link and demonstrates that our two murder victims were, at the very least, acquaintances at the university.'

Danny was impressed. 'That's great work, both of you. As a top priority, I want Tina and Rachel to go to Nottingham University tomorrow morning. I want you to establish who the other two men in the photograph are. Brian, I want you to start researching incidents that occurred at Nottingham University at the time our two victims were there. If, as appears likely, the killer's motive is revenge, and the only link we can find between the two victims is their time spent together at university, it's not a vast stretch of the imagination to think their murders could be in direct revenge for something that happened when they were both there. Tina, how did you get on with Vanessa Hall this morning?'

'She was much better today, sir. I took a full statement from her, but there's not too much detail. I think the shock of seeing her husband like that has clouded her memory; she could remember very little about the assailant. One thing she does recall quite vividly is seeing what she describes as a huge hunting knife being held in front of her face by the intruder. Dr Gillender informed me that after such a traumatic experience the memory can become vague, but that it does sometimes improve after a period of time. I think it would be prudent to revisit Vanessa Hall in the near future to see if she has regained any more memory.'

'I'll make a note of that, Tina; thank you. At least we now have some idea of the kind of weapon used. Sounds like Seamus Carter's opinion wasn't too far off the mark.'

The debrief continued for another half hour, but nothing else of any major importance was revealed.

When every detective had reported their findings, Danny turned to the team and said, 'Good work, everyone. We're starting to make progress, but there's still plenty more to be done. I want everybody back here at six o'clock tomorrow morning. Before you all go home, there's something you all need to be aware of. Just before we started the debrief this evening, I was informed by the control room that a police officer has gone missing whilst on duty. PC 212 Colin Moreton was working a day shift at Southwell. He should have gone off duty at six o'clock this evening. Both he and his vehicle have been missing since around three o'clock this afternoon. I asked the control room if they wanted us to stay on duty to help locate the officer, but the duty inspector told me that he had all the manpower needed to search the area tonight, and that there was a real possibility that staff from the MCIU may be required tomorrow morning. So, all of you, get off home, but be aware that tomorrow, in all probability, some of you will be seconded from this enquiry to assist with enquiries into the disappearance of our colleague. Let's wait and see what the night brings. I'll see you all in the morning.'

There were murmurings of concern for their missing

colleague from the detectives as they made their way out of the briefing room. It was an extremely unusual occurrence and one that rarely had a good outcome. Most of the officers were already fearing the worst for the missing constable.

30

9.00pm, 29 March 1986
Teversal Manor, Cotgrave, Nottinghamshire

Paul Fencham rang the ornate doorbell again.
This time, a light came on in the hallway of the grand house. He had parked his small Datsun car on the road outside the house, then walked up the gravel driveway. He'd been amazed at the size of the palatial residence. Since leaving the army, Geoff Naylor had really done well for himself.

Fencham had been stunned when, out of the blue, he had received the telephone call from Naylor. Of course, he had already heard about the murder of Geoff Naylor's son, Cavalie, from the news desk. As a crime reporter for the *Nottingham Evening Standard*, it was his job to know about any major enquiries being undertaken by the police.

The telephone call had still surprised him, though. He didn't understand why Naylor, the successful businessman, had called him to say he had information for a story.

He hadn't seen Geoff since they were both demobbed from the army back in the fifties. Both men had served in the same regiment during the Korean War. They had been close during their time in the service, but, as is normal for people, they had drifted apart when they returned to civilian life. He hadn't seen Geoff Naylor at any of the Korea Veterans reunions he'd attended over the ensuing years.

He'd been shocked that Naylor even knew he was a reporter.

Paul Fencham was a realist who understood that, at his time of life, he was never going to get that lucky break. He knew that the one big story that would set him up, enabling him to become a top reporter for a national Fleet Street paper, was never going to happen.

He was now the wrong side of fifty and had started drinking heavily after his divorce five years ago. He was a short, squat man at least three stone overweight. He couldn't afford to buy a suit, so he wore a tatty tweed jacket with leather patches on the elbows, a grimy blue shirt, a garish mustard-coloured tie and scruffy, stain-ridden black trousers. His brown brogues were scuffed and devoid of any polish. He had a permanent five o'clock shadow, and his once-blonde hair was now grey and receding rapidly.

All in all, Paul Fencham was a mess, and more tellingly, he knew he was a mess.

He could now hear footsteps from inside the house, approaching the double front doors.

A lock was turned from within, and the right-side door opened. Geoff Naylor stood there with a cut-glass tumbler, full of whisky, in his hand. Involuntarily,

Fencham licked his lips at the sight of the amber-coloured liquor.

'Well, don't just stand there, Fenchers, come inside,' said a clearly tipsy Naylor.

Fencham stepped inside the grandiose hallway. Naylor closed the door and said in a slurred voice, 'This way, old friend; follow me.'

Fencham followed him along the hallway and into a huge lounge.

'Grab a seat, Fenchers. Can I get you a drink?'

It was the second time Naylor had referred to him by his old army nickname.

'I'll have the same as you.'

'Yeah, course you will. Good man.'

Naylor, who had ignored his doctor's strict advice against drinking while he recovered from his recent angina attack, poured a huge measure of single malt whisky into a tumbler and handed it to the newspaper reporter.

Fencham took a huge gulp of the fiery liquid, smacked his lips and said, 'Ah, that's better! I was sorry to hear about your son. Is that why you've asked me to come over? Is it something to do with his death?'

'The fucking police aren't taking me seriously. I've already told them who's done it. Virtually handed them the case on a fucking plate, and they're still not interested. That bastard Christopher Baker killed him. The cops arrested him this morning; then just before I called you, I heard that the useless fuckers have already let him go again. I don't understand what's going on. I want to know what the fuck they're playing at.'

'If the cops have questioned and released this Christopher Baker already, I'm sure they've got their reasons. Perhaps they've let him out on bail until they get more evidence.'

'Yeah, that could be it. He's a devious, clever bastard alright, killing that poor fucker over in Beeston just to cover his tracks.'

Fencham was aware of the other murder in Beeston, but there was no suggestion anywhere that the two murders were linked.

Naylor stood up on shaky legs, poured himself another huge measure from the dark green Glenfiddich bottle, and said, 'Want another, Fenchers, my old mate?'

Fencham quickly gulped down the remaining whisky in his glass, then handed it to Naylor, who promptly filled it to the top again. He took the glass back from Naylor and took another big mouthful. He could feel his cheeks starting to flush as the whisky raced into his system.

'Geoff, why exactly do you think your boy was murdered by this bloke Baker?'

'Because I know he was after Cav's money, pure and simple. The police aren't telling your lot everything about the murders, are they? They're being very selective, right? I bet they haven't even told you about the message left on the walls, have they?'

Fencham thought Naylor had finally lost it. He was obviously pissed and was making no sense. Then the old habits of the news reporter kicked in. Fencham put his drink down on the coffee table. He needed a moment to think.

'What message on what wall?'

'That bastard Baker wrote a message on the kitchen wall in Cav's house, using my precious boy's blood.'

'What was the message?'

'It didn't make any sense. It was just a row of random numbers and letters. Gobbledegook to throw the cops off the scent. It's all a load of bollocks, and I wouldn't be surprised if he hasn't done the same when he's slotted that other poor bastard in Beeston. If the message is there as well, that's surely got to prove that evil fucker Baker did them both. Am I right, Fenchers?'

'You're dead right. What else do you think Baker did at both the murders?'

The alcohol, mixed with his strong medication, was beginning to take a heavy toll on Naylor. He mumbled, 'I don't know, mate. I want you to talk to the cops for me. Make them see sense. Can you do that?'

Naylor was now slurring his words so badly that it was hard for Fencham to understand clearly what he was saying.

'Of course. I think you need to have a rest now, mate. Get your head down and sleep off some of that whisky. I'll see myself out.'

Geoff Naylor lay down on one of the plush settees, and within seconds, he was snoring loudly.

Fencham was now deep in thought. Leaving Naylor asleep in the lounge, he walked back out into the hallway and spotted a telephone on an antique occasional table. Picking up the phone, he quickly dialled a number from memory.

'Hello, mate, it's Paul Fencham. How would you like to earn yourself fifty quid?'

There was a pause before Fencham spoke again. 'It's easy money, Dave. Just answer me one question: Did you work on that murder at Beeston the other day?'

Another pause.

'You did, that's brilliant. Listen, I know you take photographs of everything on them jobs. A little bird tells me something may have been written on the wall. What was it?'

A longer pause.

'Come on, Dave, it's the easiest money you'll ever make. Let's say seventy-five quid.'

Fencham then exploded down the phone, 'Fuck off! I'm not paying you a hundred quid, you grasping shit!'

A few seconds later, Fencham spoke in a more acquiescent tone: 'Don't be too hasty, Dave. Alright, a hundred it is. But for that money, I want to know exactly what was written on the wall.'

A broad smile spread across the reporter's features. He grabbed the small notepad and pencil that were always in his jacket pocket.

He scribbled down what he was told, then repeated it back: 'EC21V2425. Are you sure that's all it was? What the fuck's that supposed to mean?'

There was another pause while Fencham listened to his informant talking.

'How do you think, Dave? I'll post you the cash as normal. You haven't moved to a new house, have you? No? Well, stop fucking panicking; you'll get your money. I've never let you down before, have I?'

Fencham slammed the phone down, then picked it straight back up and dialled the number for the night desk at the *Nottingham Evening Standard*'s office. 'I've got something I need you to look at urgently. It's a series of random letters and numbers … EC21V2425. I want to know exactly what they mean; get on it. I'm coming back to the office right now, and I want to know what it means by the time I get there.'

Fencham walked back into the lounge, where Naylor was now fast asleep. The snoring had subsided a little and had changed into the slow rhythmic breathing of a deep sleep. Fencham finished his whisky, then poured himself another large one.

He swallowed the fiery liquid in one go. Raised his empty glass and said, 'Cheers, Geoff. I don't know who the fuck Christopher Baker is, mate, but thank you so much for the tip-off about the serial killer.'

He walked out of the house, along the gravel driveway and back to his car. He had a warm glow; he couldn't tell if it was the effects of the single malt whisky or the fact that he'd just been handed the biggest opportunity of his newspaper career.

All he had to do was figure out the meaning of the message on the walls, and then he could make some serious money, selling the story to the red tops.

31

4.00am, 30 March 1986
Farnsfield, Nottinghamshire

PC Colin Moreton was shivering cold.

He was grateful it had stayed dry, but the flip side of being dry was the way temperatures had plummeted overnight beneath a clear sky. He was also thankful that he'd decided to put a jumper on beneath his tunic before he went on patrol yesterday.

As the first light of dawn began to creep over the horizon and the birds started to sing, he glanced down at his wristwatch. It was awkward to see the watch face clearly because his wrists were twisted at a strange angle because of the handcuffs. Eventually, he could make out the time. It was just after four o'clock, which meant he had been propped against this tree for over twelve hours. It was time to try to get moving.

His head still ached from the blow, but at least he no longer felt like he would pass out if he tried to move. He was grateful that he'd only been knocked unconscious. When he had been forced to kneel, with his back facing that nutter with the gun, he'd been convinced he was about to be shot and killed.

The worst thing about the whole incident was that he still had absolutely no idea what the hell it was all about. Initially, he'd thought the bloke had broken down; then he'd noticed that he was sweating profusely and breathing hard, as though he had been running. The last thing he had expected when he got out of the police car was to be confronted with a handgun.

His head ached a little more as he tried to work it all out.

It was time to stop thinking about what had happened and do something. He'd been sat in the same position for way too long.

He forced his back into the trunk of the tree, then tried to lever himself off the ground by pushing with his legs. It was difficult because of the handcuffs and the uneven ground, but eventually he managed to get to his feet. He moved his head from side to side, and his neck felt sticky. He could feel that his shirt collar was damp. The wound to his head must have bled badly for his shirt to feel that wet. It was getting lighter now, and he could just about make out the layby through the branches of the trees.

Very gingerly, he took a couple of steps; he fully expected a new wave of nausea to rush over him and cause him to collapse again.

Nothing happened.

He gave a triumphant little grin as he took another step, then another.

He stepped onto the tarmac of the lane just as the first rays of the sun crept over the horizon. He knew it was psychological, but just feeling that weak sunlight on his face made him automatically feel warmer.

He looked both ways along the lane. There was no

sign of the black Range Rover or his police car. Had there been two offenders all the time? Had he completely missed an accomplice?

A glint of sunlight reflecting off a metal object on the road caught his eye. He shuffled slowly over to the object and saw that it was the smashed remnants of his personal radio.

After a few minutes, he got his bearings and remembered exactly where he was. Still feeling unsteady, he started to walk in the direction of Farnsfield, trying to ignore the throbbing pain building inside his head.

He had staggered along for about fifty yards when he suddenly felt dizzy and nauseous. He stopped for a rest, took some deep breaths, and looked along the lane.

Away in the distance, he could just make out a vehicle being driven very slowly in his direction. Now that the sun was creeping ever higher, the vehicle only had its side lights on. As the car slowly approached and got closer, his face suddenly creased into a wide grin. He could now clearly see the blue light bar on the roof of the white vehicle. He realised it was a police patrol car.

They must be out searching for me. That's why it's going so slowly, he thought.

Raising his manacled hands above his head, he tried to attract the attention of the officers in the patrol car.

The action of raising his arms brought on another dizzy spell. This time, it was enough to make him slump to the ground. He didn't have the energy or strength to try to stand again, so he remained sitting, cross-legged, at the side of the lane as he willed the throbbing pain in his head to stop.

Through the pain, he heard the roar of the patrol car's engine as the officers finally spotted him sitting at the side of the lane. The driver accelerated along the lane to reach him.

The car screeched to a halt. He heard doors open as the officers jumped out and ran towards him.

With relief in his voice, PC Moreton muttered out loud, 'Thank fuck for that!'

32

4.30am, 30 March 1986
Mansfield, Nottinghamshire

Danny Flint stood in his kitchen. He was just about to pour the hot water from the kettle onto a tea bag when he heard the key slide into the Yale lock of the front door.

He pushed open the door that led from the kitchen into the hallway just in time to see his fiancée, Sue, walking in through the front door.

Danny instinctively glanced at his watch. It was now four thirty in the morning. Sue's shift at King's Mill Hospital should have finished at two o'clock.

'You're late, sweetheart. Been busy?' he asked.

'There's been a bad accident on the motorway: three cars, a van and a lorry. We had four serious casualties brought into our department just after one o'clock. They're all stable and on the wards now, though, thank goodness. No fatalities this time. I'll never understand why people insist on driving so fast in the fog. That level of stupidity never ceases to amaze me.'

'The kettle has just this second boiled, if you want a cuppa?'

'Ooh! A cup of tea would be lovely, thanks, sweetheart.'

Danny finished making both cups of tea, then joined Sue sitting at the breakfast table in the kitchen.

Sue held the mug in both hands and took a sip of her hot tea. 'That's bloody lovely. Just what the doctor ordered.'

'Yeah, literally.' Danny laughed.

'Anyway, Detective, why are you up at this ungodly hour?'

'It's hectic at the minute. We've had two murders come in this week, and even though they were at different ends of the county, they appear to be linked. It looks like we've got another nutter on the loose. It could be like Jimmy Wade all over again.'

'That sounds awful. Have you any idea at all who you're looking for?'

'It's early days yet, but at this moment in time, we know very little. On top of that, just before I left work last night, I was informed that a uniform cop who works at Farnsfield was missing. He's completely vanished along with his patrol car. I haven't had any messages overnight. So I've no idea if he's been located, or if something nasty has happened to him.'

'So it looks like being a long day for you?'

'More than likely. Why?'

'Had you forgotten about our little appointment with the vicar this evening, at six o'clock?'

'Bugger! I'm so sorry, Sue, I'd totally forgotten. I might be able to slip away for a little while. Even if I can't make it, you can still go, can't you?'

Sue said, 'Of course I can still go. I think the idea of the vicar wanting to see both the bride and the groom was so he could talk to us both about the sanctity of marriage.'

Danny grinned and said, 'He knows we've both been married before. What do you think he's going to try to tell us?'

'Oh, I don't know, Danny. Maybe "better luck this time"!'

They both giggled and sipped their tea.

Sue smiled and said, 'Seriously, sweetheart, don't worry if you can't make it tonight. I'll let you know what the vicar said later. What I will say is this: You and your best man had both better be at that church on May 7.'

'I'll definitely be there, sweetheart. I don't know if Rob will be able to get time off from work, though. Apparently, the bloke he works for is a complete knob!'

'Funny, I'd heard that too. Shouldn't you be at work by now, Chief Inspector?' Sue replied dryly.

Danny grabbed his suit jacket from the back of the chair, took a last drink of tea, and made for the front door.

He stopped halfway, spun around, and walked back into the kitchen. He grinned and said, 'Nearly forgot,' before kissing Sue gently on the mouth.

She responded to the kiss before saying, 'I should think so, too.'

Danny said, 'See you later, sweetheart. Say hello to the vicar for me.'

'Get to work, Danny, before I change my mind!'

33

4.30am, 30 March 1986
Rampton Hospital, Nottinghamshire

Jimmy Wade lay on top of the hard bed in his cell at the high-security hospital. He was wide awake, staring at the ceiling.

It amused him how the staff all referred to the cells as *rooms*. Who were they trying to fool? Rampton Hospital had the highest security he'd encountered since his arrest. That included the maximum-security prison in New South Wales, where he'd been held while the British police arranged to take him back to the UK to stand trial.

Wade still cursed his luck every day. He still didn't understand how he'd failed to spot that spineless twat Dave Smedley at the Beltana mine. He lay in the dark and replayed in his mind the moment the Australian detectives had arrested him, in the pit canteen, after his shift. He had literally taken one bite from his sandwich, when three of the biggest and strongest men he'd ever seen grabbed him and threw him to the floor before handcuffing and arresting him.

Everything after that initial moment of capture had been a blur.

He hadn't said a word to Detective Inspector Flint or his sidekick Detective Sergeant Buxton throughout the entire journey from New South Wales to England. He'd refused to speak to them during the hours of interviews as well. He knew he was fucked and just had to accept the inevitable.

That feeling of inevitability changed at Leicester Crown Court when he had first seen Melissa Braithwaite in the public gallery. He'd been mesmerised by her. It wasn't the old urges he felt when he looked into her beautiful, soulful eyes, which already held so much pain. He wanted to be with her. He found her attractive and beautiful; he had no inclination or urge to snuff out her very existence.

Ever since her first visit at Wakefield prison while he was on remand, he'd been totally besotted. He was amazed at her loyalty. Even when confronted by overwhelming evidence to the contrary, she had always maintained that he was innocent. She was convinced that the real guilty party was Sergeant Michael Reynolds.

He hadn't wanted to burst her bubble, so he'd played along with her theory and insisted she was right. He had allowed her to believe that he really was an innocent man.

He'd been delighted when, after his conviction and subsequent whole life sentence, she had continued to visit him at Rampton Hospital. Throughout the many visits, their special bond and friendship had grown stronger.

When he'd first mentioned his plan about the concrete unit working party and the possibility of him getting out, she had been overjoyed and promised to help.

She had fulfilled that promise today.

He got up from the hard bed and made his way over to the small sink in his cell. Kneeling on the floor, he reached up behind the sink, fingers searching. Right at the back, in the small recess between the sink and the wall, his straining fingers found the crochet hook.

Having retrieved the hook, he started to work on the thin sheath of plastic that surrounded the metal inner rod. Using his teeth, he stripped away the plastic until he was left with a metal rod. It was the same diameter as a knitting needle, but only half the length.

The unpainted bricks near the tiny window of his cell were very rough in texture. He spat on one of the bricks, then began to draw the metal rod back and forth through the spit. There was a scraping sound, but it wasn't too loud. Unless somebody was standing directly outside the cell door, he was in no danger of the noise being heard outside his cell.

He walked over to the locked door, straining to see as far as he could along the corridor. His view was limited, as the window was merely a slit in the heavy metal door, but he could see that no lights were on.

He returned to the window and began working the crochet hook on the rough brick.

After an hour of painstaking, slow work, the harmless crochet hook had been turned into a lethal metal spike. He then used folded toilet paper to put a pad on the blunt end of the crochet hook before nestling it into the palm of his hand. He allowed the spike to protrude five inches between his middle and ring fingers. He bunched his fist around the makeshift weapon, then punched the spike into the pillow on his bed.

The spike penetrated the pillow easily, and the padding on the blunt end meant there was little discomfort in the palm of his hand.

Having satisfied himself of the effectiveness of the home-made weapon, he secreted it in the same place behind the sink.

He lay back down on the top of his bed, interlaced his fingers, placed both hands behind his head and smiled.

As he lay in the darkness, he thought of all the people he would visit when he finally got out. Some people would have to pay for the way they had either disrespected or deceived him.

First on his list were the two sadistic nurses who had regularly beaten him when he first arrived at Rampton. He'd taken great pains to establish their names and identities and was now aware that they were both single men. Fred Barnes, the older of the two, lived in Retford, and Jack Williams lived in the small village of Dunham. They would both pay, heavily, for the way they had treated him.

He stared at the ceiling and played out their deaths in his mind over and over again. Both men would suffer horribly. He would see to that.

Next on the list was that mealy-mouthed, skinny bastard Stewart Ainsworth, the social worker.

Wade had told him countless times about the beatings, and he hadn't done a thing. Not once had he tried to help him. As far as Wade was concerned, by his inaction, Ainsworth was complicit in the beatings. The weakling social worker had been more interested in taking Melissa to task over visiting him. Well, he would pay for his ineptitude and cowardice. He had something incredibly special lined up for Stewart Ainsworth. He too would suffer a terrifying ordeal. He would soon realise that he had crossed the wrong person.

Revenge would taste so sweet.

Finally, there was Rachel Moore. The beautiful, enigmatic detective who had cheated death at his hands and then provided the clinching evidence to secure his conviction.

It would soon be time for her to pay. He would make sure that this time, there would be no escape.

He closed his eyes and thought of tomorrow's events, playing out various scenarios in his mind. One more day to wait.

34

4.30am, 30 March 1986
Farndon, Nottinghamshire

The sound of dripping water began to seep into the consciousness of Frederick Reece.
As he began to come around, he realised just how freezing cold he was. He had no idea where he was and felt totally disoriented. He tried to stand up but found he'd been bound in such a way that he was prevented from being able to stand.

He also quickly realised that he'd been gagged.

Using his tongue and teeth, he tried to move the sticky tape that covered his mouth. Despite his best efforts, he couldn't shift it. Thankfully, he could still breathe through his nose.

He tried to shout, but the gag stifled his cries.

His hands had been bound tightly behind his back, and his wrists and shoulders ached because of the strained, unnatural way his arms had been pinned. He rolled his head from side to side, then up and down, trying to alleviate the ache in his shoulders.

There was no blindfold, and now, as dawn broke, light started to filter into the building. He was able to look around the room that was, in effect, his prison cell.

He was being held in what appeared to be a decrepit, disused building. The concrete walls were a drab grey, discoloured in places by various water marks, stains and random obscene graffiti. The building looked as though it had once been used as some sort of industrial unit, possibly agricultural, judging by the smell.

He wrinkled his nose. *What is that smell?*

It was like rotting rancid flesh; he'd never smelled anything quite like it. It was disgusting and made him want to vomit. He fought the urge to be sick. He knew vomiting behind the gag would be catastrophic, and he didn't want to die choking on his own sick.

He strained his ears.

Above the constant drip of water, occasionally, he could hear a rumbling noise in the distance. He soon realised what the sound was. There must be a road close by. The rumbling noise was being caused by heavy goods vehicles being driven at speed.

The realisation that he was still close to civilization raised his spirits briefly. That brief feeling of euphoria quickly disappeared when Reece realised that he desperately needed to urinate.

His stomach was pained and cramped; he couldn't hold the urge to pass water any longer. He felt a warmth envelop his lower waist and thighs as he urinated. He screwed up his face in disgust, both at the smell and the thought of wetting himself. The warmth he initially felt disappeared as his urine-soaked trousers and underpants quickly became cold.

Feeling totally helpless, he felt tears start to burn his

eyes. He felt them trickle down his cheeks until they reached the tape that covered his mouth. He cried out in anger and frustration, the noise a strangled, muffled plea.

Questions raced through his mind.

Who is that maniac? Why has he brought me here? Why is this happening to me?

Unfortunately, for Frederick Reece, the answers would come soon enough.

35

6.00am, 30 March 1986
Clumber Park Caravan Site, Nottinghamshire

The Watcher felt good.
It was the Lord's Day, a day of rest.
He filled the kettle with water, then placed it on the small stove in the caravan. He lit the gas, then popped a tea bag and a spoonful of sugar into a mug. As he waited for the kettle to boil, he opened the caravan door and drew in huge lungfuls of the cool, crisp morning air.

Reaching skyward, he stretched his arms, scratched his head and wondered at the beauty of the sunrise. The sun was now rising steadily. Its early morning rays, diffused by the tree branches, looked eerily beautiful.

He held his hands out in front of him, palms facing up, and said in a whisper, 'Defend me, your humble servant, in all assaults of my enemies: That I, surely trusting in thy defence, may not fear the power of my adversaries, through the might of Jesus Christ, our Lord. Amen.'

Just as he finished his prayer, he heard the whistle from the kettle. He stepped back inside the caravan, poured the boiling water into the mug, splashed in some long-life milk, stirred in the sugar, and took a sip of the hot, sweet tea.

He placed the mug on the table next to the Ordnance Survey map. He studied the map and soon found what he was looking for. Just outside the small town of Farndon, he could see the map symbol for a chapel. He knew he would be a stranger in the congregation, but it didn't matter. Everyone was always made welcome in the house of the Lord.

As he sipped the tea, he formulated his actions for the day.

He would go to church first; then on the way back he would drop into the disused maggot farm and check on his captive. As he thought of Frederick Reece, he chuckled at how very apt it was that Reece was now incarcerated in an old maggot farm. He considered the fat, bloated solicitor to be no better than a filthy maggot, one that he would soon crush.

But not today. The Watcher refused to work on the Lord's day.

Today, he would just check on Reece. He needed to ensure he was still securely bound so he could answer for his ungodly sins tomorrow morning.

He finished the mug of tea, grabbed his small toiletries bag and made his way to the toilet block. If he was going to chapel, he needed to have a shower and a shave. He needed to look smart and presentable.

36

6.00am, 30 March 1986
Major Crime Investigation Unit, Mansfield

Danny Flint stood and addressed his team, 'Good morning, everyone, thanks for getting here early. We've got another busy day in front of us. The first thing you need to know is that PC Moreton has been located. He's alive and, although injured, is expected to make a full recovery.'

There was murmured approval that the officer had been found. 'He was located by a patrol car, just over an hour ago, not far from the village of Farnsfield,' Danny continued. 'I've only got sketchy details from the control room, but it appears he was attacked by an armed man after he stopped to check what appeared to be a broken-down Range Rover.'

A voice from the back of the room asked, 'Was he badly injured, boss?'

'His injuries are considered serious, but not in any way life-threatening or life-altering. He was hit on the back of the head with a handgun and knocked unconscious, but as I said, he's expected to make a full recovery. The information I've got is that after being struck down, he was handcuffed using his own cuffs. He was then propped against a tree and left for dead. Again, I only have sketchy details, but it would appear the wound to the back of his head was very nasty, and PC Moreton lost a fair amount of blood overnight. From what the doctors at the hospital are telling us, it seems that our colleague's lucky to be alive. The enquiry into this assault, quite rightly, looks to be heading our way. The chief constable has insisted that the attack on PC Moreton will be treated as an attempted murder. This means the MCIU will commence the investigation, on top of our two current murder enquiries.'

This caused more murmuring around the room. Danny raised his hands for silence, then continued, 'Rob, I want you and DS Wills to get across to King's Mill Hospital straight after this briefing. I want you to get a first-hand account from PC Moreton, establishing exactly what happened to him. I understand he's conscious, so while I know he'll be resting after his ordeal, I want you to speak with him as soon as you can.'

'Okay,' said Rob.

Danny continued, 'In the meantime, I want as much information as possible from Nottingham University. I know it's the weekend, but their security teams will still be on the campus. DC Moore and Sergeant Prowse, I want you to get over to the university this morning and liaise with their head of security, Jim Cronin. He's a retired detective, a first-rate man, who'll assist you wherever he can. Don't be shy; call out anybody you think may be able to help you. Your priority is to establish the identities of the other two men in the photograph. While you're there, I also want you to find out if there were any incidents that occurred at the university while Naylor and Hall were students there. Don't forget, the probable motive for these two murders is revenge. We need to try to establish exactly what is being avenged by the killer. So keep an open mind, please. See if Jim Cronin can shed any light on what Naylor and Hall were like while they were at the university. We now know Naylor was gay. I want you to be subtle, but try to ascertain if there was any sign of that while he was a student.'

Rachel and Tina both nodded. Rachel said, 'Understood.'

Danny now turned to Brian Hopkirk, the other detective inspector on the team. 'Brian, I want you to organise the teams that are left, to look at the rest of the outstanding enquiries. I want a team to concentrate solely on the personal life of Edward Hall – was he a lady's man, etc.? You know the stuff I'm looking for. I want another team to look deeper into the business dealings of Naylor and anything else that came out of the interview with Christopher Baker yesterday.'

'No problem. Just picking up on what you said to Rachel and Tina, I'd like a couple of detectives to remain here to research any sexual assaults that happened in and around Nottingham University at the time Hall and Naylor were students. Nothing fuels the thirst for revenge like a sexual offence.'

'That's a good call. I'll leave you to organise the teams for each of the outlined enquiries. I've got to work on the details of the press conference. It's due to go out at eleven o'clock this morning, and I've got to run it by Bill Wainwright first.'

'Don't worry, I'll get everything sorted.'

'Thanks. Finally, I want everybody back here at two o'clock this afternoon for an update. Thanks.'

37

7.00am, 30 March 1986
King's Mill Hospital, Mansfield

Dr Anil Paratha was not budging.

'I'm sorry, Inspector, Mr Moreton needs to rest. He's suffered a major trauma to his skull that resulted in severe concussion. He's suffered heavy blood loss and now has a wound that required twelve stitches. If you couple the shock involved with those injuries and the fact he spent the night out in the cold and was borderline hypothermic when he was found, your colleague's extremely lucky to be alive.'

Rob Buxton was not easily put off. He replied, 'Doctor, I fully understand everything you're telling me, and I really appreciate the fact that you're caring for my colleague so well. Will he be in any physical danger if we talk to him for just five minutes? I must balance the fact that PC Moreton needs to recuperate with the fact that there's a gun-wielding maniac out there who's already shown he's a danger to members of the police force as well as the general public. All I'm asking for is a quick five-minute chat.'

Dr Paratha tutted loudly, looked at his watch and said, 'Very well, Inspector, you've got five minutes – and I mean five minutes. I'll be back then, and I will insist that you leave so your colleague can rest.'

'Thank you, Doctor. I really appreciate it.'

Rob and Andy walked into the small side room on the admissions ward.

PC Moreton was awake. He was sitting up in bed, his head heavily bandaged. He was sipping sweet, tepid tea from a plastic beaker, through a straw.

'It's the CID. I wondered how long it would be before you guys got here.' PC Moreton grinned.

'Colin, I'm Detective Inspector Rob Buxton, and this is Detective Sergeant Andy Wills. We're from the Major Crime Investigation Unit. I know you want to rest, but we need to know exactly what happened to you yesterday so we can set about catching this lunatic before he hurts anyone else. First and foremost, how are you feeling? Are you up to answering a few questions?'

'My head still aches, sir, but apart from that I'm fine, so fire away.'

'Exactly what can you remember about yesterday?'

Colin Moreton took another sip of tea and said, 'I'd just resumed mobile patrol after taking my meal break at Southwell nick. I drove over to Farnsfield. The town centre was quiet, so I drove out of town along the back lane. I'd gone about half a mile when I saw a black Range Rover parked in a small layby.'

Rob said, 'Can you tell us anything about the Range Rover?'

'It was black and looked fairly new. It had one of

those cherished registration number plates. I think it was 440 FDR.'

'Are you sure that was the number? You seem pretty certain.'

'I'm sure. I spend my working life memorising car registration plates. Cherished plates are easy.'

'That's great. What happened next?'

'I remember seeing a bloke standing in the road, at the side of the Range Rover. My first thought was that he'd broken down or something, so I stopped to see if he needed any help.'

Colin Moreton put his hand to his bandaged forehead and winced.

'You're doing great, Colin, go on,' encouraged Rob.

PC Moreton paused, took another sip of the lukewarm tea, then said, 'There was something weird about the bloke. He looked totally out of place. He was smartly dressed, wearing a dark suit, white shirt and dark blue tie, I think. The weird thing was, he was sweating like fuck, like he'd been running.'

'Can you remember anything else about his appearance?'

'He was late forties, early fifties, quite short and stocky ... he looked very strong. Not like a bodybuilder, but naturally powerful. I remember he had piercing blue eyes. His hair was a steel grey colour; it was thick and brushed back. He had a ruddy complexion, like he spent a lot of time outdoors.'

'Anything else?'

'Yes, he was Scottish. Well, he spoke with a Scottish accent, anyway. The accent was more Sean Connery than Billy Connolly, if you know what I mean.'

'What did he say to you?'

'When I first stopped, he gave me some bullshit story about hitting a fox or something, but when I got out of my car, he went quiet. It was like he was appraising me, sussing me out almost. This guy knew exactly what he was doing. He pointed the gun at me and said that if I did as I was told, he wouldn't hurt me. He also said he'd kill me in a heartbeat if I messed him about. I looked into his eyes; I knew he meant it. He marched me off the road into the woods, made me kneel with my back to him; then he belted me. That's the last thing I remember until I came around again. He'd handcuffed me with my own cuffs and propped me against a tree.'

'That's great, Colin. What can you tell me about the weapon he had?'

'It was a black handgun – an old revolver, I think.'

The door to the room opened, and Dr Paratha walked back in. 'Time's up, Detectives. I'm sorry, but that's all for now. Your colleague needs to rest.'

Rob turned to the doctor. 'Thank you; it's been a massive help.'

As the two detectives started to walk out of the room, PC Moreton spoke again: 'One other thing you should know before you go, sir. In my opinion, this wasn't a new situation for this guy. He was totally at ease with what he was doing, almost professional. It was matter-of-fact for him.'

'Thanks. Now do as the doctor says and get some rest. We'll chat again when you're feeling better. Well done out there. It sounds like you handled the situation exactly right.'

'I didn't handle anything, sir; that nutter was in control at all times. The only reason I'm still alive is because it didn't suit him to kill me.'

'Thanks, Colin. Get some rest.'

As soon as they left the room, Rob turned to Andy. 'Find a telephone, ring the control room, get that registration number checked and see if it comes back to a Range Rover. If it does, get the vehicle and description of the offender circulated immediately. Make sure you tell the control room before they put the observations out that this vehicle or the suspect is not to be approached under any circumstances. From what PC Moreton's just told us, this is one extremely dangerous individual. I don't want some young probationer getting shot going after this nutter.'

Andy nodded and said, 'I'll nip down to the medical secretary's office and use one of their phones.'

'Thanks, Andy, I just want to have a quick chat with Dr Paratha to establish what the prognosis is for Colin, and how soon we'll be able to get a written statement from him. I'll see you back at the car park.'

38

8.30am, 30 March 1986
Farnsfield, Nottinghamshire

PC Jim Miller and PC Damian Cox were on mobile patrol in Southwell. They were on the early shift and had started work at six o'clock. PC Miller was a veteran of twenty-three years' service. He was tutoring the young and inexperienced PC Cox, who two weeks ago had turned up for his first-ever shift as a probationary constable.

All the talk at that morning's briefing had been about the assault on their colleague PC Colin Moreton. It had been discussed, at length, how the patrol car had found him severely injured on a country lane just outside Farnsfield. Jim Miller had often worked alongside Colin Moreton; he was inwardly seething at the news of the assault. Damian Cox, on the other hand, was understandably feeling extremely nervous. Nobody at Dishforth Police Training College had ever mentioned anything about maniacs with guns.

It had been thirty minutes ago when they received the radio message from the control room, giving the description of the suspect wanted for the attack on Moreton, as well as that of a black Range Rover, registration number 440 FDR, that was believed to be used by the suspect. The descriptions of the suspect and the vehicle were issued with a warning not to approach either. Should the suspect or the vehicle be seen, the instruction was to call in the sighting and wait for armed backup.

Jim Miller glanced at his watch. It was now almost eight thirty. There was still half an hour to go before they were scheduled to go into Southwell Police Station to take their refreshments.

He turned to his young probationer and said, 'Let's have a steady ride back to the nick. We'll go through Farnsfield and check all the car parks. You never know, we might spot the bastard who's had a go at Col.'

Trying to maintain a confident note in his voice, Damian replied, 'Good idea.'

The young officer smiled at his tutor constable, but inside he was feeling scared and vulnerable. If by some fluke they did happen to stumble across this nutter with a gun, what would they do?

Ten minutes later, Jim Miller drove the police car into the car park at the rear of the Co-op store in Farnsfield. The entrance to the car park was through an old archway. Unless you knew the village, it would be easy to miss it, behind the store.

'Jim, look over there, in the far corner,' said Damian.

Sure enough, parked on its own in the far corner of the car park was a black Range Rover.

'What do you think, Damian? Can you see anybody inside it?'

'Not through the tinted glass.'

'Let's have a quick look, shall we?'

'I don't know, Jim; control said this bloke's armed. Shouldn't we wait for backup?'

If Jim Miller had been alone, there was no way he would have waited. He was still seething about the attack on his friend and colleague. He wanted to catch the bastard responsible for putting his mate in hospital, but he had his probationer to think about. He slowly reversed the police car into the archway until it effectively blocked the entrance to the car park.

'You're right. We'll wait for armed backup. Did you manage to see the registration number?'

'Yeah, it's the one. The number was 440 FDR.'

'Right, get on the radio; tell control that we've sighted the suspect vehicle in the car park behind the Co-op store in Farnsfield. Ask them to do a vehicle check on the PNC. Let's see who it's registered to, shall we?'

The reply from control was immediate: 'Maintain your position; observe the vehicle only. Under no circumstances approach the vehicle. An armed response vehicle is travelling to your location from Southwell. ETA ten minutes. Control out.'

Jim Miller acknowledged the call, then asked, 'Received that, thanks. Who's the registered keeper? Is it somebody local?'

'Negative. The keeper on PNC is shown as being Frederick Reece, home address of Elderflower Cottage, Rankin Lane at Beckingham. Control out.'

'Beckingham, near Newark?'

'That's correct, why?'

'It doesn't appear as though anyone's still with this

vehicle. Are you sending an armed team to the keeper's address as well?'

'Stand by.'

There was a brief pause; then the control room operator spoke again: 'Control to PC Miller, affirmative. An armed team from the Special Operations Unit are travelling to the address at Beckingham right now. Control out.'

'Thanks, control. Out.'

With his eyes fixed firmly on the Range Rover, Jim Miller smiled, then said to his young probationer, 'Well, mate, what do you reckon? Does Reece sound like a Scottish name to you?'

'Could be, I suppose. Where the fuck's the armed backup?'

'Relax, young un. The offender's long gone. We're looking at a harmless chunk of metal.'

A few minutes later, two high-powered traffic patrol cars came to a stop behind them in the archway. PC Miller got out of his car, walked over, and spoke to the traffic officers, leaving PC Cox staring at the Range Rover.

From metal boxes within the boot of the traffic patrol cars, the four officers removed weapons and ammunition. Having donned their bullet-resistant Kevlar vests, they quickly formulated a plan to best approach the vehicle.

Approaching on foot was dangerous, but allowed an element of surprise. It could be that the suspect was asleep inside the vehicle. The problem for the armed officers was the Range Rover's tinted glass – they had no view inside the vehicle. They moved forward tactically: Two officers had their weapons aimed at the vehicle at all times as the other two moved forward.

They alternated this action until they were virtually on top of the suspect vehicle.

One of the officers went forward, staying low beneath the tinted windows. As the other officers trained their weapons on the vehicle, their colleague reached up and opened the rear door. Nobody was lying on the rear seat. The process was repeated with the front door, then finally the boot.

It had taken the armed team ten minutes to clear the Range Rover. There was nobody inside the vehicle. The vehicle had been unlocked, and there were no keys in the ignition.

One of the armed traffic officers contacted the control room. He requested a full lift for the Range Rover so it could be removed to the forensic bay at police headquarters for examination.

While they waited for the vehicle examiners to attend and remove the vehicle, the officers chatted in the car park.

Jim Miller said, 'Is there anything known about this Frederick Reece character?'

One of the traffic officers replied, 'As we were travelling here, we got a message saying there was no record of him on any of our systems. So it looks like he's never come into contact with the police. It's a bit strange, to go from nothing to assaulting a cop with a gun, but stranger things have happened.'

Jim nodded. 'You're right, it does seem a little strange. I expect it will become clearer when the SOU lads have raided his house and got him in custody.'

39

9.30am, 30 March 1986
Beckingham, Nottinghamshire

When news of the Range Rover sighting had first come through to the MCIU, DI Brian Hopkirk had readied a team to travel to Farnsfield. Danny had stepped in and made the decision that Brian and his team should travel to the keeper's home address at Beckingham instead. That way, they would be ready to take the owner of the vehicle, Frederick Reece, into custody.

Brian and his team of three detectives now sat in their car on Rankin Lane. They were situated well back from the small thatched building that was Elderflower Cottage. The detectives watched as the men from the Special Operations Unit prepared to raid the cottage.

Dressed entirely in black, the armed officers approached the front door of the cottage behind a ballistic shield while their colleagues trained weapons on the windows of the building and covered the door at the rear.

A team of officers forced the front door and stormed in.

Brian could hear shouts of 'Clear!' emanating from within the cottage.

Within a minute, a message came over the radio: 'The building's clear, Inspector. You and your men are safe to approach now. There's no sign of Reece. The cottage is empty.'

Brian turned to the detective behind the wheel of the car. 'Let's go.'

The CID car pulled up outside the cottage, and Brian Hopkirk walked inside. The SOU sergeant held a bundle of documents in his hand. 'You need to see this, sir. Frederick Reece is a solicitor; he's got office premises on Spittle Row at Southwell.'

Brian looked around the cottage. There was a newspaper on the table with a photograph of a fat balding man standing next to the mayor of Nottingham. Brian grabbed the newspaper and read the article. The fat balding man was Frederick Reece.

Brian walked back to his car, reached for the radio in the car, and said, 'Detective Inspector Hopkirk to control.'

After a brief pause, the radio crackled into life. 'From control, go ahead.'

'From Detective Inspector Hopkirk, can you get a message to Chief Inspector Flint and let him know that Frederick Reece is not the man who assaulted PC Moreton? I'm at his home address and have found pictures of Reece that bear no resemblance to the description given by PC Moreton. I'm travelling to his office premises to confirm this. Can we stand down the armed team, please?'

'From control, will do. Instruct the armed team to redeploy to Southwell to remain as backup for you when you go to Reece's office premises. Over.'

Brian acknowledged the instructions from the control room, then turned to the SOU sergeant. 'Right, I need your team to regroup, then travel with me to the office address in Southwell. You and your team are to remain in the area on standby while I make enquiries at the office.'

The burly sergeant immediately started to bark instructions at his men. They hurried back to their vans, carrying all their equipment.

Brian turned to his own team of detectives. 'Right, Phil and Martin, you stay here and start a search of the cottage. I'll arrange for someone back at the office to drive up here with exhibit bags and labels. They can assist you with the search, then transport you back when you've finished. Nigel, as you're driving, you can come with me down to Southwell. We'll keep the exhibits kit in the car with us in case we need it down there. Phil, if you find anything here that's important, contact me via the control room. Okay?'

'No problem, sir.'

The SOU sergeant shouted, 'We're ready to resume if you're good to go, sir!'

'Okay, Sarge, we're ready. Let's go.'

The two SOU vans sped off down the country lane, followed by the CID car.

40

10.30am, 30 March 1986
Southwell, Nottinghamshire

Brian Hopkirk was sitting in the car, watching the front door of Richmond Legal Enterprises Limited in Southwell town centre.

The radio in his car crackled and burst into life: 'Control to DI Hopkirk. Over.'

'Go ahead, control. Over.'

'Sir, I've got a message from DC Harper. The message is as follows; they've found several more photographs of Frederick Reece in the cottage at Beckingham. He confirms that there's no possibility Reece is the man who attacked PC Moreton.'

'Thanks, control. For your information, the office here at Southwell is locked. Can you check the keyholder list for Richmond Legal Enterprises Limited and arrange for a keyholder to attend as soon as possible? Could you also inform DC Harper that DC Helen

Bailey is travelling to his location at Beckingham, with a vehicle and an exhibits kit. She shouldn't be long.'

'Okay, sir. Control out.'

He was just about to replace the radio handset when once again it crackled into life: 'Control to DI Hopkirk.'

'Go ahead.'

'The keyholder for Richmond Legal Enterprises is listed as Miss Mandy Bannatyne. She lives locally and will be with you within the next five minutes. Over.'

'Thanks, control.'

Five minutes later, a small Mini Cooper was driven into the yard at Spittle Row. A young woman with short blonde hair got out of the vehicle, clutching a bunch of keys.

The two detectives got out of their car and approached the woman.

Brian held out his warrant card and said, 'Mandy Bannatyne?'

'Yes.'

'I'm Detective Inspector Hopkirk, and this is DC Singleton. We're looking for Mr Reece, and we need to have a look round the office, please.'

'Of course. Is there a problem?'

'No problem. When did you last see Mr Reece?'

As the young woman unlocked and opened the door, she said, 'Yesterday morning. He always visits his mother at a nursing home in Edingley on Saturday. Is he alright?'

'Have you heard from him since yesterday? Any phone calls at all?'

'No, nothing, sorry.'

Brian walked into the small office behind Mandy Bannatyne.

His eyes were immediately drawn to a framed photograph on one of the two desks.

The photograph depicted four men smiling at the camera from beneath their mortar boards. All four men were dressed in black graduation robes. Brian had seen the photograph before. It was identical to the one he'd recovered from the office at the Grosvenor Hotel.

Brian immediately picked up the photograph and said, 'Is this Mr Reece?'

Mandy smiled and pointed to one of the men in the photograph. 'That's him. I don't know who the others are; just mates from his days at Nottingham University, I think.'

'May I use your phone, please?'

'Of course, Detective.'

Brian picked up the telephone and dialled a number from memory.

Danny Flint answered the phone on the first ring. 'MCIU, Danny Flint.'

'Boss, it's Brian. I'm at Reece's office. Reece isn't here, but there's a photograph on his desk that's identical to the one I recovered from Edward Hall's office at the Grosvenor Hotel. I think the attack on PC Moreton and our two murders are all connected. His secretary has just confirmed that Frederick Reece is one of the men in this photograph, so I reckon it's fair to say he's just become our third victim, and the man who attacked PC Moreton is probably our killer.'

'That's great work. It makes it even more imperative that we identify the fourth man as soon as we can.'

'It looks like we're on the right lines, with the link from university, sir. We just need to establish what these men are supposed to have done while they were there.'

'That's exactly right. The team you set up here, researching sexual offences around that time, have already come up with several interesting possibilities. I'll circulate Frederick Reece as a missing person, then chase up scenes of crime. I want that Range Rover forensically examined as soon as possible.'

'One other thought, sir. Has anybody established whether the description given by PC Moreton is similar to that given by Vanessa Hall? I know she described the offender wearing a mask, but has she been asked about her attacker's voice? Moreton described a strong Scottish accent. I just wondered if that question had been asked of Vanessa Hall.'

'It's a good point, Brian. I know it was difficult to get anything from Vanessa Hall initially. I know that Rob and Andy are stymied at the hospital for the time being, as the doctors won't let them take a statement from PC Moreton. I'll instruct Andy to travel to Beeston, speak with Vanessa Hall and ask those questions. I've got the press conference to do with Chief Superintendent Wainwright at eleven o'clock; it's good that I can now give him some positive news. Good work, Brian.'

'Thanks, sir, I'll search this office and see if there are any diary appointments for yesterday, that sort of thing.'

'See you later at the debrief. I think we're finally getting somewhere.'

41

**10.30am, 30 March 1986
Clifton, Nottinghamshire**

Paul Fencham smiled at his own reflection in the mirror.

For the first time in years, he felt like a winner. The dingy, scruffy bedsit he stood in didn't bother him today. He couldn't give a shit about the discarded, half-empty cartons of Indian and Chinese takeaway food, or the pile of smelly, dirty washing stacked at the foot of the disgusting single bed with the stained duvet on.

After today's press conference at police headquarters, he would be on the up.

It had been three o'clock that morning when he'd finally realised the meaning of the coded message. He now fully understood what the message painted on the walls of the murder victims' houses meant.

It had been so simple when he finally stumbled on the answer.

After hours of racking his brains, he had cried out loud in frustration, 'Oh, for God's sake!'

In that instant, the answer had come to him in a blinding flash of inspiration.

That was the answer. *For God's sake.* God was the answer.

He suddenly remembered all those long, boring Sundays as a child, when his deeply religious parents forced him to go to Sunday school instead of allowing him to play football on the local recreation ground with his pals.

He vividly recalled the painful memory of being given a Bible reference every week that he then had to study. Ready to repeat the passage it referred to verbatim the following Sunday.

The message scrawled on the walls was a Bible reference, pure and simple.

As soon as he had added the correct punctuation to the numbers and letters that had been written in blood, it became clear.

With punctuation in place, the message now read **E.C21.V24–25.**

Feeling elated, he grabbed the Gideon Bible that he'd stolen from a hotel some years earlier. Excitedly, he thumbed through the pages of the Old Testament.

There it was.

The book of Exodus, chapter 21, verses 24 to 25.

He had stood in his vest and underpants and read the verses aloud, 'An eye for an eye and a tooth for a tooth, a hand for a hand and a foot for a foot. Burning for burning, wound for wound, stripe for stripe.'

He had danced around the room with joy before another lightning bolt of inspiration had come to him. It was the book of Exodus. The red top newspapers loved to give a serial killer a nickname, or a cluster of murders a title. He grabbed his well-worn Olivetti typewriter, put in a clean sheet of A4 paper, and began to type.

The first words he typed in capital letters were '**THE EXODUS MURDERS**'.

An hour later the typewriter keys again fell silent. It was the best article he'd written for years – decades even.

He had spent the entire morning on the telephone, trying to sell the story to the crime desk editors of various tabloids. The *Daily Mirror* had made him the best offer. They had agreed to pay him the huge amount of ten thousand pounds immediately after the press conference being held at police headquarters that morning. This offer was made on the single proviso that the police didn't disregard the theory out of hand. The *Mirror* were going to send their top crime writer to ask questions at the news conference. He would be the sole judge as to whether the story Fencham was trying to sell had any credibility.

Fencham already knew the story was credible. By midday, he would be a wealthy man. Who knows? There might even be a future for him, working for the prestigious *Daily Mirror* newspaper.

He splashed hot water on his face in preparation to shave. He wanted to look his best at police headquarters. After all, today was all about him. It was his big day.

He couldn't wait for the press conference to start at eleven o'clock.

42

10.30am, 30 March 1986
Farndon, Nottinghamshire

The Watcher had changed his mind. He'd decided to check on the huge maggot that was Frederick Reece first. He had stopped off at the disused maggot farm before he went to the chapel to celebrate the Lord's day.

He didn't want to be distracted in his worship by thinking about Reece. He knew if he checked on him first, he would then be able to forget about him until the following morning.

As he drove the Land Rover down the dirt track towards the disused buildings, he constantly checked the surrounding area. Nothing had changed. There were no fresh vehicle tracks heading towards the drab concrete buildings. His training and background caused him to constantly review, to check everything, and leave nothing to chance. Observational prowess was just one of his skills. It was one of many that had been instilled in him over the years. Being able to kill another human being, without a moment's hesitation, was another.

He parked his vehicle behind the buildings so it couldn't be seen from the main road that ran past the farm entrance just four hundred yards away.

Taking care not to mark his smart suit on the filthy Land Rover, he got out and walked to the entrance of the building. The door had long gone; the entrance was now covered by a sheet of corrugated iron. The ground was quite firm underfoot, but it was still a dirt path. He'd taken great pride in getting his clothes and appearance looking smart for church. He didn't want to undo all that good work by being careless where he trod now.

He pulled back the sheet of corrugated iron so he could gain access into the decrepit building. He stepped inside, paused and allowed his eyes time to adjust to the gloomy light before walking further into the building. He eventually came to the room where he'd imprisoned Reece.

Reece was awake; his eyes widened with fear when he saw the Watcher walk in.

Saying nothing to his captive, he walked over to a plastic carton that was full of water. He picked up the water and walked back to where Reece sat on the cold floor.

Reaching forward, in one decisive movement, he ripped off the brown gaffer tape that covered Reece's mouth. He grabbed a handful of the man's receding hair and forced his head back.

He poured the water from the carton directly into his captive's open mouth, forcing him to drink. The solicitor managed to swallow two big mouthfuls of the cold water before he almost choked.

Reece spluttered and coughed as the water trickled

down his windpipe.

The Watcher waited for him to stop coughing before returning the water to the other side of the room. He then picked up the roll of brown gaffer tape, ready to gag his prisoner again.

Reece took the opportunity to speak before the gag was reapplied. 'Who are you? Why are you doing this? I haven't done anything to you.'

The Watcher ignored the questions, stepped forward and reapplied the tape across the mouth of Reece. Before he stood up, he checked that he'd left his prisoner's nose clear of the tape so he could breathe.

He started to walk out of the room, but heard Reece screaming muffled cries at him.

He stopped, turned and reached inside his jacket pocket, taking out a small, laminated photograph.

The Watcher said nothing. He squatted down in front of his captive and held the photograph directly in front of the fat solicitor's face.

Reece turned from being angry and arrogant into a cowering, trembling wreck.

He shook his head, then began to cry and sob into the cloying gag. Tears now streamed from his eyes and rolled down his cheeks.

The Watcher stared straight into Reece's terrified eyes and said with a low growl, 'Tomorrow you will pay.'

He then stood up and replaced the photograph in his jacket.

As he watched his captor leave the room, once again the terrified Reece could feel the warmth of his own urine around his groin as he emptied his bladder. This time, the warmth was accompanied by the disgusting stench of his own faeces as the contents of his bowel also spilled into his trousers.

43

10.30am, 30 March 1986
University of Nottingham, Nottinghamshire

DC Rachel Moore and Sergeant Tina Prowse had accessed the vast campus of Nottingham University through the north entrance, driving in from Derby Road.

Tina said, 'Aren't there any security barriers to go through?'

Rachel replied, 'No, the university is an open site; anybody can come onto the campus at any time. They have quite a few problems because of it, more so in the summertime than now.'

'How come you know so much about the university?'

'Before I transferred to Mansfield, I was stationed at Hyson Green. Although it's not in the Hyson Green area, I was often called over to the university when a policewoman was needed.'

'How did you find working at Hyson Green?'

'Honestly, I hated every minute of it. The best thing I ever did was transfer to Mansfield. Working with DCI Flint is brilliant; he gives everyone a chance and treats everyone the same.'

'What was it like working on the "coal killer" enquiry?'

'At the time, it was bloody hard graft. It's something I try not to talk about too much, for obvious reasons.'

'Oh God! I'm so sorry, Rachel. I totally forgot what that creep, Jimmy Wade, did to you. I can be such a clumsy cow at times.'

'Don't worry, Tina, it's all water under the bridge now. Wade's locked up in Rampton and will never set foot outside those walls again. I try not to think about what happened too much. I refuse to let that psychopath ruin the rest of my life.'

'I'm going to embarrass you now. You were one of the main reasons I asked to spend some time on the MCIU. As soon as I realised that under the graduate entry scheme, I could cherry-pick which departments I wanted to experience, I applied to come onto the MCIU. I don't think you're aware just how highly regarded you are by other policewomen in the force.'

'Yep, that's done it. You've officially embarrassed me.'

Both women laughed; then Rachel said, 'One piece of advice, just work hard while you're here. Everybody knows that the only reason you're on the unit is because of the graduate entry scheme, but nobody resents you being here. If you keep coming up with little gems like the link you established yesterday, you'll fit right in. Let's see if we can find Jim Cronin, shall we?'

Rachel drove onto Cripps Hill, then along Cut Through Lane and down onto East Drive before finally parking the car outside the old Nissen hut that served as the university security's control building.

Before the women left Mansfield Police Station, Rachel had phoned ahead to the security office and established that Jim Cronin was indeed working that morning.

The two detectives walked into the hut, and sitting at his desk waiting for them was Jim Cronin.

Cronin stood up to greet the two women. He was well over six feet tall and weighed over eighteen stone. He had a full head of hair, which was now snowy white. The hair was the only giveaway of the man's age. He was still extremely fit and strong despite his sixty-plus years.

He held out a huge hand in greeting towards Rachel. 'Detective Moore, how lovely to see you again, and looking so well after that dreadful business.'

It was the second reference that day about the attack made on her by Jimmy Wade, and although she showed no sign of discomfort outwardly, inside, she cringed.

'It's good to see you too, Jim; you look extremely fit, as ever. You'll have to let us ladies have your secret, minus the white hair, of course.'

Jim smiled. 'It's clean living, ladies, pure and simple.'

'Jim, let me introduce you to Sergeant Tina Prowse. She's recently joined the MCIU, so I'm guessing you two haven't met.'

'Good to meet you, Tina.'

The same massive hand was once again offered in greeting; then Jim said, 'Right, before we get down to the reason for your visit, I was about to make myself a coffee. Can I get you anything to drink?'

Rachel looked at Tina. 'Coffee?'

'That would be lovely, thanks.'

'Two coffees, please, Jim.'

'How do you take it?'

In unison, Rachel and Tina chorused, 'White, no sugar, thanks.'

Jim laughed. 'Sounds like you two have been working together for ever!'

Five minutes later, all three were sitting at a briefing table in the same hut, drinking their coffees. Rachel took out the small framed photograph of four men standing in their university robes.

'Do you know any of these men, Jim?' she asked.

'Unfortunately, I know them all, lass. That's the four musketeers. They were a royal pain in the arse when they were here, getting up to all sorts of mischief. They always knew just how far to push things, but they came awfully close to being expelled on a couple of occasions.'

'What was the main issue with them?' asked Tina.

'Their gross attitude to female students and women in general was the problem. A couple of them thought they were God's gift, and sometimes wouldn't take no for an answer, if you know what I mean.'

'In what way?'

'Any female student was considered fair game to them – the more attractive, the better. There were numerous complaints about inappropriate sexual advances, but it was never enough to chuck them out.'

'Can you remember their full names?'

Jim Cronin took the small photograph in his huge hand. His index finger moved across the photograph, from left to right, stopping at the different faces as he identified them. As he pointed out the men, he said their names.

'This first one, on the end of the photo, is Cavalie Naylor. He was the quietest of the bunch, but easily led.

He was doing business studies and got a first-class degree. Standing next to him, holding his mortar board in his hand, is Frederick Reece. He was a real pain in the arse. He was the ugliest, most unfit one of the group, but thought he was a proper Casanova. Loved the ladies, did that one. He studied law and achieved an incredibly good degree. The next man is Edward Hall, another one who was a real smooth operator. I dealt with a lot of complaints about him. At one time, I thought he might have been dabbling in drugs, but I could never prove anything. He was another arrogant, cocky bastard who thought he could get away with anything and everything. He was doing a degree course that was in some way related to the leisure industry. Out of the four of them, he was the only one who left with a shit degree. He was a lazy sod.'

Jim Cronin then tapped the photograph, his index finger drumming on the face of the last man.

'Last and most definitely the worst, Maurice Dennington. I'm surprised you didn't recognise him, Rachel. He's in the job.'

'The only Dennington I've ever heard of on the job is a superintendent.'

'The very same, Superintendent Maurice Dennington. I don't know what he's like now, but back then, the man was an arrogant pig. He had zero respect for women. I lost count of the number of complaints I had to deal with because of his self-obsessed attitude and the aggression he displayed to any woman who rebuffed his advances. I tried, unsuccessfully, on several occasions to get him chucked out, but nobody was listening. Academically, he was a brilliant student. He left here with a first in law. For some reason, unbeknown to the rest of us, the vice chancellor always appeared overly impressed by him.'

Tina was thoughtful, then asked, 'Apart from Reece and Dennington, the four of them were all studying for different degrees. How come they were so close? Did they have something else in common that pulled them together?'

'Apart from all being a pain in the backside, you mean? The thing that brought them all together was rugby. All four played rugby union for the university team. Dennington was an outstanding fly half, who at one time was being tipped to play for England, but then he suffered a serious knee injury, which put paid to that. Even after the injury, he continued to play for the university team, but any thought of international honours had gone. Now I think about it, that was probably why the vice chancellor let him get away with so much crap.'

'Was there a natural leader of the group?'

'Dennington was the leader. Without a doubt, he was the driving force behind most of their escapades.'

'Thanks, Jim, this is all really helpful,' said Rachel.

'Rachel, can I ask why you want to know so much about these four idiots?'

'It's no real secret. Two of them, Cavalie Naylor and Edward Hall, are now dead. They were murdered. Can you think of any reason why somebody would want to kill them?'

'Ordinarily, I would be shocked at news like that, but with these characters, a part of me isn't at all surprised.'

He looked thoughtful for a second, then echoed aloud what Rachel had said: 'Can I think of a reason why somebody would want to kill them? Not off the top of my head, I can't. But while they were here, these four individuals must have made a lot of enemies ... they upset an awful lot of people.'

'Upset enough for somebody to want them dead?'

'The thing is, with this four, anything's possible. I can't prove anything, but I genuinely believe they were involved in a lot of incidents that were never identified as being down to them at the time. I can think of several serious sexual assaults that happened around that time that still remain unsolved.'

'Any incident that sticks out for you?' asked Tina.

Jim Cronin looked troubled. He stroked his chin thoughtfully. 'There is one incident that sticks in my mind. A dreadful assault on a young girl during the Freshers Week of 1977.'

'Tell us about that,' pressed the young sergeant.

Slowly, he stood up and walked over to a large set of grey drawers. He opened one of the drawers and thumbed through some old files. Eventually, he found the file he was looking for. He removed a mustard-coloured folder and walked back to the table.

'This won't make for pleasant listening, I'm afraid.'

'Go on,' urged Tina.

Jim Cronin opened the file and began talking as he scanned the contents. 'Freshers Week, 1977. A young student just down from Scotland, Jean Mackay, had been in Nottingham with a couple of other students, enjoying a few drinks for the Freshers celebrations. Miss Mackay had only arrived in Nottingham that week. She wasn't a drinker, so at ten thirty, she decided to catch the last bus from town. The bus she caught that night travelled from the city centre along Derby Road to the university. Her friends decided to stay in town, intending to go on to a nightclub. Anyway, from the enquiries made at the time, it would appear that Jean caught the bus okay. Her journey was uneventful, and she got off the bus on Derby Road, outside the north entrance. She was staying at the Hugh Stewart halls of residence, so began walking along Cripps Hill. The poor girl never made it to her halls of residence. She was found, just after midnight, on the Downs by one of my security patrols.'

'What are the Downs?'

'The Downs is an area of open grassland that bisects the campus and runs alongside Lenton Hall Drive. Back then, a lot of it was quite overgrown and was pitch black at night.'

'What had happened to Jean Mackay?' asked Rachel.

'She'd been subjected to a vicious sexual assault by four men. I know that four men were involved, because when she was examined later by a police surgeon, the doctor found four different blood groups in the swabs he took. Four different blood groups mean four different semen samples, which means four different men. In those days, there was no such thing as this newfangled DNA that I've been reading about.'

'What could Jean Mackay tell the police about the attack and her attackers?'

'Absolutely nothing. The poor woman couldn't speak, the attack traumatised her so badly, she just withdrew into herself and never uttered a word. Look in your police records; you'll find far more detail there than I've got. I just remember it was an awful attack. When she was found, she'd been stripped naked, subjected to a number of serious sexual assaults, savagely beaten and left for dead in pitch-black darkness in the middle of a field. It was horrendous. One of the worst assaults I've seen, both in my police career and my time on security here.'

'Was anybody ever charged?' asked Tina.

'No. This attack happened a few years after I came here, I'd only been left the force three years, so I still had a lot of contacts in the CID. They kept me informed, on the quiet, how things were progressing with the enquiries. I know the CID did a lot of enquiries here at the time, interviewing people, getting statements. The problem was they had very little to go on, and the university authorities wanted the enquiry closed as soon as possible. That kind of publicity wasn't what they wanted for the prestigious Nottingham University.'

Tina shook her head and said, 'That's a disgusting attitude.'

'I know, lass, but that's how it works here. The university relies on the fees paid by students, foreign students in particular. The publicity generated by that sort of incident would be very damaging to the precious reputation of the university. The whole incident was effectively swept under the carpet as soon as possible. Once it had all died down, I was tasked with improving the lighting around the campus and ensuring there were more security patrols around the site during the hours of darkness.'

'What about your so-called "four musketeers"? Were they ever questioned?' asked Rachel.

'I believe so; your police records will confirm it. I just remember that they couldn't be connected to it at the time. Personally speaking, I wouldn't have put it past them. Back then, Maurice Dennington was an arrogant, nasty piece of work with an ego the size of a small African country. The other three would follow him like pathetic sheep and do anything he told them to.'

'And what about Jean Mackay? What happened to her?' asked Tina.

'She dropped out of her course. She was here to study medicine; I believe her dream was to become a doctor. The attack affected her so badly, there was no way she could continue her course. Eventually, when she was well enough to be discharged from hospital, her mother took her back to Glasgow.'

'What about her father, Jim? Did he travel down as well?'

'I don't think he did. I seem to recall he was in the military and couldn't get here, but I'm not a hundred per cent sure on that. I've got the parents' details somewhere here in the file.'

Jim glanced at the file in his hands and said, 'Let me see, mother is Glenys Mackay, and father is Ben Mackay.'

'Thanks, Jim. You said her mother took her back to Glasgow. Is that where she was from?'

Jim Cronin looked at the documentation in front of him again and said, 'I've got her home address in the file. It's from 1977, but it might still be relevant.'

'What's the address?'

'It's 16 Crosshill Road, Bishopton. If memory serves me right, I think Bishopton is a small town just outside Glasgow, not far from the airport.'

Tina quickly noted down the address and said, 'Thanks.'

Jim replaced the folder in the filing cabinet, turned to Rachel and said, 'Do you think the other two in the photo, Reece and Dennington, could be in danger?'

'I really don't know; it's early days yet. The murders of Naylor and Hall could be totally unconnected. This is just one of many lines of enquiry we're looking at.'

'Well, if you need anything else, just give me a ring or, better still, come and see me. My door's always open. Before you leave, I'll take you both over to the Downs and show you the Hugh Stewart halls of residence, just so you can get an idea of the layout of things.'

'That would be great, thanks.'

Half an hour later, after seeing the Downs and the halls of residence for themselves, the two detectives were driving out of the university.

'Rachel, can I ask you something?'

'You can ask me anything you want.'

'Why did you tell Jim Cronin that we still didn't know whether the murders of Naylor and Hall were connected?'

'It's just a habit I've developed. You always need to play your cards close to your chest. I know Jim's an ex-detective, but I also know that whatever I tell him will be all over this campus within two days. Never tell anybody anything that hasn't already been released to the press. If you do and it comes out later, it can seriously bite you on the arse.'

44

**11.30am, 30 March 1986
Nottinghamshire Police Headquarters**

Danny Flint took his seat next to Detective Chief Superintendent Wainwright and stared out at the television cameras and assembled reporters from various newspapers. He hated press conferences with a passion, but he was pragmatic enough to realise that there were occasions where the media, and the press in particular, were a huge help to the police. There were several very well-documented cases where a press release had helped to drive an investigation forward.

He'd discussed with Bill Wainwright exactly what to provide the press with on this occasion.

The information that Frederick Reece's secretary had identified her boss as being one of the four men in the photograph came in just minutes before they were due to meet the press. The two senior detectives were satisfied their enquiries were being channelled in the right direction. They both believed that as soon as they established the reason behind the attacks, they would establish the identity of the killer.

Neither man could see any benefit in linking the murders at this stage. They were only too aware of the media frenzy whipped up whenever the possibility of a serial killer being on the loose was revealed.

Danny was satisfied they were not random killings and that only the four men in the photo were at risk.

Chief Superintendent Wainwright was prepared to back his detective chief inspector's judgement.

It was Wainwright who started off the press conference by giving a brief overview of the two murders they were currently investigating. He kept detail to a minimum and made it clear to the media at the end of his presentation that there was nothing to suggest, at this time, that the two murders were linked in any way. He then made a general appeal to the public to come forward if they had seen anything, at either Underwood or Beeston, that they believed to be unusual or in any way suspicious.

As he concluded his part of the presentation, he said, 'I'll now hand you over to Detective Chief Inspector Flint of the Major Crime Investigation Unit. If you have any questions, please address them directly to him.'

A hand was raised at the back of the room, which Danny acknowledged.

'Sally Green from the *Daily Mail*. Chief Inspector Flint, how certain can you be that the two murders aren't linked? It seems a bit of a coincidence that two murders were committed within a few days of each other in the victims' own homes.'

'We do not believe these murders are linked at this moment. Obviously, we always keep an open mind on such things.'

Another hand was raised.

'Bill Prentice, the *Express*. I understand you've made an arrest already. Was that person arrested in connection with the Underwood enquiry, the Beeston enquiry, or both?'

'That's true, we did make an early arrest in connection with the Underwood enquiry. That person cooperated with us fully and is currently on bail pending further enquiries. Are there any other questions?'

A white-haired man sitting on the front row slowly raised his hand.

Danny pointed to the man and asked, 'Yes, on the front row. What's your question?'

'Todd Galpin, *Daily Mirror*. Chief Inspector, why haven't you released details of the identical messages painted on the walls at both the murder scenes?'

Danny was totally shocked by the question. It showed, as he remained silent.

'Chief Inspector, I can already see by the expression on your face that my information's correct. What significance do you put on the messages that were painted in blood at the scenes?'

There were gasps from the other reporters.

The white-haired man continued, now warming to his theme. 'Are you still maintaining these murders aren't linked?'

Bill Wainwright tried to intervene. 'That will be all for now, thank you. No further questions at this time. Our investigations are ongoing, and we'll keep you appraised of any new developments. Thank you.'

The man on the front row was not about to be put off so easily. 'Chief Inspector, the *Daily Mirror* newspaper, which I represent, will be running a front-page story tomorrow morning, under the headline "The Exodus Murders". Do you have any comment?'

Bill Wainwright stood up, virtually pulled a stunned Danny to his feet, and said in a raised voice, 'We have no further comment at this time. Thank you.'

Sitting at the back of the room, behind the assembled reporters and television cameras, Paul Fencham grinned. There was no way he wouldn't get paid for his story now. He had to admire Todd Galpin, the chief crime reporter from the *Daily Mirror*. The way he had played the two detectives was masterful.

Away from the press conference and out of earshot of any reporters, Bill Wainwright turned on Danny. 'What the fuck just happened? What was all that about, Danny?'

'I don't know, sir.'

'Well, I fucking know! Someone in your team has been talking out of turn. Somebody's leaked confidential information to the fucking press, and I want to know who!'

'Sir, none of my team would do that.'

'Really? Well, somebody has, Chief Inspector; I suggest you make it your fucking mission to find out exactly who!'

'Yes, sir,' said a totally crestfallen Danny.

'And while you're doing that, I'll go and see the chief to try to explain this fucking debacle. I've never been so fucking embarrassed in all my service! Get this fucking mess sorted, Danny, now!'

Bill Wainwright stormed off, leaving a shell-shocked, bemused Danny alone in the corridor.

Danny walked slowly back to his car, his mind racing.

Mentally, he began compiling a list of the people he knew had attended both scenes. It was useless. Everybody in the MCIU knew that the messages on the wall were at both scenes.

He had to face facts. Somebody had tipped off the press, and at that moment in time, Danny had no idea how he was going to discover who it was.

He dreaded reading the story in the newspaper tomorrow. His mind raced as he speculated about what other details linking the two crime scenes had also been leaked.

Danny was worried that any leaked information would have a massive detrimental effect on the enquiry.

The reporter who had asked the embarrassing questions had stated he was from the *Daily Mirror*. Danny decided that his only course of action was to call the editor of that newspaper as soon as he got back to his office and try to establish exactly how much detail to expect in tomorrow's paper.

Somehow, he had to attempt a damage-limitation exercise.

The last thing the enquiry needed was for details of the messages to be published. This could unleash the real possibility of copycat killers or people making false confessions to the crimes, tying up valuable resources.

Maybe he could get the editor of the *Daily Mirror* to delay publishing all the details. He might be satisfied with releasing a limited amount of information at this time, in return for the promise of exclusivity once the killer had been caught.

Danny knew he had to try something. As he drove back to Mansfield, he rehearsed his planned conversation with the editor of the newspaper.

45

2.00pm, 30 March 1986
Major Crime Investigation Unit, Mansfield

The entire MCIU were assembled in the large office, waiting for the afternoon debrief. Brian Hopkirk's team had returned from Southwell and Beckingham, having completed their searches of Frederick Reece's home and office.

Rachel and Tina had returned from the university. Rob was back from the hospital after finally being allowed by the doctors to obtain a full statement from PC Moreton. The last one to arrive was Andy Wills, who had travelled back from Beeston after speaking to Vanessa Hall.

Danny opened his office door and shouted, 'Rob, Brian, get in here!'

There was an edge to Danny's voice that everybody in the room immediately picked up on.

The two inspectors walked into the office; Rob closed

the door behind him.

'Sit down, both of you; this is for your ears only. We've got a fucking mole!'

'What?' asked Rob.

'The press conference this morning was a fucking nightmare. I was totally ambushed. Somebody out there has leaked information to the press about the writing in blood on the walls. The *Daily Mirror*'s running a story on the morning of the first of April under the headline "The Exodus Murders". They intend announcing to the world that we've got a serial killer on the loose here in Nottinghamshire.'

Brian exclaimed, 'Bloody hell, sir, that's just what we don't need. Any idea who it is?'

'No, I haven't. You two are much closer to the people in your respective teams than I am. I want you to find out who the fuck it is. I want a name. A unit such as this can't survive if information is constantly leaked to the press. I won't tolerate it.'

Both men nodded; then Rob asked, 'How are we going to prepare for the shit storm when that story hits the streets?'

'I've been on the phone for an hour, trying to negotiate a deal with the editor of the *Daily Mirror*. He's agreed to hold off releasing all the detailed information they've been given for a day, in exchange for exclusivity on the story, as and when we catch our killer. Basically, we've got another twenty-four hours to catch our man, or the full details of both murder scenes will be published in the morning edition of their fucking rag!'

Danny fought hard to keep his growing anger in check, saying quietly, 'Brian, for the rest of the day, I want you to concentrate on nothing else but getting to the bottom of this leak. Talk to everyone who had access to both scenes. Start by talking to Geoff Naylor. He's the only civilian who's seen the writing. It's just possible he's said something to somebody.'

'Okay, sir, I'm on it. There's another possibility we need to consider, though.'

'Which is?'

'The killer has spoken directly to the press himself.'

Danny shook his head in frustration. 'The editor of the paper assured me that the information they have was from a legitimate source, which he wouldn't divulge. I think he would have been overjoyed to tell the world that the killer himself had been in touch with the fucking *Daily Mirror*! If nobody else has got any bright ideas, let's get the debrief started.'

It was a harsh slap down, and Brian felt both admonished and a little ridiculed, but he didn't protest. He could see Danny was in no mood to listen to his protestations.

All three detectives walked back into the hushed briefing room.

There was still an edge to Danny's voice as he said, 'Brian, tell us about the development linking the two murders to the attack on PC Moreton.'

Brian, ignoring the embarrassing flush he still felt, said, 'It would appear that the attack on our colleague was carried out by the same person responsible for killing Cavalie Naylor and Edward Hall. You've all seen the photograph of the four men at Nottingham University, the one recovered from Edward Hall's office. Well, an identical photograph has been recovered today from the office of a man called Frederick Reece. Reece has been missing since yesterday afternoon, and we believe it was his Range Rover that was being checked by PC Moreton when he was attacked. It's fair to assume that Reece is the latest victim of our killer. As we have no body yet, we have to consider the possibility that he's still alive. Three of the four men in the photograph have now been identified. They are Cavalie Naylor, Edward Hall and Frederick Reece.'

Rachel Moore spoke up: 'Sir, we've now identified the fourth man as well. The head of security at the university says that he's Maurice Dennington, who is now a serving police officer.'

Danny said, 'Do you mean Superintendent Maurice Dennington, the man in charge of the newly formed Sexual Offences Investigation Team?'

'Yes, sir.'

Danny took a minute to digest that information, then said, 'Is there anything else from the university?'

'All four men were well known to the university security team when they were students. They were all members of the university's rugby union team and were very troublesome. Their behaviour was often rowdy, and there were numerous complaints involving the four of them. Their attitudes and overtly sexual conduct towards the female students caused a lot of issues.'

'Anything in particular involving them?'

'No, sir, but the head of security did recall a particularly vicious sexual assault on a young Scottish student that happened at the time these four men were at the university. The attack couldn't be linked to them at the time, but he strongly suspected them of being involved.'

'What was the name of the student?'

'Her name's Jean Mackay. The effect of the attack on her was so bad, she had to leave the university and went home, abandoning her studies. The university provided me with the last address they had for her. She lives in a small town called Bishopton, near Glasgow Airport.'

Danny was deep in thought.

'Right. The team researching sexual assaults for the

dates Hall and Naylor were at university – have you found any details of this attack on Jean Mackay?'

DC Fran Jeffries spoke up. 'I've been researching that very assault. It was horrific, sir. Four men attacked her during Freshers Week. She'd only been at the university just over a week when she was attacked. Her mother came down to Nottingham after the attack, and as soon as the girl was well enough to be discharged from hospital, the mother took her back to Glasgow.'

'What are the details of the attack, Fran?'

'From what I can gather from our records, Jean was out celebrating Freshers Week in Nottingham with a couple of friends. She wasn't a big drinker, so decided to catch the bus from town to the university gates and then walk to the halls of residence while her friends stayed in the city to go on to a nightclub. Jean was attacked in the grounds of the university; she was found about a hundred yards from her halls of residence on an area of open land called the Downs. The attack was sustained, violent and degrading. The poor woman was raped anally and vaginally, beaten and left for dead. The clothes she had been wearing were scattered all over the Downs.'

'What enquiries were done at the time, Fran?'

'It was a major enquiry at the time, and the CID did a mass of work. They put a great deal of time and effort into finding her attackers, but to no avail. There was little forensic evidence at the time, and no witnesses. I've checked with property; there are no surviving samples from the attack.'

'Were the four in the photograph questioned at the time?'

'I checked for Naylor and Hall. They were only ever interviewed in the same way as many other male students were questioned. I will recheck after the briefing to see if it was any different in respect of Frederick Reece and Maurice Dennington. There's no record of any arrests ever being made in connection with the attack. Certainly, the records I've seen that relate to Naylor and Hall had them giving alibis for each other. I will check for Reece and Dennington now, but I suspect it will be a similar scenario.'

'Thanks. Keep digging. I want you to find out everything you can about that particular attack.'

'Yes, sir.'

Danny then turned to Andy Wills. 'Andy, you've been to see Vanessa Hall again. Could she remember anything else about her attacker?'

'Nothing else description-wise, but interestingly, she did recall that when he spoke to her, it was with a very distinctive Scottish accent.'

'So that's Vanessa Hall and PC Moreton who've said our man speaks with a Scottish accent.'

Danny furiously scribbled notes into his large notebook, then said, 'Fran, you said that Jean Mackay's mother had come to collect the daughter. Rachel, when you were at the university today, could Jim Cronin give any information about the girl's parents? In particular, anything about her father?'

'I asked him that very question this morning. From memory, he thought her father was in the army or similar, and that was why he wasn't available to come and see his daughter. From the university records, next of kin were recorded as being Glenys Mackay, mother, and Ben Mackay, father.'

Danny was deep in thought for a while, then said, 'Rachel, I want you and Tina to go home and get an overnight bag. Contact East Midlands Airport; I want you on the next available flight to Glasgow. I'll make a call to the Special Branch office at the airport so we can waive the normal boarding procedures. Contact the CID in Glasgow and arrange for an officer to meet you at the airport with a car. I want you to visit the address in Bishopton, interview Jean Mackay and ascertain everything you can about this horrendous assault. I realise it will be a delicate enquiry that runs a real risk of opening old wounds, but it's an enquiry that needs to be done. I want you to liaise with me regularly about all developments while you're in Scotland. Fran, I'd like you to also research Glenys and Ben Mackay. I want to know everything there is to know about them. In the meantime, I want everybody to keep doing what you're doing. Things are starting to come together. Brian, you know what I want you to concentrate on. Rob, you and I need to go and speak with Superintendent Dennington.'

Danny and Rob walked back into Danny's office.

Danny sat down heavily and said quietly, 'Close the door.'

Rob closed the door and sat down.

Danny said, 'Do you think I was out of order, slapping Brian down like that?'

Rob was thoughtful for a second, then said, 'If I'm being honest, yes, I do. Don't worry about it, though, he's a professional; he'll just get on with the job. If anyone can find the leak, it will be him, especially now he's stinging a bit after your rebuke. He's a big boy, Danny; he'll soon forget it. I've no doubt that he'll already have admitted to himself that it was a pretty stupid suggestion.'

'Okay, I'll talk to him later anyway. Thanks.'

Danny picked up the telephone and dialled the number for the control room.

'Do you have the contact details for Superintendent Dennington of the Sexual Offences Investigation Team?'

There was a pause.

'Okay, I understand. Contact him at home, please, and tell him to contact me on this number as a matter of urgency. Thank you.'

Danny replaced the phone and said to Rob, 'It's his day off today.'

Rob grinned and said, 'What's a day off?'

Less than two minutes later, the telephone in Danny's office began to ring.

Danny picked up the phone. 'Chief Inspector Flint, can I help you?'

'Chief Inspector, it's Superintendent Dennington. I've just been asked to contact you by the control room. What's the problem?'

'Thanks for calling so promptly. I appreciate it's your day off, but I need to talk to you as a matter of urgency about a delicate situation that's developing.'

'I don't appreciate you talking to me in riddles, Chief Inspector. Tell me what the problem is.'

'It's not a conversation I'm prepared to have on the phone, but it is urgent, and I need to speak with you today.'

'Very well. I'll meet you at my office in one hour.'

Danny hung up the phone and turned to Rob. 'He's driving over to his new offices at Carlton in Lindrick and says that he'll see us there in one hour. Pompous git!'

'Good of him to grant us an audience.'

'Isn't it just.'

46

3.00pm, 30 March 1986
Teversal Manor, Cotgrave, Nottinghamshire

Brian Hopkirk was still quietly seething. The more he thought about it, the more he realised it had been a dumb suggestion. He was fully aware of the guidelines newspaper editors had to adhere to when dealing with information provided by a criminal source. He knew they had an obligation to disclose any communication from a person suspected of a criminal act.

He had only been trying to help when he spoke up. If he'd been alone with Danny, it wouldn't have mattered so much, but it felt wrong to be verbally slapped down in such a condescending manner in front of his friend and colleague Rob.

He wouldn't dwell on it now; he would talk to Danny about it later, in private.

Right now, he needed to concentrate on having a

conversation with Geoff Naylor. Brian was acutely aware that it was still a very raw time for the old man, and that he was only recently out of hospital. He knew he would need to be tactful and tread carefully.

Having walked up the long gravel driveway, he pulled down hard on the ornate doorbell.

He waited a minute or so, then pulled again. This time there was movement within, and he heard a croaky voice shout, 'Just a minute!'

Brian waited patiently at the door; a few minutes passed before he heard someone approaching.

The door slowly opened. Standing there, looking unwashed and dishevelled in crumpled clothes, was Geoff Naylor. His skin looked ashen, his eyes were red-rimmed and bloodshot, and Brian could immediately smell stale whisky emanating from the grieving father. He held out his warrant card and said, 'Mr Naylor, my name's Detective Inspector Brian Hopkirk. I'm one of the officers making enquiries into the death of your son. Something's come up that I need to speak to you about as a matter of urgency.'

Without speaking, Naylor turned and started to walk back down the beautifully decorated hallway. He waved his hand, indicating the detective should follow him.

Brian followed the shuffling man into the vast kitchen.

Naylor took a pint glass from one of the cupboards and filled it with cold water from the tap. He drank a full glass, then repeated the process. He took a small pillbox from his pocket and slipped a black pill under his tongue; he then sat down opposite the standing detective.

At last, Geoff Naylor spoke. 'Please sit down, Inspector. What can I do for you?'

Brian sat down and said quietly, 'Mr Naylor, are you

okay? Is there anyone I can ask to come here and be with you?'

'My son, Inspector. Can you get my son?'

'No, I can't do that for you, and I'm sorry.'

'What is it that you needed to talk to me about?'

'There's been a development that you should be aware of. Unfortunately, the media have now got hold of some of the details surrounding Cavalie's death.'

'That was always going to happen, Inspector. What's that got to do with me?'

'It's a problem because it could really hinder our investigation. They're aware of certain details we would have preferred to keep back.'

'Surely, the press knowing everything can only help your enquiries?'

'Sometimes it does, but on this occasion, it can only hamper us. Has anybody asked you any questions about your son's death?'

Geoff Naylor was quiet for a moment; then he said, 'Look, I'll be honest with you, Inspector. The other night I'd had a few drinks too many, and I rang a friend and had a conversation with him. Unfortunately, I can't recall too much of what was discussed. Let's just say I'd had more than a few drinks.'

'Who did you call?'

'I called an old army buddy who now works for one of the local papers.'

'What was it that you needed to discuss with him?'

'It was nothing much, really. I was just so bloody annoyed when you lot released that bastard Christopher Baker so quickly. I didn't understand how you couldn't see that he's the person responsible for Cav's death.'

Brian could see that the old man was close to tears, and he didn't want to push him too hard in his fragile state. He chose his words carefully.

'Would you mind if I had a quick word with your friend?'

'Of course I wouldn't. His name's Paul Fencham; he works for the *Nottingham Evening Standard*. If you give me a minute, I've got his phone number here somewhere.'

The old man stood up and left the room. He returned a few minutes later, clutching a piece of notepaper with a telephone number scribbled on it.

Brian took the piece of paper from the old man's shaking hand and said, 'Are you sure I can't get somebody to come and stay here with you, Mr Naylor?'

'No, I'll be fine, Detective, thank you. My nurse will be over soon to check on me and prepare my evening meal. I'm sorry if I fucked up with Fenchers. I was only trying to help.'

'Don't worry, Mr Naylor; it's nothing we can't fix. You take care.'

As Brian walked down the driveway towards his car, he grinned and said aloud, 'Right, Paul bloody Fencham, let's see what you've got to say about who our mole is, shall we?'

47

3.30pm, 30 March 1986
Sexual Offences Investigation Team, Carlton in Lindrick, Nottinghamshire

Rob Buxton drove the CID car through the permanently open gates and into the grounds of the newly opened Sexual Offences Investigation Team offices.

The modern, spacious development had a large car park at the front of the building. The car park was freshly marked out; the parking bays were surrounded by mature shrubs and bushes. There were CCTV cameras on the perimeter of the property and on the building itself.

Carlton in Lindrick is a small village, and there had been strong resistance from the villagers when the new development was first proposed. The locals had wrongly suspected that sex offenders would be brought into the village on a regular basis, to be dealt with at the new police building.

Several open meetings had taken place, where it had been stressed to residents that the new property was being built as a centre of excellence to help the victims of sexual offences and that no offenders would ever be brought to the facility.

In the late seventies, there had been overwhelming and justifiable criticism of the police service over their handling of the victims of rape and other serious sexual assaults. The SOIT had been set up to try to improve that situation. The only people using these offices would be detectives, medical personnel, administration staff and the victims of sex crimes.

The offices had been opened at the end of January amid a fanfare of publicity, and everything still looked brand new.

Rob parked the car in the vacant bay situated next to the parking space that had been specifically marked SUPT.

Already parked in that bay was a silver Mercedes saloon with the registration plate MWD 651.

Rob said, 'Looks like Superintendent Dennington got here before us, boss.'

'I would've been surprised if he hadn't. He only lives just down the road at Ranby. His house is a bit of a palace, by all accounts.'

'That's probably why he didn't want any South Yorkshire riffraff, like me, visiting him at home, then.'

'Yeah, you're probably right, Rob.'

'It's a good job I'm thick-skinned!'

Danny laughed. 'Or just thick! Come on, let's go and have a word with Superintendent Dennington.'

The two detectives walked up the stone steps that led to the front doors of the building. Rob used his standard-issue police key to enter the premises. It was Sunday, so the main reception area was closed. As they walked into the foyer of the building, Superintendent Dennington was walking down the stairs to greet them.

'Chief Inspector Flint, what's this all about? What's so urgent that I had to meet you on a Sunday?'

Danny knew Dennington had used his full rank to emphasise the fact he was a rank higher. He was also aware Dennington had totally disregarded the presence of Rob Buxton.

'Superintendent, this is Detective Inspector Rob Buxton. I don't think you two have met. Is there somewhere we can talk?'

'We can use my office. Follow me.'

Dennington led the way back up the stairs. The first door they came to had a brass plate with the name SUPT DENNINGTON on it.

The superintendent opened the unlocked door and walked into his office. Everything inside smelled of newness; the desk was huge with a computer terminal on one side. It had an immaculate leather desktop pad in the middle; stainless-steel document holders marked IN, PENDING and OUT were on the other side.

Along the entire length of one wall was a large bookshelf that contained row after row of leather-bound law books.

The chair behind the desk was made of black leather, which matched the two smaller chairs in front of the desk and the two-seater settee that took up the other wall. Dominating the office was the large picture window that overlooked the car park at the front of the building.

That explains why he was on his way down the stairs as we walked in. He was looking for us, thought Danny.

Dennington remained standing behind his desk and

said, 'Sit down, Chief Inspector; let's get on with this, shall we? I haven't got all day.'

Danny looked around the office and remained standing. 'Nice office, sir, very impressive. I need to ask you a few questions about some associates of yours from your days as a student at Nottingham University.'

'I knew a lot of people at university, Chief Inspector. Who exactly are you referring to?'

'Cavalie Naylor, Edward Hall and Frederick Reece.'

'Yes, I knew them; we all played in the university rugby team. What's the problem?'

'The problem, sir, is that Cavalie Naylor and Edward Hall have both been murdered, and Frederick Reece is now missing. We believe he's been abducted by the killer of the other two.'

Dennington was already aware of the two murder enquiries, but never batted an eyelid. He said calmly, 'Obviously, I'm sorry to hear that, but what exactly has that got to do with me?'

Danny maintained eye contact and said, 'One line of enquiry we're looking into is whether or not anyone would have a motive of revenge for these murders. Maybe seeking retribution for something that happened to them while they were also at university.'

'I see. I knew the three men you've named, but I wouldn't say we were particularly close. Yes, we played rugby together, but that's about it.'

Dennington had tried hard not to show it, but Danny could see the superintendent had been disturbed by what he'd been told. He remained arrogant and haughty, trying to dismiss the matter out of hand.

Danny was having none of it. 'How was university for you, Superintendent?'

'What sort of question is that?'

'One that requires an answer, sir.'

'If you must know, I thoroughly enjoyed my time at university.'

'Did you achieve a good degree?'

'Well, let's see, Chief Inspector … it was good enough for me to get on the accelerated promotion course at Bramshill, good enough for me to be a superintendent at thirty years of age. So I'd say, yeah, it was pretty good. What's your point?'

'Did you get into many scrapes while you were there?'

'None that I recall.'

'Any issues with the security staff?'

'No.'

'I know what some of you students can be like.'

Danny grinned; he was deliberately goading Dennington.

'Listen to me, Chief Inspector, I haven't come here on my day off to stand here and listen to you asking inane questions about my time at university. Say what you've come to say, or this meeting is over.'

Danny ignored the overbearing tone and said, 'Have you stayed in touch with any of the men who were your friends at university? I'm obviously referring to Naylor, Hall and Reece in particular.'

'No, I haven't. We all went our separate ways when we left.'

'When was the last time you saw any of them?'

With an air of boredom, Dennington replied, 'I really can't remember.'

Rob pointed to a small photograph on the wall of the office. 'This photograph of you and three other men in your university robes. Is that a picture of you, Naylor, Hall and Reece on your graduation?'

'Yes, it is.'

'Coincidentally, the very same photograph was

found at the offices of both Edward Hall and Frederick Reece.'

'How thrilling for you, Inspector.'

'If you weren't that close, why have you all still got the same photograph?'

'Inspector, take a moment and look around this office. You'll see there are a lot of photographs. They are all memories of different times, different places, different people. I really think you both need to look for an alternative theory. I can assure you nothing happened at university, involving the four of us, that would make somebody to want to kill these men.'

Danny stared hard at Dennington. 'The thing is, Maurice, if the reason for their abduction and murder is because of something that happened back then that involved the four of you, then you could also be in serious danger. Let's not beat about the bush here: Your life could be at risk.'

'Chief Inspector, off duty or not, I don't recall giving you permission to address me by my Christian name. The rank I have achieved is superintendent. Use that title or address me as "sir", as you wish. I've already told you that nothing happened at university, so I know I've got absolutely nothing to be worried about. Your whole theory is ridiculous, and in my opinion, a complete waste of police time and resources.'

Danny continued to stare at Dennington. He ignored his reply and said, 'I'm going to organise an immediate twenty-four-hour, round-the-clock surveillance on you, purely for your own protection, you understand.'

'Out of the question. I won't hear of anything so preposterous. Like I've already said – on two occasions now, Chief Inspector – you're wasting your time and resources continuing to look down this line of enquiry.

Maybe I should have a word with your line manager and let him know my views on the subject.'

Danny walked towards the door. 'Feel free to have a word with whoever you like, Maurice. I'm running the investigation into these two murders, and I'll be organising full protective surveillance on you. I would hate for anything nasty to happen to you.'

'I meant what I said, Flint: No surveillance!'

Danny and Rob left the office and made their way back outside to the car park. As they reached the car, both men glanced back towards the building and saw Dennington standing at the window, staring at them.

Rob said, 'Look at the arrogance of the man. Standing there with his hands on his hips, like some lord of the manor staring down at his serfs.'

'I know what you mean, Rob; he's a piece of work alright. He's sweating, though – something's definitely wrong there. I'm even more convinced that this is all to do with something that happened at Nottingham University. All we need to do is find out exactly what. We do that, we find our killer.'

'What do you want to do about Superintendent Dennington?'

'I want a surveillance team on him. I don't give a shit what he says. The man's an arrogant prick.'

48

4.00pm, 30 March 1986
Sexual Offences Investigation Team, Carlton in Lindrick, Nottinghamshire

Maurice Dennington sat alone in his brand-new office, pondering over the visit of Danny Flint and his ignorant sidekick.

He had heard about the murder enquiries involving Naylor and Hall, but the abduction of Reece had come as a massive surprise. There was no way he could afford to let Flint see that he was gravely concerned about the recent events. He couldn't agree to the surveillance being placed on him, either, without admitting that he was aware there was a connection binding the four men in the photograph.

Ever since Flint had left, Dennington had sat in the gloom, quietly going over his time at university. He had sat there quietly replaying events from his recent past. His mind kept taking him to one event in particular. The memories burst into his brain, like flash bulbs exploding. One dark night on the Downs with his three friends. The sounds of guttural laughter, the smell of the whiskey they had all consumed. The swearing and cajoling. The frightened face of the girl. The sound of fabric tearing as clothing was ripped off, the sight of white flesh. Muffled crying and then silence.

He shook his head, dismissing the memories and taking a moment to steel himself.

There would be no surveillance. He would put Flint back in his place.

So what if somebody had got to Hall and Naylor? Whoever it was wouldn't find Maurice Dennington such an easy target.

He muttered out loud to himself, 'I'm a police superintendent, for Christ's sake, not some soft businessman or weak hotel manager. Let whoever's doing this come. I'll be ready, and they'll be the one getting a big surprise.'

49

5.00pm, 30 March 1986
Clifton, Nottinghamshire

The drive from Cotgrave to Clifton had only taken twenty-five minutes, but for Brian Hopkirk, it seemed as though he'd travelled to a different country.

After a quick telephone call back to the MCIU office to carry out a reverse telephone directory enquiry check, he had tracked Fencham down to an address in Clifton.

He had gone from standing outside a palatial country manor house to standing outside a stinking two-bedroomed flat on one of the worst estates in Nottingham.

Using the fleshy part of his bunched fist, he hammered on the door. Just as he thought nobody was at home, the door suddenly flew open. Standing in the doorway was a short, overweight man with a pot belly and receding hairline. He was wearing an ill-fitting jacket, beige-coloured trousers and scruffy brown brogues. On the floor of the hallway, immediately behind the man, Brian could see a suitcase.

'Paul Fencham?' asked Brian.

'Who wants to know?'

Producing his warrant card, Brian said, 'Police. I think you and I need a little chat, mate.'

Brian stepped into the hallway and closed the door behind him.

'Police or not, you can't just walk in here like you own the place. Come on, get out! I've got a plane to catch.'

Brian turned to face Fencham and snarled, 'How about we have this conversation down the nick? That way I make sure you miss your fucking plane!'

'Alright, alright. There's no need to get all heavy. What's this all about, anyway?'

'Please! Don't waste my time, Fencham; you know exactly why I'm here. I want to know who gave you the information about the murder scenes, that you've since sold to the *Daily Mirror*. I presume you've sold the story; where else would you get the cash for an overseas trip?'

'Look, selling a story to another newspaper isn't illegal. That's my job. I'm a news reporter. I get paid to sniff out a story.'

'I'll ask you again, where did you get that information?'

'I got a phone call from a mate. Just somebody I knew from when I was in the army.'

'Leave your suitcase where it is. We're going to the nick. I'm not pissing about with you all day.'

Fencham raised both hands in a mock gesture of surrender. 'Let's not be too hasty here! I swear I'm telling you the truth. Look, the mate's Geoff Naylor. I went to see him after he phoned me the other night.'

'And exactly what information did Geoff Naylor give you?'

'He told me about the writing on the wall at his son's house. Then he said he thought the same writing was on the wall at Beeston.'

'That's all well and good, Fencham. But who gave you the information about the content of the writing? Because we both know that wasn't Geoff Naylor.'

'I don't have to give you my source.'

'No, you don't, but I'll make life so uncomfortable for you that within a week, you'll be wishing you had. We can start today – right now if you like. Paul Fencham, I'm arresting you for attempting to pervert the course of justice and for police obstruction. Come on, let's go!'

'Wait a minute, Detective. Just let me think about this.'

Fencham stepped back, away from the angry-looking detective.

His mind was in overdrive. He hadn't yet paid Dave Whitham the hundred pounds he'd promised him. If he gave the detective his name, he wouldn't have to pay him. He didn't have to say that he'd offered him any money; he could just say it was somebody who owed him a favour. Whitham couldn't say any different, or he'd be in even deeper shit.

A sly smile flashed across his features, and again, he held his hands up innocently. 'Alright, Detective, I'll tell you. It's no big deal anyway. The guy who gave me the info owed me a favour; it was a one-off.'

Brian took a step forward and said menacingly, 'Just give me the name, Fencham!'

'Alright, alright. It's a bloke I know who sometimes works as a photographer on your Scenes of Crime teams. His name's Dave Whitham. I did a favour for him ages ago. He owed me.'

'Exactly what information did he give you?'

'He confirmed what Geoff Naylor had told me about the writing on the wall. He also told me that it was at both murder scenes and that it had been written using the blood of the victims. He told me the message was EC21V2425. I worked out what it meant by myself. I realised it was a Bible reference; that's the truth.'

'Has any money changed hands between you and Whitham?'

'No, definitely not.' *At least that's the truth,* thought Fencham.

He looked shiftily at the detective. 'Am I still under arrest, or can I go and catch my plane?'

'You were never under arrest, you shithead! Just out of interest, Fencham, how much did you get paid by the *Mirror* for the story?'

Fencham allowed himself a greasy smile. 'I got ten grand. It's going to be sangria, sun and sex all the way for me now, Detective.'

Brian Hopkirk stepped out of the stinking flat, followed by Fencham, who was now clutching his suitcase.

After Fencham locked the flat door, Brian turned and grabbed the fat reporter by the lapels of his jacket. He pushed him backwards into the wall and said, 'Enjoy your holiday, Fencham, but get this into your thick head. If I ever hear about you putting the squeeze on any of our people again, I'll make your life a misery. Do you understand me?'

'Honestly, Detective, it was a one-off; there was no squeeze. I fully understand. I'm thinking about trying to find work in Tenerife while I'm over there.'

'Now that's the best news I've heard all day,' said Brian as he released the lapels of Fencham's coat.

Grabbing his suitcase, Fencham scuttled off along the walkway of the flats. He constantly glanced behind him to see if the big detective was following him.

Brian took out his cigarettes and lit one. He took a deep drag and exhaled before slowly walking back to his car. He glanced at his watch; it was now almost half past five in the evening.

Danny had tasked him with finding the mole at two o'clock. Less than four hours later, he knew it was Dave Whitham, a civilian Scenes of Crime photographer. Even Danny would have to admit that was quick work.

He smiled, took another long drag from the cigarette, then tossed it away as he exhaled the smoke.

As he got back into his car, he felt relieved that the leak hadn't come from one of the detectives on the MCIU. He was really going to enjoy telling Danny Flint exactly who the mole on the department was.

50

6.00pm, 30 March 1986
16 Crosshill Road, Bishopton near Glasgow

Rachel Moore and Tina Prowse had been lucky. They had managed to book seats on a flight from East Midlands Airport that had arrived at Glasgow Airport at quarter past five that day.

A telephone call made by Danny to the Special Branch office at the airport had meant the two detectives could forego the normal stringent checks and board the aircraft quickly.

Another phone call to the CID in Glasgow meant that arrangements had been in place for the two women to be met at the gate by a detective at Glasgow Airport.

Everything had gone to plan, and as Rachel and Tina emerged through the gate, they had been met by Detective Constable Davy Sinclair.

He had introduced himself and said, 'What's the address you're going to, ladies?'

Rachel introduced Tina and herself, then said, 'We need to get to 16 Crosshill Road at Bishopton, thanks. Have you been waiting long?'

'Nah, ten minutes max. My car's parked at the Special Branch office; it's only a couple of minutes' walk from here. At this time of night, we should be in Bishopton for just after six o'clock. Is it something interesting you're dealing with?'

'A double murder back in Nottingham,' said Tina.

'Ah! the Malky!'

'The what?'

'The Malky! It's a slang term we Scots use for murder.'

Davy was pleasant company as he drove through the countryside between the airport and Bishopton. He kept the conversation light and never enquired about the details of the murder investigation.

He drove into the small town of Bishopton, quickly found Crosshill Road and parked the car outside number sixteen.

He turned to Rachel and said, 'My instructions are to wait for you here. Do you need any help with your enquiry, or do you want me to stay with the car?'

'We'll be fine, thanks. I don't know how long this might take though, we might be a couple of hours, or we might be back in a couple of minutes.'

'Well, anything you need; I'll be right here. I hope you're successful.'

Rachel and Tina walked up the short garden path to the front door of the white-painted, semi-detached house. It was a pleasant enough street; the gardens and houses all looked neat and tidy.

Bishopton appeared to be a nice, quiet town.

There were lights on in the house, but the curtains were already drawn against the darkening skies. There was a strong smell of soot in the air, and looking up, Rachel could see smoke coming from the chimney.

Tina used the heavy black knocker on the door to let the occupants of the house know they were there.

A young woman's voice called out, 'Just a minute; I'll be two ticks!'

Rachel glanced over her shoulder and smiled at Davy sitting in the car, giving him the thumbs up. He smiled back and wound up the window of the car.

The door was opened by a young woman in her thirties. Her hair, tied back in a ponytail, was an ash-blonde colour. She wore no make-up and had clear, bright-blue eyes. She had a cooking apron on over a dark blue skirt and a knitted top that was a similar colour of blue.

She smiled at the two detectives and said, 'Can I help you, ladies?'

Rachel and Tina held out their warrant cards, and Rachel said, 'I'm sorry to disturb you; we're police officers from Nottinghamshire. We were hoping to speak to Jean Mackay.'

'I'm sorry, but you've had a wasted trip. Jean and her mother don't live here anymore.'

'Did you know Jean?'

'Aye, I did. I knew her and her family well enough. Look, where are my manners? Why don't you step inside so we can talk properly?'

'Thank you, that's very kind. I'm sorry, I didn't catch your name.'

'My name's Nichola, Nichola Brown. Please step in out of the cold.'

Nichola showed the two detectives into the living room, where there was a blazing fire in the hearth. The room was beautifully decorated, clean and tidy. Rachel and Tina sat on the comfortable settee, and Nichola sat in one of the two armchairs.

'Can I get you a cup of tea or something?'

Tina answered, 'No, we're fine, thanks. We don't want to take up too much of your time; you look busy.'

'Oh, the apron, I was just fixing my fella's supper. He works at the airport down the road. He should be home in about half an hour.'

'What can you tell me about Jean?' asked Rachel.

'I went to secondary school with her. She was such a clever girl; none of us were the least bit surprised when she got offered a place at university. She was always brilliant at science and wanted to be a doctor. I saw her just after she came back from Nottingham. She was never the same girl after what happened down there. My husband and I bought the house from Jean's mum, Glenys, after I found out they were moving back down to England.'

'Why would they want to go back to England after what happened?'

'Glenys was very poorly – some sort of cancer, I think. All I know is she wanted to go and stay with her sister, so if anything happened to her, she knew her sister would be there to take care of Jean.'

'How long ago was that?'

'We've lived here for two years now. Just a second; I'm sure I've still got an address for Glenys's sister back here somewhere.'

Nichola walked out of the living room, then returned a couple of minutes later, carrying a red-and-black address book.

'It's here. The sister's name is Maggie Fraser. Her address is 45 Gateford Road, Worksop, Notts.'

Rachel made a note of the address and said, 'Thanks, Nichola. Have you heard from Jean or her mother since they moved down south?'

'No, not a thing. People just move on, don't they? It

was such a shame what happened to Jean.' She shook her head slowly, then continued, 'Those animals were never caught, were they?'

'No, they weren't. Did you see much of Jean's parents when you were kids?'

'I saw her mum loads; Glenys is a lovely woman. Thinking about it, I never saw much of her dad, though. He was in the army or something. He was always away somewhere; I know Jean really missed her dad when he was away.'

'Anything else you can tell us about Jean?'

'No, not really, that's about it. Like I say, I haven't seen her for at least a couple of years.'

The two detectives stood up, and Rachel said, 'Thanks, that's been really helpful.'

'Can I ask why you want to speak to Jean? Have you found those bastards who attacked her?'

'We're working on it, Nichola; we're working on it. Thanks again for your time.'

Rachel and Tina walked back to the car.

As the two women got in the car, Davy started the engine and said, 'That was pretty quick. How did it go?'

Rachel said, 'Bit of a wasted trip, really; the woman we wanted to see left the address two years ago. But we know where she's moved to, so it hasn't been an entirely wasted journey. Davy, would you drive us straight back to the airport? We need to be on the next flight south.'

'No problem, buckle up.'

Three-quarters of an hour later, they had said their goodbyes to Davy Sinclair and were booked on the nine o'clock flight back to East Midlands Airport.

Rachel found a telephone at the airport and dialled the number for Danny's office.

It was now almost seven thirty at night.

Danny answered on the second ring.

'Boss, it's Rachel. I'm afraid it was a dead end here in Glasgow. We went to the address, but Jean Mackay and her mother sold the property two years ago. We got lucky, though; the woman who lives at the house now knew the Mackay family well; she went to school with Jean. Anyway, it seems that Jean and her mother moved back down to Worksop a couple of years ago so they could stay with Jean's aunt after the mother was diagnosed with cancer.'

Danny asked, 'Have you got the aunt's name and an address in Worksop?'

'Yes, we have. Her name's Maggie Fraser. She lives at 45 Gateford Road, Worksop.'

'Good work. Have you managed to book a flight back tomorrow?'

'I can do better than that. We're on the nine o'clock flight tonight. We should be landing at East Midlands at a quarter past ten tonight.'

'That's great. I'll make sure someone's there to pick you up. Tomorrow morning, I want you and Tina to swerve the briefing and go directly to the address in Worksop. I want you knocking on Maggie Fraser's door at six thirty tomorrow morning. Okay?'

'No problem. Talk to you tomorrow.'

51

7.45pm, 30 March 1986
Major Crime Investigation Unit, Mansfield

Danny saw Brian sitting on his own in the briefing room. He glanced at his watch. It was now a quarter to eight. There was still fifteen minutes to go before the debrief. He'd got time to have a quick word with his detective inspector; he wanted to apologise for his abrasive manner and the comments he'd made to him earlier in the day.

Danny had been rattled after the press conference, but he knew it had been wrong to take out his anger on one of his team. There was no excuse.

He stuck his head around his office door and said, 'Brian, can I have a word, please?'

Brian stood up, walked across the briefing room, and stepped inside Danny's office.

'Close the door and grab a seat.'

Brian closed the door and sat down.

'I wanted to apologise to you for lashing out earlier. It was a reaction to the shit press conference, but I shouldn't have taken it out on you. It was unfair and I'm sorry.'

'Thanks, but there's no apology needed. As soon as I made that comment, I realised how stupid it was. Anyway, the good news is I've managed to find our mole. I know exactly who leaked the information to the press.'

Surprised at how quickly his inspector had got to the root of the problem – and with a real sense of trepidation – Danny said quietly, 'Okay, who was it?'

'Well, the good news first; it's none of the lads and lasses on the unit. Nobody has talked out of line. The bad news is that it was a civilian photographer employed on a temporary basis by our Scenes of Crime department.'

A huge sense of relief washed over Danny; he had been dreading being told it was one of the detectives on the new unit. After an audible sigh, he said, 'That's great work. How did you find out so quickly?'

'As you suggested, I started by going to see Geoff Naylor. It turns out that he'd spoken to one of his old army buddies, who now works as a reporter for one of the local papers. Anyway, I tracked down this reporter, a bloke called Paul Fencham, to a shitty little flat over at Clifton. I was ever so slightly unpleasant, and we quickly came to an understanding. Apparently, the information was leaked by a bloke called Dave Whitham. As I said, he's a civilian who occasionally works as a photographer with our Scenes of Crime teams. I've checked the logs; he took the photographs at the Beeston murder scene. He passed over the coded message that had been left on the wall at Beeston to the reporter. After his conversation with Geoff Naylor,

Fencham already knew that the same message had been left at Underwood. Somehow, he worked out that the message was a Bible reference. He then put two and two together after reading the passage from the book of Exodus it referred to.'

'Has any money changed hands between Paul Fencham and Dave Whitham?'

'Fencham says not, but that's probably bullshit. He's been paid ten grand for selling the story to the *Daily Mirror*, and is now on his way to the airport, ready for a break in Tenerife. After our conversation today, he's under no illusion what will happen to him if he ever approaches any more of our staff.'

'That's great work, Brian; thank you. I'll talk to Chief Superintendent Wainwright; he can deal with Dave Whitham. I haven't got either the time or the inclination to start going after him. I'm just so relieved it wasn't any of our staff. The thought that someone on this unit couldn't be trusted was really depressing. I can do without those sorts of problems on top of everything else.'

'Have I missed anything while I've been chasing down our mole?'

'I haven't spoken to all the teams yet, but it looks as though everyone's back now. Let's start the debrief and find out exactly where we are.'

The two men walked into the main briefing room, where the various enquiry teams had gathered.

Danny spoke. 'Okay, everyone, let's have a bit of hush. I'll give you all a quick update first from Rachel and Tina, who are still up in Glasgow. They've visited the last known address for Jean Mackay. Unfortunately, Jean and her mother, Glenys Mackay, left that address two years ago and moved down to Worksop to stay with Jean's aunt, a woman by the name of Maggie

Fraser. I've already tasked Rachel and Tina to visit the address in Worksop, where, hopefully, they can speak to Jean and her mother.'

DC Fran Jefferies coughed loudly and said, 'I'm afraid that's not going to be possible, sir.'

Surprised at the interruption, Danny said, 'Go on, Fran. What's the problem?'

'After researching the assault on Jean Mackay as you requested, the natural progression for me was to research Jean and her family this evening. There are some interesting findings.'

'Go on.'

'Sadly, Jean Mackay's dead, sir. Her body was found in woods near Worksop eight weeks ago; she had taken her own life. I've read the coroner's file that was prepared for the inquest. It appears that she drank a full bottle of vodka to wash down three large packets of paracetamol. The next of kin, at that time, was shown as her aunt Maggie Fraser. The funeral was held at Worksop six weeks ago.'

'Why was Maggie Fraser shown as next of kin? What about her mum and dad?'

'The research I've carried out shows that Glenys Mackay passed away shortly after moving down to Maggie Fraser's address. I can't find out why her father wasn't shown as the next of kin. There's no death certificate in existence for Ben Mackay, so he's definitely still alive. I can find no record of him passing away. The father's full name is Ben Fitzgerald Mackay, and the last record I could find of him was his military service. He served in the Royal Marines Mountain and Arctic Warfare Cadre, a trained sniper and an expert on escape and evasion techniques. I couldn't ascertain whether he ever worked with the Special Boat Service or the Special Air Service. The person I spoke to at Naval Intelligence was quite evasive. Reading between the lines, it seems that Ben Mackay was probably involved in any number of deniable operations, overseas.'

'That would explain why he was never around the family home. That's good work, Fran. When did Ben Mackay leave the service?'

'According to the records, he left the service in 1980. He seems to have slipped off the radar since then. I still need to do some more digging on that.'

'Keep at it, please. I want to know everything there is to know about Ben Mackay. After what you've told me about Jean's suicide, he's definitely a person of interest.'

Danny turned to Rob Buxton. 'Rob, I want an up-to-date photograph of Ben Mackay as soon as possible, and see if we can obtain his fingerprint records from the military. I'd like to get them compared with any marks found at the crime scenes or the Range Rover recovered from Farnsfield.'

'Will do.'

Danny went through the rest of the teams, taking their information and making notes of anything relevant. At the conclusion of the debrief, he said, 'Well done, everybody. I think we now need to concentrate on Ben Mackay as a priority. I want him traced, interviewed and eliminated from this enquiry as soon as possible. I want you to finish up anything you have left to do this evening; we shall reconvene at six o'clock tomorrow morning. I know it's another early start, but we're making excellent progress. I want Ben Mackay traced by tomorrow evening at the latest. If he is our man and he's got Frederick Reece stashed away somewhere, it's vital we find him sooner rather than later.'

Danny looked over towards Rob Buxton and indicated for him to follow him into his office.

Rob walked in and sat down. Danny said, 'Quick

question, how did you get on with the surveillance team on Dennington?'

'They've been on him since he left his office at Carlton in Lindrick earlier. No issues at the moment. He's now at home, and the surveillance team are outside.'

'That's good. I want him watched twenty-four seven. I've got a bad feeling about this. If Ben Mackay's our killer, and he does go after Dennington, we're going to seriously have our work cut out trying to stop him, with his military background and training.'

Rob nodded. 'Before I go home, I'll contact the surveillance team to let them know what they could be dealing with. If nothing else, it will keep them alert and on their toes.'

'Thanks.'

'Did Brian have any luck with his enquiry?'

'He certainly did. Suffice to say we don't have to worry about anyone on this department, and Bill Wainwright will be dealing with it.'

'Bloody hell, that was quick!'

Danny winked and said, 'Well, I put my best man on it, didn't I?'

Rob laughed. 'See you in the morning, boss.'

52

10.30pm, 30 March 1986
East Midlands Airport, Castle Donnington,
Leicestershire

It had been a long day.

Tiredness washed over Danny as he waited patiently at the airport arrivals hall. He sipped a bitter-tasting, triple-shot cappuccino from the nearby coffee bar in an attempt to stave off the weariness he felt.

He glanced up at the information board and noticed that the status of the Glasgow flight had changed. It was now flashing 'Bags in Hall'.

He knew Rachel and Tina had only taken hand luggage, so he expected them to be first through the automatic doors. Sure enough, the first person to come through was Tina, quickly followed by Rachel.

Rachel smiled. 'Hello, boss! When you said you'd

make sure someone was here to pick us up, I didn't expect it to be you.'

'Well, consider yourselves honoured. I'm going to be in big trouble when I get home. I should have gone with Sue to a meeting with the vicar this evening, to discuss our wedding in May.'

'She's going to kill you.' Rachel laughed.

'Probably, although I did phone her to let her know I wasn't going to be able to make it.'

'I bet that went down well.'

'She always says the same thing: "Just make sure you're there on the seventh of May".'

'Oh, the joys of a relationship with a cop.' Tina laughed.

'Anyway, enough of my domestic bliss. I didn't pick you up because you're my favourite two detectives. I needed to give you an urgent update before you go and see Maggie Fraser at Worksop tomorrow morning. I'll tell you all about it in the car, where there's no chance of anyone overhearing our conversation.'

Ten minutes later, the three detectives were in the CID car as it pulled out from the airport car park and headed for the M1 motorway.

Once they were cruising along the motorway, Danny said, 'Right, before you go to Mrs Fraser's address in the morning, you need to know that Jean Mackay and her mother, Glenys, are both dead. Glenys died from cancer shortly after arriving in Worksop a couple of years ago, and Jean committed suicide, eight weeks ago, in woods near the aunt's home.'

There was silence in the car as Rachel and Tina absorbed the information.

Rachel broke the silence: 'Exactly how did Jean take her own life?'

'She took an overdose of paracetamol, washed down with vodka.'

There was a brief pause; then Danny continued. 'I still want you to go and see Maggie Fraser tomorrow morning. I want you to find out everything you can about the circumstances surrounding the suicide. I want you to try to establish what triggered it. Had she'd tried to kill herself before? It's also imperative that you find out from Mrs Fraser everything you can about Jean's father. We know his name's Ben Mackay and that he has a military background. I also want a recent photograph of Ben Mackay, if Mrs Fraser has one. I want to know, did he attend his daughter's funeral? What was the relationship like between Jean and her father? Most importantly, I want to know, where is Ben Mackay now?'

Rachel looked thoughtful and asked, 'Do you think Jean's father could be our killer?'

'It's certainly a possibility.'

'What if we turn up at Mrs Fraser's house in the morning and Ben Mackay's there?'

'That's a good point.'

Danny was quiet and thoughtful for a moment; then he said, 'If that's the case, and Ben Mackay is at the address, I want you to tell Mrs Fraser that the reason for your visit is purely and simply to check on her welfare. Tell her that it's normal practice following the suicide of a loved one. Do a few welfare questions, then make your excuses and get out of the house. I don't want either of you taking any risks with Ben Mackay. If he's our man, remember how ruthless he was with PC Moreton. Just get out and arrange for backup. Is that clear?'

Rachel replied quickly, 'Crystal clear.'

'I've called the briefing for six o'clock tomorrow morning. I don't want you there. As soon as you come on duty, I want you to get a car and head straight up to

Worksop. I want you to be knocking on Mrs Fraser's door by six thirty at the latest, and an update on the telephone from you by seven thirty. This is important: If I haven't had a verbal update from you by seven thirty, I'll be sending an armed response unit to the address. So make sure you call in even if you have to do it from a phone box.'

'I'll call, boss, don't worry,' said Rachel.

53

5.30am, 31 March 1986
Clumber Park, Nottinghamshire

The early morning mist drifted slowly across the heather-covered slopes, caressed into movement by the slight breeze.

At a distance of one hundred and fifty yards, standing upwind and on the opposite slope across the valley, was a handsome fifteen-pointer stag.

There wasn't a sound. The air was perfectly still.

The sun emerged briefly from behind the dark, threatening rain clouds. It was higher in the sky now, rising slowly above the distant hills. It had rained heavily earlier, bringing a freshness to the air. The clean, cold air, mixed with the subtle scent of heather, produced a heady, aromatic combination.

The two men who stalked the stag were dressed from head to toe in camouflage clothing. They paused just below the brow of the hill and lay stock-still. The younger of the two men had a rifle with a telescopic sight at his side.

The stag lowered his huge head to the ground, hoping to find another tasty morsel to eat. The shoots of heather were covered in the fresh rain and early morning dew.

The younger man fidgeted with his rifle, causing an almost inaudible click.

Immediately, the stag reared its huge antlered head and looked across the valley in the direction of the two men.

In a voice less than a whisper, the older man breathed, 'Be still, Your Highness.'

A minute passed before the stag looked back over his shoulder, away from the camouflaged men.

Satisfied he was alone on the slopes, the animal resumed eating.

In the same whispered tones, the younger man said, 'Is it time, ghillie?'

'Yes, Your Highness, it's time, but move carefully. The slightest noise will spook the beast.'

Painfully slowly, inch by inch, the man manoeuvred the rifle towards him.

Finally, the rifle was in position, and the young prince allowed the butt to nestle comfortably in his shoulder. He lowered his head into position so he had a natural line of sight through the telescopic sight.

Through the powerful magnification of the scope, the stag suddenly appeared close enough to touch. The young royal could see the individual hairs that made up the distinctive red fur, the dew glistening on the snout of the animal and the moisture sparkling in the animal's huge, dark brown eyes.

The ghillie whispered, 'He's yours now, Your Highness. Remember to aim where I taught you, just behind the shoulder. The bullet will pass directly through the animal's heart, and it won't suffer.'

Again, the stag raised his head from the heather. This time he snorted, tilted his head back and roared. The ghillie smiled. He knew this was a good sign, that the stag was totally unaware of the hunters' presence.

'Breathe as I taught you, Your Highness, be as one with the rifle and take the shot.'

There was total silence in the glen.

Suddenly, the big rifle barked into life. The stag's legs crumpled beneath its body, and it dropped like a stone.

A clean kill.

The ghillie jumped to his feet, whooping with delight.

'That was a fantastic shot, Your Highness! A perfect kill! You're a natural shot, so much better than your father.'

The young man got to his feet and pulled off the hood, revealing his short dark brown hair.

'I've had a bit more practice than my father recently, ghillie. Don't forget, it's not that long ago I was spending hours on the ranges at Lympstone.'

'Aye, that's very true, Your Highness, and it's gratifying to know that the Royal Marine Commando instructors can still produce fine marksmen. That was a wonderful shot.' The ghillie beamed.

'Thank you, ghillie, you tracked him like a master. What do we do now?'

'You can leave the rest to me, Your Highness. I'll arrange for the stag to be brought down from the hills. Let's get down to the house and tell the Duke your good news. Then you can celebrate with your folks properly.'

The clouds above blotted out the sunshine, and the

rain started to fall again. In no time at all, the far slope of the valley was no longer visible.

The rainfall got progressively harder and harder.

The rainfall pounding the peaty soil slowly merged into the noise of the heavy rain hammering down onto the roof of a caravan.

Suddenly, the Watcher was dragged back from his dream, back to reality.

He sat up in his sleeping bag, rubbed his eyes and glanced at his watch. It was almost half past five; it would soon be time for Frederick Reece to answer for his sins. Only when that had been achieved would it be time for him to snare the main architect of the evil deed that had made his mission a necessity.

From a small table at the side of his sleeping bag, he picked up his Maglite torch and a photograph. He switched on the torch, illuminating the photo, and whispered, 'Not long to wait now, sweetheart. With the grace of God, your tormentors will all soon be banished back to the hell they came from. Then I'll be free to see you and your mother again.'

54

6.30am, 31 March 1986
Farndon, Nottinghamshire

The Land Rover bumped its way along the rutted dirt track.
 The heavy rain that had fallen earlier had turned the dusty track into a muddy, sodden quagmire. At least now that it was starting to get light, the water-filled potholes were easy to see. The vehicle was built for such atrocious conditions and ploughed through the mud with ease. The Watcher had engaged the four-wheel drive of the vehicle as soon as he had turned off the tarmac road.

Once again, he parked the vehicle at the rear of the disused buildings. The grey walls looked even bleaker and darker, saturated by the heavy rain.

The rain had stopped briefly, but the Watcher still allowed himself a smile. He knew the threat of more inclement weather that morning meant there was very little chance of him being disturbed at the derelict buildings.

Having parked the Land Rover, he pulled the hood of his camouflage jacket over his head and moved to the rear of the vehicle, where he removed a black bag and a large axe.

The Watcher moved the sheet of corrugated iron to one side and made his way into the crumbling single-storey building.

The stench of the building's previous use was still evident, even after the torrential rain of the previous night. The building itself was now a crescendo of dripping noises as the leaks in the roof of the abandoned building were found out by the rainfall.

He made his way through the warren of drab concrete until he came to the room where he'd left Frederick Reece bound and gagged.

He could see Reece in the dim light. The solicitor was shivering with cold, and his eyes were half closed.

The Watcher walked over and slapped the prisoner's face, hard.

Instantly, Reece was wide awake, his face stinging from the brutal slap.

He opened his eyes and saw the Watcher standing in front of him. His eyes widened with fear, and he started mumbling beneath the brown gaffer tape.

Reaching forward, the Watcher ripped the tape from the face of Reece. As soon as the tape had been removed, the fat solicitor started to beg and plead for his life. 'I'm so sorry! Please show me some mercy.'

'Maybe I should show you the same mercy you showed my daughter?'

'Please. I'm begging you; there's no need for you to do this.'

'You know exactly what you did back then, and today you will finally pay for your sins.'

The Watcher bunched his huge fist and punched Reece hard on the forehead.

The force of the single concussive punch knocked Reece unconscious, and he slumped forward.

The Watcher moved quickly now. He untied his prisoner's hands, then walked across the room and picked up four large concrete building blocks.

He carried the four blocks over to Reece and put them down at the unconscious solicitor's side. He grabbed Reece and turned him onto his back, then extended his arms away from his body until he was in the crucifix position.

He used the brown gaffer tape to position the concrete blocks – one each side of the arm at the elbow joint.

Once the blocks were taped into position, the arms could no longer be moved. The weight of the blocks was far too much for an already weakened Reece to lift. As he started to regain consciousness, he gamely tried to move his arms, but he was powerless to lift the heavy blocks. Reece realised that he was trapped in that position and gave up trying to shift the blocks.

He could see the Watcher standing over him, with the large axe resting on his shoulder.

The Watcher saw that Reece was fully awake and placed the axe on the floor.

For a second or two, Reece entertained the idea that the maniac standing before him had changed his mind about killing him. That scant hope of a reprieve evaporated when he saw his captor reach into the black bag and take out a small blowtorch.

Using a disposable lighter, the Watcher lit the blowtorch and adjusted it until the flame was showing as a small stream of white-hot gas. He placed the lit blowtorch on the floor and lifted the huge axe above his head.

He looked into Reece's eyes and shouted, 'The scriptures have taught us, through the book of Exodus, that revenge shall only be complete with an eye for an eye, a tooth for a tooth, an arm for an arm and a foot for a foot!'

He brought the large axe down forcefully. It severed Reece's right hand between the wrist and the elbow before biting into the dusty concrete floor.

Reece screamed in pain, but was powerless as he watched the man step over him. The Watcher repeated the chopping motion. The axe fell onto the solicitor's left hand with the same devastating result.

A second agonised scream pierced the silence of the dingy concrete space.

The Watcher dropped the axe, letting it clatter to the floor. He then picked up the blowtorch and used the white-hot heat to cauterise both stumps. The raw, exposed flesh sizzled under the molten heat of the blowtorch. The open blood vessels were seared shut, and the bleeding instantly stopped. The agonising pain caused by the hot flame of the blowtorch screamed through Reece's body, and mercifully he passed out.

Smoke hung in the air of the small room; the cramped space was now filled with an almost overpowering stench of burnt flesh, stale urine and faeces.

The Watcher turned off the blowtorch and placed it on the floor to cool. From within the black bag, he removed two large ziplock bags. He picked up the two severed hands, which were still twitching on the floor, then dropped each one into a separate bag.

The index finger on one of the severed hands continued to contract and extend, as though the hand had developed a life of its own. Eventually, the nerves died too, and the twitching stopped. The Watcher sealed the two bags and dropped them into the larger black bag. He waited for the blowtorch to cool down completely before placing that in the same black bag.

Casually, he walked back over to the unconscious Reece and began to peel away the gaffer tape from the blocks. Once the tape had been removed, he moved the four blocks away from the stinking, blackened stumps.

Having removed the blocks, the Watcher dragged Reece upright and propped him against the wall. He squatted down on the floor, opposite Reece, and waited patiently for him to recover consciousness.

Twenty minutes passed, during which time the Watcher's eyes never left the fat solicitor.

Finally, Reece began to stir. A low, mournful moan emanating through gritted teeth was the first sign he was regaining consciousness. Another five minutes passed before Reece fully opened his eyes. The realisation of his situation was instantly apparent, and he began to sob.

The sobbing turned to crying, which changed to howling, then finally transformed into a single, long, piercing scream as the pain from his scorched, mutilated arms racked through his body.

The Watcher said cruelly, 'You can scream as loud as you like. There's no one to hear your pitiful wailing.'

'Why are you doing this?' screamed Reece.

'You know why, Reece. The only question you have left to answer is this, do you want to repent your sin before God?'

Reece slowly nodded his head. 'I'll do whatever you want me to do. You don't have to kill me. Have mercy! You've already maimed me.'

'Have mercy? Don't you understand that giving you

this opportunity to repent before the Lord is the only mercy I'm prepared to show you? Then I'll deliver justice and God's will.'

Reece was pleading now. 'You have to understand, none of what happened to that girl was my fault. All of it was Dennington's idea. He made us do it; he made us attack her. He told us that it was her fault, that she deserved it. We didn't kill her; she didn't die. You can let me live; please let me live.'

He was babbling now.

'Yes, you did. You don't know it, but you and your evil friends have killed her,' said the Watcher flatly; he then stepped in front of Reece.

He held the lethal blade of the Suminagashi knife in front of Reece. The solicitor let out a mournful cry as he saw the weapon.

The Watcher pushed Reece's head back and allowed the razor-sharp blade to slice across the fat solicitor's throat.

He felt the warm blood as it burst from the severed blood vessels and cascaded down over his hand. He turned the blade and drew the knife back in the opposite direction, almost severing the head.

The fat solicitor bled out rapidly over the filthy floor of the disused maggot farm. The Watcher took a step back from the rapidly spreading pool of blood.

He wiped his bloodstained hands on Reece's trouser legs, then gathered up his tools and placed them in the black bag.

Finally, he took out the two-inch paintbrush and dipped it into the steaming pool of Reece's blood. He painted the same Bible reference on one of the cold, grey concrete walls.

Picking up his bag and the axe, he said a whispered prayer, 'Defend me, your humble servant, in all assaults of my enemies: That I, surely trusting in thy defence, may not fear the power of my adversaries, through the might of Jesus Christ, our Lord. Amen.'

With Reece dispatched, the Watcher finally allowed another name to enter his thoughts.

Maurice Dennington.

Just the thought of the man's name repulsed the Watcher.

Thanks to the newspaper clipping left for him by his daughter, he knew exactly where he would find that particular demon.

As he walked out of the maggot farm and back to his vehicle, he salivated at the prospect of finally being able to deliver justice to that hypocritical pig.

Superintendent Maurice Dennington, of the Sexual Offences Investigation Team, would soon pay the ultimate price for his own cruelty and deviance.

55

6.30am, 31 March 1986
Gateford Road, Worksop, Nottinghamshire

Rachel Moore rubbed the sleep from her eyes, then rapped the car keys on the small glass windowpane in the front door of 45 Gateford Road, Worksop.

She had hardly slept last night, worrying about visiting this address. Her mind was racing now. She was struggling to push the tangible fear she felt to the back of her mind. Usually, she could mask it very well at work, but ever since Jimmy Wade had attacked her in her own home, she had lost a great deal of self-confidence. She couldn't get past the fact that without the intervention of her brother, Wade would have killed her that day.

Tina Prowse had picked up on Rachel's anxious mood. 'Rachel, are you okay?'

'I'm fine, thanks.'

'Why don't I handle things this morning? You try to relax a little.'

Rachel nodded, tightened her lips a little, then rapped a little harder on the glass pane.

A light appeared from an upstairs window. Although dawn was breaking and it was starting to get light, the sky was still gloomy and threatening more rain.

The window opened. A woman leaned out and said, 'Who's there?'

Tina stepped back, away from the door, and looked up at the woman. 'We're police officers. I'm really sorry it's so early, but we need to speak to Mrs Fraser. Is she home?'

'I'm Mrs Fraser. Just a second. I'll come down.'

There was a short delay before Tina and Rachel heard the key being turned in the lock of the front door. The door was opened by Maggie Fraser. She was dressed in a cream-coloured towelling bathrobe, and her greying blonde hair was still in tight curlers. A plump woman, she stood only five feet tall and looked to be approaching her sixties.

'You said you're from the police. Is something wrong?'

Tina held out her warrant card to reinforce the fact that they were indeed police officers, then said cleverly, 'I'm so sorry to disturb you and your family, Mrs Fraser, but we need to have a chat with you about your niece, Jean.'

'There's nobody else in the house, lass, just me. You do know my niece is dead, don't you?'

It felt like a ton weight had been lifted from Rachel. She now knew Ben Mackay wasn't in the house.

Tina pressed on, 'Yes, I was aware of that, Mrs Fraser, and I'm very sorry for your loss. Would you mind if we came inside for a few minutes? We do need to ask you a few questions, as a matter of urgency.'

Maggie Fraser was intrigued. 'Of course. Come in, come in.'

She stepped to one side, then said, 'You'll have to excuse me. It's so early, I've still got my bloody curlers in!'

Tina smiled. 'I'm sorry we've had to call at such an early hour, but like I said, it's urgent.'

Maggie ushered the policewomen into the front room of her terraced house. There was a dark green settee and a matching armchair. They were all arranged so they faced the television in the opposite corner. There was a sideboard that had several photographs placed at intervals along the top, and a small coffee table between the settee and the gas fire. Maggie walked over and turned on the gas fire; the room still held the night's chill.

She gestured for the detectives to sit on the settee, then said, 'I don't care how urgent it is, lass, I can't function without a cup of tea in the morning. Would you both like a drink?'

Rachel said, 'I'd love a coffee, please. White, no sugar, thanks.'

Tina said, 'A cup of tea, no sugar, would be lovely, thank you.'

Maggie shuffled out of the room to go and make the drinks. Tina took the opportunity of her absence to turn to Rachel and whisper, 'Well, at least we know Ben Mackay isn't here.'

Rachel replied, 'So she says. Stay alert.'

Tina nodded.

Minutes later, Maggie returned to the small lounge, carrying the three hot drinks on a tray. She passed the detectives their mugs of tea and coffee, who in turn put them down on the coffee table in front of them. Her own drink was in a delicate bone china cup and saucer.

Sitting down in the armchair, still holding the cup and saucer, Maggie said, 'I know what you're both thinking: a cup and saucer, really? I just can't get used to drinking out of a big pot mug. I like my dainty little teacup.'

She took a sip of the hot tea from the bone china cup. Her little finger was raised, as though she were sipping tea at a royal garden party.

She faced Tina and said matter-of-factly, 'You said it was urgent about our Jean, lass. What can be so important now the poor wee girl's dead?'

Tina said, 'We're investigating a number of incidents that may or may not be connected to what happened to your niece when she was a student at Nottingham University. We need to ask you a few questions about that.'

'Well, ask away.'

'After the horrendous attack on Jean when she lived in Nottingham before, why did her mother bring her back down to Nottinghamshire to live?'

'After she was attacked by those bastards, our Jean was never the same girl. She became totally withdrawn, refused to speak, and would hardly eat. It was as though she'd completely given up on life and just wanted to die. My sister, Glenys, looked after her twenty-four seven, and gradually, Jean started to recover slightly.'

'So why bring her back down here? Closer to where the attack happened?'

'Just when things were starting to improve a little with Jean, my sister was diagnosed with cancer. The doctors told her that she had stage 4 pancreatic cancer.

The prognosis they gave her was that she only had months, rather than years, to live.

'Glenys immediately sold everything in Scotland and brought Jean down here to live with me. She did it so I could continue to take care of Jean after she passed away.'

'Why couldn't Jean's father take care of her?' asked Rachel.

'Glenys had been separated from her husband, Ben, for a number of years, so that was never going to happen. Glenys knew I'd recently lost my husband, Eric. She thought that Jean would be good company for me too. You see, Jean and I always got on really well. She's a lovely girl.'

A tear formed in the older woman's eye. 'Was a lovely girl. Sorry.'

'So, when did Glenys and Jean come down here to live with you?' asked Tina.

'They sold their house and came down to stay with me a couple of years ago. My sister's condition deteriorated quickly, and she passed away less than a month after they had arrived here. It was a really hard time. Jean regressed a little after her mum's death. But over the last eighteen months, she'd really started to improve again. I began to see glimpses of the old Jean, of how she was before the attack. She looked healthy, smiled a lot and was eating properly. Like I said before, Jean and I always got on really well. We were having a good time; things were going well.'

'How was Jean's relationship with her father?'

'Her father's a good man. Ben is deeply religious; some might say devout. Although he was estranged from Glenys, he never, ever stopped loving or providing for Jean. The only reason Ben and our Glenys separated was because of his work. He was some sort of specialist soldier, always away from home. In the end, Glenys couldn't take the long absences anymore, and they separated permanently.'

'What do you mean, "specialist soldier", Mrs Fraser?' asked Rachel.

'Please call me Maggie,' the older woman said. Then, to Rachel's question, she added, 'I'm not sure, really. I know he was in the Royal Marines and that he was a brilliant shot, but then he joined something different and was forever being sent overseas at a moment's notice. He would be gone for months sometimes, and there was never any contact back to Glenys. She never had any idea where he was, or what he was doing. Twice he came back wounded, but as soon as his wounds healed, he would be sent away again. Even when he was home, he could never talk to Glenys about where he'd been or what he'd been doing. I think it was that silence that caused them to split up in the end. The separation hit my brother-in-law hard, because he was absolutely devoted to Jean – he worshipped his daughter. He even left his beloved job in the army to try to win Glenys back, but it was too late.'

'What did Ben do when he came out of the army?'

'He got a job working for the Royal Family as a ghillie, a stag hunter. He still works up at Balmoral. He's very well regarded up there.'

'Do you have any photographs of Ben?' asked Tina.

'I've got some here somewhere.'

Maggie stood and stepped over to the sideboard. She opened one of the drawers and took out a black photo album. She placed the album on the coffee table and turned the pages. There were a couple of photographs of Ben in his Royal Marine dress uniform and one of him in a ghillie suit.

Finally, she found the most recent photograph.

Ben Mackay was standing outside a chapel with a sombre expression on his face, dressed in a black suit, white shirt and black tie.

'This one's the most recent. It was taken at Jean's funeral about six weeks ago.'

'Do you mind if I borrow this photograph, Maggie?'

'Of course I don't mind. But can I ask why?'

'I'm really sorry, but I can't say at the moment. I can let you have it back tomorrow, and I'll tell you then, if that's okay?'

Without saying a word, she handed the photograph to Tina, closed the album, returned it to the sideboard and sat back down.

'Thank you, Maggie. I really appreciate it.' Tina smiled.

Rachel said, 'Maggie, you said earlier that Jean was doing well. Do you know what caused the change in her? I suppose what I'm really asking is, why do you think she did what she did?'

'I've thought about that so much, and I'm convinced it was that bloody newspaper article that caused her to go backwards. After seeing that report in the paper, it was as though she had regressed right back to the day after the attack.'

'What newspaper article?'

'I've still got a copy of the newspaper; I'll fetch it and show you.'

Once again, she stood up from her armchair and left the room. She returned a couple of minutes later, clutching an old copy of the *Worksop Chronicle*. She placed the newspaper on the coffee table, then opened it to the pages that held the article.

There was a full-page story reporting on the opening of the new Sexual Offences Investigation Team offices at Carlton in Lindrick.

In the very centre of the page was a photograph of Cavalie Naylor shaking hands with Superintendent Maurice Dennington. Both men smiled into the camera. The article outlined how it was Naylor Properties Limited that had built the new state-of-the-art offices, and how Superintendent Dennington had been selected to lead the dedicated new team.

Maggie pointed at the article. 'It was as though reading about the type of offences that would be investigated there tipped our Jean right back over the edge. I found her sobbing her heart out, just staring at the article. I tried to talk to her, but she wouldn't or couldn't speak. She took herself off to her room and stayed in there crying for a long time. She must have dropped off to sleep, eventually, because the crying stopped.

'After a couple of hours, I went upstairs to her room and told her through the door that I had to go out that afternoon. I had to go to the dentist, but I needed to go over to Mansfield and see a specialist about my wisdom teeth. To this day, I still blame myself for what happened. If I hadn't gone to see that bloody dentist, our Jean would still be alive.'

Rachel walked over to the armchair to comfort her. She put an arm around the old woman's shoulders and asked gently, 'What happened, Maggie?'

'When I got home from the dentist, I found a note from Jean on the dining table. It just said, "I need to think, gone to the woods for a walk". I knew she meant Farriers Wood – it's a large wood that's quite close to here. There's a path that runs through the middle of it. It's a beautiful spot … well, it was a beautiful spot. I went straight to the woods; I had a feeling that something was dreadfully wrong. I found Jean lying under an oak tree, just off the path. There was an empty vodka bottle at her side. At first, I thought the poor wee girl was drunk, but then as I tried to rouse her, I saw the empty packets of paracetamol all around her. I couldn't wake her up; I knew she was dead. I walked as fast as I could to the nearest phone box and called the police.'

She was sobbing steadily now.

'I'm sorry. I know this is still very painful for you.'

'It's like it happened yesterday, lass. I still cry every night. It was all so needless ... if only she had talked to me, we could've worked through it.'

'What about her father? When did you inform him?' asked Tina.

'That evening, I phoned Ben's work and left a message. He came straight down that night and stayed with me until after the funeral. He was noticeably quiet after the service, so I thought it would be a good time to give him the letter Jean had left for him.'

'What letter?'

'When I was sorting through Jean's things in her room, I found a sealed envelope addressed to her dad. I can tell you, Detective, I've never seen such a tough man break down so badly. Ben cried like a wee bairn as he read the letter. He wouldn't let me see it. He just folded the letter, put it in his jacket pocket and asked me to show him the newspaper article.'

'This newspaper article?'

'Yes. That's a different copy; I bought this newspaper afterwards, for the inquest. Ben kept the original one, the one Jean had read.'

'You've got no idea what was in the letter from Jean to her father?'

'No, he wouldn't show it to me. He stayed until the funeral, then left the next day and went back up to Scotland.'

'Didn't he stay for the coroner's inquest?'

'No, he didn't want to. He did say something strange before he left, though.'

'What was that?'

'He said that he didn't need a coroner to pass judgement on what had happened, that the Lord God had made a judgement already. He said that God had told him exactly what had happened to Jean and what needed to happen now. I didn't really understand what he was saying. I just put it down to his grief.'

Rachel glanced at her watch. It was now almost twenty past seven. She had to contact Danny before seven thirty.

She squeezed Maggie's shoulder and said, 'Maggie, Tina's going to stay here with you. She's going to take a statement from you. I've got to nip over to the police station in the town centre; then I'll come back. Are you going to be okay?'

'Aye, lass, it's still very upsetting, that's all. Jean was such a lovely wee girl.'

Rachel took the photograph of Ben Mackay from Tina, put it in her pocket, and left the house.

56

7.30am, 31 March 1986
Ranby Village, Nottinghamshire

'Come here, you silly cow, and see for yourself! Look, they're out there, parked up on the lane!'

The woman slowly got out of bed and joined her husband standing at the bedroom window.

'I can't see anything,' she said sleepily.

Maurice Dennington grabbed a handful of his wife's long auburn hair and pushed her face against the cold glass of the window. With his other hand, he punched her hard in the kidneys, then screamed in her ear, 'What's that red Fiesta down there then? Fucking scotch mist?'

He pulled her away from the window, slapped her on the back of the head, and threw her back onto the bed.

Liz Dennington curled up on the bed. She drew her knees up to her chest, gasping for breath. She was still winded from the blow to her kidneys. She fully expected the beating to continue as her enraged husband stomped around their luxurious bedroom.

He was muttering to himself; she could just make out the words *Flint* and *surveillance*, but that was all. She desperately wanted to cry, but she knew from bitter experience that if she attracted any attention to herself, her brute of a husband would definitely resume his physical assault on her.

So, like she had done countless times before, she buried her face in the pillow and remained silent.

Liz Dennington had met her husband just before he was due to go to Bramshill Police College. At that time he was charm personified and a very good-looking man. When she had first seen him, he was walking through West Bridgford town centre in his sergeant's uniform, and she had thought he looked amazing.

Liz Dennington was still an extremely attractive woman, but back then she had been stunning, with long auburn hair and bright, sparkling green eyes. At that time, she also had a figure to die for. So, when she began chatting to the handsome sergeant, he had been only too pleased to engage in conversation with her.

It was a whirlwind romance; they had married six weeks after that first meeting. Liz was an only child, and at the time she met Maurice, she still lived with and cared for her elderly mother. Her father had passed away when she was still a toddler. Her mother had warned her against marriage, saying she was moving too fast in the relationship. Liz had thought she knew better, and had ignored her mother's advice.

It was on the night of his promotion party to inspector, six weeks after they had married, that the veneer of normality finally slipped away from her husband.

As soon as they returned home from the celebration,

and for no obvious reason, he launched into a vicious verbal tirade, which was quickly followed by a physical assault. He was clever and calculating during the assault, only landing punches where the bruises wouldn't show. Feeling sore and bruised the next morning, she had considered going to the police station to report it, but had decided against it, fearing no one would believe her.

From that day on, the beatings had become a regular occurrence. Liz felt as though she was living with two different men. Whenever they were in company, he was perfectly charming; when they were alone together, he was a brutal, depraved monster.

After her mother died, the bullying and psychological intimidation got worse. Her husband effectively cut her off from any remaining friends. By now, the assaults were not only confined to physical beatings, as he also regularly abused her sexually. He would force her to commit gross, disgusting, painful acts at the threat of another beating.

With her mother now dead and no friends to confide in, she felt totally trapped. If she had tried to leave, there would have been nowhere for her to go. She remained a virtual prisoner in her own home, without the confidence to do anything about her parlous situation.

He had often left her defiled and bloodied on their marital bed, the same bed she was now curled up on, trying her hardest to become invisible.

Finally, she breathed a sigh of relief as her husband stalked out of the bedroom, stormed down the stairs and picked up the telephone in the hallway.

Liz crept from the bed and listened in on the call.

The house they owned was a palace. It was decorated beautifully and was located at the top of a hill looking down over a sloping garden towards a country lane. Beyond the lane were open fields as far as the eye could see. There were ornate metal gates that opened from the lane onto the York stone paved driveway.

For Liz, the house had always been nothing more than a gilded cage.

She listened in as her angry husband said, 'Good morning, sir, Maurice Dennington here. Sorry it's so early.'

There was a pause.

'I'll tell you what's so urgent, sir, it's that snide bastard Flint. Against my explicit instructions, he's placed a twenty-four-hour surveillance team on me. He's got his goons watching my every move. I won't stand for it. You need to speak to him today and get this surveillance off my back. It's bloody ludicrous.'

There was a longer pause.

'There's absolutely no reason for it, sir. Flint's a jealous little fucker who resents the fact that I went to Bramshill and that I'm ahead of him in the game. He's just trying to score points against me and my department.'

Another pause.

'Well, I'm sure you do think he's a good detective, but I won't stand for it, and one way or another, I'm going to put a stop to it. You need to speak to Flint this morning, sir, or I'll be making a direct complaint about his conduct to the chief constable.'

Dennington smashed the telephone back on its cradle.

He grabbed his coat, document case and car keys, and stormed out of the house, slamming the front door behind him. He used the fob on his car keys to remotely open the electric metal gates, then walked down the lane to the red Fiesta.

As he approached the car, he could see it had two

occupants, both male.

Tapping on the roof of the car, he indicated for the driver to wind the window down.

It had now started to rain; a heavy drizzle was falling.

The driver of the car lowered the window a fraction, and Dennington launched into a tirade: 'What the fuck do you two think you're doing?'

The driver showed his warrant card and said, 'DC Lorimar, sir. We've been ordered to keep an eye on you, make sure you're safe and everything's okay, sir.'

'On whose orders?'

'Our boss, Chief Inspector Flint, sir. He told us there was a strong possibility that your life could be in danger.'

Dennington scoffed, 'My life in danger? I've never heard anything so preposterous. If I see either of you two clowns again, any time today, I'll have your fucking jobs. Is that clear?'

'But, sir, our orders are to stay with you at all times.'

'I don't give a flying fuck about your orders, Detective! I've just telephoned Chief Superintendent Wainwright and put Danny Flint's bollocks in the mangle for setting up this surveillance. If you two don't want to be the subject of a formal complaint yourselves, you'd better disappear right now. Understood?'

'Is that an order, sir?'

'Yes, it's a bloody order!'

The detective started the car and drove off along the lane, away from Dennington's house.

Dennington stalked back up the drive and got into his Mercedes.

As he drove the silver-coloured saloon out of the driveway, he cursed out loud: 'Fucking Danny Flint! I'll crucify the little wanker!'

57

7.30am, 31 March 1986
Ranby Village, Nottinghamshire

From the bedroom window, Liz Dennington had watched the drama unfold. As she watched her pig of a husband drive away, a feeling of despair and helplessness overwhelmed her. She felt her legs buckle beneath her.

She sat on the bedroom floor and sobbed softly, a broken woman.

The years of abuse, physical and mental, at the hands of her brutal husband had reduced her to a quivering wreck who couldn't think for herself.

She felt trapped and violated beyond repair.

Deep in her heart, she knew there was only one way she would ever escape her husband's control and this hell on earth.

Maybe today would be the day Liz Dennington finally found the courage to end her nightmare.

58

7.28am, 31 March 1986
Worksop Police Station, Nottinghamshire

Rachel walked into the deserted CID office at Worksop Police Station. She grabbed the nearest telephone and dialled the number for Danny Flint's office.

It was answered on the first ring: 'Chief Inspector Flint.'

'Sir, it's Rachel. Everything's okay at the Gateford Road address. Ben Mackay isn't there.'

'You were cutting it fine, Rachel; I was beginning to get worried.'

'Sorry, sir, I didn't mean to leave it so late. I think we're definitely on the right lines, though.'

'What do you mean?'

'Ben Mackay could easily be our man. It seems that Jean Mackay committed suicide soon after seeing a newspaper article about the opening of the offices for the new Sexual Offences Investigation Team. The article had a big photograph of Cavalie Naylor shaking hands with Superintendent Dennington in his police uniform. The aunt thinks it was reading about the types of offences that would be investigated there that caused her niece to go downhill so quickly, but what if it's because she recognised the two men in the photograph? The aunt also said her niece had been perfectly fine before she saw the article, and was almost back to being her old self. Back to how she'd been before the attack.'

'What about Ben Mackay? What can Mrs Fraser tell us about him?'

'From how she describes it, I'd say he was definitely in some sort of Special Forces set-up.'

'Does she know where he is now?'

'After the funeral, he went straight back up to Scotland.'

'What's he doing in Scotland?'

'You're going to love this, boss. Mackay now works as a ghillie, hunting stags with the rich and famous on the Queen's estate at Balmoral.'

'Bloody hell!'

'There's one other thing you need to hear: Mrs Fraser told me that Ben Mackay said something weird before he left after his daughter's funeral. Just a second – I made a note of it.'

Having found the note in her pocketbook, Rachel continued. 'He told her that he didn't need to hear a coroner pass judgement on what had happened. The Lord God had made a judgement already, and that God had told him exactly what had happened to Jean and what needed to happen now.'

'Has Mrs Fraser seen him since the funeral?'

'No, boss.'

'Anything else?'

'Yes, I've managed to get a recent photograph of Ben Mackay. It was taken six weeks ago at his daughter's funeral. He bears a very strong resemblance to the description given by PC Moreton of his attacker.'

'Fantastic work. I'll get onto the royal household at Balmoral and see what they can tell us about Ben Mackay. I want you to go straight to King's Mill Hospital and show that photograph to PC Moreton. You can go back and collect Tina from Gateford Road later. This is now the top priority, Rachel; I need to know if PC Moreton can identify Ben Mackay as being the man who assaulted him. Quick as you can, please.'

'Okay, boss, I'm on my way.'

59

7.45am, 31 March 1986
Major Crime Investigation Unit, Mansfield

Danny had just put the telephone down after the call from Rachel when it immediately began to ring again.

He picked it up straight away. 'Chief Inspector Flint.'

'Boss, it's DC Lorimar. I'm calling from Ranby nick. We've just been ordered off the surveillance.'

'What do you mean ordered off? Who by?'

'Superintendent bloody Dennington, that's who. He's given us both a right bollocking and said he'd spoken to the chief super. He said we were to stop the surveillance straightaway, or he would make a formal complaint about our conduct.'

'So let me get this straight, you're at Ranby nick, and nobody's watching Superintendent Dennington?'

'Yes, sir, Dennington was mad as hell. I'm sorry, boss. We had no choice.'

'I know, Glen. I want you and Wayne to stay put at Ranby. I'll speak to the chief superintendent and try to get to the bottom of this. Hopefully, I'll have you two back on the surveillance as soon as possible. It's not your fault; I know you had no choice but to back off. Stay in the CID office and wait for my call.'

Danny replaced the phone, picked it up straightaway, and dialled the number for the switchboard. 'Good morning, it's Detective Chief Inspector Flint at the MCIU. I need you to find me the phone number for the Balmoral Estates at Ballater, Aberdeenshire. If possible, I'd like a direct line number for the Secretary of the Royal Household.'

There was a pause.

'Okay, I'll wait for you to call back.'

Less than two minutes later, the phone rang again. It was the operator on the switchboard. Danny picked up a pen and scribbled a telephone number down on his blotter.

Danny hung up and dialled the number he'd just been given. The call was answered very promptly. 'Good morning, the Balmoral Estate, Sir Jarvis Eccles speaking.'

'Good morning, Sir Jarvis. My name's Detective Chief Inspector Danny Flint from the Nottinghamshire Constabulary. I was hoping to speak with a ghillie who works on the estate, a Mr Ben Mackay.'

'I'm afraid that's out of the question, Chief Inspector. Mackay is currently on leave following a recent bereavement in his family.'

'I see. Can you tell me when he started his leave, please?'

'Just a second, I'll find the paperwork.'

Danny heard a filing cabinet open and close, then papers being shuffled.

'Here we are, Chief Inspector. Mackay started his leave on March 15; we're expecting him back on April 15. Is there a problem? Is the man in any trouble?'

'I don't know at this moment in time. What can you tell me about Ben Mackay?'

'Mackay's an absolutely superb ghillie, probably the best I've ever seen. He came to us highly recommended when he left the military. He had served in the Royal Marines, then with distinction in the Special Boat Service. He's extremely well liked by both Her Majesty and the Duke.'

'Does your paperwork there say where he intended to go during his leave?'

'No, it doesn't, I'm afraid. I did talk to Mackay before he left, as he had requested the use of one of the Land Rovers from the estate. He told me that he intended going down south, somewhere in Derbyshire, I think. He wanted to finalise some issues that remained outstanding after his daughter's death. I believe he may have mentioned that he also wanted to spend time walking in the Derbyshire Dales.'

'Did you allow him to take the vehicle?'

'I thought it would have been churlish to refuse the man, bearing in mind the recent loss of his daughter. The poor chap was obviously suffering – he told me he needed it for his "mission", not his "leave". I put the fact he used military jargon down as a slip caused by his grief. So, the answer to your question is yes, he's got one of our vehicles.'

'Can you let me have details of the vehicle he's using, please?'

'Yes, I've made a note of that on the paperwork. He's taken one of our older vehicles; it's a bit battered, I'm afraid. Here it is: He's got a Land Rover Defender, registered number FJH 591.'

'What colour's the vehicle?'

'My dear chap, all the vehicles here are the same colour. It's British racing green, of course.'

'Have you had any contact with Mr Mackay since he left Balmoral?'

'None whatsoever. We agreed to him having a month off because of his bereavement, so I wasn't expecting to hear from him. You have me a little concerned now, Chief Inspector Flint. If Mackay is in some sort of trouble, I'd like to be kept informed, please. As I said earlier, Ben Mackay is one of the Royal Family's favourite employees.'

'As soon as I have any more information, Sir Jarvis, I'll let you know straightaway. In the meantime, if Mr Mackay returns to Balmoral or contacts you, would you please give me a call at Nottinghamshire Police Headquarters, as a matter of urgency?'

'Of course. If there's anything else I can do for you, please don't hesitate to call.'

Danny put the phone down. His mind was racing.

He now knew for definite that Ben Mackay had all the skills needed to have carried out the murders. It had now also been confirmed that he was back in England at the time they were committed. He had transport that matched the sighting of a vehicle mentioned during the Beeston enquiry and, most importantly, he had a genuine motive to commit the murders.

He just needed PC Moreton to identify Ben Mackay as the man who had attacked him; then he would be able to circulate him on the PNC as wanted.

Ten minutes passed slowly by as Danny paced up and down in his office. He heard a quiet tap on the door, turned, and saw Chief Superintendent Wainwright coming into the office.

Wainwright looked worried. He said, 'Good morning, Danny. I think you and I need to have a conversation.'

'Don't tell me, sir: Superintendent Dennington's been on the phone, bending your ear.'

Bill Wainwright smiled a wry smile and gestured for Danny to take a seat. Both men sat down.

'Spot on. Maurice Dennington's been on the phone, alright. He's spitting feathers about you. He was raging when he called me first thing this morning. What the fuck is all this about a surveillance on him? Detectives from the MCIU sitting outside his house, watching his every move?'

'It was for his own good, sir, but the idiot has just forced the two detectives to back off. I've got them on standby at Ranby Police Station.'

'For Christ's sake, just explain to me what's going on!'

'Right, sir, the theory we're currently pursuing is that Maurice Dennington was possibly one of four men involved in the serious sexual assault of a young woman at Nottingham University back in 1977. Two of the four men believed to have been involved were Cavalie Naylor and Edward Hall. The third man of the group is believed to be Frederick Reece, who we think has been abducted by the same man who assaulted PC Moreton and left him for dead. The victim of the sexual assault in 1977 was a young woman called Jean Mackay. She committed suicide recently after seeing a photograph in the local paper of Maurice Dennington and Cavalie Naylor at the opening of the Sexual Offence Investigation Team's new offices. Her father's a man called Ben Mackay, who's an ex-Special Boat Service operative, who now works for the Royal Family at Balmoral as a ghillie. Literally, just before you came in, I was on the telephone to the Secretary of the Royal

Household, Sir Jarvis Eccles. He has just confirmed that Mackay is now somewhere in the East Midlands on a month's compassionate leave. He has access to transport, as he's borrowed one of the Land Rovers used on the Balmoral Estate.'

'Bloody hell, Danny! What a fucking mess.'

The telephone began to ring again. Danny grabbed it on the second ring: 'Chief Inspector Flint.'

'Boss, it's Rachel. I've just broken every speed limit getting to King's Mill Hospital. I'm on the ward with PC Moreton now, and he's just positively identified Ben Mackay as the man who attacked him.'

'Great work, Rachel. I want his written statement before you go back to Gateford Road. Tina will be okay; she'll just have to wait.'

Danny put the phone down.

'Well, that's just confirmed our theory, sir. PC Moreton has just positively identified Ben Mackay as the man who attacked him at gunpoint.'

'Where exactly is Dennington's surveillance?'

'Like I said, they're on standby at Ranby Police Station, sir.'

'Get on the phone and tell them to get their arses over to Carlton in Lindrick. I want that surveillance back on Superintendent Dennington immediately. If he protests about it again, put him onto me.'

'Yes, sir.'

Danny picked up the phone, dialled the number for Ranby Police Station, and ordered the two detectives to travel to Carlton in Lindrick immediately and resume surveillance on Dennington.

Chief Superintendent Wainwright stood up and said, 'I'll give Dennington a call. I'll tell him what the situation is. If he doesn't like it, he can take it up with the chief constable.'

60

7.50am, 31 March 1986
Sexual Offences Investigation Team, Carlton in Lindrick, Nottinghamshire

Superintendent Maurice Dennington was still seething as he drove his Mercedes through the open gates and into the SOIT car park. It was still early, and there were only two other vehicles in the car park.

He grabbed his leather document wallet from the front seat and got out of the car. He walked purposefully towards the stone steps that led up to the front doors of the building. He paid no attention to the man with steel grey hair who walked down the steps straight towards him.

As they drew level, the man with the grey hair stopped and said quietly, 'Superintendent Dennington?'

'Yes, that's me. Do I know you?'

'You'll know who I am soon enough; do as I tell you, or I'll kill you right here.'

For the first time, Dennington saw the black handgun the man was holding. The weapon was then firmly pressed into his ribcage. He had been so angry about the imposition of the surveillance that he had failed to pay attention to his surroundings as he walked across the car park. Now it was too late. He was faced with a gunman, and there was nothing he could do.

Dennington blustered arrogantly, 'I don't know who you are, or what the fuck you think you're doing, but you won't get away with this.'

The gunman growled, 'Shut your mouth, Dennington! Speak again and I'll spread your guts all over this car park.'

He nodded his head in the direction of a dark green vehicle and said, 'Walk towards the Land Rover.'

As realisation dawned on Dennington that the man wasn't bluffing, the colour drained from his face. He obeyed the man's instruction and walked slowly towards the scruffy Land Rover parked in the very corner of the car park.

Once they were at the vehicle, the Watcher kept the handgun pressed into the ribs of Dennington, then he reached forward and opened the back door.

Through gritted teeth, he hissed, 'Get in.'

Dennington dropped the document holder he was carrying, then said in a voice edged with panic, 'You're totally mad! You won't get away with this! Look around you, man; there are security cameras everywhere!'

The Watcher responded by smashing the barrel of the gun into Dennington's mouth. He then used the heavy grip of the pistol to deliver a more concussive blow to the back of the policeman's head.

As Dennington slumped forward, stunned by the

two blows, the Watcher grabbed him and bundled him into the back of the Land Rover. He climbed in after Dennington, bound his hands and feet with cable ties, then gagged him using gaffer tape.

He climbed back out of the vehicle, quietly closed the back door and looked around the car park. There wasn't a soul about. There had been no witnesses to the abduction. He wasn't concerned about the CCTV cameras. By the time they were checked, it would be too late for Dennington.

The Watcher got into the driver's seat, started the engine and slowly drove out of the car park.

From start to finish, the abduction of Superintendent Maurice Dennington had taken just two and a half minutes.

61

8.15am, 31 March 1986
Major Crime Investigation Unit, Mansfield

Rob sat with Danny in his office. They were discussing possible locations where Frederick Reece could be imprisoned. Now that PC Moreton had positively identified Ben Mackay as the person who had assaulted him, it was almost certainly Mackay who had been responsible for the abduction of Frederick Reece. If Reece wasn't dead already, he had to be hidden somewhere near the abduction point.

'It's an impossible task. It literally is like looking for the proverbial needle in a haystack.'

'I know it's difficult, but at least we now know Mackay's using a green Land Rover Defender. I can't help thinking we missed a trick there. Do you remember the old lady who lived across the road from Edward Hall, how she mentioned seeing an old Land Rover?'

'You mean Mrs Hughes. Yeah, I remember that sighting. We checked all the available CCTV cameras, and at the time, there was no sign of any similar vehicle. The house-to-house enquiries didn't reveal anybody else who'd seen a Land Rover.'

'You're right, Rob. Hindsight's always twenty-twenty vision.'

'Her sighting of that particular vehicle couldn't be connected to what had happened.'

Danny nodded. 'I want you to start at the Co-op in Farnsfield, where the Range Rover was found, then work your way out, checking any CCTV you can find. You never know, we might get lucky and pick up a sighting of the Land Rover.'

There was a knock on the office door, and a very worried-looking Chief Superintendent Wainwright walked in.

Rob stood up to leave.

'It's alright, Inspector, this won't take a minute. Danny, is the surveillance back on Dennington?'

'Yes, sir, the team arrived at Carlton in Lindrick just after eight o'clock this morning. The superintendent was already there; his car was parked in the car park. Is there a problem?'

'I'm not sure. I've been trying to call him, and he's not picking up the phone. I'm worried, Danny. If his car's there, why isn't he answering my call?'

Danny picked up the phone and called the control room. 'Hello, it's Chief Inspector Flint. I want you to contact DC Glen Lorimar, call sign MQ73, tell him, from me, to go inside the SOIT offices and make sure that Superintendent Dennington is at his desk. Call me straight back once they've responded.'

After five tense minutes, the phone rang. Danny snatched up the receiver. 'Chief Inspector Flint.'

'It's the control room, sir. MQ73 have just called in. There's no sign of Superintendent Dennington in his office. They're saying that none of the staff working there have seen him today. On the way into the offices, one of your officers has found what appears to be the superintendent's document case in a corner of the car park. They're awaiting your instructions, sir.'

'Tell them to start checking the CCTV in the building. The place is surrounded by cameras. If they see anything at all suspicious on those cameras, they're to call me in my office immediately.'

'Yes, sir.'

Danny replaced the telephone and turned towards Bill Wainwright. 'Dennington's not there. He's not in his office and not in the building. His car's in the car park, but no one's seen him there this morning. I think there's now every likelihood that Mackay's got Maurice Dennington and Frederick Reece.'

Wainwright looked shocked. 'Right, Danny, get back onto the control room. I want an armed team travelling immediately to the Carlton in Lindrick area. I want them on standby. I take it the description of Mackay and the details of the Land Rover have already been circulated.'

Danny nodded. 'Yes, sir.'

'As soon as we get a sighting of Ben Mackay or the Land Rover, I want the armed police units deployed. I think we're rapidly running out of time.'

'I'll get it organised, sir.'

Wainwright left the office, and once again Danny reached for the telephone on his desk.

As soon as he'd arranged the armed response units to be deployed, Danny turned to Rob and said, 'Get a vehicle, Rob. I want to be out there on the ground. We're going up to Carlton in Lindrick. Tell Brian to man the telephones here; I want to know the minute anything comes through. Make sure the vehicle you get is fitted with a VHF radio so we can monitor the control room radio traffic.'

62

9.00am, 31 March 1986
Rampton Hospital, Nottinghamshire

Breakfast in the large hall had been the same as usual: cornflakes and toast with a mug of strong, sweet tea. Jimmy Wade had eaten his food almost automatically. If today went as planned, it would be his last meal inside this dreadful place. He felt calm and in control. He knew exactly what he needed to do to get out of there.

Clive Winstanley sat opposite him, loudly chewing a slice of toast. His mouth was wide open as he chewed. Jimmy could see the masticated toast being hurled around the huge mouth before it was swallowed with an equally loud gulp. The toast was washed down noisily with a mouthful of tea.

'For fuck's sake, Clive, is everything you do loud?'

The huge West Indian grinned, showing teeth that were still covered in remnants of toast.

'Jimmy man, you should hear me when I'm with a girlie. I make the bitches squeal, man, believe me.'

Jimmy shook his head in disgust. He normally wouldn't tolerate being in the same vicinity as Winstanley, but he knew that for his plan to succeed, he would need to stay on the right side of the giant paedophile.

Today, they were both on the roster to work at the concrete slab-making facility.

The facility was located near to the lowest perimeter fence of the high-security hospital.

Three men were down to work on the concrete slabs that day; the third man was the serial arsonist Lester Silwell. An effeminate man, Silwell was considered a grass by every other inmate, so Jimmy hadn't mentioned any of his plans to him. He'd ensured Winstanley didn't breathe a word of the plan to Silwell by making a promise to the big West Indian that he would get him out, too.

It didn't bother Wade that Clive Winstanley was considered a nonce by other inmates at the hospital.

Wade knew Winstanley had been imprisoned ten years ago for the vicious abduction and rape of three schoolgirls in Northampton. He was now almost fifty-five years of age, but was still extremely strong and powerful. He'd been sentenced to be detained indefinitely, and realistically, there was no chance of Clive Winstanley ever being released from Rampton Hospital. He truly was criminally insane. However, over recent years, he had portrayed a placid image to the social workers and nurses. That was the main reason he had managed to get himself on the concrete working party on a regular basis. He was also selected because he was such a naturally strong man. His work rate was second to none; he could lift and manhandle the heavy slabs with ease.

Wade leaned forward and said, 'How many nurses will be watching us today, Clive?'

'Normally, it's two nurses for every one of us. So, coz Silwell's coming too, I reckon there'll be six nurses with us.'

'Are you going to do exactly what I tell you to do?'

Winstanley roared with laughter. 'Yeah, man, of course! I'll be drinking beer in the pub tonight, entertaining some hot bitches!'

Jimmy leaned forward and hissed, 'For fuck's sake, Clive, keep it down. I've told you we've got to be all meek and mild until it's time to act. If you're serious about wanting to get out, you've got to do exactly what I tell you, when I tell you! Have you got that?'

'Yeah, man, I got it. You eating that toast, Jimmy?'

Jimmy pushed the plate containing the last slice of toast towards Clive and grinned. 'It's all yours, mate; it's all yours.'

He reached down and slipped his fingers inside his boot. He felt around for the sharpened crochet hook in his boot lining and smiled when he felt the hard steel.

63

8.55am, 31 March 1986
Worksop, Nottinghamshire

The Watcher had parked the Land Rover near to the entrance of Farriers Wood.

The last time he'd been to this woodland was on the day he buried his daughter. He had wanted to see for himself the very spot where his precious daughter had taken her own life.

He and Maggie Fraser had come to the wood straight after the funeral. They had held each other and wept beneath the oak tree where Maggie had found Jean, lying dead, two weeks earlier.

He looked through the windscreen at the woods, wiped a tear from his cheek and zipped up his jacket. He had been waiting patiently for Dennington to regain consciousness, but he could now hear him spluttering and whining beneath the brown gaffer tape.

It was time.

He got out of the Land Rover and glanced up and down the street. Fifty yards from the entrance to the wood, on the other side of the road, there was a row of four terrace houses.

Farriers Wood was located on the very edge of Worksop. Directly opposite the entrance, there was nothing but open fields.

Satisfied there were no prying eyes watching his every move, he walked to the rear of the vehicle. He opened the door and was immediately met with grunts of protest from a bound and gagged Dennington.

He reached past Dennington, grabbed a black grip bag and a large axe. The head of the axe was wrapped in a black bin liner.

The Watcher placed the two articles at the rear of the vehicle, then leaned back inside and whispered to Dennington: 'I'm going to remove the cable ties from your ankles and the gag from your mouth. If you make any attempt to run or shout for help, I'll kill you on the spot. You and I are going for a walk into the woods, where we can talk without being disturbed. Is that clear, Superintendent?'

The thought that all was not lost flashed through Dennington's brain. If they were going to talk, he felt sure he could make this lunatic listen. He suddenly felt a renewed confidence that he would be able to get out of this predicament.

He quickly nodded that he understood.

The Watcher took a large hunting knife from a scabbard attached to his belt and sliced through the cable ties that bound his captive's feet.

He returned the knife to its scabbard, then removed the handgun from his camouflage jacket pocket.

He shoved the pistol into Dennington's face and said through gritted teeth, 'If you try anything, I won't hesitate to put a bullet through your brain. Do you understand me?'

Dennington nodded.

The Watcher removed the gag from his prisoner's mouth and dragged him from the back of the vehicle.

Dennington didn't protest. He just asked quietly, 'Who are you?'

'Never mind who I am. Just walk slowly, two paces in front of me. Go through the entrance, then walk along the path towards the woods.'

The superintendent looked wide-eyed at the black handgun in the Watcher's right hand. He was so transfixed by the handgun, he never noticed the large axe resting on top of the grip bag being held in the Watcher's left hand.

'Start walking, Dennington.'

The Watcher followed behind Dennington. The two men moved slowly along the path and made their way deeper into Farriers Wood.

After ten minutes walking, the Watcher suddenly said, 'Stop there. Turn left off the path, then start walking again.'

Dennington did as he was instructed.

After another fifty yards, he heard the Watcher's voice again: 'Stop there.'

Having put down the black grip bag and the axe, the Watcher stepped in close behind the terrified policeman and used the razor-sharp knife to slice through the cable ties that bound his captive's wrists.

The Watcher then barked an order. 'Strip! Get that uniform off. Now!'

The superintendent started to protest, but immediately felt the blade of the skinning knife slice across his cheek.

'This isn't a fucking debate! Do exactly what I tell you!'

Dennington's hand shot up to his cheek. He felt the warm blood on his fingers, then felt it start to trickle slowly down his face. Slowly, he began to get undressed. As he hurled his uniform onto the ground, he said, 'I thought we were going to talk?'

'Oh, we're going to talk alright, but only when I'm ready. Get a move on!'

After removing his underpants, Dennington stood there naked. He instantly felt vulnerable and cold. His police uniform lay in a crumpled heap at his feet.

In a voice that was flat and devoid of all emotion, the Watcher said, 'Lie on the ground, face down, and put your hands behind your back.'

Dennington could still feel the blood on his cheek from the first protest, so he did as he was told.

The Watcher moved in close and once again bound Dennington's hands and feet with cable ties. As soon as the cable ties were tightly secured, he grabbed a length of strong blue nylon cord from his bag. He tied the cord very tightly around the naked man's knees.

Having effectively immobilised his captive, the Watcher lifted Dennington up and dragged him over to the base of a large oak tree. He sat him upright, so his back leaned against the rough bark of the old tree.

He then returned to the discarded black bags.

First, he took the axe out of the bin liner and propped it against a tree before stuffing the empty bin liner inside the leather grip bag.

Dennington couldn't take his eyes off the wooden-handled axe that was just five yards in front of him. The bright steel of the honed edge was mesmerising.

He knew he had to try to talk his way out of the situation. There was nothing he could do physically.

'You said we were going to talk. Are you going to tell me what this is all about?'

The Watcher grinned malevolently. 'You still don't know, do you?'

'I've no fucking idea. I don't even know who you are!'

Reaching into the breast pocket of his camouflage jacket, the Watcher removed the small photograph. He stepped over to Dennington and said with a snarl, 'But you know her, don't you, Superintendent Dennington?'

He held the photograph twelve inches from the face of the now cold and shivering Dennington.

'I don't know her. Who is she? This is ridiculous; I've never seen that woman before in my life! Why don't you untie me? Then we can work this out. I know I'm a police officer, but I'm prepared to turn a blind eye to your actions so far.'

'That's funny, because your friend Cavalie Naylor was also prepared to turn a blind eye. Which was convenient for me, as I now have both his eyes in a ziplock bag. I pulled them from his face while he was still drawing breath, just as the scriptures demanded. Then I slit his throat and let him bleed to death.'

'What are you talking about? How could you even imagine doing something as disgusting as that?'

As he spoke, the shock at what he was hearing was evident both on Dennington's face and in his voice.

The Watcher continued, 'Before Naylor died, he told me everything that happened on that night, all those years ago, at Nottingham University. He told me the names of the other men involved. He told me whose idea it had been – he even told me who did what. Has your selective memory allowed you to recall the beautiful young woman in the photograph yet?'

Dennington had known exactly who the girl was,

just as he had known instantly what incident the maniac was referring to, but he continued to act as though he had no idea.

Trying to maintain an even voice, he said, 'Look, this is all madness. I don't know who you are, and I've no idea what Naylor told you, but I wasn't there that night. I do remember her face, but I don't recall ever having a conversation with her.'

'I've already visited your friends: Cavalie Naylor, Edward Hall and Frederick Reece. They're all dead now. None of them refused to repent their sins. What about you, Dennington? Are you going to seek forgiveness from the Lord?'

Dennington was trying to think fast. 'You've got to help me understand why you've brought me here. What did those three men do to that poor woman?'

'We both know it wasn't just those three men. You and your friends accosted her, raped her, sodomised her and then left her naked in the middle of a field to die. You and those other three pigs treated her worse than an animal. You debased her in every way possible, for no other reason than because you could. That beautiful, innocent young woman was my daughter, and the time has now come for you to pay for your sins.'

Dennington was panicking. In a trembling voice, he pleaded, 'Listen, I don't know what Cavalie Naylor told you about me, but he's always hated me. He's a liar. He told me about him and Hall attacking that woman.'

'That woman was my daughter!' roared the Watcher.

'Sorry, your daughter. Yes, she's your daughter, a beautiful girl. It wasn't me; it was those two. Naylor told me that it had been his idea. I had nothing to do with any of it; you've got to believe me.'

The Watcher felt bile rise in his throat as he listened to Dennington making his puerile attempts to lay the blame on his two friends. He felt the rage building within him, and he had a strong urge to kill him there and then, but the scriptures demanded that he control that rage. He had to give the demon one chance to atone for his sin before he was dispatched back to the hell he had crawled out of.

Dennington blustered, 'Let me talk to your daughter. I'll make sure she's listened to. I'll get those two bastards prosecuted for what they did.'

Through gritted teeth, the Watcher replied, 'My daughter's dead. The sight of you, dressed in your fancy police uniform, the head of a sex crimes unit, was too much for her to take. She ignored the teachings of the Old Testament; your actions made her weak, and she took her own life. Be under no illusion, Dennington, you and your three friends killed my daughter just as surely as if you had taken a gun to her head and pulled the trigger.'

The Watcher shook his head before carefully replacing the precious photograph in his breast pocket.

He sat down on the trunk of a fallen tree, opposite Dennington. He closed his eyes and said softly, 'Lighten our darkness, we beseech thee, O Lord; and by thy great mercy defend us from all perils and dangers of this night; for the love of thine only son our saviour, Jesus Christ. Amen.'

Suddenly, Dennington shouted at the top of his voice, 'Help me!' The plaintive cry echoed around the trees.

With lightning speed, the Watcher removed the razor-sharp Suminagashi skinning knife from its scabbard. He stepped over to Dennington and dragged the blade slowly across the man's naked chest.

There was an agonised howl of pain as blood started to seep from the eight-inch gash across his chest. The cry was quickly stifled as the Watcher wrapped gaffer tape around the naked man's head. There would be no more cries of help from Dennington, nor would anybody hear his screams of agony. The brown tape was wrapped tightly around his head, completely covering his mouth.

The Watcher had heard enough vile words spew from Dennington's mouth; he knew he would never repent for his sins. It was now clear that the others had told the truth before they died. Dennington had been the leader of their group. He had been the one urging them all to commit atrocity after atrocity upon his beautiful daughter.

He stepped over to the now-terrified policeman. He leaned in close, until his mouth was only inches from his ear.

He shouted directly into his ear, 'Devil, can you hear me?'

Dennington jerked his head away from the shout and nodded.

'My daughter's name was Jean Mackay; my name is Ben Mackay. I want those two names to be the last names you hear before I dispatch you from this earth and back down into hell. In the name of the Lord God Almighty, this day I shall complete the work demanded by the scriptures. Very soon, you will join your fellow demons in eternal damnation. As it demands in the book of Exodus, so shall it be.'

Ben Mackay walked back to the fallen tree, sat down, closed his eyes and began to pray.

Dennington watched his every move, his eyes widening with fear.

64

9.00am, 31 March 1986
Worksop, Nottinghamshire

PC Phillip Trenchard was on foot patrol in Worksop. He had covered the shopping area of his beat and was now doing a check on the very perimeter.

He was just out of his two-year probationary period and enjoyed being on foot patrol. He had worked this same beat for almost six months. He relished the fact that he now knew it like the back of his hand.

People had got used to seeing his face, and he would spend most of each day shift exchanging pleasantries with the residents and shopkeepers on his beat.

He turned the corner that led onto Farriers Row, a small terrace of four Victorian houses. These four houses were the last on his beat and the last in Worksop. After this, there was nothing but open fields on one side of the road, and the public park, Farriers Wood, on the other.

As he strolled around the bend in the road, his eye was immediately drawn to the mud-covered, dark green Land Rover parked directly outside the entrance to the public park.

He stepped back around the corner, keeping the vehicle in his line of sight. He took his pocketbook from the breast pocket of his tunic and scanned the last scribbled note he'd made.

There it was in black and white: FJH 591, dark green Land Rover.

The radio message he'd received from his control room earlier was clear. Under no circumstances was anyone to approach this particular vehicle. The occupant, Ben Mackay, was believed to be armed and dangerous.

The young policeman strained his eyes and tried to make out if anyone was still with the vehicle. From his position, he couldn't tell – it looked empty, but he wasn't sure.

He stayed out of sight, reached for his personal radio, and said, 'Three three five to Worksop control. Over.'

'Go ahead, three three five. Control over.'

'I'm on Farriers Row, near to the entrance of Farriers Wood. I've found that dark green Land Rover, FJH 591. It's parked up directly outside the entrance to the wood. I can't tell if anyone's still with the vehicle. It looks abandoned, but I can't be sure. Over.'

'Control to three three five, maintain a visual on the vehicle only. Do not under any circumstances approach the vehicle or any of its occupants. Armed units are travelling to your location; their ETA is ten minutes. Control over.'

65

9.00am, 31 March 1986
Cuckney Crossroads, Nottinghamshire

Danny and Rob were driving towards Worksop along the A60 when they heard the message of the Land Rover's sighting being passed over the VHF radio. The force control room had contacted the armed units on standby at Carlton in Lindrick and ordered them to travel to Farriers Wood at Worksop to check on the sighting of the dark green Land Rover FJH 591.

Danny said, 'Farriers Wood. That's where Jean Mackay committed suicide.'

Rob gunned the engine and sped through the crossroads at Cuckney village.

'I know where Farriers Wood is. We can be there in ten minutes.'

Danny grabbed the radio handset. 'Chief Inspector Flint to control.'

'Go ahead. Control over.'

'Show myself and DI Buxton also attending Farriers Wood, ETA ten minutes. Who's in charge of the Special Ops units that are travelling?'

'C Section of the Special Operations Unit are attending. Sergeant Turner's in charge, sir. Their ETA is roughly the same as yours.'

'I'll liaise with Sergeant Turner on our arrival. Over.'

'There's another message for you, sir. We've just been asked by DC Lorimar to inform you that the CCTV at Carlton in Lindrick has been checked. It clearly shows that Superintendent Dennington has been forced into the back of a Land Rover at gunpoint. The vehicle used in the abduction was the green Land Rover, Foxtrot Juliet Hotel Five Nine One. Control out.'

'Received, thanks. Chief Inspector Flint, out.'

Danny gripped the dashboard and said, 'Put your foot down, Rob. I've got a nasty feeling this isn't going to end well.'

66

9.00am, 31 March 1986
Rampton Hospital, Nottinghamshire

'Wade and Winstanley, I want you two to shift this pile of concrete slabs from the stack near the fence to the main store. We've got all day, so take your time. There's no rush.'

The order had come from Staff Nurse Pete Timmons. He was in overall charge of the working party.

'Okay, boss man,' said Clive Winstanley before smirking at Jimmy Wade.

'Silwell, I want you to stay here and count the slabs as they move them. I need you to make sure that you keep a record of how many slabs we've got in the main store. Can you manage that?'

He clutched the clipboard close to his scrawny chest and said in his lisping voice, 'Yeth thir.'

Wade looked at Winstanley. That hadn't been factored into his planning. He couldn't afford to have

Lester Silwell watching their every move. As he mulled over the problem of Silwell, he had a flash of inspiration.

He suddenly realised how he could deal with Silwell and reduce the number of nurses supervising them, both at the same time.

He picked up one of the heavy concrete slabs and set to work.

Wade and Winstanley worked at a steady pace, lifting and carrying the heavy slabs. The six nurses who had been detailed to watch them as they worked soon got bored. They smoked cigarettes and chatted amongst themselves, paying little attention to the three men in their charge.

Near the main store, Jimmy turned to Silwell and said quietly, 'Lester, do me a favour, mate – can you tell me the colour of this slab? It's covered in dust, and I want to make sure I put it on the right pile.'

'Of courthe, Jimmy, it'th a beige one. It needth to go over there.'

'Thanks, Lester.'

Jimmy turned to walk towards the stack of slabs Lester had indicated; then he slammed the heavy slab directly down onto the top of Silwell's foot.

Silwell howled in pain and dropped to the floor, clutching his now broken foot.

As he hadn't been tasked with doing any lifting, he wasn't wearing steel toe cap boots. All the toes on his right foot had been crushed.

Jimmy shouted, 'Over here, boss! There's been an accident. Lester's hurt his foot.'

Two of the nurses quickly made their way over to the two men. Silwell rolled around on the ground, clutching his foot. He was obviously in a great deal of pain.

Wade looked suitably horrified and said, 'It was an accident, boss. I turned around and Lester was right behind me. He bumped into me and I lost my grip on the slab. I think it landed on his foot.'

'For fuck's sake, I can see where it landed, Wade! Come on, Silwell, I think you're going to have to see the doctor. That looks bad.'

Wade couldn't resist a slight smirk as he said, 'Sorry, Lester.'

'Fuck off, Wade! You did that on purpoth!' snarled Silwell.

'Get back to work, Wade. I want all of those slabs moved by the time we get back.'

Two of the nurses grabbed hold of Silwell by the arms and hoisted him up. They supported him as he hopped along with them.

Now there were only four nurses watching Wade and Winstanley.

The pile of slabs they were moving had previously been stacked directly next to the perimeter fence. Very cleverly, the two men had moved the slabs in such a way that the slabs that remained now acted like steps up towards the fence.

It was nearly time for Wade to make his move.

The perimeter fence at this location was chain link and only seven feet high. It was topped with strands of rusting barbed wire; beyond the fence was open countryside. The only thing that now stood between himself and freedom were the four male nurses.

Jimmy Wade looked at Clive Winstanley and nodded almost imperceptibly.

Winstanley grinned, then walked over to two of the nurses. At the same time, Wade sidled his way behind one of the others.

Without warning, Winstanley suddenly punched one

of the nurses full in the face. The force of the blow knocked the unsuspecting nurse to the ground. The other nurse immediately grabbed the giant West Indian around the neck.

Winstanley threw the second nurse over his shoulder before disabling him with a karate chop across his windpipe. Before the other two nurses had time to react to Winstanley's actions, Wade plunged the home-made chiv deep into the first man's eye.

The nurse instantly dropped to the ground, going into spasms as he clutched his face.

The sharpened point of the crochet hook had gone straight through the eyeball and plunged deep into the man's brain.

Wade then leapt at the last nurse. He held the chiv against the terrified man's throat and growled, 'Take off your coat.'

The nurse quickly removed his heavy coat and dropped it on the ground.

Winstanley picked up the coat, then scaled the slabs to the top of the chain-link fence. He draped the jacket across the barbed wire at the top of the fence, climbed over, and dropped down the other side.

'Come on, Jimmy man, we need to get going. The other two nurses will be back soon.'

Wade grinned, then slowly pushed the sharpened crochet hook deep into the throat of the nurse he was holding. He twisted the metal spike in the wound, then let the man drop to the ground. The wounded nurse desperately grabbed at his gashed throat in a futile bid to stop the bleeding. Jimmy ran up the slabs to the fence, then jumped over the final hurdle to freedom.

Both men were wearing the navy-blue work overalls they had been issued for the working party.

As they ran across the open fields, Winstanley

shouted, 'We need to find somewhere to ditch these clothes, man.'

They reached the first drainage ditch, and both men waded through the knee-high water.

Wade turned to Winstanley and said aggressively, 'Fuck off, Clive! I don't want you staying with me. You're going to stand out like a sore thumb around here, whatever you're wearing. How many six-foot-six Rastas do you think they've got around here? Now fuck off and don't follow me. Got it?'

'Fuck off yourself, Wade! I don't need you, man.'

'Course you don't, Clive. Good luck, mate. You're going to need it.'

'Fuck off, Wade!'

Winstanley then turned and sprinted away.

Jimmy marvelled at the older man's pace; he was extremely fast for such a big man. It was just a pity that he was now running back towards the main entrance of the hospital.

Wade grinned at the stupidity of the man, then jogged steadily along the bottom of the next ditch, heading away from the hospital. He knew exactly which direction he needed to go. In the days and weeks leading up to the escape, he'd visualized this moment repeatedly in his mind.

He knew it would only be a matter of time before Winstanley was recaptured. He was determined that he would not suffer the same fate.

He looked down at his bloodstained hands and the bloody chiv. He stopped jogging, bent down, and washed the blood from his hands in the little brook that ran along the bottom of the ditch. The palm of his hand had an inch-long gash in it, caused by the base of the crochet hook. It had dug into his hand as he plunged the makeshift weapon through the eye of the first nurse.

The wound had then been made worse as he pushed the spike into the second nurse's throat.

He took a handkerchief from his pocket and wrapped it around his injured hand. He slipped the sharpened crochet hook into his pocket and resumed a steady pace as he jogged away from Rampton Hospital.

The mournful wail of an air raid siren rose to a crescendo in the distance.

The siren was only ever sounded in the event of an escape from the maximum-security hospital. It served as a warning to the surrounding villages and farms that an inmate or inmates were on the loose, and appropriate precautions should be taken.

It meant parents in the immediate vicinity would now be making sure their children were accounted for and indoors.

Local farmers would start checking and securing their outhouses and barns.

For Jimmy Wade, it meant he had to quicken his pace. He had a rendezvous to keep.

67

9.10am, 31 March 1986
Worksop, Nottinghamshire

The young constable stood in the middle of the road and raised his right arm.

Rob braked hard and came to a stop just in front of the officer's knees. Exasperated, Rob wound the window down and said, 'What do you think you're doing? I almost knocked you flying!'

'Just pull in here, please, sir. This is the designated RV point. The Special Ops vans are over there, and Sergeant Turner instructed me not to let anyone get any closer. I've already had to tell the ambulance crew to wait further down the street.'

Danny got out of the car, his warrant card in hand. 'You're doing a great job, son. I'm Detective Chief Inspector Flint, and this is Detective Inspector Buxton; we need to liaise with Sergeant Turner urgently. Where is he?'

'He's over there, near the first van, sir.'

'Thanks. Come on, Rob.'

The detectives walked over to the two unmarked white Transit vans, where a dozen stern-faced men were donning Kevlar body armour, checking MP5 semi-automatic weapons and Smith & Wesson .38 revolvers. Three of the men grunted as they lifted the heavy ballistic shields from the rear of the van.

Sergeant Graham Turner was in his late thirties, but still incredibly fit. He maintained his fitness levels by running and regular gym sessions. He, too, was fully kitted up in the black overalls and body armour. He made the final checks of his own personal weapons. He was very much a lead-from-the-front man, who wouldn't ask his men to do anything he wouldn't do himself.

Danny had met him on a couple of occasions and had the utmost respect for him.

Sergeant Turner saw the two detectives approaching and walked over to them.

'You're going to have to wait here, sir, just until we clear the Land Rover. I can't get a visual on it to see if anyone's still in the back of the vehicle. We've got to clear that before we even think about going through the woodland. I'll be honest with you, boss; this entire scenario is our worst nightmare. I was given the background on this guy Mackay this morning, and being tasked to search woodland for a man like that, with his undoubted skill set, is just about the most dangerous situation we could face. Personally, I think searching the woodland is asking for trouble. To make matters worse, we haven't got a dog handler available to assist us. They've all just been diverted to Rampton for an urgent shout up there.'

Danny replied, 'I hear what you're saying, Graham,

but it's just been confirmed that Mackay's got Superintendent Dennington. The CCTV at Carlton in Lindrick has been checked, and it shows Dennington being abducted at gunpoint and put into this Land Rover.'

'Right, sir, that forces our hand a little. Let's get this Land Rover cleared first, then see where we're at. There's some spare body armour in the back of the van. Both of you put it on.'

It wasn't a request, and both detectives quickly donned the protective clothing.

Danny and Rob then watched from a safe distance as a group of four SOU officers approached the Land Rover behind the cover of ballistic shields.

While two men covered the doors and windows of the vehicle with their semi-automatic weapons, the other two men tried the doors. All the doors of the vehicle were unlocked, and very quickly the vehicle was cleared.

There was no sign of Superintendent Dennington or Ben Mackay.

After clearing the vehicle, every member of the Special Operations Unit team advanced to the Land Rover.

Sergeant Turner conducted a quick briefing with his men, then waved Danny and Rob over.

'Chief Inspector Flint, we're going to start advancing through the woodland. I've got to insist that you remain at least twenty yards behind our skirmish line. We're going to be moving forward fast. My personal advice would be for you to remain here, but I know you're not going to want to do that.'

Danny replied, 'Ordinarily I would gladly take your advice, but I believe Ben Mackay has returned here specifically because it's the place where his daughter committed suicide. Pass me that map of Farriers Wood. I can show you exactly where she was found.'

'That's all very well and good, sir, but it's only a theory. We will still have to advance towards that point tactically, using cover as we go. Normally, we'd never advance like this towards a loaded gun. On this occasion, it sounds like one of our own's in serious danger, so we're left with little or no choice. I'm going to put PC Matt Jarvis with you two. He will be there to look after you. I know you've both completed a basic handgun course, but I don't want you getting too close. Matt will be responsible for your safety. Do exactly what he tells you to do, without argument. Rank doesn't count here, Chief Inspector, got it?'

'I understand. We'll be guided by PC Jarvis.'

Graham Turner then turned to his men. 'Right, you know the drill, move tactically and swiftly. Use whatever cover you can find, and watch out for each other. At the first sign of movement, don't be shy, I want to hear a shout of contact. Understood?'

There was a chorus of acknowledgement from the men before they made their way cautiously into Farriers Wood, with PC Matt Jarvis, Danny and Rob bringing up the rear.

68

9.15am, 31 March 1986
Worksop, Nottinghamshire

Ben Mackay stood in front of the cowering, naked Dennington. He picked up the axe that had been propped against a tree and began to slowly swing it back and forth. It looked like a lethal pendulum counting down the seconds of Maurice Dennington's life.

He paused for a moment, deep in thought, and replaced the axe against the fallen tree.

Reaching for his skinning knife, he sliced the gaffer tape away from his captive's mouth.

Dennington was crying. 'Please don't do this to me. I never meant things to go as far as they did. I'm truly sorry. We were all young and stupid back then. It was only ever meant to be a bit of a fun.'

'Do you truly repent for your sins, Dennington?'

'Of course I do. I just said sorry, didn't I? Can't you just let me go, please?'

Mackay shook his head. He recognised platitudes when he heard them. The demon was tormenting him.

Well, enough was enough.

He walked back over to the fallen tree and picked up the axe.

Striding back towards the whimpering, terrified Dennington, he raised the axe high above his head before bringing it down, hard. There was the sound of bone splintering, then the still air was shattered by the piercing scream that erupted from Dennington's mouth. The right leg of the superintendent had been completely severed mid-shinbone, with one blow of the axe.

Without pausing, Mackay raised the axe again. This time, he brought it down onto the left leg, just below the knee. The axe failed to sever the leg in one blow, so for a third time the axe was raised. This time, the axe did its work, and the left leg was severed.

Mackay threw the axe down behind him, then picked up the two severed feet, holding them above his head.

He looked down at Dennington and said, 'You are dying; your life blood is leaving your body. This is your last chance to repent.'

Dennington's eyes had already glazed over. His entire body had lapsed into massive shock, caused by the trauma and huge blood loss. He tried to mouth a word, but it only emerged as an inaudible rasp.

'Then descend into hell,' said Mackay.

Suddenly, he could hear movement behind him. Somebody was approaching through the trees.

Instinctively, he ducked low and moved into cover behind the tree that supported Dennington's dying body.

69

9.22am, 31 March 1986
Worksop, Nottinghamshire

The black-clad figures of the Special Operations Unit were weaving their way through the woodland. Their pace had quickened even more after they heard the blood-curdling scream that came from deeper in the wood. Danny and Rob struggled to keep pace with PC Jarvis as the men moved forward with urgency and purpose, led by Sergeant Turner.

Suddenly, there was a shout from the man leading the way into the wood: 'Contact!'

Almost immediately after the shout, there was the sound of a single gunshot.

The bullet slammed into the trunk of the tree next to the officer who had shouted the contact. Every man in the team instantly dropped to the ground and rolled into cover.

Matt Jarvis grabbed Danny and Rob, hauled them both to the ground, and shouted, 'Down!' All three of them then rolled behind the cover of a fallen tree.

The next shout was from Graham Turner: 'Report contact!'

The reply came back: 'I can see Superintendent Dennington, boss. He's badly injured. We've come under fire, and I haven't got eyes on the shooter.'

A third voice then broke the silence. This voice was calm and had a distinctive Scottish brogue. 'All of you stay down and don't move! I could have killed any one of you with that shot, but I didn't. I have no quarrel with any of you, and I don't want to have to hurt any of you. Dennington isn't quite ready to leave us yet, so I can't let you approach him. I will shoot dead the first man who tries. Trust me when I say I'll not miss.'

Graham Turner was in good cover behind the thick trunk of a sycamore tree. He crawled slowly around the tree trunk until he could see the stricken Dennington. He could see the catastrophic injuries to the police officer's legs and the huge blood loss from those wounds.

Guided carefully by Matt Jarvis, Danny Flint crawled forward until he was at the side of Turner. He, too, could now see the obviously dying Dennington.

Danny whispered to the Special Ops sergeant, 'Graham, let me see if I can talk to Mackay.'

'Okay, Danny, but if any of my men get the opportunity for a shot, they'll take it.'

Danny nodded. 'We can't get near Dennington anyway. It's got to be worth a go.'

Danny shouted, 'Ben Mackay! My name's Chief Inspector Daniel Flint. It's not too late to stop this. Let me help you out of this mess. Put your weapon down and allow my men to administer some first aid to that wounded man.'

'Daniel, is it? And here you are in the middle of the lion's den; how very appropriate. I won't allow any of your men to approach or get any closer. Just stay back.'

'The man is dying, Ben.'

'This is no man, Daniel! Dennington and his friends were responsible for the assault, rape, sodomy and subsequent death of my beautiful daughter. Now, as the scriptures dictated, they have all paid the price for their sins. Reece is already dead; you'll find him where I killed him at the disused maggot farm.'

'Ben, I promise you, I'll make Dennington pay for his crimes, police officer or not. Let justice deliver his punishment. Don't let him ruin your life as well.'

'Don't you understand, Daniel? My life was ruined on the day my daughter took her own life. Do you think I care to remain in a world where evil men like Dennington can rise to positions of power? Where hypocrisy is rife? How could this rapist scum be placed in charge of a Sexual Offences Investigation Team? Anyway, all this talk is academic now. Dennington has bled out; he's finished. Even as we speak, he's descending into hellfire. I know that my beautiful daughter and my lovely wife are waiting for me. The Lord will forgive me for what I have to do now.'

Danny shouted, 'Don't do it, Ben!'

The loud crack of a single gunshot echoed around the dark forest.

Then total silence.

Graham Turner turned to Danny and said, 'Wait here.'

He then looked at Matt Jarvis and whispered, 'On me, Matt. Let's move forward and see what's happened. Take it very steady.'

The two men moved slowly forward, their weapons

trained on the tree where they had last heard Mackay's voice.

Graham Turner found Ben Mackay lying on the far side of the tree Dennington was propped against. He had blown the top of his head off with a single shot through the roof of his mouth.

Turner recovered the black handgun that had fallen to the side of the body. He made the weapon safe, handed it to PC Jarvis, and shouted, 'Chief Inspector Flint, you can come forward now! Mackay's dead.'

Danny ran forward to where Maurice Dennington lay propped against the tree. He thrust two fingers into his neck, seeking a pulse. It was there – faint and slow, but it was there. Danny shouted, 'Get some tourniquets on his legs and call the paramedics forward. He's got a pulse.'

Two Special Ops officers began to render first aid to the catastrophic injuries to Dennington's legs, using their own belts as makeshift tourniquets to try to stem the bleeding.

Pools of thick blood already lay beneath the leaf litter surrounding the stumps where Dennington's feet had been.

Graham Turner looked at Danny and said, 'He's not going to make it, sir. Both main arteries have been severed. He's lost too much blood already.'

Danny felt for a pulse again. It was even more feeble, as Dennington's body began to shut down and the massive shock induced by his injuries took hold.

He cradled Dennington's head and said loudly in his ear, 'Maurice, you're close to the end. Do you have anything you want to say?'

The dying man's eyes flickered, and Danny placed his ear next to his mouth.

In a voice that was barely a whisper, Dennington

gasped, 'I never meant it to go that far.'

Danny shouted, 'What? What didn't you mean to go that far?'

'The girl.'

Dennington's head slumped forward; his eyes took on a glassy stare.

Danny's fingers could no longer find a pulse.

Turner said, 'He's gone, boss.'

Danny stood up, leaving Dennington propped against the tree. 'Rob, start calling in the circus. This is a murder scene now.'

Rob nodded. 'Will do.'

The two detectives looked down at the two dead men either side of the oak tree. Danny said, 'This was only ever going to end one way. I'm just relieved that Mackay didn't decide to take a few of these men with him. It would have been so easy for him to do that.'

'You're right, Danny, it would. It's clear that all this was always about revenge. His quarrel was with the four men who defiled his daughter, nobody else. Talking about four men, we know where three of them are … what was it Mackay said about a maggot farm?'

'He said that Reece was still where he'd killed him, at a disused maggot farm.'

'Well, there can't be too many of those knocking about, can there?'

'Come on. Let's get back to the car and start getting things organised for the murder scene.'

Danny walked over to Graham Turner. 'Thanks, Graham. You and your men did a fantastic job today. It's tragic that two men have died, but I'm glad nobody else got hurt.'

'You and me both, sir. That really was a nightmare scenario – he could have taken out as many of us as he wanted to. That was bloody scary shit, boss.'

70

5.00pm, 31 March 1986
Major Crime Investigation Unit, Mansfield

Bill Wainwright sat opposite Danny in his office at the MCIU. The two men were discussing what had been a very eventful day.

Danny leaned back in his chair and said, 'We've recovered the body of Frederick Reece from a disused maggot farm just outside Newark.' He quickly summarized the details, concluding with, 'God knows how long the poor bastard was alive before he had his throat cut. The same Bible reference had been painted on the wall using his blood.'

Bill shook his head slowly. 'Jesus Christ, Danny, what a fucking mess.'

Danny continued, 'When we searched the Land Rover, we found a key and documentation for a caravan site in Clumber Park. I've had a forensic team examining the caravan, which the key fitted, all afternoon.

They've recovered what are probably going to be Naylor's eyes and Hall's teeth in individual ziplock bags. The hands hacked from Frederick Reece were found in a bin liner in the back of the Land Rover.'

'So the severed feet of Dennington would have completed the demands of the Old Testament reference, is that it?'

'That's how I see it, sir. I think Ben Mackay was so devoutly religious that the rage and madness brought on by the suicide of his daughter manifested itself through the demands of the Old Testament. In particular, the book of Exodus. He didn't see his conduct as brutal, cold-blooded murder; he thought he was ridding the world of four evil men.'

'From what your enquiries have revealed so far, Danny, he probably wasn't far from the truth.'

'Unfortunately, with the skills Mackay possessed, once he'd set this train of events in motion, those four men were always dead men walking.'

'And Superintendent Dennington? How could we have allowed this to happen?'

'Are you asking me about his acceptance into the police, his accelerated promotion at Bramshill, his appointment to head the new Sexual Offences Investigation Team or his murder, sir?'

'His murder. The chief constable's the one who's going to have to find an answer for all the other questions.'

'In my honest opinion, I believe Maurice Dennington was the architect of his own demise. If he'd allowed the surveillance to continue, he would probably still be alive. If he'd told us the truth about the assault on the woman when he was at university, he would still be alive. If he hadn't been a misogynistic, raping bastard, he would still be alive.'

'Point taken, Danny. I know the chief's already having cold sweats about tomorrow's press conference. They're going to want to know how one of our superintendents became the final victim in the last of the Exodus Murders. Talk about egg on face for him and the force. The man he appointed to be in charge of the Sexual Offences Investigation Team was nothing more than an unconvicted rapist!'

'With the greatest of respect, sir, that's the chief's problem. I'm glad it's not mine. Don't forget we still owe the editor of the *Daily Mirror* first disclosure on this story.'

'Bloody hell, I'd forgotten about that, Danny. You'll be pleased to hear that I've already dealt with that disloyal bastard Dave Whitham. Suffice to say, he won't be working on any crime scenes for the foreseeable future.'

'Quite right, too. We can do without those kinds of problems. To be perfectly honest, I'm more concerned about the people left behind, who are now suffering because of this mess. I think about Vanessa Hall and her kids, her husband and their father gone. Geoff Naylor and Christopher Baker, who both loved Cav Naylor. The elderly Mrs Reece, a Parkinson's sufferer, who'll never get another visit from her son. Then there's Liz Dennington. I've just got back from seeing her at the family home. To say she's stunned would be the biggest understatement ever – the poor woman couldn't speak. The fallout and devastation caused by those four men, committing that despicable act all those years ago, has been simply horrendous.'

'Who was it once said, for every action, expect a reaction?'

'I couldn't tell you, sir, but it's absolutely true.'

'Talking of reaction, I've also spoken to Sir Jarvis

Eccles, the Royal Family's secretary up at Balmoral. Apparently, somebody's "not amused" that the press has already got wind of the fact that the Royal Household recently employed a serial killer, who was regularly left alone with possible heirs to the throne whilst in possession of loaded firearms. Talk about a shitstorm, Danny.'

'I suppose that's the chief's knighthood up the creek for the foreseeable future, then?'

Both men smiled before Wainwright again turned serious.

'I wouldn't have wished this to happen, Danny, but we needed a case like this to test the MCIU capabilities. I've been extremely impressed with how the unit functioned. You and your team pulled the case together very quickly. Unfortunately, due to the skills possessed by the man you were pursuing, I think the outcome was somewhat inevitable. I don't think there was anything you could have done quicker or differently, which would have led to an alternative outcome.'

'That's true, sir. We were always playing catch-up, trying to piece everything together. And, like you said, somebody with the skills of Ben Mackay will always take some stopping.'

'Changing the subject: I hear your wedding day's getting pretty close now?'

'Yes, sir, only a few more weeks to wait now. The wedding's set for the seventh of May. Put it in your diary; you'll be getting a proper written invitation when I can get around to sitting down with Sue and writing them all out.'

'Well, rest assured, Danny, when you return from your honeymoon, your desk will still be here. The MCIU is here to stay. Please pass on my thanks to the team for all their hard work.'

'Will do, sir, and thanks.'

Just as Bill Wainwright stood up to leave, there was an urgent knocking on the office door.

Danny shouted, 'Come in!'

The door opened, and a breathless Rob Buxton walked in.

Rob said to the two senior officers, 'Sorry to interrupt your meeting.'

He then turned to Danny and said, 'Boss, you remember how there were no police dogs available this morning because they were all on a shout at Rampton? Well, we've just had a notification stemming from that breakout at Rampton Hospital. Four guards – sorry, nurses – were injured during the escape. One of the nurses, who received a stab wound through the eye, is still on the critical list. The prognosis is that he's not expected to survive his injuries. Apparently, the weapon used to stab him went through the eye and into the man's brain, causing a massive haemorrhage. The escape could well become a murder enquiry; that's why we've been notified.'

'Are Brian Hopkirk's team travelling to Rampton to start the enquiries?' asked Danny.

'They're already on their way, sir. The thing is, one of the two inmates who escaped was Jimmy Wade.'

EPILOGUE

7.00pm, 31 March 1986
Ranby Village, Nottinghamshire

Liz Dennington stood in the shower and allowed the torrent of hot water to cascade down her naked body. She had stood, motionless, under the hot water for twenty minutes. She closed her eyes, allowed the water to hit her face, and tried to lose herself in the steamy heat.

Finally, she reached for the chrome control unit and switched the shower off. She stood in silence, listening to the water drip from her body onto the shower tray.

She opened the glass door and took the soft white towelling robe from the hook. As she dried herself, her thoughts became a little clearer.

It had been a truly bizarre day. It had started with yet another vicious assault by her husband. Then later in the day, there had been the visit by Detective Chief

Inspector Flint and the policewoman. They had come to the house and informed her that her husband had been abducted and murdered, and that Ben Mackay, the man responsible for his death, had then taken his own life. At the time they were there, she had been unable to process all the information they had given her.

She had been unable to speak to them, unable to respond in any way.

When the senior detective left, the policewoman had stayed with her. She had been supportive, trying to coax her into speaking. At six o'clock that evening, Liz had finally responded to the policewoman's efforts and begun to speak. She thanked the officer and then asked her to leave. She had lied, telling the officer that a relation was coming to stay with her, that she would be fine and just needed a little time on her own.

It didn't bother her that she'd lied. It was true that she did need to be on her own now.

There were no tears for her brute of a husband, just a cold acceptance that he was finally gone.

Liz finished dabbing her wet hair, then wrapped a towel around her head, put it up into a turban, and began to walk around the beautifully decorated rooms of her palatial home.

As she walked through the house, she collected boxes of paracetamol tablets that had been hidden. Stashed away in secret places.

Finally, she walked into the bedroom, and from her bedside cabinet, she took out a half-litre bottle of Smirnoff vodka. She threw all the boxes of tablets onto the double bed, unscrewed the cap from the bottle and took a sip of the fiery vodka.

She replaced the bottle on the bedside cabinet, then used the towel on her head to rub her hair dry before throwing it onto the wash basket in the corner of the room.

Liz stood in front of the full-length mirror and discarded her robe.

She studied her reflection in the mirror. Her body was still curvaceous and firm. Her face, scrubbed clean and slightly flushed from the hot shower and the vodka, was still very pretty. Her tousled auburn hair was long and framed her face beautifully.

Staring at herself in the mirror, Liz Dennington knew she was still an incredibly beautiful woman.

But was it enough? Was beauty ever enough?

She slipped on a silk nightie, then sat on the bed amongst the scattered pillboxes.

Very slowly and methodically, she began to puncture each blister pack, popping each white tablet into the empty glass at the side of the bed.

When she had removed the last tablet from the last blister pack, she stared in silence at the huge quantity of tablets in the glass. She had collected them for months, carefully hiding them in places she knew her husband wouldn't discover them. Waiting for the day when she finally found the courage to free herself from her living hell.

Liz took another sip of the warming vodka, and very slowly a smile spread across her lips. It was almost imperceptible at first, but gradually the subtle smile became a beaming one.

She stood and picked up the glass that was now almost full of paracetamol tablets. Striding purposefully into the bathroom, she flushed the toilet at the same time as she poured the tablets from the glass down the pan.

Laughing out loud, she walked back into the bedroom, collapsed smiling onto the bed, and said in hushed tones, 'I've never met you, Ben Mackay, but I honestly believe you were an angel sent by the Lord. Today was going to be the day I ended my life, but now, because of you, today will be the first day of the rest of my life.'

WE HOPE YOU ENJOYED THIS BOOK

If you could spend a moment to write an honest review, no matter how short, we would be extremely grateful. They really do help readers discover new authors.

Leave a Review

ALSO BY TREVOR NEGUS

EVIL IN MIND
(Book 1 in the DI Fint series)
DEAD AND GONE
(Book 2 in the DI Fint series)

Published by Inkubator Books
www.inkubatorbooks.com

Copyright © 2021 by Trevor Negus

DEAD AND GONE is a work of fiction. People, places, events, and situations are the product of the author's imagination. Any resemblance to actual persons, living or dead is entirely coincidental.

No part of this book may be reproduced, stored in any retrieval system, or transmitted by any means without the prior written permission of the publisher.